LOGIC
of the HEART

LOGIC
of the HEART

by
Patricia Veryan

St. Martin's Press
New York

Library of Congress Cataloging-in-Publication Data

Veryan, Patricia.
   Logic of the heart / Patricia Veryan.
     p.   cm.
   ISBN 0-312-03861-5
   I. Title.
  PS3572.E766L58 1990
  813'.54—dc20   89-24104
                                           CIP

First edition

10 9 8 7 6 5 4 3 2 1

For Debbi Martin, whom I have never met,
but who is a loyal friend,
a devoted reader, and the hard-working
president of my fan club.

1

May, 1818

The day had been unseasonably chill for May, and late that evening fog began to swirl about the streets and squares and parks of London, muffling the sounds of the great city. In the hallowed portals of White's lounge, however, all was jollity, for two friends had encountered each other after a long separation. Their reunion was boisterous and enthusiastic, and became more so when they were joined by a third gentleman. Many amused glances came their way, glances not untouched by admiration, for they presented an attractive picture. Jocelyn Vaughan, who had fought with Wellington's peerless cavalry on the Peninsula, was very much the light-hearted, devil-may-care Corinthian; Valentine Montclair was of slighter frame, his rather drawn sensitive face lacking the glow of health that marked Vaughan's, but they both were judged very good-looking young men, and were as dark of hair and eyes as the third member of their group was fair. Alain Devenish lacked a few of the inches of his friends, but was so handsome as to arouse immediate animosity in other men, and adoration in women, which—combined with a rather volatile disposition—had caused his life to be an eventful one.

Delighted by this unexpected meeting, and full of youthful high spirits, they momentarily forgot their surroundings, their voices rising until some of the members began to frown in their direction. Devenish, his blue eyes alight with mischief, suggested in a stage whisper that they adjourn to his rooms in Stratton Street.

"*Your* rooms!" exclaimed Vaughan, indignant. "They're mine, you rogue!"

"Are they?" As they left the lounge, Montclair glanced curiously from one friend to the other. "Did you remove, Dev?"

"To Gloucestershire, old lad. Should've ridden up to see you long before this. Moved over a year ago."

"Did you, by Jove! Then you married your fair Yolande and are now—" Montclair paused. Devenish's handsome face had become very still, and Vaughan's gaze held a warning.

"Might we perhaps be granted a little QUIET, gentlemen?" Admiral Peterson's bushy eyebrows bristled over the top of *The Times*.

"Whoops!" muttered Vaughan, *sotto voce*. "Sorry, sir. We're leaving."

"Good," said the Admiral testily.

Devenish bowed his curly head and whispered, "Discretion being the better part of valour . . ."

Grinning like mischievous schoolboys, the three friends tiptoed to the cloakroom. They were putting on long caped coats and taking up hats, canes, and gloves, when Devenish was hailed by another acquaintance. Making no bones about the fact that he considered this new arrival a good fellow but a regular windy wallets, Vaughan hurried Montclair into the street.

"Oh, Lord," he grumbled, peering through the fog. "Only look at this beastly stuff." And because he had

2

noticed his old school friend was not in good point, he said airily, "I'll call up a hackney-carriage."

There was no such vehicle in sight, however, and the porter conveyed the information that they were scarcer than hens' teeth tonight.

"Oh come on, Joss," said Montclair impatiently. "Let's walk."

Having instructed the porter to tell Mr. Devenish to find a jervey and pick them up along the way, Vaughan hailed a hovering link boy, and they started off.

They had much to talk about, and despite the chill clammy air, the moments passed pleasantly enough, the link boy trotting ahead of them, his torch bobbing as he guided them unerringly along Piccadilly. Laughing at one of Vaughan's questions, Montclair conveyed the information that he was most definitely not in the petticoat line; and Vaughan, when asked in turn, admitted he had not married the beauty he'd been so enamoured of the last time Montclair had seen him. "Felicity married Rich Saxon," he said with a sigh.

"What—that wild man?" Montclair grinned. "Poor Joss. But you don't seem about to put a pistol to your head. Another lady?"

"Oh, any number, old fellow. I was mad for Alicia Wyckham for a whole year. Really thought I'd found my once-and-forever. But—to say truth, I begin to think I'm just not inclined to become a Benedick." He gave Montclair a sly nudge and said laughingly, "They're *all* so deuced lovely, y'know."

"I see. And—er, Dev? I collect I put my foot in my mouth just now."

Vaughan sobered. "Yes, you did rather. I thought everyone knew Yolande had jilted him. But, of course, you will persist in rusticating out there in Gloucestershire all year round and likely hear nothing of what goes on."

3

"Jilted *Dev*? You never mean it! He was always mad for her!"

"Astonishing, ain't it? She married his cousin. Some Canadian fellow."

Surprised, Montclair exclaimed, "Not Craig Winters? I'll be dashed! Dev and Craig visited me at Longhills a couple of years ago. Winters is a fine fellow. Cannot touch Dev for looks, of course, but he was at Waterloo, you know. A major with the Scots Greys. Still . . . Miss Drummond and Dev had been betrothed forever. I fancy Dev called him out, no?"

"No, as a matter of fact. Took it very hard, poor fellow, but seems to be making a recover. Now—enough of all this chitchat. Tell me of yourself. I—" They had turned into a silent and deserted Stratton Street, and Vaughan grabbed Montclair's arm as his friend staggered, and steadying him, peered at the pale face and said anxiously, "You all right, old lad?"

"Perfectly . . . fine . . ." said Montclair, sounding breathless. "Must have just . . . stumbled over . . . a paving stone or something."

Vaughan frowned into the night, but said only, "Oh. Still at your music? I fancy you're a famous composer by this time?"

"I've a few things completed. My uncle, of course, throws up his hands in horror at the thought of publication." Montclair gave a contemptuous snort. "Bad *ton,* he says."

"Good God, never say old Selby Trent still sponges off you? What became of Lord Geoffrey? Ain't he come home yet?"

"No, my brother's off in India. Hasn't been in England since Waterloo. I wish to God he'd come back so I could kick Trent and his—" He bit off the words hurriedly.

"D'you mean to tell me," said Vaughan, horrified, "that Geoff has abandoned you there with that nest of vipers while he cavorts off to hunt tigers or whatever?"

4

Montclair chuckled. "Oh, Barbara's not a viper, Joss."

"True. But—your uncle . . . and Lady Trent . . . and *Junius!*" Vaughan shuddered. "Get rid of 'em, Val. That's my advice. Quick!"

His voice low-pitched and bitter now, Montclair said, "Do you fancy I wouldn't have done so years ago, if it was possible? When my mama appointed Sir Selby to administer the estates, it was so worded that I can't kick the—I can't force him to leave Longhills without he does something criminal, or until Geoff comes back to take control."

"But—my dear fellow! The man's a wart. No, really Val, I'm sorry, but he is! And that aunt of yours scares me to death! Does Sir Selby interfere much in running the estates? I'll lay odds he does, the old skinflint!"

"My revered uncle," began Montclair grimly, "strives to—" He was never to finish the remark.

The link boy whistled shrilly, then took to his heels.

They came out of the blackness like flying wraiths. Four of them, with shabby caps drawn low over masked faces, dark coats with collars turned high, and the diminishing glow from the link boy's torch reflecting on the blue gleam of steel. With not an instant's hesitation the two friends leapt to meet the attack. They were unarmed, but both carried walking canes as was the fashion, and they wielded them as though they held sabres, meeting slash with parry and swipe with thrust, holding their own with the fierceness of desperation, until the clip-clop of hooves echoed through the dimness. "Dev!" shouted Vaughan. *"À moi! À moi!"*

A distant voice roared, "Spring 'em! Over there!"

The end of Montclair's cane rammed into a large shape, drawing forth a wheezing profanity. A gleam was flying at his throat, and he whirled aside, feeling the razor-sharp steel brush his shoulder. His left connected hard with a nose. A dark form reeled back, howling, but another was there at once to take his place. Montclair

5

ducked as a club whistled at his head. It would have brained him had it landed squarely. As it was, the night was scattered into a thousand crazily whirling fragments . . .

"I shall move!" Jocelyn Vaughan sat at the parlour table in the flat he had taken over when Devenish left it, clutching his wrist and watching Devenish bathe the gash over Montclair's right ear. "A fine neighbourhood you chose for me, Dev!"

Devenish paused an instant. Montclair sat bowed forward, his crossed arms on the table. His eyes were closed, his brows and lashes startlingly dark against the deathly pallor of his face. Devenish touched his shoulder very gently, and the dark eyes blinked open. The amber flecks in them that were a fair reflection of his mood were dulled, but the pale lips curved to a grin. "Jolly good . . . turn-up," he said faintly, then propped his chin on the palm of one hand and closed his eyes again.

Devenish exchanged a troubled glance with Vaughan. "I think you'd best send the porter for an apothecary, Joss. Val caught a proper leveller."

"What, at this hour?" Montclair forced his head up. "Devil a bit of it. I'm—perfectly fine. If you've a—drop of cognac perhaps . . ."

"Not after being popped on the noggin, old lad," said Vaughan. "I've got the kettle on the hob. Have a cup of tea for you in a trice."

"Splendid . . ." Montclair realized they were both watching him uneasily. His head hurt so badly he was half blinded, but he said, "Look at you. A fine pair! Dev, you'll have a black eye for sure. And—is your wrist broke, Joss?"

Devenish gave him a pad to hold against the cut and

turned his attention to Vaughan's damaged wrist. "They caught you properly," he said, inspecting the vivid swelling that was already starting to purple.

"Dropped my cane," grumbled Vaughan. "And it was brand new, and amber to boot!"

Devenish explored, and Vaughan cursed gaspingly. "Blasted damned Mohocks! I thought London was free of that scum."

"I can't tell if any bones are broke, Joss. You'd as well have an apothecary look at that in the morning. Did they get anything from you, Val?"

"Thanks to you—no," said Montclair.

"Nor from me." Vaughan rolled down his sleeve and muttered thoughtfully, "Funny thing. When I went down, I took one of the bastards with me. But the other fellow didn't attempt to take my purse. He went straight to help his cronies. Odd behaviour for that breed."

"Jove, but that's right," said Devenish, drying his hands. "When we drove up there were three of 'em having at you, Val."

"I'm only grateful you came when you did," sighed Montclair.

The kettle began to whistle and Vaughan came to his feet. "Come on, Val. You can rack up here for the night. Use my man's room, since he's off to Cardiff 'til Monday."

Montclair offered little argument, and stumbled away, having said his good nights to the wavering shape he vaguely supposed was Devenish.

When Vaughan came back into the cozy parlour carrying a teapot, Devenish was stretched out in an armchair, his feet propped on an occasional table. He opened one eye and asked drowsily, "You give Val his tea?"

"He was asleep before I got him into bed." Vaughan waved the teapot. "Want some?"

Devenish looked at him.

7

Vaughan grinned and went to fill two glasses at the sideboard. Carrying one to Devenish with his left hand, he returned to claim his own cognac, then sat on the littered sofa and stared at the fire. "How long must we wait for the Runner? I thought you sent the jervey off after him?"

"Did. And I don't mean to wait all night, I can tell you." After a minute he asked quietly, "What's the matter with him, Joss?"

Vaughan shook his head. "Don't know. Trent-itis, probably."

"Good Lord! Is he still playing host to that unlovely crew? Where's his noble lordship? Womanizing in France still?"

"Geoff's in India, Val thinks. And he can't kick his uncle out 'til Lord Geoffrey Montclair comes home and claims his rights. Poor old Val. Well—it's a big house, that's one thing."

Devenish grimaced. Longhills Manor was very large indeed, and famed as being one of the loveliest of England's many lovely great homes, but he said, "If it was Versailles it wouldn't be big enough. I wonder he doesn't just leave."

"Can't do that, dear boy. His charming uncle would have a free hand with the estate. Val may bury himself in his music and not know half the time whether it's Monday or last Spring, but he loves Longhills. He'll fight Selby Trent every step of the way before he'll turn tail and run."

"As Geoff has done," said Devenish rather grimly. "Val's stuck there with that loathsome crew, trying to protect estates he'll never inherit, and damn near isolated into the bargain. No one in his right mind would set foot under a roof with the Trents in residence!"

"Pity," nodded Vaughan. "Val should've been the heir."

8

Devenish smiled faintly. "He'd give you an argument on that one. Don't want it. Besides, he thinks the sun rises and sets on his big brother."

Vaughan said, "Perhaps it's just the strain of all the argumentations."

"No, it's more than that, Joss." Devenish frowned. "He's definitely down-pin. Looks awful. Didn't you notice?"

"I noticed when he almost measured his length on the flagway. Said he tripped over a loose stone or some such thing. Wasn't no loose stone."

There was a brief silence. Devenish broke it. "They weren't Mohocks, of course. They were after Val."

"Plain as the nose on your face. But—why?"

"Has he any enemies?"

"The man that don't has to be a clod. And old Val's temper ain't always—er— But—murder. . . ? No, I doubt that."

Another pause. Then Devenish said reluctantly, "If Lord Geoffrey should die—Val would come into the title and fortune, I fancy."

Vaughan nodded. "But the Trents ain't next in line, if that's what you're thinking. Four or five before them, as I recall. To pop off that many would be stretching credibility more than a little, eh my tulip?"

"Hmm . . ." muttered Devenish. There was a long silence broken only by the tick of the clock on the mantel.

"The devil with this! That rascally jervey likely never went after the Runner at all!" Devenish stood, touching his lurid eye with an investigative hand. "My poor orb is complaining, and I'm for my cozy bed at the Clarendon. I shall leave you, my pippin, to the joys of my former home!"

"Wait up a bit." Vaughan went into the kitchen and began to rummage in the small pantry. "I'll see if I've a beefsteak for that eye."

9

Devenish trailed after him. His eye felt twice its size and a few minutes' delay would be worthwhile.

Vaughan turned, peering dubiously at the small package he was unwrapping. "Don't have any steak, I'm afraid. D'you suppose this trout would fit the bill? It ain't too ancient, and we could cut it open and clap it on—" Blasphemously interrupted, he listened until Devenish ran out of breath. "Trouble with you, Dev," he pointed out, "is that you want for a proper sense of gratitude."

The Bow Street Runner arrived late next morning, just after Devenish had joined his friends, and was bedevilling them with the details of the excellent breakfast he had enjoyed at the Clarendon.

The Runner, a ponderous gentleman who introduced himself as Mr. W. Wilkins, adopted a no-nonsense air, and demanded the details of the previous evening's mayhem. His manner underwent an immediate thaw when Devenish asked if he was acquainted with Major Paisley, and if he knew how the major went on.

"He is quite recovered, sir," said Mr. W., sketching a bow. "Very busy, in fact, sir. Account of this here Masterpiece Gang. Hot after 'em, he is, by what I hear."

"Masterpiece Gang?" echoed Montclair.

The Runner stared at him.

Vaughan said excusingly, "Mr. Montclair lives in the country."

"Oh. The country." The Runner nodded his understanding of such desolations, and explained ponderously, "Well, they're a gang of very clever thieves, sir, what specializes in, as you might say, masterpieces. National treasures, some of 'em. Items of rare and partic'ler value took from the homes of peers and such like, or from museums and galleries. Paintings, sir. Works o' art in gold, silver, crystal; what, as you might say, have you. They won't take nothing but the best. Pass over shelves of silver and gold, and take only the cream, as you might say, of the crop. So the Powers that Be are, if you'll forgive the expression, a'burning of their crumpets! And when there's crumpets burning at the top, down comes the smoke to Bow Street. And poor Major Paisley, he gets proper smoked out, as you might say. What with all this here vicious smuggling getting worse day by day, and the Masterpiece Gang, upsetting of His Royal Highness, and the Quality. To say nothing of attacks on fine gentlemen like yourselves, sir, on London's very own thoroughfares! Terrible the crime is nowadays! Fair terrible!"

Fascinated by this flow of eloquence, Montclair asked, "Has this Major Paisley been successful in recovering the stolen goods?"

"Not so much as a speck of oil paint, nor a chip of porcelain china, sir. Once something of great value gets stole, we—Bow Street as you might say—usually gets word of it popping up somewhere in this here globe, sir. But—not with this lot! Two years they been at it. Musta stole a king's ransom, they must. But if they been and gone and sold it, no one knows where. It's like it had disappeared off the face of the earth with not a trace, sir! Not a whiff. Not, as you might say, a whisper!"

"Or a suspicion," put in Devenish solemnly.

Mr. W. drew himself up. "I wouldn't go so far as to say that, sir. We—meaning Bow Street—have plenty of suspicions. Proof—well, that's another mug of mice."

"Or tray of trout," said Vaughan agreeably.

Devenish snorted, and Montclair put a hand over his lips.

Mr. W. directed a hard stare at the culprits and took

11

out his notebook. "Now as to this here assault, gentlemen . . ."

He left half an hour later, having told the three friends, at great length, nothing they did not already know. The apothecary, entering shortly afterwards, came upon such hilarity that he thought at first he had come to the wrong house and was only reassured by the assorted cuts and bruises offered for his inspection. He was as meek and unassuming as the Runner had been self-important, and having told Devenish that his eye was undamaged, and expressed the opinion that Vaughan's wrist harboured no broken bones, proceeded to examine Montclair's damaged head and pronounce it a "nasty cut but likely no more than a mild concussion." He eyed the young man thoughtfully, and added, "Are you feeling quite up to par otherwise, sir?"

"Perfectly, thank you." Montclair stood, turning to his friends with a bright smile. "I'm afraid I must be on my way. I've some business waiting at home that has already waited much too long."

They paid off the apothecary and said their farewells, promising to meet soon at Devencourt near Stroud, or Greenwings in Sussex, or at Longhills Manor near Tewkesbury, and Montclair took his leave.

Glancing out of the front windows, Vaughan said idly, "That apothecary fellow waited for Val."

Devenish wandered to join him, and they watched Montclair converse briefly with the little man, then walk briskly towards Piccadilly. The apothecary looked after him, shook his head, and went off in the opposite direction.

It was a warm morning. It was, in fact, now midday. The remaining occupants of the parlour discussed sustenance, decided on the merits of ale, and having filled two tankards, carried them to the sofa and sat down in a companionable but vaguely troubled silence.

12

"Devencourt ain't too far from Longhills," observed Vaughan at last.

They looked at each other.

Devenish raised his glass in a mute acknowledgement.

"If I might have your card, sir," said Deemer, clinging to his dignity even as he was pushed back across the sunny entrance hall of Highperch Cottage.

The large man in the very tight green coat gave the frail elderly man another shove and turned a broad, red, and amused face to his companion. "Is it a butler, Junius? Don't dress like a butler. Don't look like a butler. Looks more like a greengrocer!" His friend emitting a howl of mirth, he went on aggrievedly, "Wants my card, old boy. D'you have a card we can give the poor clod?"

"Damme if I ain't left m'cardcase at home!" The younger of the two intruders, tall and well built, with a pair of powerful shoulders, administered a third shove that sent the grey-haired man staggering. "Getting absent-minded, Pollinger," he said laughingly. "You should watch me more carefully. As for you, fellow, do not be annoying your betters. We want to see your mistress. The naughty widow. She is here, so don't give us no argumentation."

Looking at once shaken and outraged, Deemer, who was butler/groom/major domo at Highperch Cottage, said, "Since you have no cards, gentlemen—"

"Didn't say we don't *have* cards," said the man called Pollinger.

"Said we wasn't giving *you* one," grinned his friend. "You may tell the, er—lady, that Lord Montclair's representatives have come to see her." His unusually large

13

blue eyes flickered around the shabby hall. "Think we'd best not sit down whilst we wait, Poll. Looks damned dirty. Furthermore"—he aimed a glossy topboot at a dusty but graceful Hepplewhite chair, sending it crashing across the hall—"dashed rickety. Look at that! Damned leg fell off!"

Both the young men laughed uproariously. Halfway up the winding staircase, Deemer paused and glanced back, the lines in his thin face deepening. Mrs. Susan should not have to deal with those two boorish Bucks. They meant trouble, if ever men did. "If only Mr. Andrew was here," he whispered to himself, hurrying along the dusty upstairs hall. But taking advantage of the lovely June weather, Mr. Andrew Lyddford and the Bo'sun were off on the barge; Señor Angelo had left just after luncheon to drive Mrs. Starr, the housekeeper, and little Miss Priscilla into Tewkesbury, so Mrs. Susan Henley was just at the moment protected only by himself and Martha, their solitary abigail-cum-parlourmaid, who was simple, poor girl, and would likely fall into hysterics did those two downstairs raise their voices again.

He proceeded worriedly along a musty-smelling corridor, treading on faded threadbare carpet, the daylight coming dimly through the dirty windows at each end. The door he approached swung open even as he reached it. Mrs. Susan Henley stepped out and the dingy hall seemed brightened.

A tall willowy young woman, she wore a dark mulberry riding habit, the train caught up over one arm. A jaunty little matching hat with a pink feather was perched on very thick near-black hair that was worn long and perfectly straight, being tied back from her face with a mulberry ribbon. Gloves and riding crop in hand she smiled at Deemer, but the smile faded at once from the generous, ruddy-lipped mouth, the dark low-

14

arched brows drew together, and a frown came into the clear grey eyes. "What is it?" she asked, in a quiet, musical voice.

"Two—men, Mrs. Sue," said the butler, trying to keep his voice from trembling.

"And they have upset you, I see." The firm chin set, and the dark head swung up a little. "No cards, Deemer?"

"No, ma'am. I—I think it were best if you did not come down. They're ugly customers, if ever I—"

"No names, either?" she interpolated coolly.

"They said they were from his lordship, ma'am. One is named Pollinger, I think."

"Is he indeed?" Mrs. Henley drew on one black kid glove, her lip curling. "If it is Sir Dennis Pollinger, his reputation precedes him. And—the other?"

"Mr. Pollinger—or Sir Dennis perhaps—called him 'Junius.' Mrs. Sue, please do not go down there. I'll run down to the river and see if *The Dainty Dancer's* in sight yet. Perhaps I can signal Mr. Andrew and—"

"And we'll have a small war on our hands, I fancy. If his lordship has sent these men to intimidate us it will be as well they learn at the outset where we stand." She flashed a sudden smile that banished the worry from her oval face, and walked past him.

"A moment, ma'am, I beg." The butler hurried into another room and emerged carrying a long-barrelled duelling pistol. "I'm coming with you," he declared bravely.

Mrs. Henley chuckled. "Not carrying my brother's horrid great cannon! Give it me."

He protested, but she appropriated the pistol and slipped it into the deep pocket of her skirt. "Never worry so," she murmured. "Gentlemen are always alarmed to see firearms in the hands of a woman, and besides, Lieu-

15

tenant Henley taught me how to repel boarders!" She thought, 'If nothing else!' and went to the stairs.

Deemer looked after her worriedly, wishing he was younger, and stronger than his last illness had left him. Then he ran quickly to the rear staircase.

Mrs. Henley heard the loud voices from the landing and as she followed the curve of the stairs, her eyes took in the two young men who strolled about inspecting the hall with arrogant criticism. 'A fine pair of blackguards,' she thought. 'Likely typical of Montclair's cronies!'

The younger of the two was somewhere in the neighbourhood of thirty, and quite handsome, but she was not drawn to the big, beefy type, and she thought his eyes too large, his lips too thick and voluptuous, and his fair hair was arranged in a dandified style that she could not like. She had seen him somewhere . . . In Town, unless she was mistaken. She wrinkled her brow. Deemer had said his name was 'Junius.' Junius . . . Trent! Mr. Junius Trent! In that case, her opinion of the gentleman was not shared by the majority, for he was widely admired by London's ladies, his sarcasm put down as cleverness, and his impudence as wit. He was a reckless gambler whose luck at the tables was legendary. He commanded a large circle of friends and hangers-on, by whom he was described as a bruising rider to hounds, a fine man with the fives, an excellent shot, a general all-round sportsman. His friends chose to overlook the fact that he had been denied admission to White's Club, and that his popularity in certain quarters appeared to have dimmed of late. This might perhaps have been ascribed to odd little rumours that were beginning to be whispered, and also to the fact that his way with a team and carriage left a great deal to be desired, his quick-tempered impatience having cost a groom his life when he was thrown from a curricle Trent had contrived to overturn.

16

Mrs. Henley slowed her steps and appraised the second man narrowly. Despite his fine build and the fact that he looked to be no older than five and thirty, he already showed marked signs of dissipation. The flush on his broad face proclaimed the heavy drinker and the beginnings of a paunch curved his green and white striped waistcoat. His lank hair was straight and of an indeterminate brown. His features were regular but undistinguished and the loose mouth and rather neighing voice caused her to marvel that any woman could be swept off her feet by such a one.

Her eyes fell on the overturned chair then, and she frowned.

". . . no business here," Trent was saying loudly. "Besides, who cares what *he* says? The fact remains it ain't legal, and by God, I mean to—"

"You wished to see me?" said Mrs. Henley, her cold voice cutting through his words.

Both men jerked around and stared up at her.

She stood on the stair, one hand lightly resting on the handrail, her head high, her thick brows a little arched, her mouth haughtily drooping, and the sunlight which slanted through the grubby window of the half-landing awakening a sheen on her luxuriant raven locks.

"Now . . . by heaven . . . Juno is come among us!" breathed Trent, staring.

His friend pursed his lips, eyeing Mrs. Henley's tall aloofness without marked approval. "No, d'you think so?" he said dubiously.

"A veritable Venus!" Trent paced forward, lifting a jewelled quizzing glass and scanning her from head to toe with bold admiration.

A glint came into Mrs. Henley's candid grey eyes. "I expect," she said in her calm way, "when you have finished with your impertinence, you will tell me why you are here—gentlemen."

17

Trent chuckled. "A spirited Venus, you'll note, Poll," he remarked. "Just how I like 'em."

"Perhaps," Mrs. Henley turned her gaze to Pollinger, "you can be more lucid, Mr. Poll."

Pollinger's shifty brown eyes fell away before her cool stare. "Do but mark the hauteur of it, dear boy," he sneered, with a giggle that did not equate with a man of his size and years.

"And—the shape," murmured Trent, the quizzing glass busy again.

"Good day—gentlemen," said Mrs. Henley, contempt in her voice.

"No, no! You cannot throw us out, m'dear," drawled Trent, sauntering nearer. "Ain't polite. 'Sides, we ain't been so much as introduced as yet. Allow me, ma'am, to present my friend, Sir Dennis Pollinger."

Sir Dennis offered a great flourishing bow.

"Silly fellow," murmured Trent, amused.

"I expect you know best," said Mrs. Henley tranquilly.

"Be dashed!" protested Sir Dennis.

Trent laughed. "And I am Junius Trent," he said, bowing also. "May I assume we address Mrs. Burke Henley? I was—acquainted with your late husband, ma'am."

She met his mocking gaze levelly. "Yes. I had heard you shared his weakness for gaming."

"Hah!" roared Pollinger, vastly diverted. "That gave you back your own, Junius!"

Trent pointed out, "It is only a weakness does one lose, dear ma'am. And your husband, regrettably, did so often—lose. Save, 'twould appear, in one respect."

The famous blue eyes were slithering over her again. Mrs. Henley began to feel soiled. "You will forgive me if I cut short this fascinating conversation. Friends are waiting for me, and—"

"They must be waiting a long way off," said Trent,

18

drifting ever closer, "for we saw no sign of 'em as we rode up. And why anyone should wish to be any distance from your lovely self . . ."

Mrs. Henley stepped back. "You oblige me to be blunt, sir. Say what it is your master sent you to say, and then be so good as to leave."

"Your *master*," hooted Pollinger, slapping his thigh delightedly. "There's a rib tickler, by Jove!"

"I was given to understand," said Mrs. Henley, her pulse quickening as she saw the sudden glint in Trent's eyes, "that you are come in behalf of Lord Montclair, who seems to labour under the delusion that I live here illegally."

"What sauce, and for such a pretty mouth," said Trent. With a sudden pounce he was facing the widow at the foot of the stairs. He put his right hand on the baluster beside her, and said smilingly, "Lord Montclair is perfectly right, m'dear. This house is part of the Longhills estate."

Mrs. Henley slipped one hand into her pocket and closed her fingers around the reassuring butt of the pistol. "My father-in-law purchased this property long ago, and—"

"Ah, but he cancelled the sale, and sold Highperch back to Lady Digby Montclair. Had you—ah, forgot that trifle?"

"To the contrary, sir. My man of business in London has a copy of the Deed, and it—"

"Was found to be in error, ma'am."

"Which is why," pointed out Pollinger, grinning, "her la'ship returned Henley's funds and voided the sale."

"So . . . much as I regret it," said Trent softly, "you must go away, pretty one. Montclair might be willing to—"

She stepped back once more but even as he spoke, like a striking snake, his left arm shot out and trapped her

19

against the stair railing. He smiled down at her seductively. "You are not exactly beautiful. At least, not in the accepted sense. You are too tall, but most generously formed. And although your hair should be curled it is exceeding silky, and I like the way it comes to that charming peak in the centre of your brow. Let's have your hat off," he reached up, "so I can better admire it."

"Let's have your hands off," said Mrs. Henley, drawing and levelling the pistol under his ribs, "before I decide to fire it."

"Hey!" cried Pollinger, starting forward, alarmed.

Trent looked down at the pistol, then looked up into the young lady's steady grey eyes. His hands still raised and his own eyes very wide, he muttered, "By God, but I believe you would."

"Have you ever wondered how many people would attend your obsequies?" she asked chattily. "Were I you, sir, I would lower my hands very slowly. This is cocked and my brother tells me it has a hair-trigger—whatever that may mean."

Pollinger gave a little yelp and retreated.

Trent's eyes narrowed. "Why, you little trollop," he breathed. "With your reputation, you dare—"

"Have a care, Junius!" cried Pollinger nervously. "Woman. Pistol. Looks like a Boutet. Very touchy, y'know. Very."

"Your friend is perfectly right," said Mrs. Henley. "I am sure I do not know how long I can hold this thing, so—"

"What the devil—"

A tall young man exploded through the rear door and came down the hall on the run. He wore work clothes and heavy hip boots, and a Belcher neckerchief was tied carelessly about his throat. Very dark, with thick curly hair and a fine physique, he was yet of much slighter build than the pair who confronted Mrs. Henley. "Get

20

away from my sister, you filthy swine!" he roared, his grey eyes narrowed and murderous.

Mrs. Henley's gaze flashed to him. Junius Trent's hand flailed downward and smacked the pistol to the side. It went off with a roar that purely astounded the widow, who had really thought it to be unloaded.

Pollinger grabbed the newcomer's arm, swung him around, and collected a tightly clenched fist in one eye. Staggering, he howled curses.

Trent wrenched the pistol from Mrs. Henley's grasp, whirled, and brought the butt down hard on the back of the newcomer's dark head.

Mrs. Henley whispered, "Andy!" as her brother crumpled to the floor. Starting for him, she was caught by the wrist. "Coward!" she flung at Trent.

He laughed rather breathlessly. "I do not care to be shot at when I come calling," he said, and jerking her to him, kissed her ruthlessly.

She made not the slightest attempt to struggle, but stayed passively until he released her. Very white, she stared at him, a blaze in her eyes that brought his slow smile back. "Gad, but you're a fiery chit, well worth the taming," he murmured. "How the hell did you come to marry a drunken sot like Henley?"

"My husband," she said, her voice trembling with fury, "was a disgraced and dishonoured man. But compared to you, sir, he was a paragon of virtue!"

Clutching his eye, Pollinger had bent over the fallen man and now suggested, "Think we'd best be on our way, Junius."

Trent bowed. "My compliments, Mrs. Henley. You will remember why we came, I trust."

"Certainly I shall not forget two brave men who forced their way into this house, abused a lone woman, and struck down her brother from behind. I hope you may be proud of what you have to report to your master!"

"You've a wicked tongue, lovely one," said Trent, frowningly. "No man is my master. But be warned. Montclair wants you out of this house and off his land. And it does not do to oppose him. As for this young fool," he glanced contemptuously at his motionless victim. "Had you not tried to murder me I might not have struck so hard. Blame yourself, Mrs. Henley. *Au revoir.* I do not say goodbye, you'll note. We will meet again."

He sauntered from the house, shouldering Deemer aside as the butler came panting up the front steps.

The reaction making her shake violently, Mrs. Henley sank to her knees beside her brother. "Andy," she sobbed, seeking a pulse.

Deemer ran in. "Oh, my God! Please say he's not dead, Mrs. Sue!"

She looked up through a blur of tears. "No, thank G-God! But—oh, Deemer, if he is badly hurt I will take a rifle to my lord Montclair! That filthy, conniving lecher will rue the day he sent his ugly cronies after us. I swear it!"

2

onghills, for almost three hundred years the country seat of the barons of Montclair, was situated on a rolling knoll some miles north of Tewkesbury. It was an enormous Cotswold stone mansion of the late Tudor period; the kind that brought visitors to an awed halt on their first sight of it and evoked such comments as "My God! What a museum!", "Who could live in such a pile?", or "Oh, is it not heavenly?" "A palace *véritable*!" depending upon the point of view. Despite its vast size, however, it had a simple charm, for no Flemish or German artisans had been imported and permitted to desecrate it with Italian Renaissance distortions, so that the Tudor architecture remained unsullied and pure. The graceful gables and mullioned windows, the tall and beautifully worked chimneys prevailed throughout the three storeys of the main block and the two storeys of the more recent south wing, their charm embellished by the surrounding sweeps of parkland and richly wooded slopes. The *pièce de résistance* was the famous marble fountain and Montclair mermaid, rising with fairy-tale beauty from the flower gardens of the huge circular entrance court about which the mansion was erected.

As in most Tudor houses, the rooms sprang from a great hall, customarily the household gathering place. This huge chamber had fallen into disrepair over the centuries, but had been much improved by the sixth baron, Digby Montclair, the present lord's sire. It was now a delightful room, the floor of black and white marble squares spread with thick rugs, the ceiling plastered in an exquisite design of lilies and birds, with the Montclair mermaid proudly centred. The old oak panelling gleamed anew, and the two massive fireplaces, scrubbed clean of their long-worn shroud of smoke stains, revealed once again the glorious carvings wrought by skilled Tudor artisans.

Of all the rooms, the great hall was the favourite of Sir Selby Trent, who was administrator of the estate in Lord Geoffrey Montclair's absence. Sir Selby had a deep love for Longhills. He delighted in the immaculate and productive farms. The well-kept woods, the broad ribbon of the river, the three picturesque villages, the fat brown cattle chewing placidly in the lush meadows, warmed his heart and brought a fond smile to his moonlike visage. As for the mansion, there was scarcely a room that did not receive a weekly visit from him, nor one he viewed with displeasure. It was to his favourite chamber, however, that he had taken his guest on this rather sultry June afternoon, and they had settled themselves in two comfortable chairs facing the rear terrace.

They were an oddly disparate pair. Sir Selby was plump and colourless, with pale brown eyes, a pasty complexion, and pale brown hair. Even his voice was pale, for he invariably spoke in a soft monotone. This afternoon, however, he was unusually animated, for his cheeks were slightly flushed and there was a gleam in his eyes as he examined a dagger, turning it almost reverently in his pudgy hands, gazing down at the shining, razor-sharp blade, the four prongs that curved down from the hilt, and the elaborately chased counter guard.

Chin in hand, one elbow resting on the arm of the rose brocade chair, the other man watched Trent in silence. Even seated, he was clearly very tall. Of slender build, he was clad with elegance but without ostentation in a navy blue double-breasted tail coat, a white piqué waistcoat, and dove grey pantaloons. His eyes were near black, dull, and fathomless. His face, framed by lank black hair, was narrow and long, but his complexion was clear, and if pallid, showed no hint of sallowness. He had thin, very graceful hands, marred only by the black hairs which presented a rather unpleasant contrast to the excessive whiteness of the skin. Watching Trent's rapture, his full red lips curved to an expression of faint distaste. "It pleases you?"

Trent tore his eyes from the dagger. "It is exquisite. A *main gauche*. Spanish. Early seventeenth century, I fancy. You are too good, Monteil."

Imre Monteil clasped his hands before his chest, and inclined his head. "I reward those with whom I—contrive."

Trent's gaze had returned to his prize, but at this his head lifted once more. There had been the barest trace of condescension in the remark, and it irritated him. "You make us sound dishonest," he murmured with a smile.

Monteil shrugged. "Such considerations are of no consequence. It is a left-handed dagger. You comprehend, *sans doute*?"

"Of course. Used with a rapier in duelling."

"And you would like very much the matching rapier to add to your collection."

25

Trent's eyes glinted. "I would indeed. But to find its mate would be nigh impossible, I'd think."

"Nothing is impossible, *mon ami*." The white hands of the Swiss wrung gently. "Though *you* would seem to have encountered a—difficulty, *oui*?"

Sir Selby returned the dagger to its sheath, deposited it lovingly upon the table beside him, and smiled again. "A—delay, shall we say? It will be dealt with. I sent Junius up there this morning, in fact. With young Pollinger."

Monteil's hands formed themselves into a church steeple. Over them, his dark eyes remained unblinkingly upon his companion. "And Montclair? You have again approached him about the cottage?"

"I thought it best to delay until we have resolved the present rather unexpected development." Trent gestured apologetically. "His music obsesses him, you know, and his mood is so unpredictable that one is obliged to handle him carefully. Especially at present."

The Swiss pursed his lips. "Do you know, I question this desire to become a composer. *Tiens!* It is not good *ton,* I think."

"It most assuredly is not! A gentleman of his position? Nonsense! You cannot think I would permit such a disgraceful thing."

"And—forgive, *mon cher,* but—will your permission be asked? He is of age surely, and seems to be rather, shall we say—stubborn?"

"Yes. Regrettably. And has a nasty temper. But—one must be charitable. The poor lad's illness—" Trent tapped his temple meaningfully.

Imre Monteil shook his head. "Such a pity. And in so young a man. How fortunate that—" He glanced up, leaving the sentence unfinished as a footman carried a golden salver into the room.

Sir Selby took the card and glanced at it. Up went the

26

pale brows. "Show the lady into the morning room and offer my apologies that I must keep her waiting a minute or two." He handed the card to Monteil as the footman made his stately departure. "The minx does not want for impudence," he murmured.

Monteil read aloud, "Mrs. Burke Henley." He smiled and stood with lazy grace. "Well, well. She carries her battle to the enemy's gates. But how intriguing. I shall come and see what our intrepid trespasser looks like."

Coming to his feet also, Trent shook his head. "No, Imre. I think it better I should see the chit alone."

"Do you?" Monteil accompanied him to the door. "Even so—I shall come," he said blandly.

Susan Henley had not paid much heed to the beauties of Longhills as she drove through the muggy afternoon, all her anxiety being with her brother. Thank heaven Bo'sun Dodman had always longed to be a doctor and while serving aboard Grandpapa's East Indiaman had learned so much from the apothecary that he might almost qualify as one himself. The short, square, powerfully built man had come up from the barge in a rush when Deemer had called him, and having pronounced Andrew merely stunned, had thrown the young man's inanimate form over one sturdy shoulder and carried him up to his bedchamber. Her brother had come to his senses while the Bo'sun was bathing the cut on his head, and ignoring his own injury had been full of concern for Susan. To see his face so pale and his fine eyes narrowed with pain had put her in a flame. Deemer had helped her to ready their solitary old phaeton, and when Andy was between the sheets and the Bo'sun sitting watchfully beside the bed, she had driven out alone, guiding Pennywise and Pound Foolish by way of the public road so as to approach the manor from the formal front entrance, and in such a rage she'd scarcely noticed her surroundings.

Not until she rounded the curve in the drivepath and passed through the wide-open lodge gates did she receive the full impact of the great mansion, and for several seconds she let her eyes rove in awed admiration around the sweep of the mellow stone buildings that glowed like pale gold under the afternoon sun. "Lud," she whispered, "'Tis a palace!"

Two gardeners looked up curiously, and a stableboy was running, gawking his astonishment at the sight of a lady driving herself, with neither groom nor abigail beside her. Squaring her slim shoulders, Susan sent the team clopping their elderly and nondescript hooves around the towering plumes of the fountain as brashly as though they were high-spirited Thoroughbreds.

The icy, liveried, and powdered footman who swung open the great door looked pointedly for her servant, and she wished with all her heart that she had brought one of the men with her. But Deemer was becoming rather frail and had looked white and shaken, and she'd thought it imperative that the Bo'sun should stay with Andy, in case any sort of relapse occurred.

She fully expected to be denied the master of the house, but the footman asked her to wait in a quietly regal hall, then returned to conduct her up a pair of stairs to a landing from which twin curving staircases wound left and right to the galleried first floor. Up the left-hand stairs they climbed, along a noble corridor, passing wider stairs leading to the second floor. Susan caught a glimpse of a stupendous and beautiful room leading off to the right, which could only be the great hall; then the corridor jogged left again into a smaller hall, on one side of which she saw a dining room with mahogany furnishings that gleamed like dark rubies.

28

She was ushered into the opposite chamber, desired to wait "a minute or two," and again abandoned.

Resisting the impulse to sink timidly onto the nearest straight-backed chair, she wandered about. What a glorious house! Not that she'd wish to live in such a gigantic place—Lud, but one might go for days without meeting another soul. Still, it *was* a thing of beauty. Only look at the panelling in here; the ancient oak had been painted pale blue, which she thought regrettable but was the fashion, and the panels were ornamented with splendid carvings.

Before the windows a round fruitwood table was spread with a delicate lace cloth on which stood a statuette; a mermaid again, of translucent pink jade and exquisite design. She was admiring that work of art when from the corner of her eye she saw a flutter of pale blue. She crossed to the open casements and looked down on lush emerald lawns studded with flower beds and great old trees. A girl, rather on the plump side and weeping heartbrokenly, was running wildly down the terrace steps. A slim dark-haired young man sprinted after her, and swung her to face him, allowing Susan a view of mousy brown curls hanging untidily about a pale unremarkable countenance, not improved by reddened eyes and tear-streaked cheeks.

"I tell you I won't!" the girl sobbed hysterically. "I'd sooner be dead! Does it mean nothing to you that I don't *want* to marry without love?"

"Don't be a little fool!" He shook her hard, and said something in a low angry voice of which Susan only heard ". . . know very well you'll do exactly what . . ."

"I won't! I *won't*! How can you expect—"

"Mrs. Henley?"

The cool, cultured enquiry came from behind her, and Susan spun around, knowing her face was reddening, and vexed to have been caught eavesdropping.

A short, rather stout gentleman stood in the doorway, regarding her through an upheld quizzing glass. He was clad in shades of brown and had wisely avoided the tight coats and snug breeches favoured by younger men. His features were pallid and nondescript, his thinning hair pale brown, and his manner coolly disdainful.

"Yes." Rebelliously, she made no attempt to return a curtsy for his sketch of a bow. "Lord Montclair?"

Amusement danced very briefly in the brown eyes. "I am Sir Selby Trent, ma'am. Allow me to present my friend, Mr. Imre Monteil."

Susan glanced at his tall companion and encountered black eyes that glittered like two jet beads in the long white face. Unusually red lips curved to a smile. As graceful as he was elegant, he bowed his dark head, and said admiringly, "My *very* great pleasure, ma'am."

Trent threw a sharp glance up at him.

Susan was suddenly put in mind of a fungus growing furtively in the shade of a dark and twisted tree, and for a moment she was afraid, but she speedily dismissed such nonsensicalities. "I am aware that my visit is improper, but I have urgent business with Lord Montclair."

A sudden outburst of sobs from the garden brought a frown to Sir Selby's smooth forehead, and he moved quickly to close the casements. "Lord Montclair is not available," he said rather sharply, glaring at the pair on the steps below.

Monteil purred, "But Sir Selby administers the Longhills estates and I am sure would much wish to be of assistance to so lovely a lady." He crossed to pull out a graceful Hepplewhite chair and gestured to it invitingly.

Susan ignored the offer. "In which case," she said, with her firm chin elevated and her grey eyes flashing scorn, "you may care to explain, Sir Selby, why his lord-

30

ship should have sent two brutal men to invade my home this morning, bully my servants, and—"

Monteil interposed an aghast *"Mon Dieu!* Did Montclair authorize such an atrocity?"

"I most sincerely hope not, but . . ." Trent shook his head dubiously. "Madam, I can only convey my regrets. My nephew has a—ah, rather unpredictable disposition at best. He is besides extreme concerned about your illegal occupancy of his house, and—"

"My occupancy is *not* illegal, sir! My late husband's father purchased Highperch Cottage from Lady Digby Montclair seven years ago and—"

"And sold it back again just before my dear sister-in-law's death."

Susan responded hotly. "The purchase money was never returned to Mr. Ezra Henley. Therefore the property now belongs to me!"

"Coming to you as a bequest from your—ah, late husband?"

She flushed. How softly the baronet had spoken those words, yet the faint mockery in his eyes told her as clearly as though he had shouted it that he was fully aware of Burke's disgrace and eventual suicide. "Just so," she said defiantly.

"I would think the matter easy of proof," said Monteil in his slightly accented voice. "Surely there must be legal papers? A receipt—et cetera?"

Susan nodded. "We have filed our proofs with the court. But there appears to have been some confusion at the time of Lady Digby Montclair's death, and the case has been delayed and delayed by one legal manoeuvre after another."

"Come, come, Mrs. Henley." Sir Selby looked bored. "Is it not true that your late father-in-law was—er, ill and mentally confused for some years prior to his death? Further, I hope you will pardon my saying that it seems

31

remarkable that your husband made no move to claim any ownership of Highperch during his lifetime."

Susan stood very straight and tall in the quiet room, her head well up, her cheeks flushed, the light of battle in her eyes. "You imply, I think, sir, that *I* am the one making a claim, and that I know it to be fraudulent?"

His usually dull eyes brighter than ever, Monteil watched the sunbeam which slanted through the window to flirt with the toe of one of Mrs. Henley's rather scuffed riding boots. "Harsh words, dear ma'am. Say rather—an honest mistake, eh, Trent?"

"We may say whatever we wish, Imre," replied the baronet. "The fact remains that Montclair is adamant and will do exactly as he chooses. He intends that you be evicted, Mrs. Henley, and I most strongly recommend that to avoid any possibility of more such regrettable incidents, you should remove as soon as possible."

Quivering with wrath, Susan said, "That sounds remarkably like a threat, sir."

"Then I am being clumsy, ma'am, for I had meant it purely as a warning."

"I do not frighten easily, Sir Selby. Especially since I know my claim to be an honest one! You may inform Lord Montclair that his methods are cowardly and despicable, and that I have no least intention of removing from the home my husband left to me. You may further inform his lordship that we intend to bring suit for assault, battery, and—and intimidation, against Lord Montclair and Longhills! And that if he takes one more step against us prior to the court hearing, the entire matter will be well publicized in the newspapers! I am very sure Lord Montclair will be proud to have his fine old name flaunted throughout England as the type of ruffian who would evict a helpless widow and her little daughter from the only home they possess! Good day to you, gentlemen!"

And with a toss of her long black hair and a swirl of her habit, she was gone, marching through the door a most titillated lackey swung open, and traversing the hall like a ship of the line with all her flags flying.

As the door closed behind her, Sir Selby tugged at his lower lip. "Dear me," he muttered. "What a very pushing creature. One might think she could have sent a gentleman to handle matters for her."

Imre Monteil, who very seldom betrayed the slightest interest in the joys or griefs of any lady or gentleman of his acquaintance, chuckled softly. "How fortunate for us that she did not," he argued. "A truly glorious young woman. This becomes interesting."

The 'truly glorious young woman,' meanwhile, had reached the lower landing just as two ladies climbed from the ground floor. One of these was the girl she had seen in the garden. A closer view revealed her to be about nineteeen, with the most tragic pale blue eyes Susan had ever seen. The second lady was tall, middle-aged, and angular, with tightly crimped brown curls rather suspiciously untouched by silver. She was impeccably gowned in a rose velvet tunic over a paler rose sarsenet gown having the new high neckline. Her cheekbones were prominent, her mouth small and tight under the thin nose that swooped down towards her pointed chin. She paused when she saw Susan, and narrowing a pair of hard blue eyes, scanned her up and down critically.

"If you are the applicant for the position of upstairs maid," she said in a harsh, high-pitched voice, "you should have used the servants' stairs."

"Mama!" whispered the girl, embarrassed.

"If you are the housekeeper," riposted Susan coldly, "I would not wish to work here!"

"How *dare* you!" shrilled the woman. "I am Lady Selby Trent!"

"Good day, ma'am. *I* am Mrs. Burke Henley!"

"Good . . . heavens!" Lady Trent swept her train aside as though fearing it might be contaminated, and pushing her daughter before her, said, "Hurry along, child! Imagine! The brazen effrontery of it! Disgraceful!"

Susan continued on her way, eager to be gone from under my lord of Montclair's roof, smarting with resentment of Lady Trent's scorn, and plagued by the guilty knowledge that however ill-used she may have been, Papa would have been shocked by her rude response to an older lady. She could not help but be sorry for the unhappy Miss Trent, however. Just before she had been hurried away, the girl's big blue eyes had met her own in an anguished look of apology. There had been something else in those stricken eyes, and Susan was still trying to think what it was when the stableboy walked the team back and shyly handed her up into the phaeton. Starting off along the drivepath, she suddenly identified that expression, and she looked back thoughtfully at Longhills Manor.

Miss Trent dwelt in one of the loveliest homes in the land. She had probably not once in her life known what it meant to have to pinch pennies to pay the bills and the servants, or to lie awake at night wondering what was to become of her loved ones. And yet Miss Trent had looked at the shocking Mrs. Burke Henley with—envy!

Longhills faced northwest and in the far southeastern corner of the first floor, behind the conservatory, were the two large and charmingly irregularly shaped chambers that constituted Valentine Montclair's study and music room. It was towards the latter that Sir Selby Trent now made his way, frowning because of the angry voices and sounds of strife that emanated from within.

He opened the door to a bright airy room, its tall mullioned windows open to the warm afternoon air. Although it was cluttered, it was a comfortable chamber, dominated by the harpsichord set in one of the two deep bays on the east wall; a magnificent double keyboard instrument, long and graceful, the case intricately carven and gilded. Across the room, several armchairs and occasional tables were grouped around an impressive marble fireplace. A long reference table piled high with musical scores in various stages of completion stood in the second bay and nearby was another grouping of a sofa and chairs, one of which crashed over as the two young men locked in combat plunged past.

"Stop this at once!" the baronet commanded.

He was ignored. Junius Trent broke from his cousin's strong hands and sent his muscular fist in a deadly jab to the jaw. Montclair swayed nimbly aside and his right rammed home under Junius's ribs, neatly doubling him in half.

"Have done!" shouted Selby Trent.

Breathing hard, Montclair stepped back. A head shorter and of far more slender build than Junius, his hair had tumbled untidily over his forehead and the amber flecks in his dark eyes flamed with wrath. "The— next time," he panted, "you feel moved to . . . vent your spleen on something, dear cousin—"

Sir Selby raised the top of the harpsichord an inch or two and let it fall.

The resultant reverberating crash brought Montclair's head jerking around.

"Might one enquire as to the reason for yet another vulgar brawl?" enquired Sir Selby.

Montclair glared at him and crossed to lift the top of the instrument and peer anxiously at the quills.

Junius laughed breathlessly and contrived to

35

straighten up, leaning one hand on the reference table. *"Et tu . . . Brute?"*

His father regarded him coldly. "Should I interpret that to mean you also have laid hands on your cousin's harpsichord?"

"Not—er—hands exactly, Papa."

"A dead bird," said Montclair, throwing a look of disgust at Junius.

"Anything—to muffle the sounds of your . . . cacophonous efforts, dear coz."

Sir Selby was not amused. "You outdo yourself, Junius. First, that fiasco at Highperch, and now you must upset your cousin, and engage in fisticuffs, well knowing he is ill and—" He paused, then finished acidly, "I almost said unable to defend himself."

Junius flushed. "My attention was diverted when you arrrived, sir," he said sullenly.

Montclair snorted with contempt and carefully lowered the harpsichord top. "This house is sufficiently large and well built that the sounds of my playing do not carry very far, especially since a harpsichord lacks the volume of a spinet. Your quarters are in the south wing where they cannot be heard at all. One might hope you would confine yourself to that wing. Or better yet, remove from Longhills altogether."

"Ah, but I would purely loathe to give you that much pleasure," sneered Junius.

"Then you may give *me* the pleasure of picking up that chair before you remove yourself from this room," said his father. "I have business with Montclair."

For an instant Junius hesitated, then he shrugged, restored the fallen chair, and sauntered out, leaving the lackey to close the door after him.

"Val, dear lad," murmured Sir Selby, "I am sorrier than I can say, but—"

With a peremptory gesture Montclair said harshly, "What's all this about Highperch?"

36

"Alas," Trent's plump shoulders drooped. "You are impatient. As ever."

Montclair sat on the bench of the harpsichord. "I have been patient these five years since I came down from University, uncle."

"And I longer than that, Valentine. My own estates are neglected whilst I administer Longhills as—"

"Then by all means don't let 'em languish an instant longer, sir!"

Trent shrank before the sardonic tone and his head lowered. He wandered to the window and with his back to the room said in a voice that quivered with emotion, "You know very well that it was your dear Mama's wish I should—"

"My mother set you up as administrator until Geoff reached the age of five and twenty. He passed that four years since."

"How true. And if *only* he would come home to relieve me of my task! But I'll not betray my trust whilst my brave nephew is off fighting for his country."

"Pshaw! We are three years past Waterloo, and Geoff's been in India these two years and more. If he could be bothered to answer my letters I might know what the lamebrain's about, but *I'll* relieve you of your task, sir. And willingly!"

"Yes. Dear boy, I know how gallantly you would take on such a burden. Even though your health—"

"Health be damned! I can manage."

Sir Selby turned and said with a rueful smile, "Aye— to run the estate into bankruptcy!"

"The devil!" Montclair sprang to his feet, gave a gasp and clutched at the harpsichord, then sat down again. "If you mean . . ." he said unevenly, "because I refused to sell Highperch to . . . your bosom bow . . ."

Trent moved closer, eyeing his nephew's suddenly white face uneasily. In a gentler tone he said, "Another attack? Poor lad, poor lad. My fault—though I had no

37

desire to upset you. But it's more than that single matter. I know how well you mean, but your plans are too grandiose, Valentine; your ambitions too costly for the estate to bear. I've managed to keep us in good financial colour all these years, despite rising costs, and—"

"You've hoarded every damned farthing, is what you mean! You *cannot* just—" Montclair paused, and drew a trembling hand across his eyes. "*Damn* this . . . confounded dizziness," he whispered.

Trent hurried to rest a consoling hand on the bowed shoulder. "Poor boy. I should never have scolded you." Sorrow came into his eyes as his nephew jerked away from his touch, and he said with a smothered sigh, "Dr. Sheswell says you must be calm. I'll go."

"No." Montclair pulled up his head and peered into his uncle's martyred smile. "Tell me what you meant about—Highperch."

Trent occupied the dark green velvet sofa and smoothed a crease from his sleeve. "Perhaps I should not bother you with it, dear lad, but—"

"For the love of God," snarled Montclair, "stop calling me 'dear lad' or your 'poor boy'! I am nigh seven and twenty. Say it and be done!"

For the space of a single breath the chubby hand was very still on Trent's well-clad arm. Then he said softly, "If my son ever dared use such a tone to me . . ."

"You are to be congratulated, sir. I am neither your son nor any blood relation."

"No." Trent drew a breath and smiled kindly. "You are the child of my dear wife's beloved brother. And as a good Christian, I must make allowances for your—"

"Mental lapses?"

"No, no! Never describe it thus. You have been ill and the symptoms linger—no more, no less. Now, let us talk of less grievous matters. The fact is, Valentine, that—well, not to beat about the bush, Burke Henley's widow has moved into Highperch, and—"

38

"*What?*" roared Montclair, rising from the bench like a rocket. "Were our keepers and gardeners asleep? How the hell did she manage it?"

"I've no least notion, but it is an isolated piece of land. Perhaps she moved overnight. She might even have had her effects shipped by way of the river. The—er, worst of it is, she claims her papa-in-law never received his funds from the resale of Highperch, and—"

"By God, but he did! Old Ferry's got Ezra Henley's signed receipt locked in his safe!" Montclair began to stride about the room. "When I think of how that wretched old humbug bothered my mother! From the moment he bought the property he did nothing but complain. He never would keep to the public road, but insisted on driving clear across Longhills to reach Highperch. When Mama learned the description on the Deed was at fault, it was her chance to declare the sale invalid, which she did promptly enough, I can tell you."

"I knew the sale was voided, of course. But how was the description at fault?"

"The property was described as being in Gloucestershire whereas in point of fact that small parcel is across the county line. That's why it was never included in the entail. A few years before her death my Grandmama decided she wanted Highperch for a Dower House. Lord knows there was no need, and none of us wanted her to go, but she persisted, had the entire place redecorated, lived there about a year, and then declared it too lonely." Smiling nostalgically, he sat down again, then drove an impatient hand through his hair. "Lord—why did I tell you all that? You know it as well as I!"

"With your papa and my dear wife having been estranged for so many years, I had little opportunity to know the old lady." Trent shook his head. "She always was eccentric, I understand."

"Then your understanding is at fault," snapped Montclair.

39

"I had intended no criticism," said Sir Selby with a crushed air. "I merely thought it a sad waste of money." He saw the immediate spark of anger in his nephew's dark eyes, and added hastily, "After my brother-in-law died I wonder your mother did not simply have High-perch torn down."

"That was her intent, but I always liked the house and begged her not to level it. She agreed, with the proviso it should never be a charge on her, and made it over to me." Montclair's face darkened. "Dammitall, had I restored it and moved in, as I meant to do, this wretched widow would never have been able to slither into possession!"

"Instead of which, you were too busy guarding Long-hills from the depredations of your unworthy uncle," said Trent wryly. His nephew merely glaring at him, he added, "I had hoped to persuade Mrs. Henley to leave, but she is a brazen hussy and—"

"You've *met* the lady?"

"There is a great difference my b— Valentine, between a lady and a woman. She called here this after-noon. Alone, if you can believe such boldness."

"Blast it! Why wasn't I told?"

"We were unable to find you." Trent added with a bland smile, "Perhaps you were discussing wedding plans with my daughter."

Montclair flushed but met his eyes steadily.

"At all events," went on Sir Selby, "Madam Henley is full of threats and says she means to bring suit against us for every crime imaginable, and drag your name through the mud. The vulgar harlot! I'll tell Ferry to have an eviction—"

"Thank you—no. It is *my* house, sir. I'll ride over to Highperch first thing in the morning and have a little discussion with our avaricious widow. She'd as well learn as soon as may be that she must practice her chicanery elsewhere!"

40

Susan guided the team mechanically, angered because she was trembling and shaken by the ugly encounters in the great house. It was cooler when they entered the woods. The sunlight danced through the leaves, painting a roof of varying greens above her, the lazy shifting of the branches creating an ever changing pattern on the broad backs of Pennywise and Pound Foolish—a pattern Susan viewed through the blur of tears.

She groped for her handkerchief and wiped her eyes fiercely. She *would* not cry! She *would* not be defeated! Not now. It had been so hard to keep them all together after Burke died. Andy and the Bo'sun had tried to help, and together with the money she'd raised by selling her jewellry, they'd been able to stay in the house in Town until the lease expired. It had been a necessary but not happy arrangement. Priscilla, innocent of any wrongdoing, was shunned by the neighbourhood children until, bewildered and hurt, she'd invented her own little excuses for her unpopularity. Not one of those viciously virtuous matrons who dwelt in the Square would so much as pass the time of day with the widow of a man who had gambled away a fortune, been dishonourably discharged from the Navy, and had then so disgracefully ended his own life. To make matters worse, Andy had brought them more notoriety by calling out a gentleman who had sneered a little too openly.

When they'd gone through Burke's papers and come across the Deed to Highperch Cottage, it had seemed the answer to their prayers. Only, the next day further investigation had disclosed that the Deed was clouded. She and Andrew had laid the whole matter before the aging solicitor who had handled all Grandpapa's affairs. The old man had glanced through the various papers, examined the Deed, and said that certainly there would be a battle to prove that Mr. Henley had never been refunded the purchase price on the cottage. Well aware of their circumstances, he'd cocked a shrewd eye at Andrew and said, "Incidentally, it's my understanding no one has lived at Highperch for several years. Possession being nine-tenths of the law, was you to slip in there, Lyddford . . . under cover of darkness perhaps . . ."

Andy had laughed delightedly, but Susan had been shocked and had said with considerable indignation that she had no intent to do anything illegal. It was the Montclairs who were behaving in an unlawful way, argued Andy, by having failed to make proper restitution to her late father-in-law. "Besides," he'd added thoughtfully, "the cottage sits on a bank right above the Severn. Be jolly fine for *The Dainty Dancer*." And, with a gleam of mischief in his grey eyes, "Seems almost as though it was intended for us, don't it, Sue?"

The phaeton left the trees and plunged into warm sunshine again, following the ribbon of the road as it wound across the fragrant meadows towards the last low hill, aesthetically crowned by the little belt of ash and elm, that sheltered Highperch Cottage. Susan's throat tightened when at last the gables of the house came into view. She'd loved the poor old place the instant she saw it standing in proud if rather forlorn dignity on its eminence above the river, the widespread inverted U-shape of the two-storey building so much too large for the term 'cottage,' the red sandstone walls a burnished glow in the light of the full moon. It had been shamefully neglected, and she'd fancied it was lonely, waiting for the warmth of a loving family to make it feel wanted again.

Well, it was wanted. But Lord Montclair was a rich and powerful man and she was only a disgraced widow. If the courts ruled in the baron's favour, she and her little 'family' would have to move again. Wherever would she find so perfect a home for them all?

Pennywise and Pound Foolish slowed as they plodded up the drivepath. The scent of roses drifted from the weedy flower beds. The front door burst open and Priscilla hopped down the steps and danced joyously to meet the phaeton, Wolfgang prancing at her heels. Edwina Starr, dainty despite her dusty apron, walked onto the terrace and waved a greeting. Beyond the sprawl of the old house the great river wound its sparkling way to the estuary, and far away loomed the unchanging hills of Malvern.

An invisible hand clamped around Susan's heart and her throat tightened. She thought achingly, 'We cannot lose it! We *cannot*! He has so much—must he cheat us out of this dear old place, when he never even cared enough to keep it in good repair?' And she knew she would fight with every weapon at hand to prevent High-perch Cottage being stolen from them.

3

The morning was windy but warm. With much to think about, Montclair rose early and having advised Gould that he would be walking over to Highperch later, was dressed in fawn breeches, a green nankeen jacket, and topboots.

Gould, a tall middle-aged man slightly stooped from rheumatism, was a rather dour individual, and seeing the frown in his master's eyes made no attempt to engage him in conversation. Valentine Montclair would have been a disappointment to any Town valet with aspirations to rise in his profession. He was, thought Gould, a perfect representation of the artistic temperament: impatient with the demands of Fashion and anything that smacked of the dandy; impatient with the inanities of snobbish small talk and gossip; impatient with the lovely young ladies who fluttered their lashes and their fans at him, and whose vapid giggles and flirtatious chatter had been known to drive him to a precipitate retreat from the parties his aunt so delighted to preside over.

Not an easy young man. But oddly enough, Montclair

never quite disgraced his valet. In the throes of composition he might wrench at his neckcloth until it was all awry, or drive his long sensitive fingers through his dark locks until they tumbled untidily over his high forehead, yet with not the least inclination to do so, he always looked well turned out. Mr. Junius Trent, who spent a small fortune on his wardrobe, invariably found himself in some inexplicable fashion cast into the shade by his cousin, with the result that Mr. Trent's man was forever dodging boots or bottles hurled at him in a frustrated fury.

Aware of some of the crushing burdens carried on those slim shoulders, Gould had a deeper sympathy for his employer than Montclair would have dreamed. To sympathy was added another emotion. Prior to entering Montclair's service, the valet had enjoyed hearing the band play in the park, and he'd even gone to Covent Garden once or twice, mostly to see the opera dancers, of course, but paying more attention to the music than many in the audience. When first he came to Longhills, he'd soon learned that Sir Selby and Lady Trent had only disdain for Mr. Valentine's musical talents, and that Mr. Junius Trent was revolted by them. When guests came to dine, however, my lady invariably pinched at "dear Valentine" until he agreed to play. It was said with much amusement in the servants' hall that this was a mixed blessing to Lady Trent, for her attempts to talk throughout her nephew's performance were all too often ignored, and she had once actually been "shushed" at. The applause and the praise showered on Montclair were gall and wormwood to her, and on the evening when a *grande dame* was moved to tears and embraced Valentine, saying he was a true master, hilarious footmen relayed the information that my lady's smile appeared to have been applied to her face with rusty nails. Intrigued by all this, Gould crept one night to where he

45

could hear his employer play, and since then he eavesdropped as often as he dared and was frequently so moved that he could scarcely refrain from expressing his admiration. Had anyone suggested that he was deeply fond of his unpredictable master, he would have scoffed, but had he been offered twice his already generous salary, he'd have given not one instant's consideration to leaving Valentine Montclair's service.

He watched the young aristocrat walk briskly to the door, and wondered what particular problem was causing the black brows to draw into such a scowl this morning. The door closed, and Gould shook his head worriedly. Mr. Valentine had fought hard to overcome the unknown malady that had afflicted him in March, but here it was June and he still suffered dizzy spells, and did not look—

The door burst open, and Montclair's dark head was thrust inside. "Forgot," he said, with a grin that banished the grimness and took years from his lean face. "Good morning, Gould."

"Good morning, sir," said Gould gravely. The door was slammed shut, and the valet smiled and began to hum as he started to tidy up the shaving paraphernalia.

Montclair asked a hovering lackey to bring toast and coffee to his study, and made his way to that ever welcoming haven. He crossed at once to the harpsichord and stood with one hand on the lid, staring blindly at the keyboards. In Town, good old Jocelyn and Dev had been concerned about him, he knew. Dev had ridden up twice since then, and it was a good two hours' ride— even the way Dev rode—for Devencourt was situated high in the Cotswolds and the private road was far from easy. Had they suspected, as he suspected, that the Mohocks had not been Mohocks, but hired assassins? Or had his friends merely been concerned because he was obviously not in the pink of health? "Damn!" he snarled explosively, and sat on the bench.

46

He began to play a piece by the incomparable Mr. Mozart. His fingers flew and the old harpsichord vibrated. Lost in his music, he didn't hear the lackey come in with his breakfast, and when he sensed a presence beside him, he whirled, crouching low, his fists clenched and his face so murderous that the lackey came near to dropping the tray. He deposited it nervously on the top of the harpsichord and fled, pale and shaken.

Pouring himself a cup of the steaming coffee, Montclair whispered a frustrated "Valentine sir, you are a blasted fool!" and scarcely noticed when the first mouthful scalded him. But *was* he being a fool? *Was* he imagining it all? Or was his greatest dread becoming reality—the ever deepening fear that the illness was seriously impairing his mind? He spread strawberry jam lavishly on a piece of toast, and glanced around with schoolboy guilt because of his gluttony, but after only two bites his mind had reverted to the incident in Town, and the toast was abandoned.

The first such incident had occurred almost a year ago, when the pole on his racing curricle had snapped. He'd come away with no worse than three broken ribs and some bruises, but both horses had to be destroyed, and one had been dear old Flinders, a friend of many years, and mama's favourite. Later, Charlie Purvis, the head groom, had told him that it was "odd" the pole breaking like that. "Looked almost as if it had been tampered with, Mr. Valentine . . ." He'd paid small heed. Who would want to do him a mischief?

A few months later, he'd been riding Allegro—not the most placid of his horses, certainly, but a joy to ride and a real goer. Topping a familiar rise at his customary high speed, he'd seen too late that the smooth downward slope was smooth no longer, but a widespread deathtrap of piled chunks of rocks and timber. There'd been no possible chance to avoid disaster. The big ugly bay stallion had made a gallant try and almost cleared the debris. Uncle Selby had said it was a miracle they both hadn't been killed, and scolded because he'd so often cautioned that 'dear Valentine' rode like a madman. Nursing a broken ankle, he'd been grateful that Allegro had fallen clear and suffered only some scrapes. The most disturbing aspect of the matter was that he followed exactly the same route several times a week, and never had there been any obstruction on the down side of that hill. It was open country, off Longhills land, and why the great pile of wreckage had been assembled there, or who had left it, could not be discovered. But not until the poacher hunting pheasants had come so damnably close to blowing his head off in March, followed in May by the attack in Town, had he accepted the possibility of a plot against his life.

He took up his coffee again and sipped broodingly. Why? He was not without enemies, his temper was quick, and his impatience with nonsense had ruffled a few feathers. But he could think of no one who would really want him dead. If he held the title, and if the next in succession was his uncle, then perhaps— But what rubbishing stuff! He did *not* hold the title, and if he ever should—God forbid!—he and poor Hampton Montclair would still stand between Junius Trent and Longhills. Seized by disgust for such basely unwarranted suspicions, he slammed down the coffee cup and launched into his new concerto. It was a fiery piece, the final movement rising into a most difficult *accelerando*, but his skilled fingers mastered the challenge. Revelling in the sense that it was good—that he had achieved something really worthwhile, he swept into the last crashing chord, and sat with head thrown back and eyes closed, exhilarated.

"Ti! Help Monsieur Valentine! Quickly!"

Montclair groaned a curse and spun around, coming practically nose to nose with the short but solidly built

Oriental who was Imre Monteil's groom and constant companion. Just before he'd come down from Oxford Montclair had met a young Chinese, and because he had an enquiring mind had struggled to overcome the accent which had made conversation difficult and tended to isolate the foreigner. His persistence had been worthwhile; he'd learned much of the Orient and its customs and had parted from the humble and softly spoken Mr. Li with the awed conviction that he had made friends with a genius. Ti Chiu was a very different proposition. Junius Trent contemptuously described his features as chunks of granite which had been so haphazardly tossed together as to hide his eyes. Montclair was not one to judge by appearances, but he had to admit that Ti Chiu was not a well-favoured man. He had never been known to smile, and seldom looked directly into the eyes of another, keeping his own downcast. His big hands were outstretched now, and Montclair recoiled, saying irritably, "I am perfectly well, thank you!"

Ti Chiu bowed and scurried back to stand, dwarfed, behind his master.

"Are you quite sure, my poor fellow?" The Swiss wandered nearer.

Standing, Montclair was once more conscious of the extreme dislike he harboured towards both this elegant gentleman and his craggy servant. "Quite sure," he said coolly. "What can I do for you?"

He was granted the wide smile that failed to bring the slightest warmth to the flat, dead eyes. "But you have already done everything—or almost everything—dear Valentine. I am come, in fact, to thank you for yet another visit most delightful."

"You are leaving us, monsieur?" said Montclair, ignoring the qualification.

"My affairs, alas, demand my presence in Brussels. I trust you will accept my invitation and visit me at some time of your convenience. *Assurément,* I may offer you more sunshine than you enjoy here in your—green and pleasant land."

"If you find England so gloomy, sir, you must be relieved that I would not sell Highperch to you."

"Ah, but one must have change, eh, *mon ami?* Do you go now to your so charming trespasser? I shall wish you good hunting with the bewitching widow."

It was the closest approach to enthusiasm that Montclair had ever seen in this man, and his dark brows lifted. "That's not how my uncle describes her, monsieur."

"Me, I am more in agreement with your cousin's impression of her, but you will judge for yourself. And when I return, my dear sir, I shall hope to persuade you to let me buy the cottage. You may change your mind, if I make a more substantial offer, *n'est-ce pas?*"

"No. Goodbye, monsieur."

"Ah, but that is much too final. I say instead *au revoir,* for we shall meet again."

Valentine acknowledged Monteil's bow with a short nod, gave a sigh of relief as the ill-assorted pair strolled from the room, and muttered, "Not if I can help it!"

Having no desire to be caught up in the involved and formal farewells that Lady Trent appeared to find indispensable, he left the house by way of the conservatory, detoured around the kitchen gardens and lodge gates, and walked into the stable block. The head groom, a sturdy little Welshman on the light side of forty, was looking up at a disgruntled-seeming individual mounted on a grey horse, with a worn valise tied to the pommel.

"A sorry fool ye are," the Welshman said in his pleasant singsong voice, "to let yerself be pushed out of a steady situation by a dumb beast!"

The rider started away, but turned in the saddle to

call, "Maybe I am. But I ain't so big a fool as you, Charlie Purvis, to stay and be chewed by the brute. I come here to work wi' horses—not be attacked by a bloody great wolf!" He drew level with Montclair, fixed him with a resentful eye, but touched his hat and muttered, "Goodbye, sir," before he rode on.

Purvis, short, dark, and with an impish look in his blue eyes, hastened to Montclair's side.

"Doesn't like my cousin's hound, is that it?" asked Montclair.

Purvis had been head groom at Longhills for twenty years, and did not feel it necessary to guard his words. "We none of us like the dog, sir, but it took a special dislike to Jim, I'll not deny. Bit him three weeks ago and again today. I will not say as I blame him fer going away, since we are not allowed to strike the creature."

"Devil you aren't! No man in my brother's service is expected to stand for being savaged by that hound and do nothing about it! I broke a stick on Soldier when he came at me last year, and he's kept his distance since. He's just a bully, and has to be put in his place."

"Like his master," said Purvis under his breath.

"What's that?"

"Er, I said he's a bastard," said the Welshman, round-eyed and innocent. "And ye're one of the family, Mr. Valentine. 'Tis a different matter fer ye, if I may be so bold as ter say so."

"You don't seem to lack for that quality," said Montclair, who had a good pair of ears.

Purvis looked chastened, but a different expression came into his face as he watched the younger man stride briskly out of the yard. He turned his glance to the great house, frowned, and spat at the cobblestones. "Past time you come home, Lord Geoffrey Montclair," he muttered. "Long past time!"

Comfortably stretched out on the shabby sofa in the spacious withdrawing room of Highperch Cottage, Andrew Hartley Lyddford turned the page of the novel he was reading and gave an amused snort.

His sister peeped into the room to see if he was sleeping, heard the snort, and—because she had selected his reading material—was somewhat puzzled. She walked over to him. "What are you giggling about?"

He closed the volume hurriedly, having first put a finger between the pages to mark his place. "Oh, it is this stupid book." His grey eyes widened as he looked up at her, and before she could comment, he asked laughingly, "What the deuce are you about, Sue? Be dashed if you don't look a fright! Whatever shall you do if Lady Selby Trent comes calling?"

Susan had been helping Mrs. Starr and Martha Reedham with the unending task of cleaning this funny old house, and was clad in her oldest gown, a grubby apron tied about her shapely middle, and an old mob-cap containing her luxuriant hair. "Swoon," she replied with a grin. "But never fear, that odious woman will not set foot in this house—unless it is with a constable to eject the brazen Widow Henley. However, if any of that horrid Montclair contingent *should* come, my lad—"

"I am four and twenty, and one year your senior, Madam Sauce. Do not be addressing me as if I were a mere snip of a child."

"—you will at once be packed off to your bed again," Susan went on, unperturbed. "We want no more pitched battles, and I cannot have you prancing about after taking such a nasty whack on the head."

She had mothered him since 1805, when their beautiful but frail mama had begun to grieve herself into an early grave. Lieutenant Hartley Lyddford had been one of Lord Nelson's most able upcoming officers, a well-born man in whom the good looks of the Lyddfords had been allied to a winning manner and a keen mind that remained cool and collected however fierce the action. The admiral had prophesied a brilliant career for Lyddford, but at the height of the Battle of Trafalgar a mizzen-topgallant mast was shot through and, falling, had written finis to that career before Lyddford reached his thirty-sixth birthday. The lieutenant had accompanied the commander he worshipped on a voyage into the hereafter, and his widow, lacking either the will or the courage to face life's struggles without him, had followed him within a year of his death.

Susan had seen her father as an heroic, beautiful, and godlike creature, and had adored him. Now, scanning the handsome features that were so very like those of her papa, she thought Andrew looked pale and rather drawn despite his cheerful grin. She also became aware that her neat bandage was missing from his dark curls, and her eyes sparked indignantly.

Not for nothing had Lyddford shared the same roof with this dauntless young woman for most of his four-and-twenty years. "My particular form of concussion," he declared hurriedly, "will manifest itself in tearing limb from limb any female who dares wrap another piece of sheet around my noble brow and turn me into a figure of fun for anyone chancing to pass by!"

Susan bent a thoughtful look on him and walked over to the window. The sky was acquiring a few clouds and a whitish look, and the treetops were tossing restlessly. She ran one slim fingertip down a leaded pane, sighed, and turned about.

"Now what has you in a pucker?" asked Lyddford curiously.

"I was looking for passers-by. There are none. Rest

there, if you please, while I go in search of a *male* to wrap a bandage around your noble brow, since it would appear that only females are denied that glorious opportunity." He laughed, and she added more soberly, "No, but you really must be good, Andy. If you cavort about and fall again I shall be obliged to send Angelo to find a proper physician."

"He wouldn't be able to pronounce it—much less find one. And besides, if all I hear is truth, physicians are far from proper!"

He had forgotten to keep the book facedown. Susan gave a small outraged cry and pounced to snatch it from his hand.

"What's this?" She read the title aloud. "*Santo Sebastiano or the Young Protector* by *Mrs. Cuthbertson?*" Unable to keep the amusement from her voice, she said in pseudo-shocked condemnation, "Andrew—Hartley—Lyddford! This is not the book I gave you! Whatever would Grandpapa have said?"

"Likely that he'd read it, and it's a jolly good book. At any rate, it's better than that awful thing *you* selected! *The Dairyman's Daughter,* indeed! If ever I read such stuff!"

"It is elevating to the mind," she said primly, holding the substitution out of his reach. "They say it has already sold over a million copies!"

"Then there are over a million Britons who are bored to distraction, and likely mobbing the bookshops demanding their money back! No really, Susan, if the people in that wretched tale aren't dying, that widgeon of a heroine is busily converting 'em! Do you know, the chit converts everyone in sight, including her sister? And the sister dies anyway! In the end, *she* dies! Jupiter! It's enough to give a man the moulding miseries!"

She laughed and waved the book at him. "Well, in *this* one everybody swoons!"

"So you've read it, you little varmint."

"Yes." She sank to her knees beside him. "Did you keep count of all the bodies thudding to the boards? I thought it so diverting. Even Lord St. Orville swoons!"

"True. Still, it's a ripping good tale for all that. I especially liked—" He stopped, a faint frown tugging at his dark brows as his sister glanced again to the window. She was not one to fret for nothing. He tugged gently at a strand of glossy hair that had escaped the mob-cap. "What are you worrying at? I've my pistol loaded and ready in case those clods should come back. And when we have our day in court we'll send Montclair to the rightabout soon enough."

"I'm sure we will," she said. But she spoke absently, and her troubled gaze was still on the window.

Lyddford watched her, his eyes sobering. If ever a girl deserved the good things of life, it was his Susan. No man could wish for a better sister; nor, he thought loyally, a lovelier one. But poor Sue's path through life had been far from easy. With the best will in the world to provide for his family, Papa had been a younger son with no expectations other than what his Navy pay and the possibility of prize money would bring him. After his death they'd been all but destitute, existing on the begrudging charity of Papa's brother, Sir John Lyddford, surely the worst piece of clutch-fisted snobbery ever created. Grandpapa Tate, as different an article to mama as could have been imagined, had left the merchantman he'd commanded for the East India Company, and come home to, as he put it, steer his daughter's children "through the shoals to the Isle of Dreams." It was Grandpapa who had moved them into decent lodgings and seen to it that they were able to enter the fringes, at least, of Polite Society. It was Grandpapa who'd presented Burke Henley to Susan, and had said he was a "fine young gentleman with a comfortable fortune behind him."

55

Lyddford had never really known whether Sue married the dashing Henley because she loved him, or for the security a wealthy young man could offer. Wherever their 'Isle of Dreams' was, however, Burke Henley had not possessed the chart to it. Good-natured and easy going, deeply in love with his bride, always full of fun and high spirits, he had willingly paid his brother-in-law's University expenses for two years. But in the third year of his marriage he had come home from sea and been stationed at the Navy Board in London, with easy access to the clubs and theatres he'd patronized before entering upon a naval career. It hadn't taken long for him to fall in with some old friends. When Grandpapa had pointed out that they were now part of a very fast crowd, Henley had only laughed at the old gentleman for his "sanctimonious preaching."

Not his wife nor any member of his family could make Henley listen to reason. After Grandpapa's death, he had been even less restrained, and had very soon whistled his fortune down the wind. Perhaps it was guilt that had made him turn to drink, or perhaps that weakness had always been there too. At all events, bad had led to worse, and now poor Henley's honour was clouded and he was dead this year and more. Susan was disgraced and rejected by the *haut ton,* and they were reduced to living in a neglected rundown old barn of a house, miles from anywhere.

Lyddford followed his sister's gaze to the window and observed, "Weather on the way, I wouldn't be surprised. Is that what bothers you? The Bo'sun knows what he's about, never fear."

She nodded, then stood. "But Priscilla doesn't."

"The deuce! Has she gone wandering off again? That little minx! Well, she'll stay away from the river, at least, after the whipping I gave her yesterday morning."

Susan glanced at him and suppressed a smile. He was

exceeding fond of his small niece, and the fear for her safety that had led him to actually deposit one half-hearted spank on her little bottom had left him pale and stricken. Priscilla had been devastated, and for a while Susan had scarce known whom to comfort first. She had no doubt that her daughter would not go near the crumbling riverbank again, which was a weight off her mind. Still . . .

"I cannot have her roaming like this," she muttered. "Angelo has gone to try and find her. I thought he'd be back by now."

"Oh, I think there is no cause for alarm. We're miles from the village, and very few people use the lane. I fancy she took Wolfgang with her, and Angelo's probably gone on with them. She'll be all right."

But after his sister had gone back upstairs to help Mrs. Starr in the linen room, Lyddford detached his tall figure from the sofa and made his way to the window. The river was a pale silver snake winding through a peaceful green and gold patchwork. It was true that they were isolated here, but one never knew where evil would rear its ugly head, and a man who would send two bullies to terrorize a helpless woman was capable of anything.

He darted a quick look at the door, then raised the window, climbed through, and started around the side of the house and southward towards the woods.

Montclair crossed the park, paying little heed to the mischievous wind that tossed his hair about, or to the great billowing sails of the cloud ships that were beginning to gather high above him. Normally, he would have been appreciative of his surroundings, for he loved this beautiful part of Britain, with its rolling hills and verdant meadows, its darkly mysterious woodland, the ever changing voice of the mighty River Severn, the timeless serenity of the proud old estate that had been his birthplace. But serenity had gone. For six years and more Longhills had been under siege, with Geoffrey—a pox on his irresponsible self!—cavorting about all over the globe because he couldn't abide the Trents, and not even coming home now that he was of an age to end his uncle's administration of the estates. Montclair scowled, hoping there was nothing wrong with the madcap brother he loved dearly. He'd tried to keep things in good case for Geoff, Lord knows. Now, Dr. Sheswell was insisting that he must rest more. But how the hell could he—

A twig snapped behind him. He halted abruptly and jerked around. He had come into the fringes of the Home Wood, and had the strongest impression that someone followed, but his keen gaze saw only the trees, calm and stately; the dappled light flirting with ferns and shrubs; a rook cawing at him from a high branch. 'Imagining things again, you dolt,' he thought, and walked on. If his health failed—now of all times—with this wretched betrothal business to be dealt with, and Babs so frantically opposed to it. Though she'd do what she was told, if—

A low growl interrupted his frowning introspection. The small clearing before him was occupied by a dog. Part Alsation and part Great Dane, it crouched with fierce eyes fixed on him, a bone gripped between its jaws, the menacing rumble of sound coming from deep in its throat.

Montclair stood still. "Soldier! Go home!" he said firmly.

The dog dropped the bone. The hair standing up all across its powerful shoulders, it presented a fearsome picture as it charged.

Montclair had neither pistol nor cane, but he knew that to back away, or run, would be fatal. He raised his voice and his fist. *"Down!"* he bellowed. For a second he

58

really thought his only chance was going to be to grab for the throat. Then, two yards from him, the savage attack halted. The dog dropped to a crouch again, barked fiercely for a minute or two, then turned, retrieved his bone, and trotted off, still growling around it.

Montclair took a deep breath. "Damned ugly brute," he grumbled, and just to be on the safe side, took up a hefty fallen branch before walking on.

His attempts to think of a way to convince Barbara seemed doomed. He had journeyed only a short way after his encounter with Soldier when another meeting disrupted his concentration. His gaze was on the ground before him and he paused when a pair of small, highly polished boots came into his field of vision.

"Mices foots chew mire?" said a tenor voice enquiringly.

A small dapper gentleman sat on a fallen tree trunk, his high-crowned beaver hat beside him. Very black hair sprang in thick glistening waves from his rather sallow but unwrinkled brow. Equally black eyebrows arched over bright dark eyes. His skin seemed to stretch over the high cheekbones, his nose was a large thin arch, his chin long and pointed. He was impeccably clad in a brown riding coat over moleskin breeches, the only incongruity being the outmoded foam of lace at his throat and wrists. Montclair guessed him to be anywhere between thirty and forty, and that he was foreign was obvious, but the language had been unfamiliar. He made an attempt. *"Pardon-nez moi, monsieur?"*

"Angelo have say," the dapper one explained, looking irked, "chew mices foots mire. Plain is not?"

'Plain is *not!*' thought Montclair, but said a baffled, "Right."

"Right!" The little man beamed, stuck out his right leg, and admired it. "Very much spense. Chew know goods, chess!"

59

Struggling, Montclair said, "Your—feet?"

"Chess. Foots." He stood on them. "Very good very nice chew mire."

"Ah. I admire your boots, is that it?"

"It? Ay! It what?"

"I mean—did you ask if I admired your boots?"

A haughty frown drew down those black brows. "Chew make the funny thing, but Angelo laugh ha-ha no! Many time this we talk. Chew say right. Now chew say it what. Theses I know about no much. Splain pliss chew doing what in trees."

'Saints preserve us,' thought Montclair. "I am walking through the woods to visit someone," he said with slow and careful enunciation. "May I be of help to you?"

"Poor cove very bad chew English spoke. Meece, Angelo, *comprende mucho*."

Montclair gave a sigh of relief. "Ah! *Se habla espagnol, señor?*"

A thin hand was flung up autocratically. The dark head tossed high. "*Inglés, por favor!* Angelo speak now goodly. But better spress mices elves soon will." He grinned broadly and put out his hand. "Angelo Francisco Luis Lagunes de Ferdinand is mices elves. Service your hat."

Preserving his countenance gallantly, Montclair shook his hand and responded, "I am Valentine Montclair. At *your* serv—"

Señor de Ferdinand whipped his hand back as if he'd been stung. *"Bandido!"* he howled, thrusting his face at Montclair's chin. He sprang back, lifted both fists in a prize-fighting attitude, and began to dance around the astonished Englishman at great speed, his head tilted far back, his legs fairly twinkling as he advanced and retreated, his fists flailing madly about, and all the time shouting variously, *"Sapristi!" "El Diablo!"* or similar uncomplimentary epithets. Abandoning these aggressive tactics, he snatched up his hat, and flung it in Montclair's

60

face. "Chew dog dirtness!" he declared, and suddenly all stately languor, stood very straight and still, his arms folded as he enquired with a bored smile, "We with the pistolas shoot. *Mañana*—er, threemorrow, chess?"

"I think you have escaped from Bedlam," gasped Montclair. "I've no least intention to fight a lunatic! And the word is *to*morrow. Not *three*morrow."

Señor de Ferdinand's black brows rose and an eager light brightened the dark eyes. "Ay, *bueno!*" He bowed with a great many flourishes. "*To*morrow! Thankschew, señor! Mices hand shoot it will true. Chew nothing feel very much!" He struck himself on the chest. "Angelo he say theses!" He clapped the beaver at a jaunty angle onto his head, and gave it a rap on the crown, whereupon it fell off. He grabbed for it, juggled it an embarrassed second or two, and then dropped it. With a rather guilty look at the fascinated Montclair, he snatched it up and hurried off.

"Well, I'll be damned!" Still incredulous, Montclair shook his head, and went on his way.

Not until later did it occur to him to wonder what the small Spanish birdwit had been doing on Longhills land.

The Montclair Folly had been built to house a madwoman. In 1362 Sir dePuigh Montclair, grandfather of the first baron, had stolen the enchanting young girl who had dared to reject him, and dragged her to Longhills to become his bride. The poor girl had been in love with the man he'd slain while capturing her; shock and grief had caused her mind to give way and her abductor had found himself saddled with a raving lunatic. A belatedly awoken sense of guilt had kept him from doing away with her. He kept her locked in an improvised suite in Longhills' second cellar for a year, while he built a tower for her in the deepest part of the forest. His wretched victim only dwelt there for eight months, however, before escaping it and life by the simple means of jumping off the roof.

Years later, when the tragic story at length began to be whispered abroad, the Montclair Folly became an object of curiosity for lovers of the macabre, and inevitably with such a background came the rumours that it was haunted. In 1624, when much of the tower was destroyed in a lightning-caused fire, the superstitious villagers said the devil had claimed his own, and after that even the family members avoided the Folly. For over a century the windowless walls still stood. But rain and mould took their toll, the insidious roots of creepers, the invasion of insects proved once again their superiority over the works of man, and early in the eighteenth century the rugged walls of the Folly at last began to crumble away. Now, all that remained were two ivy-covered half walls and assorted stone blocks scattered around the yawning pit that once had been the cellar.

Lost in thought, Montclair had not noticed his proximity to the Folly, and might have wandered past it had he not begun to be annoyed by something that felt like a stone in his boot. He was still carrying the branch he'd taken up when Soldier came at him, and he tossed it on a small heap of the blocks, sat beside it, and began to pull off his boot. He stopped abruptly when he heard a woman singing. The voice was thin and high pitched, the words indistinguishable, the melody set in a minor key and having some resemblance to a monastic chant.

The hairs on the back of Montclair's neck started to lift and a chill crept over his skin. With a pang of dread he thought that it was probably his illness plaguing him again, causing his mind to play him false, but he picked up his branch, tightened his grip on it, and walked slowly towards the great glooming ruins.

4

The singing faded away. Had it ever really been a sound outside his own head? Was he getting worse? Perhaps his family would soon be building a Folly for him . . . Revolted by this lapse into self-pity, he gritted his teeth and decided to have a closer look, just in case there *was* something more substantial than his erratic mind. He gave a gasp as the song rang out once more, much closer now, and accompanied this time by another voice raised in an unearthly wailing that turned his bones to water.

> *"Woe, woe, woe, woe.*
> *I will go*
> *And when I'm dead*
> *He'll hang his head*
> *And wish that I*
> *Am here instead*
> *Woe, woe, woe, woe!"*

He hadn't imagined all that! He felt the blood drain from his face. "Dear God!" he whispered, and stood motionless, quite incapable of taking another step.

63

The dark walls towered above him. The mournful wind wailed softly and set the branches rustling. The air seemed to have become icy.

An oddly penetrating voice wailed, "Who comes to my tower?"

He sent a swift glance around the clearing. He was quite alone. So there really *was* a ghost! He knew he was behaving like a spineless coward, but his one thought was to run. He obeyed the impulse, spun about, took a long stride, collided with something, and a piercing screech rang out. The trees seemed to ripple before his eyes.

"Now see what you've gone and done!"

The voice came from the ground at his feet. He looked down and relief was overwhelming.

A small girl lay sprawled on her back, looking up at him reproachfully.

"Oh—Jupiter . . ." he gasped.

Her solemn little face was framed by a lopsided sunbonnet from which untidy dark brown curls strayed erratically. A bent pair of spectacles hung from one ear, and two big grey eyes frowned at him. "I 'spect you're prayering to be forgiven," she said. "While you're talking to the angels you better ask my papa to help me. You hurt me. Very bad."

"I'm so sorry." He knelt beside her and retrieved the spectacles. "I didn't know you were there."

"Yes you did. You heered me singing and comed. I creeped round and hid 'hind you, just a'case."

She seemed remarkably self-possessed for such a small girl. "Just in case—what?" he asked.

"Just a'case you were bad. Are you bad?" She hooked the spectacles around her ears and scanned him, her head tilting, her face anxious as she awaited his reply.

He thought, 'She can't be much more than five or six.'

"I don't think so," he answered, smiling at her. "At least, I try not to be. Sometimes, I'm afraid, I don't try hard enough."

A moment longer those grave eyes searched his face, then all at once she beamed sunnily. "I know," she said, sitting up. "When you hasn't tried hard enough to be good, you have to make 'mends. So I'll rest here and be brave, and you can mend my toe. But you better wait while I make myself 'spectable."

She leaned forward, arranging the skirts of her pretty pink muslin frock with great care, then ruining the effect by sticking her foot in the air and directing the beam at him once more. "Mend it now, if you please," she commanded.

The dress, he noted, was of excellent quality and workmanship, and when he removed her little shoe he found that it also was of fine leather and design.

"You've got pretty hands," she remarked.

"Thank you." The toe of her shoe was caved in, and her stocking was torn. He set the shoe aside, and touched her foot gingerly.

"Is my toe all broke into hund'eds 'n thousands of pieces?"

"I certainly hope not." He looked up in alarm. "Does it feel like it?"

"It feels squashed. I shall prob'ly die. And it'll serve him jolly well right!" She added with a thoughtful nod, "Then he'll be sorry, and he'll come to my grave an' cry buckets'n buckets."

"Who will?"

"My Uncle Andy. He whipped me with a great club. With spikes onto it. And I din't do anything *very* bad, 'cept go near the river." The great eyes came tragically to meet his, and she appended, sighing, "He'll beat me again if he finds I've goed out 'stead of doing my sums. Don't you tell him, will you?"

"I think he's far more like to beat *me*," he said bracingly, "for knocking you down."

She considered that and agreed it was very likely, adding the warning that if Uncle Andy did come, it would be better to run away quick, "'Cause he's hugeous big an' fierce as four lions."

Montclair grinned and wiggled the tiny big toe with care. "Does that hurt?"

"Hidjus. I'd scream an' have the foggers if I wasn't so brave."

Foggers . . . He suggested dubiously, "Vapours. . . ?"

"Oh, that's right. Is my shoe full of gore?"

"No. But a hurt can be just as painful even if it doesn't bleed. I think you're very brave, and I really am sorry for being so clumsy."

She giggled. "I was trying to fright you. I was 'tending to be the Fury. I 'spect you'll say I din't fright you. Grown-ups always do. But"—she giggled again—"you should have seen your face!"

"I think you're a rascal, miss," he said with a twinkle. "And you see what happened because you played a trick on me. You might have been really hurt when I knocked you down."

"I *is* really hurt," she declared indignantly. "You stamped all over me with your grown-up feet. Did you fall down too?"

She was looking at his knuckles, which had become skinned when they'd connected with his cousin's jaw during their battle yesterday.

"Something like that." He straightened out the toe of her shoe. "May I replace your dainty slipper, madamoiselle?"

She looked at him wistfully. "When you hurt someone you're s'posed to kiss it better."

He at once obliged. She sighed rapturously, and gave him permission to replace her shoe, and after he had been instructed not to buckle the strap so tightly that her poor foot couldn't "breathe," she allowed him to help her stand up and to brush the twigs and dirt from her dainty frock.

"Thank you," she said politely, and tucked her hand trustingly into his. "You can come and see my special place if you like." She turned back to the bleak tower. Montclair frowned and hesitated. She tugged impatiently, then pushed up the spectacles which had slipped down her infinitesimal nose, and peered up into his face. "I'll help it," she said. And before he realized what she was about, she'd pressed a kiss on his damaged hand.

He stared at her, touched.

"Don't be sad," she said kindly. "You'll be all better, quick as a bird. Only look at me!" She stuck out her foot and wriggled it so vigorously that she lost her balance and Montclair, laughing, had to restore her.

"I like your face," she told him with the open candour of childhood. "You're not so han'some as my Uncle Andy is, and I really p'fer my gentlemen to have golden hair. But yours curls a bit, and you've got d'licious eyes when you laugh only they're a bit lonely inside when you don't."

Montclair gave her a rather startled glance, but she was prattling on artlessly.

"Mama says eyes are 'portant, you know, and that I must choose my friends by their eyes, so I'll have you for a friend, if you like, and then you c'n be happy." Her lips drooped. Suddenly, she was incredibly forlorn. "I'm lonely too. I hasn't got any little friends."

"Well, you have a new grown-up friend," he said, bowing low.

She gave a delighted laugh and clapped her hands joyously.

With an answering grin he asked, "Why have you no little friends?"

"When we lived in London, the children next door laughed at me 'cause I'm—read-ishy, or something."

"Bookish, perhaps?"

"Yes. That. It's 'cause I wear specs, the Bo'sun says. So I throwed 'em away. But Uncle Andy found them."

"And did he beat you with that great club again? He must be a wicked man."

"No he's not! He's the bestest uncle what I ever had!" She scowled at him fiercely, saw the twinkle in his eyes and giggled, her small face becoming pink. "Oh, you're teasing. Did you know I made that up a teensy bit? He din't really beat me. But he *did* spank me. Not 'cause I hid my specs, though. He said he quite und'stood 'bout that, and that the other children were jealous, that's all. But"—she sighed, despondent again—"they're not really."

"But you can wear your—er, specs now that you've moved away, is that it?"

"No. I weared them there, too. I can't see to read 'thout 'em."

She seemed awfully young to be able to read. He stared down at her sad but resigned little face, intrigued by its mixture of solemnity and childishness. "How old are you?"

"Oooh! That's rude," she said, cheered by this evidence of faulting in the man she thought rather scarily splendid. "I asked the Countess Lieven how old she was once, and Mama made me beg pardon."

'The Countess Lieven.' Then her family must be of the Quality. He could well imagine the formidable countess's reaction to such a question, and his lips twitched. "Your mama was quite right. And I beg your pardon."

She beamed at him and imparted, "I'm six in December." She again tugged at his hand. "Come on."

Resisting, he said, "Now that we're friends, I must warn you. You shouldn't come to the Folly. It's a bad place."

"No it isn't! It's a nice place. And it's not folly!"

"That's what it's called, Mistress—er . . . I think we haven't been properly introduced, have we? May I present myself? My name is Valentine."

She swept into a rather wobbly curtsy. "How de do? That's what my Bo'sun says." She lowered her voice to a 'manly' growl, repeated, "How de do?" then laughed merrily. "Just like that."

"Is your Bo'sun a sailor?"

"Yes. Well, he was a long time ago. He sailed with my gran'papa for hund'eds of years, but now my gran'papa's moved up to heaven so the Bo'sun lives with us an' keeps asking Starry to be his missus but she won't. I'm P'scilla. I c'n say my name now, 'cause my tooth growed back. Last month I couldn't say it right, and everybody laughed when I tried. D'you want to see? It's bright and new!" She halted, holding up her face and opening her mouth wide.

He admired the small, pearly new tooth and told her that they all looked very nice. "I expect you clean them every day."

"Yes." She sighed. "But they don't grow much. I wish they were bigger. Like Wolfgang's. His are pointed. I asked my Uncle Andy to file mine into points, and he said he would, but Mama wouldn't let him. An' Starry— she lives with us—Starry said everyone would think I was a Fury. And Furies are drefful bad creatures, you know. 'Sides, Mama said I wouldn't be able to chew jam tarts if my teeth was all made into sharp points, and I saved a *special* place in my tummy for jam tarts. So I 'spect I better not have pointy teeth."

"I agree," said Montclair, and reserving his musician's curiosity as to the naming of Wolfgang, took up his branch once more and asked, "Where do you live, Mistress Priscilla?"

"In London."

"Do you stay with relations, then?"

69

"Oh yes. But we won't be here long."

"Don't you like the country?"

She considered this, then said judiciously, "I been looking it over. It's pretty, but there's a awful lot of it."

"Very true. But you shouldn't go looking it over all alone, child."

"I don't. Wolfgang was with me, else Mama wouldn't let me go out. He's my 'fierce an' 'vincible guard dog,' Uncle Andy says. Wolfgang the Terrible he calls him 'cause Wolfgang 'tacks anyone who comes near me."

"He sounds terrible indeed." Montclair glanced about, wondering with a touch of unease if Wolfgang was as antisocial as Soldier, or whether he was another figment of this extremely bright little girl's obviously fertile imagination. "Where is he?"

She glanced around, then called shrilly, "Wolf . . . gang. . . !"

Almost at once there was a rustling in the undergrowth. "Here he comes," said Priscilla fondly.

Wolfgang plunged into the clearing, then paused, scanning Montclair with ears alert and eyes unblinking. "Stand very still, Mr. Val'tine," whispered the child: "An' p'raps he won't bite you very bad!"

Montclair, who had instinctively tightened his grip on the branch, regarded 'Wolfgang the Terrible' in silence. The dog was white with liver markings. His eyes and ears were large, he was about seven inches tall at the shoulders, and he probably weighed in the neighbourhood of ten pounds. He advanced on Montclair without marked hostility although the ratty tail did not wave a greeting. Montclair saw the somewhat protruding dark eyes fixed on the stick he held. He tossed it aside, and Wolfgang took three quick leaps to the rear. Dropping to one knee, Montclair called, "Here, Wolfgang. Come, old fellow."

Wriggling, the dog inched forward. His ears flattened

70

themselves against his head, and his tail was wagging so fast that it was almost invisible. He licked Montclair's outstretched hand, then flung himself down and presented his stomach for inspection. 'A fine guard dog you are, sir,' thought Montclair, troubled, as he caressed the small head.

Priscilla, however, who had watched this meeting with her hands tightly clasped and an anxious look on her face, gave a sigh of relief. "Thank goodness he likes you," she whispered. "He can be dreffully awful!"

"I'm sure he can." Montclair stood up, took her hand tightly in his, and led her among the decaying slabs to the very edge of the pit. "Do you see her?" he whispered.

Her eyes very wide, for she had not dared venture this close, Priscilla adjusted her spectacles, peered downward, and whispered back, "No. Who?"

"The Fury. She lives down there, only she comes out if she hears little girls. Especially little girls who sing. She likes the taste of them."

He felt the small hand tremble, and she shrank closer against his leg.

"A real—*Fury*?" she whispered. "Is she bad and wicked and ugly?"

"Very bad. And very ugly. She does cruel and awful things to children who come here alone."

A pause. Then she quavered, "Wolfgang wouldn't let her. He takes care of me. He's braver than anything!" She thought, then added reinforcingly, "He could bite the King, I 'spect."

"Perhaps he could. But the King is only a man. The Fury is a witch. A wicked witch with no heart and a big hairy wart on the end of her nose. So I want you to promise me you will never come here again, Priscilla. As one friend promises another."

She looked up at him, her eyes very big behind the spectacles that made her face seem even smaller. The

71

sunbonnet slipped down to cover her left ear. She asked, still in that hushed whisper, "Isn't you 'fraid of the Fury?"

"Yes, I am. She must be asleep or she'd have heard us and pulled us both in there. That's where her cooking pot is. Down at the bottom." The child was beginning to look quite pale with fright and he thought he'd made his point, so drew her back. It was more important that she get safely to her family than that he see the Henley woman today. He sat on the blocks again and discovered that a sharp stone had worked its way into the boot sole under the ball of his foot. "I'll just get this out," he said, pulling off the boot. "Then, I'll take—"

A sudden gust of wind sent a branch tumbling into the pit. Priscilla heard the scraping rattle and jerked around, pale with fright. "She's *coming!*" she screeched, and was off, her frock flapping. Wolfgang the Terrible scampered after her, uttering the high-pitched howls Montclair had heard when the child was singing.

He sprang up, started to run after her, but trod on a rock and swore. Hopping, he turned back for his boot. "Wait! I'll take you home!" he shouted, but she had already vanished into the trees.

Undoubtedly Mistress Priscilla had known the benefits of upbringing and a rather surprising amount of education. Pulling his boot back on, he racked his brain trying to think whom the child and her mama visited, and decided her 'Uncle Andy' must be Major Anderson, whose fine big farm was located about a mile east of the Longhills boundary. He began to run in that direction, calling her. It was too far for her to walk alone, even with the protection of the fierce and invincible guard dog.

"It is quite the most wicked thing I ever heard of," declared Mrs. Edwina Starr, extracting Welcome from the blankets and slipping a hand mirror between the sheets.

Susan had just piled those sheets onto the now immaculate shelf in the linen room, and she watched her diminutive companion/cook/housekeeper uneasily. "I think he is a very young cat, Starry. He'll learn in time."

"Time is what he may not have, does he persist in forever being where he shouldn't." Mrs. Starr looked grimly at the little tabby who had walked in with them when first they arrived at Highperch Cottage and had since shown no inclination to leave. "But I was not referring to that particular creature, Mrs. Sue." She took a blanket from the chair beside her with marked suspicion in her bright hazel eyes. "No Christian landlord should permit such a creeping, oozing, smelly bog to lurk about the village where little ones play. And him the Squire and a Justice of the Peace besides! A fine justice *he* dispenses! This blanket needs to be patched. He should have drained that bog long ago! He must be a bad man! A very bad man!"

"He most certainly is. I think I may have seen him whilst I was at Longhills—or at least, the back of him. From what I could tell, he was berating Miss Trent because she does not wish to wed him."

"Hah! Who would, I should like to know?" Mrs. Starr shook out another blanket and sniffed it, her dainty little nostrils twitching so that she looked like a busy rabbit. "I only wish I had been here when his wicked friends or servants or whatever they were dared lay their hands on you and break dear Master Andy's head!" She paused, her brow wrinkling with renewed indignation at the very thought of such dastardly behaviour. In her mind's eye she still saw Andrew as a pale, silent eleven-year-old, crushed by the death of his father and bewildered by the impending loss of his mama. When Captain Tate had asked her to care for his daughter's orphans she had agreed eagerly, and had lavished upon them all the love she would have given the children de-

73

nied her when her young husband was killed in the same great sea battle which had ended the life of Lieutenant Hartley Lyddford. Andrew had been sickly as a child, and her tendency to fuss over him had not diminished when he grew into a robust and well-built young male animal full of pride and energy.

"Only to think of it fairly makes my blood boil!" she went on. "And all that wicked violence over a house which his evil lordship obviously never sets foot in, else it would not have come to such a sorry pass! Which reminds me, Master Andy found a dreadful dark painting he thinks might be better than that one hanging in the withdrawing room. The frame is quite nice and if you don't object, it might do was it cleaned. I shall set that lazy George Dodman to it so soon as he comes home."

Susan helped her refold the apparently acceptable blanket and set it aside to be sprinkled with powdered alum before it was put into the storage chest. "The Bo'sun has been working very hard, Starry," she pointed out placatingly. "Between helping Deemer with the horses and doing most of the gardening, to say nothing of his work with the barge, the poor man scarce has time to breathe."

"Señor Angelo helps also." Mrs. Starr sniffed disparagement. "One might think the Bo'sun ninety-five and being starved into his grave to judge by his glummery!"

"If he is sometimes downhearted, I suspect one does not have to look very far to find the cause," said Susan with a teasing smile.

Her companion, who at eight and thirty was still a very pretty little lady, blushed and changed the subject hastily. "From what the woman in the grocer's shop had to say—her being a proper tattle-monger you understand—the whole estate has been let go to rack and ruin since the old lord died. Like the flood, for instance. It seems there was a bore tide two years back that caused it all, and it was months before the water was pumped out of the catacombs under the church, no matter how the Village Council begged and pleaded with his lordship's steward."

"Is that how the swamp came to be?"

"So they say. Half the hill behind Longhills itself came down on the old family chapel, only because a lot of trees on the hillside had been damaged in the great storm the year before and no one at Longhills lifted a finger to have them tended and replanted. Thirteenth century the chapel was, and one whole wall smashed in and windows broke that are irreplaceable works of art. The villagers call it justice, and do not grieve about it, you may be sure!" She pulled the mirror from between the sheets and scanned it with suspicion.

Susan said indignantly, "Well, I think it dreadful that works of art such as that should be lost because of carelessness or pennypinching. The Montclair chapel is famous, and really belongs to England more than to the family. Martha cleaned out this cupboard on Tuesday, Starry. It is quite dry, I'm sure."

"It is not the cupboard I question. Aha! Just as I thought! Mist on the mirror! See there! The sheets are damp. Natural they would be, coming down the river on that nasty boat of Master Andrew's." Mrs. Starr tugged at the neatly disposed pile. "All have to come out again and be aired, just as I thought. Every blessed one! No! Don't you touch them, dear girl. You're all over cobwebs! And you must be fairly worn out. Go downstairs and make yourself a cup of tea, do!"

Susan hesitated, but she really was rather tired, and the thought of a cup of tea was heavenly. Having won a promise that her devoted retainer would soon join her in the kitchen, she made her weary way to the stairs.

Montclair's wrath built steadily as he limped up the drivepath. Having grown up in a house where a small army of servants eliminated dirt before it dared settle, where two full-time maids did nothing more than arrange fresh flowers every day and it was the sole task of three lackeys to clean the silver, he had no comprehension of the amount of time it could take three women to set to rights a house that had stood gathering dust for several years. It appeared to him as if his beloved old cottage had been taken over by a band of gypsies. The front terrace was littered with boxes, rolled-up rugs, sad-looking articles of furniture, and a large and battered child's doll house. The Henley woman and her unpleasant clan, he thought angrily, had lost no time in desecrating the house with their rubbish. Lord only knows what it would be like inside! They likely had pigs settled into the withdrawing room!

Fuming, he hurried up the steps. The front door was open, and he marched inside. The main hall was cluttered and deserted. He swore softly, and stamped through the chaos, up the two steps and into the upper hall.

A maid halted, halfway down the stairs, and stared at him. He thought her inordinately tall; almost as tall as himself. Her apron was a disaster, her grimy mob-cap hung askew, and many wisps of dark hair had escaped it to straggle untidily about her dirty face. She clutched a dustpan and brush in one hand, and a broom in the other, and she was evidently as dim-witted as she was slovenly, because she made not the slightest attempt to address him, but stood there perfectly still, gawking at him.

Frozen with dismay, Susan saw a slim young man

gazing up at her. She received a swift impression of attractively tumbled black hair, a pair of rather stormy-looking but remarkably fine dark eyes set in a pale face with a firm nose and chin, a high intelligent forehead, and a grim but shapely mouth. He was dressed with expensive good taste but without ostentation, and aside from the fact that for some peculiar reason he was carrying a sturdy branch, he was undeniably a gentleman.

Her heart gave an odd little jump. She thought despairingly, 'Oh, I am filthy! Whatever must he think?' and started to snatch off her mob-cap.

In her confusion she quite forgot that she held a full dustpan in that hand . . .

Stalking towards her, Montclair received the full benefit of a cascading pile of dust, cobwebs, and debris. He uttered a shocked cry and reeled back, his eyes painfully full.

"Oh, my heavens!" Aghast, Susan ran to help him. "Here, let me brush your coat!" Briskly, she began to wield the brush, which was unhappily full of cobwebs.

"Woman—*desist!*" roared Montclair. "By Gad! You're a full"—he gasped—"a full-fledged . . ." Uttering an explosive sneeze, he tripped over a croquet mallet. "Disaster!" he finished, prone.

Susan threw one hand to her cheek and moaned faintly.

Snatching out his handkerchief, Montclair sat amid the rubble and sneezed. Between sneezes he strove not very successfully to chastise the lunatic. She watched him, seemingly completely undismayed by the fact that her thick hair now hung in a straight dark curtain past her shoulders with only one comb on each side holding it back from her face. Her eyes were very wide and her lower lip hung down. He brandished his handkerchief at her and tried to speak, only to sneeze again.

"I do apologize," said Susan, recovering herself. "I didn't hear you knock."

She spoke in a cultured voice that surprised him. 'Probably the family idiot,' he decided, clambering to his feet and trying to dislodge a timber that seemed to have invaded his eye. "The front door was open," he snarled.

"So I see." Susan continued to the foot of the stairs. "I am sorry that there was no one here to receive you. Everyone is gone out. You see, a little girl is lost."

Irritated by her impertinently familiar manner, he stared at her, and, sneezing again, wondered if she referred to Priscilla.

'How cross he is,' thought Susan. He really was very good-looking and he had every right to be vexed by such a welcome. Contrite, she went on, "I suppose you must think it very dreadful. But Priscilla is astoundingly clever for her age and has a great deal of common sense in—"

So Priscilla did live here. What a pity. "A small child should not be allowed to go out alone," he interpolated sharply, "clever or no."

Priscilla had slipped away again whilst they were all so caught up in the flurry of making this funny old house fit for human occupancy. Heaven knows, she had told the child repeatedly that she was not to go out alone, but Priscilla was lonely, poor dear mite, and such a dreamer. She'd probably imagined Wolfgang into the gigantic hound she'd thought he would become, and thus decided she was not 'out alone.' The young man looked haughty and condemning, and Susan began to bristle. Who did he think he was, to force his way into her home and then lecture her about her own child?

"I am perfectly aware of that fact, sir," she said defensively. "But I scarce think this peaceful English countryside swarms with monsters and werewolves and the like!" Still, he was right, and it was good of him to be concerned, wherefore she relented, smiled, and prepared to explain.

Mrs. Henley, thought Montclair, would do well to hire better-trained servants. He had not so much as been asked for his card or his identity, and this Madam Dementia was apparently in the habit of standing about chatting with her mistress's callers. He should not be surprised, of course, but her cavalier attitude toward Priscilla's absence infuriated him. "You appear to find the loss of a child amusing," he said sternly.

"Amusing!" echoed Susan, her smile fading.

"One reads in the newspapers every day," he went on, "that some poor helpless innocent has been stolen to be sold into a lifetime of slavery and degradation. It is not to be wondered at when half the time their scatter-wit parents—"

"Oooh!"

"—are too busy frippering about where they've no business being, and paying more heed to their coiffures and their cards than to their offspring! And furthermore, my good girl—"

"I am *not* your good girl," she flashed, sparks of wrath appearing in her big grey eyes.

"One might think you'd be ashamed to admit it," he said sardonically, advancing to shake a finger under her elevated nose.

Her breath momentarily snatched away, Susan prepared to give this insufferable intruder the blistering set-down he deserved, but she was too late.

"Furthermore," he swept on, noticing despite his frown that this odd creature had quite pretty eyes, "there may not be monsters or werewolves as you so facetiously point out, but there are places in my woods that are—"

"In *your* woods?" she interrupted, stiffening. "Pray, who are you, sir?"

"I would think it about time you enquired. My name is Montclair. I have come to see your mistress."

Montclair? Susan stood rigid. So this was the hard-hearted lord of the manor! And he had dared, he'd *dared* to march in here and add insult to injury! She'd scatter-wit him!

"Horrid!" she squealed, flailing her mob-cap into his face. "Wretch! Loathsome—*viper!*"

Retreating with stunned incredulity, Montclair seized the mob-cab and wrested it away.

Having suffered one assault at the hands of his men, the widow was not about to be abused again, and rapped her brush smartly over his head.

"Ow!" he cried, and involuntarily recoiling from madness, promptly tripped over the steps to the lower hall and went staggering back.

Susan followed, flailing at him vigorously. "How *dare* you send your beastly creatures here to try and frighten me?" Whack! "How *dare* you—"

Off balance, Montclair made an abortive snatch for the brush, which eluded him and landed a telling blow on his ear.

"Ow!" he repeated, backing away in horror from this frenzied apology for a housemaid.

"Breaking into our house—" she shrilled, her arm flying.

"Your house?" he gasped, ducking. "It is—yike!—*my* house! And— Ouch!"

He could imagine few things more disgraceful than for a gentleman to engage in hand-to-hand (or -brush) combat with a female, and striving rather unsuccessfully to protect himself, retreated across the entrance hall, and beat a hasty and inelegant exit.

The side of his forehead hurt, his ear felt on fire, and he had given his elbow a fine crack when he fell. Glaring ragefully at the virago in the open doorway, he shouted, "You may tell your mistress she will be hearing from me!"

"One can but hope it will be from a great distance," she riposted. A thought struck her. "And furthermore, if you cared a scrap for your country you would take more care of your windows!" The door closed with a bang.

It was a clear confirmation of his suspicions. "Good God," whispered Montclair, rubbing his elbow and backing away. "She's short of a sheet all right! Poor creature . . ."

Susan whipped the door open once more. "And *I* am the mistress of this house!" she announced, then threw his branch after him, and slammed the door again.

She was the notorious trespassing Mrs. Henley? That tall, dirty woman with her mass of straight hair and her horrid dustpan was the creature Imre Monteil had come near to mooning about and had spoken of as 'the bewitching widow'? Montclair gave a contemptuous snort. It followed! Monteil was just the type to admire what any reasonable man must only find appalling!

He had come here with an open mind, he thought aggrievedly, and not only had he been disgracefully abused, but the creature had for some reason become annoyed. There was small point in trying to talk to her now. Well, he'd been willing to give her the benefit of the doubt, but from this point on Ferry could deal with her. Serve her right!

Making his disgruntled way to collect his branch, he reflected that it was small wonder poor little Priscilla wanted for friends. Very likely the parents of any possible playmates were well aware that her mother was a raving lunatic. A strong raving lunatic, he thought, tenderly feeling a lump above his right eye. He was mildly surprised to find that the mob-cap was still in his left hand. He stared down at it. Egad, but he'd been shocked when the wretched woman had flung it into his face. Recalling the rage in those wide grey eyes, he grinned. She'd admitted she was not a "good girl." He'd scored there. Of course, she in turn had called him a horrid wretch and a loathsome viper. Hmmn . . . He stuffed the cap into his pocket and took up his branch.

The wind was getting colder and grey clouds were mingling with the fluffy white ones. He walked faster.

He'd be lucky to get home before it rained. Jupiter, but this had been a crazy day! First, the repellent Monteil; then, Soldier and his stupid bone; that Spanish idiot in the woods; little Priscilla—poor babe. And to cap things off nicely, the virago-ish Widow Henley. It would be miraculous did he reach Longhills without being captured by cannibals and boiled in oil!

Leaving the Highperch drivepath, he struck off across the meadows, and was starting down the rolling slope when he came face to face with three people. One was the Spanish idiot; the second was a tall, darkly handsome young fellow, carrying a small girl piggyback. So the child was safe, thank goodness!

Priscilla gave a squeal. "Mr. Val'tine!"

The little group halted. The Spanish idiot muttered something darkly and glowered at him. The tall young man set Priscilla down and asked, "You know this gentleman, scamp?"

"Yes," she trilled. "That's the man who hurt me in the wood!"

Montclair's day continued true to form.

5

lancing up from the chess board as Susan came slowly into the withdrawing room, Lyddford drawled, "That's the third time she's called for you. Is my niece still at daggers drawn with me because I knocked down her new 'friend'?"

Susan returned to her chair and pulled the branch of candles closer. "The poor babe keeps having nightmares," she said, taking up her workbox. "Starry's going to sit with her for a little while. From what I can gather our gallant Lord Montclair entertained himself by terrifying her with stories of a Fury who lives in the woods."

"Now damn the wretch!" exclaimed Lyddford, ramming his clenched fist down on the table and sending chessmen flying. "What sort of glower and grim would resort to such tactics only to keep a little girl from daring to set foot on his confounded sacrosanct property?"

"Chaw move was it," sighed Señor de Ferdinand, retrieving a queen's pawn from Welcome, who'd experienced a joyous embarrassment of riches and was ferociously chasing the flying pieces about the room.

"Oh, egad! My apologies, Angelo. But—Jove!" Lyddford's grey eyes fairly shot sparks. "To think I've been reproaching myself because I hit him when he wasn't looking!"

It would have been difficult to find a more ardent sportsman than her brother, and this admission of so flagrant a breach of the rules of fair play caused Susan to stare at him in horror. "Andy! As if you would do such a thing!"

His eyes fell away. "I—er . . . Well, the fact is that he was watching Priscilla. When she said he had hurt her, I don't mind owning I saw red! And what's more, had I known he'd been terrifying my niece into having nightmares day and night— Dammit, when I meet the bas—er, the knave, I blasted well might just put a period to him!"

"Andy—no! You'd have to leave the country! How ever would we go along without you?"

He scowled at her, frustrated by the truth of her remarks.

"Needing is not for," declared de Ferdinand airily. "Angelo first dealings shot knave's heart throughout." He took up a castle and sighted it with grim intensity. "Missings pips never."

Susan watched him, wondering if she would ever become accustomed to his erratic use of English. He had come into their lives four months ago, the victim of a shipwreck in the Channel. Despite high running seas, Andy had managed to bring *The Dainty Dancer* alongside the oarless dinghy, and take the sole occupant aboard. Soaked to the skin and thoroughly chilled, Señor Angelo Francisco Luis Lagunes de Ferdinand had been able to tell them his name and not much more. He had developed an inflammation of the lungs and, since his identity could not be ascertained, he had been installed at the London house. After making an excellent

84

recovery, he had shown no inclination to leave. His very poor command of English had made it difficult to discover either where he lived or what had been his destination, but it had soon become apparent that his imagination soared to even giddier heights than did Priscilla's. His home was alternately a palace near Madrid, a chateau in the south of France, a villa in Italy, a chalet in Switzerland. His childhood would seem to have come straight out of an *Arabian Nights'* dream, and he made vague references to hundreds of servants, countless horses and carriages, several yachts, and innumerable hair-raising adventures. When Andrew burst out laughing at these boastings, de Ferdinand not only took no offence but was quick to join in the hilarity. There were not very many years between the two young men who soon became fast friends. The Spaniard, who had no visible means of support, was somehow able to contribute a sum to the household expenses that had become well-nigh indispensable. He was devoted to Priscilla, always willing to help with the barge or the horses, and had rapidly become a fixture. Susan was inclined to the belief that he had been involved with smugglers. She liked the young man and hoped he did not decide to go away, but it would be nice if she could more often understand what he said.

"He says he can shoot the pips from a playing card and not miss," translated her brother.

"Good gracious, señor. Do you say you also are to fight a duel with Lord Montclair?"

He sprang up and bowed. "Chess. All so. Mices elves. Angelo Francisco Luis Lagunes de Ferdinand. Firstings from other one else." His arms swept out to embrace the room. "Chew—mices friends good. Montclair—him dog dirtness!"

Lyddford asked with a grin, "Did you tell him that?"

The Spaniard bowed again. "His mouths into mices hat I have hove!"

"Did you, by God! Would that I'd seen it! Well, I'll second you, Angelo, and you can do the same for me."

"Meeces fightings. Yust *meeces!* There be no chew fightings!"

Lyddford said with a chuckle, "Well, whether it is just you, or both of us to face the bounder, I fancy Montclair's friends will be calling here to arrange matters. If the beastly fellow has any, that is!"

"D'you know what I think?" said Junius Trent, directing a sly grin up the dining table to his cousin. "I think Montclair tried for a kiss from the wicked widow, and she levelled him and then galloped her horse over his face."

Considering several of the more fiendish methods of torture, Montclair chose one and gave Junius a sympathetic smile before returning his attention to his roast beef. His jaw ached, the right side of his mouth was swollen and discoloured, and his conviction that he must look ridiculous had been borne out when he'd reached home and sat at his dressing table. Gould had met his dismayed gaze in the mirror and with his usual cool impassivity had suggested that Mr. Montclair might prefer to have his dinner carried up to his room this evening so that he could retire early.

Montclair had positively yearned to accept the suggestion. The thought of facing his family and their boring guests, of enduring the perpetual gossip about their 'friends,' had been anathema to him. But he'd encountered his cousin Barbara in the conservatory as he'd attempted to slink through to the side stairs. The unhappy girl had been restricted to her room since yesterday, but

86

had whispered that she was permitted to dine with them tonight, and had pleaded with him not to desert her. There had been no time for more talk, because she'd heard her mother approaching and, paling, had fled.

Montclair had been obliged to cover that panicked flight and had thus fallen victim to his aunt's spleen. She had, Lady Trent shrilled, "a very important guest" arriving momentarily. A leader of the *ton* whom she'd been trying to snare for years. Of all nights, why must Montclair pick this one to come home in "so disgusting" a condition? He'd been tempted to agree to her suggestion that he not put in an appearance, but Barbara's imploring eyes and tragic little face haunted him, and he knew he couldn't abandon the poor chit to the wretched pack.

And now here he was, seated as his brother's representative at the head of the table in the small dining room, with one fire quite unnecessarily adding more heat to the warm room, the flames awaking flickering shadows in the fine plasterwork of the ceiling, the candlelight playing on snowy napery and reflecting in sparkling crystal and silverware.

From the third chair on his left, the slumberously inviting eyes of the much admired the Honourable Jemima Merriman-Jones turned frequently to Montclair's damaged features. Lady Spindle, her vast aunt, had just concluded a long-winded and stern homily on the deplorable frequency with which some young men (of whom one *might* have expected better things!) engaged in vulgarities such as fisticuffs, this having afforded Junius his excellent opportunity to snipe. And from both sides of the long table, amused faces turned to Montclair.

"Noticed you was a trifle battered, Valentine," bellowed Colonel Ostrander, seated next to Lady Spindle. "Whatya say happened? Didn't quite hear the details."

"And I'll wager dear Valentine don't mean to relate 'em," whispered Junius in the ear of Mrs. Rodenbaugh, the colonel's perpetual companion, this witticism causing the amply endowed widow to giggle hilariously.

Montclair said, "A slight difference of opinion, sir. With a fellow I found on my lands, and who had no business being there."

"Is that so, begad," piped Lord Spindle in his piercing falsetto. "Think it was one of these curst smuggler fellas, Montclair? They're becoming a confounded plague! Ought t'be took out and shot, every last one! And what do the authorities do? I ask you. Nothing! When's Geoffrey going t'put a stop to it, that's what I'd like to know? He's the Squire, after all."

"You must have forgot, my lord, that Geoffrey is out of the country at the moment," said Lady Trent with the gushing sweetness she reserved for anyone above the rank of baronet.

Montclair sprang at once to his brother's defence. "Besides, I doubt there'd be anything for him to do, sir. There's not much smuggling up here. That's more along the south coast, surely."

"Beg to differ," put in Lord Thornleigh, his volume rattling the glasses. "They've expanded, by what I hear. Quite a surge of activity in the west country of late. I believe the authorities suspect a distribution centre somewhere between Bath and Bristol. Right, Spindle?"

His lordship agreed, said it was a scandal, a national outrage, and that there was a deal more to it than smuggling brandy and the like. "Probably all part of this Masterpiece Gang," he added gloomily.

Montclair's ears perked up. In Town the Bow Street Runner had spoken of that criminal band. He tried to insert a question, but was overridden by his aunt's shrill voice, which was in turn obliterated by an imperative demand that the guest of honour be informed of the thieves.

88

It was the first time Valentine had ever seen Lady Trent shouted down. Amused, he caught Barbara's awed glance and sent a sly wink her way while my lord Thornleigh launched into a lengthy history of the Masterpiece Gang and their depredations.

"And everything they've stole is irreplaceable," growled Ostrander. "Priceless old jewellery. National treasures. Robbed Britain, is what the dirty bounders have done! Curst revolutionaries, mark my words! Selective da— er, rascals too. Cannot recall exactly what they've made off with this year, but—"

Spindle inserted, "They took a Bellini from poor old Jacob Chalfont just after Christmas. Broke the fella's heart!"

"And a couple of Tintorettos from the British Museum—Montague House, you know," said Lady Thornleigh. "Not likely to find *them* again, now, are we?

"Gad, no," agreed Spindle, allowing his wine glass to be refilled. "Last month they broke into Castle Gower in broad daylight while everyone was occupied with a garden party. Took the dowager duchess's ruby tiara. Most beautiful trinket. Seventeenth century, I think. Prinny always held it should've been kept at Windsor. He's fairly beside himself and blames the duke, instead of putting the blame where it lies—at Bow Street! And there have been other treasures too: diamonds, emerald necklaces—you'll recollect last year the Viscountess Chepstow was robbed at gunpoint in her carriage."

"And they took some fabulous early crystal from . . ." began the Count di Volpe.

Montclair did not hear the rest of the stout Italian's remark, for Madame la Comtesse de Bruinet, who had tired of the subject, enquired of him as to Geoffrey's whereabouts. He had heard much of the formidable Frenchwoman. Small but big-bosomed, she was rumoured to be five and sixty and looked ten years younger. Refusing to speak English and incredibly haughty, she was a leader of Polite Society. She had escaped Paris just before the Revolution, bringing trunks crammed with gold louis and jewels, which Montclair suspected had been acquired rather than inherited. She still showed traces of what had once been a dazzling beauty, but now her raddled cheeks were jowly, her eyelids had an almost perpetual droop, and her lips pulled down sneeringly at the corners. Once or twice during this interminable meal, however, her shrewd eyes had met his, and he'd thought to glimpse a lurking twinkle in their depths. A sense of humour would win his regard as no amount of wealth or social stature could do, and, intrigued, he warmed to the lady. If, as he suspected, she had been a highly successful courtesan, she would have reason to be amused both by her prestige in England, and by the adulation of the simpering snobs around his table.

Lady Trent was ranting on about "the late dear princess," and how deeply afflicted she had been by that young lady's tragic death in childbirth. All England had been stunned by that profound tragedy, but Montclair could recollect very clearly his aunt's screaming rage because she had been obliged to cancel a dinner party. Her remarks about the princess's folly in marrying "that prim German boy" had been so vitriolic that one would never have suspected her to be anything but vexed by Princess Charlotte's having chosen to die at so inconvenient a moment.

It chanced that by the unfailing route of the servants' hall, the tale of my lady's fury had reached the comtesse's ears. Disgusted by Lady Trent's present show of hypocrisy, she glanced at Montclair and surprised his lurking smile. With a soft chuckle she leaned to him, lifting a hand that was heavy with gems.

"Bien sûr embrasse-moi, mon petit."

Very aware that Junius's pose had slipped and that his cousin was looking daggers at him, Valentine said gravely, *"Avec le plus grand plaisir, madame,"* and saluted her fingers.

Junius tittered audibly.

Madame la Comtesse put up her lorgnette fan and surveyed him through a hushed and awful moment from which he was rescued when his mother rose hurriedly and led the ladies from the room. Demurely in the rear of the august train, Barbara's face was brightened by silent laughter.

The gentlemen lingered over their port and nuts, but at last Montclair was able to conduct the small male group across the great hall, into the south hall and thence down the steps, through the conservatory, and into the gallery where the ladies had gathered. This was not Montclair's favourite room, perhaps because of the half-a-hundred ancestors who stared down from their ornate frames. Since impromptu dances were often held in here, a fine piano-forte stood in the deep alcove midway between the vast central hearth and the rear wall, and Madame la Comtesse lost no time in observing that she had agreed to come to Longhills because she had heard that Montclair played divinely. Fixed with a basilisk stare, my lady Trent swallowed her fury, and in a voice that shook slightly implored her nephew to oblige them. "Why don't you play that new little thing you writ, dearest boy," she said, her lips curling back as though she yearned to bite him.

'That new little thing' . . . Gritting his teeth, Montclair made his way to the piano-forte. The instrument had far more power than the harpsichord; at least Aunt Marcia would be quite unable to make herself heard. The Honourable Jemima promptly volunteered to turn the sheets for "clever Mr. Montclair," but he foiled that ploy by saying with pseudo-regret that he needed no music, and thus was spared the young lady's way of pulling her chair very close, edging ever closer and flirting in the over-coy but determined way that was so appalling.

He launched into his music, losing himself in it until the roar of applause greeted the final chord. The Honourable Jemima rushed to take his hand and declare that she was "all admiration." Madame la Comtesse was ecstatic, his cousin Barbara was reduced to tears, the other guests, who wouldn't know an Irish jig from an oratorio, applauded to please the comtesse, while Junius, who admired the Honourable Jemima, seethed.

Another hour dragged by before Madame la Comtesse decreed that she had been here long enough, and departed, expressing her thanks with cold hauteur to Sir Selby and Lady Marcia, but patting Montclair's cheek, and murmuring, *"Charmant, Maestro! Le plus charmant!"* The Spindles also left, bearing the Honourable Jemima with them. The remaining guests, the Trents and their son, were avid gamesters. They settled down to their cards and since they would likely play until the wee hours, Barbara was sent off to bed, and Montclair was able to slip quietly away.

Before going upstairs, he went out onto the terrace for a breath of air. He was very weary, but the evening had not been a complete loss. Because the mighty comtesse had apparently taken a liking to him, his aunt's nose was properly out of joint, and Junius could cheerfully have rent him limb from limb.

Chuckling to himself, he glanced to the left. Deep in the shadows at the far end of the terrace, something had moved. One of the servants, likely. "Hello," he called. "Who's there?"

Save for a cool night wind that whispered among the shrubs, the silence was absolute. Montclair tensed. His eyes were very keen, and he was sure he could distinguish a darker shape, standing very still. "The devil!" he muttered. "Hey! You there!" Grabbing a flower pot he sprang forward. Perhaps his weariness and then the sudden movement set it off, and dizziness struck hard, the terrace swinging under his feet so that he weaved drunkenly. Candlelight glowed at an open upper window. Barbara's voice called a vaguely anxious, "Val? Is that you?"

Montclair had managed to reach the deeper darkness under the beech trees. He was sure that someone stood mute and still, very close to him. His vision was blurring, and he drew an impatient hand across his eyes. When he looked up the dark figure was drifting away. "Stand!" he gasped, waving his flower pot.

An arm was about him. Gould's voice, sharp with concern, asked, "Are you all right, sir?"

"Somebody . . . here . . ." he managed thickly.

Barbara called, "What is it? Is he ill again?"

Gould looked up at her. "A little too much wine I think, Miss Trent."

"I—tell you," mumbled Montclair, "there was . . . somebody . . ."

"Yes, sir," said Gould soothingly. "Let me give you a hand, Mr. Valentine. Here we go, sir. Have you in bed in two shakes of a lamb's tail."

On this sunny morning Susan had awoken to the strains of some Castilian ditty, sung regrettably off-key as usual. When she descended the stairs forty minutes later, the howls had ceased, and the perpetrator was standing on the front steps throwing his arms wide and breathing deeply.

"Good morning, Señor Angelo," called Susan.

He bowed, then announced he was "riding forego!" and marched off stablewards.

Bo'sun George Dodman came along the corridor, carrying a large painting. He greeted her in his shy way, the sunlight waking his red hair to a flame, the usual

93

cheerful grin brightening his square sun-bronzed face and deepening the laugh lines that edged the green eyes. "You're up early, ma'am, and looking mighty trim a'low and aloft, if I may say so."

"Thank you, Bo'sun. What are you going to do with that monstrosity?"

He turned the painting and viewed it without delight. "Horrid, isn't it, Mrs. Sue? But"—his voice lowered— "the little widow wants it cleaned. So—cleaned it must be. I only hope she won't be disappointed when I've done." Suddenly despondent, he sighed heavily. "I'd like to please her, ma'am."

Susan smiled. In this house of widows she was invariably referred to as 'Mrs. Sue,' while Edwina Starr was 'the little widow.' The painting looked like nothing more than a collection of dark brown swirls, but as the Bo'sun swung the kitchen door open she said encouragingly that there might be a pretty picture under all that dirt, in which case Starry would indeed be pleased.

The kitchen was bright with sunlight and fragrant with the aromas of bacon, freshly baked scones, and coffee. Priscilla, sampling a scone, turned from the stove and ran to collect her morning kiss.

"Mama! I'm so glad you waked yourself up at last! Uncle Andy has almost finished mending my doll house an' it's just 'dorable, an' I want to paint it. He said I could if I liked, but the Bo'sun won't let me have any paint. Will you make him get some out of his pot for me, Mama? Just a teensy scrinch? There must be enough for a *tiny* little house if there's enough for that *hugeous* big boat!" She looked sternly at the miser. "He's just being uncoproff'tive."

"Now Miss Priscilla, don't bother your poor mama the moment you see her," scolded Mrs. Starr, studiedly unaware of Dodman's admiring gaze. "Come and sit here, Mrs. Sue, your breakfast's all ready. Did you sleep well?

94

Such a chilly night for this time of year. Never stand there like a lump, Bo'sun. I've cut you a raw potato, it's in the bowl over there. You'll likely want to take it into the Hall where you'll have more room to work."

"Yes, ma'am." He collected the potato and proceeded with lagging steps towards the door that led into the Servants' Hall.

Her eyes very round, Priscilla asked, "Aren't you going to cook it for him, Starry?"

Susan laughed. "Bo'sun George had his breakfast already, darling. He is going to clean the picture, and the potato is a—a sort of paint soap."

"Unless," said Mrs. Starr, who had timed to a nicety the closing of the door, "the Bo'sun would care to work at the counter by the sink, and have another cup of coffee."

His eyes lighting up, Dodman fairly shot back into the room.

Susan stirred cream into her cup. "Real coffee, Starry? Can we afford it?"

Her colour somewhat heightened as she carried a cup over to the industrious man at the counter, the little woman answered with a wink. "Depends upon where we buy it, dear ma'am. This pound wasn't weighted down with government taxes, you may be sure."

Susan's brows lifted. She said innocently, "Free Traders, Starry? Here? You surprise me."

Dodman joined in the laughter, caught Mrs. Starr's eyes, reddened, and hurriedly restored his attention to the canvas.

"*I'm* s'prised that with all that paint, the Bo'sun can't spare a teensy scrinch for my doll house," sighed Priscilla, standing on tiptoe to watch the results of his efforts. "It seems very mean an' unkindly to bedredge a little child a drib of paint when she needs it so drefful bad."

"That should be 'begrudge,'" said Mrs. Starr, buttering another scone. "Come and sit down at table with your mama, now."

Priscilla clambered onto the chair beside her mother. "Don't you think the Bo'sun is a greedy great hog, Mama?" she enquired. "He's got so much paint and all I want—"

"Is a lesson in manners," said Susan. "Little girls do not call grown-up men greedy great hogs!"

"But, Mama, the Bible says 'Thou shalt not bear false witness' an' if the Bo'sun reely is a—"

Mrs. Starr turned away, a hand over her smile, then scowled and removed Welcome from the sink.

"The Bible also says 'Thou shalt love thy neighbour as thyself.'" And seeing that pretty little mouth start quite predictably to open, Susan added, "Which means friends as well. And also it says, 'Thou shalt not covet.'"

"I don't, Mama! I wouldn't never do that 'cause I don't know what a covet is."

"It's wishing you had something that belongs to someone else. And the Bo'sun has very little paint. Oh, I know it seems a lot to you, dear, but really it may not even be enough for all the work he has to do on *The Dainty Dancer,* and we can't afford another big pot. Besides," she spread some raspberry jam on her scone, "I think, if it was my doll house, I wouldn't want white paint. Have some jam, my love. Did she eat her egg, Starry?"

"Yes, I eated it all up," said Priscilla, "and Wolfgang eated his breakfast too, din't he, Starry? An' has we got some other paint, Mama? I'd 'ticlarly like red, if poss'ble."

"Red!" said Mrs. Starr, with a furtive smile at Susan. "Whoever heard of a red house?"

"The elfs did," argued Priscilla. "In that book you read me, Mama. 'Member? The elfs lived in a little shoe house an' it was all bright and red an' cosy. Red's a cosy colour, don't you 'gree, Bo'sun George?"

96

Dodman glanced uneasily at Mrs. Starr's bright eyes, which were immediately averted. "Can't say that I do, Miss Priscilla. Red's a colour that doesn't please some folks, who think that red hair, for instance, stands for bad temper." Mrs. Starr emitting a small snort, he went on innocently, "Not in my case, of course, for everyone knows that I'm a very peaceable man and like a quiet life, y'see."

Priscilla squealed delightedly, Susan could not restrain a laugh, and although Mrs. Starr tried to look indifferent, she was won to a smile. She often remarked in Dodman's hearing that she could not abide a man who was forever brawling. It was well known that the Bo'sun had often resorted to fisticuffs in the taverns near their London home. And however often Andrew would explain that Dodman was only defending the honour of the family name, and that someone had ventured a disparaging remark about Burke Henley's suicide, the 'little widow' would doggedly hold to her opinion that there was *never* a need for violence.

When Susan finished her breakfast, Mrs. Starr gave her the list of things to be purchased from Amberly Down. At once, Priscilla put in her bid for a particularly vital item. Susan explained patiently why this was not possible; Mrs. Starr tried diversionary tactics; the Bo'sun smiled and worked busily. And the end of it was that when Susan walked onto the front steps in her riding habit, a small pot of red paint (if affordable) had been added to her list.

Outside, Deemer led up Pewter, the silver grey mare snorting and sidling in her pretty way, eager to be gone on this bright morning. With a worried look the butler handed Susan a letter. "Came by special messenger, Mrs. Sue," he said.

Susan said she would read it later and rode away, waving merrily to Priscilla, who came out onto the steps to watch her leave. Once out of sight of the cottage she guided Pewter into the shade of some trees, and broke the seal. Her apprehensions were justified; the letter was from a solicitor in Gloucester, written in behalf of Lord Montclair. Brief and to the point, it stated that Mrs. Henley was trespassing on Longhills property; that Highperch Cottage had been sold to Mr. Ezra Henley in January 1811, but was bought back by Lady Digby Montclair in November of that same year, after Mr. Ezra Henley had repeatedly expressed dissatisfaction with the premises. Further, that all pertinent deeds and documents were in the hands of Messrs. Ferry, Laidlaw, and Ferry, at the above address. Wherefore, Mrs. Burke Henley was hereby formally advised that she, her family, friends, servants, and livestock must remove from the dwelling known as Highperch Cottage, a part of the Longhills preserves, prior to the 15th inst. In the event she had not vacated the premises by that date, bailiffs would be sent to effect the removal, at which time Lord Montclair would institute legal proceedings against her.

Heartsick, Susan spurred the willing Pewter to a gallop and tore through the brilliant morning trying to shut out her worries.

She found herself dwelling on the memory of a pair of angry dark eyes and two long narrow hands of surprising strength, which had appropriated her (dirty) mobcap. She had been quite aware that Lord Montclair was unprincipled and ruthless, but only a man of extremely unpleasant character would deliberately frighten a little child. And very soon now this nasty man would face her brother with a loaded pistol in his hand. Andy was an excellent shot, but . . .

Here was the lane the Bo'sun had said would take her straight to the village. Troubled, Susan turned Pewter onto the rutted surface and rode eastward.

6

It was a glorious day, the kind that comes sometimes in spring and splashes all nature with brilliance so that everything looks new-washed and sparkling. The air was cool and bracing and fragrant with the scents of June; the sky azure, with only a few puffy clouds here and there. Perfect weather for a gallop and Montclair loved to ride, yet today he rode with a frown, heedless of the beauty of colourful flower beds, laburnum trees that were a blaze of gold, the headily fragrant violet of lilacs, or the lush emerald of the park's ancient turf. Lost in thought, his dark eyes were grim, his lips set in a thin hard line. He leaned forward in the saddle, instinctively steadying Allegro as the big horse thundered towards the brook. It was a tricky jump, but the stallion soared into the air, clearing the far bank with ease and racing on unchecked.

The incident last night, thought Montclair, had been the final confirmation. If Barbara had not opened her window, if Gould had not chanced to come outside, his own tale might have been told. It was not pleasant to know that someone wanted him dead, but it must be faced. He swore angrily. So—what now? He had no proof to carry to Bow Street. Even if they believed what he told them, what could they do, save to assign one of their men to guard him? "Gad," he muttered with revulsion.

He could hire a guard privately, of course. But the vexation would be the same. And when all was said and done, what use would it be? He knew his temper; sooner or later he would be unable to stand constant surveillance, and would dismiss his protector. If the enemy had been patient, he would strike then. Besides, to a determined assassin, the presence of a guard would likely pose no problem. A pistol or a rifle could be fired from cover and bring down his quarry no matter how many guards had been hired.

He took the far hill in a blur of speed. At the summit, Allegro was beginning to blow, and Montclair reined up and gazed unseeingly on the serene beauty of the ancient village spread below them.

Junius, beyond doubting, harboured a malevolent hatred for him. Lurking under his suave and gentle manner, Uncle Selby's dislike for all the Montclairs was intense; and Valentine was quite aware that Aunt Marcia detested him as thoroughly. But withal they were of the same family, and blood truly is thicker than water. Besides, it was said that, discounting insanity, there are only four motives for murder: passion, financial gain, self-protection, and power.

He had fancied himself in love several times while he was at University, but since he'd come down he'd had small opportunity to seek the company of women, and those he'd met had done nothing to divert his mind from its preoccupations with Longhills and his music.

Nor did financial gain apply, since he was not a wealthy man. He had a comfortable inheritance that had come to him from his late grandmother, but it was scarcely sufficient to tempt anyone to murder, and besides, if he died the residue was earmarked for grandmama's favourite charity. Certainly, none of the Trents had anything to gain by his death. Junius was fourth in line of succession to the title and estates, and would become Baron Montclair of Longhills only after Geoffrey, himself, and Uncle Hampton Montclair had left this earthly coil. Furthermore, had his erratic brother taken a wife and set up his nursery during his long absence, Junius's hopes might have dwindled another step—or even two!

He started Allegro down the hill, still puzzling at it. What next? To the best of his knowledge, he was no threat to another man's life or fortune; he had witnessed no foul play, he was privy to no guilty secrets.

Lastly—power. He had none. Nor could any be gained by his demise. Except perhaps that Uncle Selby would be free to institute all the stupidly clutch-fisted economies he yearned to practice at Longhills; while the improvements he himself had fought to implement, despite his uncle's opposition, would be abandoned. It was ludicrous to imagine that Trent would have him murdered because of that opposition, and there was no one else to regard him as a stumbling block to— He frowned suddenly. In a small way, he *did* constitute a threat to someone: he had the power to evict the Henley virago and her nasty clan from Highperch Cottage!

True to its name, Amberly Down nestled under a hill, so that when approached from the west there was no sign of it until one had crested the top. The single row of honey-coloured stone cottages curved around a village green, which was very green indeed. Beyond was the larger loom of what seemed to be an inn situated near a

pond, and beyond that a dark, forbidding area that
Susan thought must be the infamous swamp, and from
which came the unpleasantly dank and foetid aroma
that assailed her nostrils. The ring of hammer striking
iron came from the far end of the street, and a farmhand
in smock and gaiters was leading a fine ploughhorse towards the open doors of the smithy.

A boy of about ten began to accompany her, keeping a
possessive eye on Pewter. He touched his brow respectfully when Susan wished him good day, and put in
his bid to hold her horse did she mean to shop.

"Well, as a matter of fact, I do wish to make some
purchases," she said, slowing Pewter to an amble.
"What a lovely village this is."

"Ar," he agreed. "Better nor some, surely. Hasn't ye
never been here a'fore, milady?"

"No. And I'm not a milady," she said with a dimple
that made his young heart warm to her. "What *is* that—
er, odour?"

He waved towards the bottom of the street. "Swamp,
ma'am. Me ma says as it be a blot on the village."

"Indeed, I agree with her. Why has your squire done
nothing about it?"

The boy seized Pewter's bridle as another lad made
towards them. "I'm taking care o' the lady, David. Hop
off!" He scowled the competition into deciding against a
closer approach, then answered in a carefully low voice,
"Lord Montclair don't do nothing, ma'am. We could rot
away, every last one of us, me dad says, for all he'd care.
Me dad says as 'twas different in the old lord's day.
Now . . ." He shrugged. "There's Miss Plunkett's millinery in this next house, or the Receiving Office what's the
grocer's as well, two doors down."

Susan consulted her list and halted Pewter beside a
mounting block. The boy handed her down, his face becoming very pink when his disgruntled competitor
hooted loudly from a safe distance.

102

"Oh, and I am also to take back some paint," said Susan.

"The ironmonger's is next to the smithy. I'd best know your name, ma'am. Case the constable thinks I've took your mare without leave."

"Of course. My name is Mrs. Henley."

From the open door to Miss Plunkett's Millinery Shop came an audible squeak, and two bonnets shot from view.

The boy's face was a study. "Oooh . . ." he whispered. "The *widder!*"

It was, Susan realized later, a foretaste of her reception at Amberly Down. Miss Plunkett, a shy, faded little lady, was polite, but her eyes were enormous. Her two customers, large and forbiddingly respectable country matrons, stood apart, whispering and staring quite rudely at the notorious stranger. Angered, Susan pointedly ignored them, choosing some ribbons quickly and matching her cotton as closely as was possible from the limited stock.

There were no letters waiting at the Receiving Office, but the sharp-featured middle-aged woman behind the counter was a very different proposition from Miss Plunkett. She smiled tightly at Susan, welcomed her to the village, and said she hoped she would have the business from Highperch. "Fer so long as ye be there, that is," she added with a bland stare.

Susan said with a spark in her eyes, "Then you may expect our business for a long time to come. Here is my list. If you will be so good as to wrap it all up I'll come back in a minute or two. Thank you." And she was gone with a nod and a swirl of her riding habit before the frustrated proprietor could say another word.

Vexed, Susan walked along the short street, passing several cottages at whose windows curtains were hastily straightened, or from which children peeped at her in frank curiosity. The King's Arms sported a sign

103

whereon was painted a fair replica of Charles I. The door was wide, and from the dim and fragrant interior a woman's voice exclaimed that it was "... downright shameful a woman of *that type* would dare show her nose in a decent village."

Hopelessness descended crushingly on Susan. She should have realized she would still be very much the outsider, but was there no end to it? Was Priscilla to be shunned, even here in this peaceful countryside? Her throat ached and tears stung her eyes. But Andy would be so angry if she let them see she was hurt. 'Pox on them all,' she thought fiercely, and jerked her chin up.

David Brewster made a wild dash for Montclair's stirrup, a great grin of triumph spreading across his small freckled face. "That'll show *you*, cocksure Jack," he shouted at his competitor. "*I've* got Mr. Valentine's Allegro!"

The stallion rolled his eyes and danced sideways.

"Have a care, halfling." Montclair swung from the saddle and with some strict instructions, gave Allegro into the boy's care. He glanced to young Jack Rogers who was walking a pretty little grey mare he didn't recognize. The mare carried a side-saddle, and he wondered which of the local damsels had ridden a new mount into Amberly Down.

Last month some unkind hand—he could guess whose—had gouged a long chip from the gilded top of his harpsichord, and Mundy, the ironmonger, had ordered some gold-leaf paint, which should have come by now. Montclair patted Allegro and strode off down the street. The villagers he encountered responded to his greeting politely enough, but with an air of suppressed excitement, or amusement, or both. When he raised his hat to Mrs. French, the old lady bobbed him a curtsy, then giggled audibly as she hurried past.

Puzzled, Montclair stooped to enter Mundy the Ironmonger's. The shop smelled of paint and putty. It was a dim overcrowded little place with dirty windows, dusty shelves crammed with tools and mysteriously shaped lengths of pipe, and countless bins and boxes full of screws and nails of every shape and size. His eyes momentarily dazzled by the contrast from the brilliant morning outside, Montclair saw that the fat little proprietor was holding a large paint pot and saying persuasively, ". . . happens as I mixed it fer Mr. Ford's new barn. It *must* be just this shade, says his missus. Until they put some on. Then she changed her mind. Could let ye have it cheap, marm. A fine bargain."

A lady said, "Thank you. I'm sure it is, but you see, I just want a—"

She had a low cultured voice that had a musical ring and sounded vaguely familiar. Montclair's view was blocked by some piled tubs on the counter, and he shifted so as to see around them.

"Let ye have the whole pot fer sixpence ha'penny," interrupted Mr. Mundy. "Ye'd spend more nor that on a little'un was I to mix it up again. My boy has to drive the pony and cart to Malvern today, and he could deliver it, if you like." He caught sight of Montclair then, and his broad, perspiring face was wreathed in a bright grin. "Mornin', sir. Fine mornin'. Ye'll be wanting that gold-leaf paint. I'll go and get it."

Montclair saw a slender back clad in a well-cut blue-violet riding habit. The pert little hat had some sort of sheer pale violet stuff tied around it that hung down behind, and it was set upon the head of a lady who wore her near-black hair *à la* ancient Egypt: long and very straight. Stiffening, he thought, 'It is the wretched

105

widow!' and he said, "No. Finish with the lady, Jed. I'll wait."

The icy drawl brought Susan's head jerking up. Of all people! He *would* have to come in here!

"Lady's buying some house paint, sir," offered the proprietor amiably.

"Indeed?" Montclair strolled forward and, determined to remain a gentleman however this hussy provoked him, removed his hat. "Do you undertake some renovations, Mrs. Henley? By way of—recompense, perhaps?"

Susan turned and encountered a bleakly contemptuous gaze. Lord, but Andrew had marked him! To say nothing of the dark bruise her dustpan brush had bestowed on his forehead. She stifled an unwarranted pang of guilt. The horrid creature deserved it all! And only look how he was curling his haughty lip at her. She said with a saintly smile, "We do what we can to restore the poor old house. I'm not accustomed to living in a pigsty, you see."

His dark brows arched. "You surprise me, ma'am."

The sardonic rejoinder fanned Susan's wrath so that she could scarcely breathe. 'You have not begun to be surprised, Baron Beastly!' she thought.

Mr. Mundy mopped his grimy apron at his heated brow and blinked hopefully from one to the other. The Wicked Widder was a luscious plum if ever he saw one, but it was clear young Mr. Valentine didn't think so. Looked ready to strangle the gal, he did, and with them devilish eyes of his and his hasty temper, it wouldn't surprise no one a bit if he was to take her 'crost his knee and whack her bottom for her. Now *that* would be a tale worth telling at the King's Arms tonight!

"This will do very nicely." Susan dazzled Mundy with her smile. "I'll take it with me." She turned her back on Montclair's scowl, and handed over her small sum so that he might not see how very little more was in her purse.

106

He did see the lid of the pot, however, liberally and luridly splashed with scarlet. "The . . . deuce!" he gasped. "Do I understand you to say you mean to paint my house with—*that*?"

"Certainly not," she replied, fluttering her eyelashes at him. "The house I mean to paint belongs to *me,* sir!" She saw his jaw drop as she swept out, clutching her purchase, laughter bubbling inside her.

Seething, Montclair caught up with her and seized her elbow. "You would not—*dare,*" he said between his teeth.

Her eyes very wide and innocent, she blinked up at him. "Sir? I fail to understand you, but do you think you should embrace me on a public thoroughfare?"

"*Embrace* you!" He glanced up and discovered at least twelve people who had not been on the street before. Releasing her arm as though it burned him, he said grittily, "Mrs. Henley, you have absolutely *no right* to interfere with my house. I warn you—if you *dare* apply that hideous paint to—"

"I would think you might be grateful to us for improving the poor old place," she sighed. "Rather than let it go to rack and ruin—as you have done. Oh!" She clapped a hand over her nose and added a muffled, "Pray excuse me, sir. That *dreadful* stench . . . it is quite suffocating. I vow I am all but overcome and in another moment must fall down in a swoon. *Whatever* would people think, I wonder. . . ? Ah, but you would catch me, of course."

Practically incoherent, Montclair snarled, "Do you know what *I* think, madam? It is that you are a—"

"Here I am," called Susan, as young Jack approached, leading Pewter. "Would you please carry this for me? Goodbye, sir."

"Oh, no, ma'am," said Montclair, clapping his hat on as she tripped away. "Not goodbye. We shall meet very soon, I assure you!" He watched her hasten into the

107

grocer's shop, tall and willowy, that long thick black hair swinging softly. "By God, but we will—you conniving Cleopatra!" he muttered.

When Sir Selby Trent had moved his family into Longhills he had declared with commendable humility that he had no wish to intrude into the private life of the Montclairs. Refusing therefore to occupy any of the many suites available in the main block, he had taken up his abode in the south wing. This decision had been viewed without regret by his two nephews, and lauded by his son. His daughter, however, had always wished to reside in the main block, for although the south wing was more modern and extremely luxurious, it was a long walk to and from the dining room.

On this bright afternoon, Barbara could only be grateful for the distance. She had emerged from her earlier hiding place in the gardens, and had been nervously arranging flowers in Valentine's study when Winnie had brought her father's summons. Now she walked with trembling knees beside her plump and comely abigail, listening without conviction to Winnie's whispered but daring observation that "no one cannot *force* you to marry if you don't choose to, Miss Barbara."

They crossed the long gallery toward the steps that led down into the side hall. "Oh yes they can," moaned Barbara miserably. "Are you sure my cousin is gone out?"

"Rid into the village, miss, so that starched-up Mr. Gould says. And he should know, being as he's Mr. Valentine's valet, though one might think from the airs he gives hisself as he was valet to the Pope o' Rome, at least!"

This criticism went unnoticed by Barbara whose entire unhappy concentration was on the forthcoming interview with her formidable parents.

A footman flung open the door that led to the south wing, and they passed through.

"They likely chose this time, knowing he was gone," Barbara whimpered. "May God help me! I am quite undone! I can never face them down alone!"

A lackey froze to attention in the broad panelled hall leading past the ballroom, and Winnie was discreetly silent until they had passed another lackey whose mission in life appeared to be to repel the attempted invasion of a small butterfly. Then she asked softly, "What could Mr. Valentine do, miss? He can't hardly tell your parents the marriage is not right for you."

Three steps up and past double doors that stood open, revealing the sun-splashed magnificence of the Venetian drawing room in which two maids were polishing busily. Barbara whispered, "I know, but he doesn't like this any more than I do. He would tell me what to say. Oh, Winnie! I'm—so *scared*! If *only* Mr. Valentine was back! They will *make* me marry him! I know it!"

"Just don't promise anything, miss. You *mustn't*!" Winnie glanced sympathetically at the pallid and drawn young face beside her. Much chance the poor little thing had with them two! "I s'pose it could be worse, miss," she pointed out, trying to make the best of a bad thing. "What if it was that there Mr. Monteil they wanted you to marry?"

Barbara shuddered.

They started up the main staircase now, the great stained-glass window on the half landing bathing the beautifully carved panelling with colour. A slim young footman, carrying a large Chinese urn down the stairs, stepped aside respectfully as Barbara passed, then gave Winnie a grin and a wink.

"Owdacious flirt," she muttered, her big brown eyes sparkling.

"Is that you, Barbara?" The high-pitched, rasping voice heralded the appearance at the top of the stairs of Lady Trent. She wore a morning dress of apple-green silk with forest-green velvet bands about the bodice and the short sleeves, and a green velvet fringe above the hem. Her coiffure was of the latest fashion, but vindictiveness and suspicion radiated from her; nothing could make her look charming, and her very presence at the top of that fine old stair seemed to cast a pall over its beauty.

Certainly she cast a pall over her daughter, who jerked to a halt, became even paler, and gripped her hands together. "Yes, M-Mama," she faltered.

"We have been waiting this age," scolded my lady, fixing Winnie with a frigid stare. "Well, never stand there as if you'd taken root, child! Hurry up, do!"

Barbara's imploring glance at her abigail was ignored. Winnie had encountered my lady's temper before, and she fled.

Quaking, Barbara followed her mother.

The study was large, bright, and airy. The curtains were thrown back, and warm sunlight slanted into the luxuriously appointed room, painting a golden bar across the dark wine carpet. Fine paintings graced the walls, and tall display cases between the windows contained a prized collection of antique weapons. Sir Selby rose from behind the graceful Hepplewhite desk and hastened to draw up a chair for his wife, who at once launched into an irked denunciation of her bold and disobedient daughter.

"N-no, ma'am, I beg you," said Barbara, perching nervously on the edge of an adjacent chair. "I came at once when Winnie told me—"

Trent murmured, "I think I did not give you my permission to be seated."

His daughter fairly sprang to her feet. "Oh! Your pardon, Papa," she gasped, wringing her hands.

"Accepted."

"You are too lenient, Sir Selby," said my lady with her toothy smile. "Insolence must be punished or there is no telling where it will end. Therefore, Miss Trent, that piece of ill manners will cost you your dinner this evening."

Barbara hung her head and yearned to be peacefully in her grave.

"You knew perfectly well you should have notified your dear papa of your acceptance long before today," Lady Trent went on.

Summoning every vestige of her courage, Barbara forced her stiff lips to obey her. "But—but Mama . . . Papa," she croaked. "I—I do not . . . w-wish to m-marry him."

There was a moment of tingling and terrible silence.

"Do . . . not . . . *wish* . . ." gasped Sir Selby, lifting his quizzing glass and through it scanning his shivering offspring as though she were some rare and repulsive insect.

My lady sprang to her feet. "How *dare* you flout your parents' authority, wretched child? The boy is well born, not unattractive, and very rich! Are you gone quite mad to balk at such a chance?"

"Never upset yourself, my dear." Sir Selby turned to his daughter, his eyes a little narrowed, his words spaced and distinct and ineffably menacing. "Barbara will obey us as a well-bred Christian girl should do. I promised that she would accept this offer, and I never break a promise. You—*do* understand me, I trust, miss?"

Pierced by his grim stare, able to feel her mother's anger, Barbara shook visibly, and tried with dry lips to respond. The words came in a sudden rush. "I—oh,

111

please, Papa! I cannot care for him in—in that particular way. I *beg* of you—do not force—"

"Heavens above, has the chit never *looked* at herself?" Her eyes sparking, her voice piercingly shrill, Lady Trent said, "All your life, Miss Barbara, you have received the very best of instruction and guidance. Much you chose to benefit from it, never regarding what a pretty penny you have cost us! Can you suppose you are a credit to your unfortunate parents, fat and drab and ugly as you are? That you should receive an offer from *any* eligible gentleman is little short of miraculous, as you would realize were you blessed with the faintest degree of Godliness and humility!"

Incapable of speech now, Barbara felt physically sick. She was painfully aware that the door was not quite closed, and had no doubt but that the lackey outside had heard every word of her chastisement and that it very soon would be giggled over by every servant at Longhills. She stood with head bowed, tears of humiliation creeping silently down her white cheeks.

"Look at your daughter, sir!" cried my lady, exasperated. "She has received an offer from a well-bred and well-to-do young gentleman, which is a sight more than I dared to hope for the silly chit, even though it was likely only made out of pity. She should be down on her knees giving thanks. And—look at her! Only *look* at her!"

"Alas, my love. How sharp is the lash an ungrateful child turns upon its parents . . ."

"No," sobbed poor Barbara. "Truly, I—I *am* g-grateful, sir, but—"

"There are no buts," interpolated Sir Selby in a quiet and awful voice. "At half past eleven o'clock on Saturday morning, you will present yourself in the great hall. You will accept with maidenly modesty and gratitude the honour that has been offered you." He lifted one

112

hand in a regal gesture, halting his daughter's feeble attempt at speech. "There is nothing more to be said. You may go and meditate upon your outrageous behaviour."

Taking her weeping daughter by the arm, Lady Trent pushed her to the door. "Stop your snivelling, do," she commanded, tightening her grip cruelly. "And furthermore, my girl, you had best not appear on Saturday with a face like an expiring bloodhound, else you will be sorry, I promise you. *Very* sorry!"

The hills were emerald, the sky intensely blue, the breeze playing like a frolicsome kitten; now quiet and hidden, now darting from concealment to dance with the treetops and riffle the grasses and run flirtatious fingers through Susan's long soft hair. The little mare tossed her pretty head and picked up her hooves as lightly as thistledown. And Susan rode with anxiety for a companion, and her thoughts on the letter that now resided in her pocket.

Had the cottage *really* been sold back to the Montclairs? Was it possible that she really *was* trespassing, and that the young nobleman who had so contemptuously sent his friends to drive her away had right *and* the law on his side? She bit her lip, frightened. What court would believe her if she said that Burke Henley may not even have known about the cottage, and had certainly never mentioned it to her? Or that, even as Sir Selby Trent had implied, Mr. Ezra Henley's mind had been clouded during the final few years of his life and he had kept many things secret and hoarded his papers, fearful of trickery, so that even Burke had known few details of his father's affairs?

If they *were* trespassers, it might take some time to

dispossess them. Grandpapa Tate's solicitor had said
something about possession being nine-tenths of the
law. If things went along as they were, within just a
little while they would have their feet on the ground
again, but it could not be accomplished within ten days
as demanded by the letter in her pocket. What was
needed was something to delay the evil baron . . .

Deep in thought, she paid no attention to her route,
allowing the mare to choose her own path. How angry
Montclair had been about the paint. She brightened.
He'd been fairly white with rage. As if she would put a
red trim on the dear old cottage! She giggled, picturing
it. The pot of paint, much larger than she'd thought to
buy, had proven too heavy and bulky to be slung from
the pommel, especially on such a warm day, so she'd
asked the boy who'd held Pewter to take it back to the
Ironmongery and tell Mr. Mundy she would like it delivered to Highperch, as he'd kindly offered. Priscilla
would be so—

She glanced up and gave a shocked gasp. Pewter had
slowed to little more than a walk. They were following a
trail beside a long line of tall birch trees, and beside her
rode the object of her thoughts. With an involuntary
jerk at the reins, she exclaimed, "Oh! Lord Montclair!"
And she thought, 'He thinks I have the paint in my parcels and has come to try and wrest it from me by force!'

"Now what has he done?" he asked in the cool drawl
that was so infuriatingly provoking.

"What has who done?"

"I thought you spoke of Lord Montclair?"

"Oh. Well, I was shocked to—to find you riding with
me."

"I'd have thought you would have expected such a development."

That sounded sinister, and Susan eyed him uneasily.
His mouth looked hard and cruel. Was she going to have
to fight him off. . . ?

114

"And I'll own myself dense," he went on. "But for the life of me I cannot see what my brother has to do with my riding beside you."

All thought of red paint left Susan's mind. She was seized by a horrible sinking feeling, and stammered feebly, "Your—br-brother?"

"Lord Geoffrey DeBrant Colwynne Montclair."

She paled. "D-do you say—that *you*—aren't. . . ?"

"No, ma'am. I am Valentine Amberly Montclair. The younger brother."

"Oh—no!" wailed Susan, horrified. "How perfectly *dreadful!*"

Despite himself, his lips twitched at this. "To be a Montclair? Or to be a younger son?"

"I thought *you* were Lord Montclair!"

"Did you? Dear me, I must warn my brother!"

Susan's brain reeled. So he was *not* the Beastly Baron who meant to force them from Highperch! 'Heavens! What have I done? I struck the wrong man!' Struggling to regain her equilibrium in the light of this shocking disclosure, she said, "Then we owe you an apology. You see, Lyddford thought—"

"I am aware, ma'am." The words fairly dripped ice. "Your brother is extreme hot at hand. But I assure you I do not molest small girls. Even if they trespass on our estate."

How coldly aloof he was. He wouldn't even let her apologize properly. Irritated, she snapped, "No, you merely so terrify them they cannot sleep at night!"

"If that is so, I am sorry for it, but—"

"*If* it is so? I do not tell falsehoods, sir!"

He gave her a long measuring look. "Do you not, Mrs. Henley? How admirable."

"More admirable than for your brother's friends to forcibly invade my home, bully my servants, and beat my brother into unconsciousness because he tried to protect me from being mauled!"

115

Inwardly appalled by this litany of abuse, Montclair frowned at the riding whip in his hand. Then he said slowly, "My brother is out of the country, ma'am. And has been for several years."

In which case she'd been right, after all. "So you act for him, I take it."

They had come to the end of the trees and were approaching a stretch of high level land with a fine view of the surrounding countryside. Charmingly flanked by two weeping willow trees, a summer house stood in the centre of the turf, the bright faces of lupins, daisies, and stocks bobbing around it.

Montclair drew rein. "It will be easier to talk inside, madam."

Belatedly, Susan asked, "Where are we?"

He had, she discovered, a perfectly horrid way of regarding her, saying nothing, but the upward twitch of one dark brow speaking volumes. His slim hand moved in a graceful but mocking gesture to the right. She yearned to strike it, and with considerable irritation glanced where he indicated.

Distantly, the chimneys of a great house peeped above the trees. Susan felt her face grow hot. "Never say that is Longhills? But—it cannot be! I started out the other way. Oh, how vexing! I suppose I did not pay heed to where I was going and must have ridden in a circle." It sounded so lame that she was not surprised by his scornful stare. Much chance she had of convincing this icicle that her trespassing had not been deliberate.

"It would appear to be a family failing," he drawled sardonically. "Your later father-in-law had the same—ah, tendency."

He dismounted in a lithe swing and tethered Allegro to a branch of one of the trees. He had fully expected an angry response to his barbed remark, but when he turned he found Mrs. Henley with hands prayerfully clasped before her bosom and eyes closed. Heaven forbid she was about to make good her earlier dastardly threat and swoon into his arms! He scanned her uneasily. "Are you well, madam?"

"And grateful," she said, blinking down at him. "I was thanking a merciful Providence. Only think—a few centuries ago had I dared set foot upon your property you might have punished me by providing me with an iron collar!" She gave a realistic shudder.

Montclair's lips quirked. Iron collar, indeed! With all her faults, the widow had spirit and a sense of humour. He drawled, "Have no fears, madam. Even were I so inclined, I own no serfs at present, and will provide nothing more threatening than an offer to help you down."

'Even were he *so inclined*?' The conceit of it! And his eyes glittered at her in a most unpleasantly piercing way, the strange amber flecks in startling contrast with the near-black iris. She contemplated refusing his help, but that would mean a clumsy dismount, and so she leaned to him. The hands that received her were strong, but held her as briefly as possible. Susan, who would have been infuriated if he'd held her longer, thought with perverse resentment that he must be afraid of contaminating himself.

The summer house was constructed on the open plan, with several wooden benches grouped under the graceful pagoda roof. Susan found it delightful, but refused to give him the satisfaction of saying so. She was surprised to find his hand supporting her elbow as she mounted the three shallow steps. The noble gentleman very obviously despised the scheming widow, but at least he remembered his manners.

"As a matter of fact," she said, unbending a little, "it is as well you followed me, for there is something I must discuss with you."

"I did not follow you, Mrs. Henley. In point of fact, I

117

was surprised to find you here. And if you wished to speak to me, I cannot but wonder why you—er, 'started out the other way.'"

She drew a deep breath. It served her right for addressing him as though he had been human. What a pity that she had hit him with the brush. She might better have used the broom! "I had intended to apologize," she said coldly, refusing to allow his sarcasm to fluster her.

"For invading my cottage? Or for your hideous scheme to redecorate it?"

"Oh, neither. For being a—just a touch put out when you came to my house."

"Just a—'touch'. . . ?" Montclair fingered his bruised forehead. "It would be diverting to see you when you are really vexed, ma'am."

She smiled at him in the way that so exasperated Andrew and which he referred to as her 'Sphinx grin.' If Montclair was exasperated, he gave no sign of it, watching her enigmatically for a moment, then turning away to dust off one of the benches, and bow her to it.

Ignoring the overblown gallantry, she sat on an adjacent bench and contemplated the view. How beautiful it was, all green and blue and gold; neat and peaceful, typical of the west country she loved so well.

There could be little doubt, thought Montclair, scanning the widow obliquely, that her reputation was well earned. She had behaved with disgraceful abandon at the cottage yesterday; she probably hoped to wound him by using that ghastly paint on the dear old place, and she had a way of meeting one's eyes that was decidedly unmaidenly. Besides, who ever heard of a lady wearing her hair so long and straight? That style was quite out of fashion—and had been for about two thousand years. She was a shapely creature, though, and was clever enough to achieve an air of tranquillity. The way her

118

hands were folded in her lap, for instance; the graceful disposition of her body . . . The breeze riffled her hair. It was, he noticed, very thick and silky-looking. He wondered if it felt silky. She turned her head so suddenly that she caught him watching her, which made him long to give himself a hard kick.

"You said we could talk," Susan reminded, smiling sweetly into his level stare.

"By all means. When do you mean to begin?"

"Begin. . . ?"

"*You* said you intended to apologize."

"True. But then I changed my mind."

"A feminine trait, I understand." He looked bored. "Why? Because you have been asked to leave my house?"

She said dryly, "You have some most unpleasant friends, Mr. Montclair."

"Forgive if I contradict a . . . lady. My friends are not at all unpleasant. But I *am* responsible for your having been roughly dealt with. For that I do apologize."

At first infuriated by that deliberate hesitation before naming her a lady, then astonished that he would deign to offer such an apology, she murmured a confused "Thank you," and looking across the drowsing valley below them asked inanely, "Does your brother own all this?"

"As far as you can see in any direction, madam. Save for Highperch Cottage."

"Your friends gave me to understand that the cottage was part of the Longhills entail." She saw the irritated flicker of his dark brows, and added, "They *are* your friends—no?"

A little muscle moved in his jaw. He answered evasively, "Mr. Junius Trent is my cousin, madam. Highperch is not a part of the entail and was made over to

119

me by my mother after she bought back the property from Mr. Ezra Henley."

"We, of course, dispute the fact that the property ever *was* bought back."

"My solicitor," he began with a weary sigh, "has all the necessary papers and—"

"Oh, yes. Messrs. Ferry, Laidlaw, and Ferry. And you may sit down if you wish, even though you mean to have your bailiffs throw me out on the fifteenth."

The impudence of the woman! Montclair sat on the adjacent bench. "You went to see my solicitors?"

"Hardly. How would I know who they are?" Susan took the letter from her pocket and handed it to him.

His eyes travelled the page rapidly. He uttered a stifled exclamation and crumpled the paper in his fist.

"I'll have it back, if you please."

Montclair muttered an apology, attempted to smooth the wrinkled letter, and returned it.

Scornful, she said, "Am I to believe you were unaware this was sent, Mr. Montclair? Faith, but you must be singularly ill informed by your man of business!"

He tightened his lips, then snapped, "It says truth."

"Does it, so? Then you believe my father-in-law, my late husband, my brother, to have been cheating thieves, and myself a conniving opportunist!" She stood, coming to her full and stately height, and regarding him from beneath haughtily arched brows.

He rose at once. "I cannot think my opinion would weigh with you, Mrs. Henley. But I will give you the benefit of the doubt and suppose you to be unaware that my solicitor holds your father-in-law's signed receipt for the return of his funds."

"Your nobility is awesome, sir," she riposted, dropping a mocking curtsy. "In turn I shall suppose *you* to be unaware that my brother and I, as well as my late father-in-law's solicitor, have branded that signature a forgery."

120

"A forgery!" Scowling, he snapped, "By whom, I should like to know?"

He looked so fierce that Susan was a little frightened, but she said bravely, "By whosoever *did* receive the funds, obviously."

"Madam, that is absolute rubbish! The funds were directly returned to your late father-in-law by special courier. Perhaps, owing to Mr. Ezra Henley's state of health, he was unable to write in his usual hand, but—"

She laughed merrily. "But how very convenient."

"The fact remains," he snarled, glaring at her, "that the funds *were* delivered. What became of them after that is not my concern."

"It is very much *my* concern, sir! What you allege is typical of the nonsense by which the business has been dragged out and delayed. We shall take you to court and—"

"And waste a good deal of time and money! Including the cost of your paint and the restitution I shall claim for any defacement of my property."

Susan cried ringingly, "Kindly allow me my say, Mr. Montclair."

She stood there, the picture of disdain, her riding crop tapping at the skirt of her habit, shapely and slim, and so regal one might suppose him to be the veriest peasant in the presence of a queen. She was an unscrupulous jade, but by heaven, she had her share of gumption! His ready sense of humour stirred, he bowed low. "Your pardon. Say on, madam."

The sudden and unexpected twinkle in his dark eyes brought the flecks of amber brilliantly alive, and his grim mouth relaxed into a faintly whimsical grin so that from a ruthless menace he became a charming young man. Again thrown off stride, Susan murmured, "Oh dear, where was I?"

"Taking me to court," he prompted obligingly.

"Yes. Thank you. And likely prove that your courier

either delivered the funds to the wrong party, or—or perhaps absconded with them himself."

"Oh, very good. But unlikely. Especially since the courier is still in my solicitor's employ. However, do not let me deter you, Mrs. Henley. If that is your best defence, by all means use it."

She eyed him uneasily. "I suppose that smug look means that you are convinced we shall lose if we do so."

"I am convinced you will lose *whatever* you do. I have said what I wished to say. If you have nothing to add, perhaps you will permit that I and my—er, smug look leave you."

"I have a great deal to add, including resentment for your arrogant and unwarranted use of the word 'defacement.' Neglect sir, constitutes far greater defacement than any painting and repairs I may contemplate."

She had struck a nerve. His hot temper flaring, he said explosively, "If you are truly so vulgar as to use *that* colour on Highperch, Mrs. Henley, I warn you that you will become the laughing-stock of the county!"

"Instead of merely being scorned and my innocent little girl ostracized because her father was a suicide?" Her lip curled. "I have survived the tender mercies of self-righteous town-dwellers, Mr. Montclair. I had hoped to find a kinder attitude among country folk, especially towards Priscilla. Apparently, my hopes were vain. But I promise you the time is past when the prospect of becoming a laughing-stock could cause me to shake in my shoes."

"How regrettable," he drawled. "It is evident, ma'am, that to prolong this discussion would be pointless. I give you good day."

Bowing, he started off, but glanced back when she called, "One moment, if you please. We have another matter to discuss."

He scowled, hesitating. But he was curious to see

what outrageous ploy she would next present, and thus went back to the bench once more.

Susan sat down and ordered her skirts. "When my brother attacked you—"

"After I molested your daughter," he interpolated, stiffening.

"Mr. Montclair, permit me to say that your manners are atrocious. Did no one ever teach you that it is very rude to interrupt? I was about to explain that it was no more than a simple mistake, and—"

He was rude again. "*Simple!* Many sins I consider forgivable, Mrs. Henley, but the man who abuses a helpless little child is utterly despicable. To have been judged capable of such conduct is not my notion of a 'simple mistake'!"

"You know perfectly well, sir, that my brother misunderstood what Priscilla said."

He shrugged irritably. "It is of no consequence. What is done, is done."

"That is nonsensical! You might just as well say that if a carriage wheel comes to rest on my foot I must not move because it 'is done'! Or that if I should accidentally set light to the curtains, I must not put out the fire because it 'is done'!"

"I am sure you can dredge up countless inappropriate similes, Mrs. Henley. The fact remains that Lyddford struck me in the face. And the Code of Honour does not permit—"

Forgetting her scold about interruptions, she threw up her hands in exasperation. "You men and your stupid Code of Honour!"

"Yes," he sneered. "I can well imagine you would find it stupid."

Susan flushed darkly. "Your *imagination* at least, cannot be faulted, sir. I suppose you are a crack shot and

123

look forward eagerly to ridding the world of a man who dared defend his little niece!"

"I believe I know one end of a pistol from the other, madam. And if I may point out—since I did not instigate the duel, your argument is ill taken."

The horrid man had a point. She bit her lip, but persisted. "Were my brother to apologize. . . ?"

"Hah! I wish I may see it! Lyddford did not impress me as being either a fool, or the type to apologize for his errors."

"If you knew him better—" she began angrily, but stopped when she saw the pitfall.

Montclair was in no mood to allow a poor move. "I would know he *is* a fool?" He clicked his tongue. "Perhaps you are right, but I think he would not appreciate your putting me in possession of that fact, Mrs. Henley."

'Wretch!' she thought, and said loftily, "The mistake was mine, for supposing I might appeal to your better nature."

"'Appeal to my better nature,' is it? Jove, but you're a rare optimist, ma'am! You illegally occupy my house; attack me like any fishwife—"

"*Fishwife* . . ." she spluttered, outraged. "How *dare* you?"

"—make perfectly vile aspersions on my character; your brother has the confounded lack of sportsmanship to knock me down when I'm looking the other way; you mean to render my house hideous by splashing scarlet paint all over it—and *you* seek to appeal to *my* better nature? By God, madam! If you hoped to turn me up sweet so as to grant you a stay of eviction, you could scarce have played your cards in worse fashion!"

Springing up, Susan gathered the train of her habit with so sweeping a gesture that she revealed the tops of her riding boots. She saw Montclair's glance flash to the embarrassment, and yearned to scratch him. "Cer-

124

tainly," she said, her voice quivering with rage, "I have wasted my time by attempting to reason with an ill-tempered boor. Good day, Mr. Montclair."

Having thus dismissed the obnoxious creature, she turned her eyes away and waited for him to depart.

He gave her the sketch of a bow and stood firm, coldly immovable.

It dawned on her then that this was *his* summer house. Discomfitted, she walked past, and down the steps, but as she approached the mare, was again discomfitted. Pewter was not a tall horse, but the stirrup was rather too high to permit a graceful mount without assistance.

Montclair watched her predicament with wicked enjoyment. Still, she had played fair in their dispute, resorting to neither tears nor hysterics, as so many of her kind would have done. Besides, she *was* a female and his breeding prevailed. "Allow me, Your Majesty." He handed her the reins, and bent, cupping his hands for her foot.

'Sooner,' thought Susan, 'would I perish!' Made reckless by anger, she flicked the reins over the pommel, and in a trice was atop the first step. It was just a little jump to Pewter, and once she had a grip on the pommel . . . She launched herself at the saddle.

Startled by such unfamiliar antics, Pewter danced away.

Bewildered, Montclair half turned, making a grab for the stirrup. Unfortunately, Susan was quite unable to stop in mid-air, and with a shocked squeal she crashed unchecked into him.

Winded, flattened, and extremely surprised, he heard faint feminine moans, and found that he was enveloped in a cloud of black hair.

Dragging herself to her hands and knees, Susan snatched the obstruction from his eyes. "Give me my hat. At once!" she demanded, kneeling over him scarlet faced, and all but weeping with chagrin. "And just for your—your information, Mr. Amberval— Oh! I mean—" His wheezing and unsympathetic laughter was typical of the brute. Between gnashing teeth, she finished sobbingly, "For your information, you are—without"—she blew a lock of hair from her eyes—"without doubt—the—the most *odious* creature I have *ever* met!"

He sprawled there. Howling.

She all but flew to Pewter, and heedless of propriety, got one foot into the stirrup and dragged herself up. Jamming the hat onto her head, she resorted to the spur she never employed, and the mare was away at the gallop.

It was no use. For what seemed miles she could still hear his loathsome laughter.

7

The day after tomorrow was Saturday. Walking in aimless distraction among the trees, Barbara thought how marvellous it would be to be a milkmaid or a governess. Anything but a lady of Quality, who must be forced into wedlock, only because the gentleman was very rich. Surely milkmaids and governesses were allowed to wed whomsoever they wished. Or perhaps, not forced to wed at all.

She had come to the little secluded glade to which she sometimes crept when deeply troubled, and she sank gratefully onto the stump of the big elm tree that had been the king of this glade until last November's great storm had wrought such havoc in the woods.

The day after tomorrow . . . Mama and Papa were determined, beyond doubting. Her tears and pleadings had only made them angry. And Junius thought it all a great joke. Val understood, and wanted this no more than did she, but even if she found the courage to follow his suggestion it would only land him in great trouble, and as it was, the expression in Junius's eyes when he looked at his cousin sometimes made her fear . . . She shivered.

So there was no hope. Unless perhaps she could do as the poor lady of the Folly had done, and jump off the roof. Or would she be too lacking in courage to commit that awful sin? Oh, how ghastly it all was! She bowed her head into her hands and wept with soft but racking sobs.

The deadly and unmistakable crack of a gunshot shocked her from grief and all thought of self. She whispered, horrified, "*Val!* Oh, my God!" And she was running.

Montclair strode through the copse, the reins loosely held, Allegro thudding amiably beside him. The warmth of the afternoon was increasing and there was a sultriness in the air that spoke of bad weather to come, but he scarcely noticed these things, his mind preoccupied with the Widow Henley. What a hoyden the woman was! Whoever heard of a lady flinging herself at a horse in so abandoned a fashion? He chuckled. Gad, but how dear old Geoff would have laughed to see him smashed to the ground by a flying female! An unscrupulous female, who was no better than a thief.

The smile faded from his eyes, and his jaw set. So they challenged Ezra Henley's signature, did they? Much good might it do them! After all these years any self-respecting judge would laugh at their case. If they really meant to bring a case. More likely they'd moved into Highperch well knowing they'd no legal claims at all, relying on using legal manoeuvrings and the slow-grinding wheels of justice to protect them for as long as possible, thus ensuring they would have a free roof over their heads. A free roof with a garish red trim. . . ! He ground his teeth.

'My innocent little girl ostracized because her father was a suicide. . . !'

Those words, so fiercely uttered, disturbed him. It was very likely true enough. People could be cruel. But that was the way of the world. Certainly, it was not his problem. Old Ferry's proofs of the resale were indisputable, and the noxious Henley clan must be made to vacate Highperch. Still, it was a *damnable* thing to have had a lone woman terrorized and her brother clubbed down on Longhills property! Papa would turn in his grave! Once again the Trents had—

Allegro snorted nervously. There was a sudden great rustling nearby; someone was riding at reckless speed. Montclair's hand flashed to the pistol in his pocket. A fine bay horse burst from the trees and charged straight at him. At the last instant the rider pulled up his animal, then sprang from the saddle in an impressive if unnecessarily dramatic demonstration of horsemanship.

Montclair thought with a silent groan, 'Oh Gad! It's the Spanish lunatic again!' but relinquished his grip on the pistol.

"Chew I foundling," declared Señor de Ferdinand exuberantly.

"Most astute," drawled Montclair at his haughtiest. "Since I live here."

"Chess." De Ferdinand directed an approving glance over woods, park, and gardens to the distant loom of the house. "Very nice small 'state. Chew theses sell?"

Speechless, Montclair stared at him.

"Chew wish 'state selling," said the señor earnestly, "I interest to buyings have."

'Good God!' thought Montclair. "Longhills," he explained, keeping his patience with an effort, "has been in my family for centuries. It is not for sale. If it were, however, the figure involved would be extremely high."

The Spaniard waved a hand airily. "Mices elves high figures havings. Meece buying Longhills."

Montclair tightened his grip on the reins and took a

pace forward. "Señor Angelo—er, et cetera—de Ferdinand, I will say this as slowly and carefully as I can. Item—Longhills is not, will not be, and never has been for sale! Item—if this is more of Mrs. Henley's nonsense, you waste your time and mine. Item—if that is all you came here to say, you have said it. I have replied. Now be so good as to take yourself off our property."

Señor Angelo, who had followed this exposition with parted lips and extreme concentration, suddenly jerked his shoulders back, bowed low, and said, "Chew say mices elves lie telling. Chess? Very good. Now we shootings." He whipped a long-barrelled and richly gilded pistol from his saddle holster, and twirled it recklessly around one finger.

"Hey!" cried Montclair, drawing back. "Have a care! That's no way to handle a duelling pistol!"

"Chew with mices elves shoot. Now. Hereupon—once at!"

Montclair, although no great hand with a pistol, had early been taught a healthy respect for such weapons. "I am engaged to fight Mr. Lyddford," he pointed out, eyeing the Spaniard's flourishings with alarm. "Put that thing down, you block, before—"

"Chew forget into chaw mouths mices hat were hoved." Señor Angelo laughed. "First mices—"

The pistol eluded his suddenly frantic clutch and swung sideways.

With a shout, Montclair leapt away and in the same instant the pistol roared deafeningly.

There was no impact; no stab of pain.

The smoke cleared, and he saw that the Spaniard had fallen to his knees and was bowed forward.

"Good God!" Montclair sprang to bend over him.

A pallid, sweating face was lifted. Dazedly, de Ferdinand gasped, "*Caramba!* . . . mices elves have . . . Angelo shootinged."

130

"Of all the stupid—" Montclair slipped an arm about him. "Here—sit back. Let me have a look."

Already, bright crimson stained the snowy shirt. Montclair unbuttoned and removed the coat, moving as quickly and carefully as possible. He glanced up and was given a faint twitching smile. The fellow was raving mad, but he had bottom, thank heaven. "Good man," he muttered, and spread the shirt.

"*Val!*" Barbara ran across the turf, holding up her gown to facilitate her tempestuous advance, her face pale with fear. "Oh, Val!" she panted. "Are you—"

"I'm all right, Babs." Montclair tugged at his handkerchief. "I'm afraid this fellow has been hit, though."

Unspeakably relieved, she took in the injured gentleman who sat leaning back on his hands and gazing at her in white-lipped silence.

Montclair had fashioned his handkerchief into a pad which he placed firmly over the wound in the Spaniard's left side. Watching the hurt man's face, he increased the pressure until the steady stream of blood stopped. De Ferdinand became whiter than ever, but did not flinch.

Barbara did. "How d-dreadful!" she faltered. "W-why did you shoot him?"

De Ferdinand murmured, "Mices elves dyings was?"

For some reason Barbara appeared to have no difficulty with the gentleman's unique way with English, and she knelt beside him also and said shyly, "No, sir. I am sure you are not badly hurt." Then, with an anxious glance at her cousin she added, "Is he, Val?"

"Just a deep groove across the side of his ribs. You're extreme fortunate, señor. I— Blast! Babs—I hate to ask, but I can't hold this and get his shirt off, and I need it for a bandage. Could you—?" He looked at her doubtfully. She was such a timid little mouse and this brave but crazy Spaniard had bled like fury. To his surprise,

131

her little hands came at once to hold his handkerchief tightly against the wound.

"Brave girl," he said, relieved, and managed to detach the hurt man from his shirt. Tearing it into strips, he said curtly, "Babs, this is Señor Angelo de Ferdinand. Señor—my cousin, Miss Barbara Trent."

Barbara threw a quick, shy glance at the Spaniard's drawn, intent face.

"Chaw incestual eyes must rest not mices decentless selves upon," he murmured, faint but gallant.

Barbara looked startled.

Beginning to wind his improvised bandage around the lean, olive-skinned body, Montclair explained, "I think that roughly translates to a request that you not cast your innocent eyes upon his indecent self."

"Oh," said Barbara, blushing, and lowering her gaze.

"And I did not shoot him," added Montclair. "Hold tight now, Babs. Ah—here we go. The fact is that Señor de Ferdinand was—" He caught the Spaniard's look of desperate entreaty, and amended hurriedly, "was—er, showing me his new pistol, er, thinking it empty, you know. Hang on, señor, I'm going to have to tug this."

"Oh dear," murmured Barbara sympathetically as the wounded man gave a gasp. "Val—do you suppose a rib may be broken?"

De Ferdinand had managed to continue to prop himself up, but now he began to sag. Barbara moved quickly to catch him and he sank into her lap. *"Dios!"* he whispered.

"Poor soul." She took up a piece of the rendered shirt and dabbed it at his sweating face.

"I think I'll leave the rest to old Sheswell," said Montclair, wiping his hands on another remnant of the shirt. "We're closer to Longhills than to Highperch, so I'll take you there, Señor de Ferdinand, if—"

The dark eyes opened. Gazing up at Barbara, Angelo sighed, "Madonna . . . chew kindly . . . most. Mices heart—words no havings. Montclair—mices thanks ways all, but chew bring the Highperch, pliss. Put horse on meece."

Their protests were unavailing. Weak and shaken he might be, but he was also—as Montclair lost no time in telling him—stubborn as any mule. Surrendering, Barbara said that she would stay with Señor de Ferdinand while Montclair rode for a carriage. In the middle of a tangled sentence denying the need for anything but his own horse, the victim checked and stared to one side.

Montclair turned his head. A man lay propped on one elbow a short way up the slope, watching them. "Well, of all the bare-faced—" Montclair began. "Hey! Get down here!"

The man stood and ambled down the slope, a piece of grass between his teeth. "Thought I'd stay near, sir," he said lazily. "Not meaning to intrude, as they say. 'Case you might need a spot o' help like."

He was tall and thin and clad in work garments that had seen far better days. A battered straw hat, perched on a mop of curly and untidy brown hair, shaded a face notable for bushy eyebrows, a jutting chin, and a pair of heavy-lidded drowsy eyes of a very pale blue.

"I should have thought it would be dashed well obvious I needed a 'spot of help,'" snapped Montclair. "You're the new gardener, I believe? I've yet to see you standing up while you work! If all your hard labour hasn't worn you out, you can bring the horses over here."

The gardener's thin lips twisted into a grin. He cast an amused eye over Señor Angelo. "Dropped yer gun, didya, mate?" he murmured innocently.

Barbara's eyes widened. The Spaniard glared at him.

"What is your name?" demanded Montclair.

"They call me Diccon, sir."

"Do they? Well that's not what I'd call you if there weren't a lady present. Get the hacks. *Now!*"

133

"Right you are!" Diccon went shambling off.

Señor de Ferdinand was eased into his coat again. When Diccon returned with the horses, Allegro stood firm, but the smell of blood sent the bay prancing in fright. Montclair pulled him down and quieted him, and Diccon all but lifted de Ferdinand into the saddle, and asked, "Would ye want as I should come with you, sir?"

Montclair refused this offer, requiring instead that he escort Miss Barbara home and that a groom be sent to Bredon immediately, to fetch Dr. Sheswell to Highperch. Señor Angelo managed to convey the information that Mrs. Henley's staff included a man of medicine. 'I wish I may see it,' Montclair thought, cynically, but rescinded his order without argument.

The ride to the cottage was accomplished with some difficulty. The Spaniard seemed to get his second wind, and jauntily proclaimed himself "a perfect fit," which caused Montclair to grin, but a few minutes later he barely caught the man in time as he started to slide from the saddle.

"I'll say this much for you," said Montclair, hauling him up again. "You may be bats in the belfry, and 'perfectly fit' you're certainly not—but you're a game one, señor."

Susan reined Pewter to a halt before they left the woods, and made an effort to restore her appearance. She had shed tears of rage and humiliation, and was still breathing too fast, and had no wish to alarm her family. She had only to recall Montclair's heartless laughter when she'd—er, fallen, and she began to seethe again, which would not do, so she sat quietly for a moment, closing her eyes and trying to compose herself. Since she spent several minutes thinking instead of what she would like to do to the wretch, composure was not at once achieved, but it was cool and quiet and peaceful among the trees, the silence broken only by the drowsy twittering of the birds, and gradually her tumultuous heart quieted. She had decided to continue on her way when she heard a man laugh.

It was not her brother's merry peal, nor the rather shrill bray of Señor Angelo's amusement, or the Bo'sun's boom. There was, furthermore, something sinister about the laugh, if only because it was obviously restrained.

The peaceful woodland glade began to seem lonely and menacing. She was quite alone and too far from Highperch for screams to be heard. If that horrid laugh belonged to Mr. Junius Trent . . . Her heart began to pound again. She stifled the impulse to spur Pewter to a gallop and make a run for safety. It was difficult to tell from which direction the laugh had come, and she had been sufficiently foolish today without capping it off by rushing straight at the very man she sought to avoid. She urged the mare forward at a walk.

She heard voices then, again low pitched. Two men, and quite nearby. Why were they talking so softly? How silly she was, imagining all this drama. They were likely nothing more threatening than a pair of poachers. Heavens, but her imagination was running away with her. And then, like the crash of doom, a horse whinnied. Poachers did not ride!

"D'ye take me for a flat?" demanded an irate and cultured voice. "We'll have to keep a very careful watch on the lot of 'em, as he said, or—"

A horse whickered, and Pewter whinnied a response. A startled exclamation. Rapid hoofbeats.

With a squeal of fright Susan drove home her heels, and the mare jumped into a gallop.

Someone shouted, "That way!"

Susan bowed to avoid a low-hanging branch. From the

135

corner of her eye she saw the shrubs to her right violently disturbed and her heart jumped into her mouth.

Then Pewter burst from the trees and was thundering across open country towards Highperch.

It was a few minutes before Susan dared glance behind her. Half expecting to see two villains riding her down, she beheld only the golden afternoon and no sign of pursuit. She gave a gasp of relief, but just the same, she galloped the mare all the way home, slowing to a canter only as they came to the drivepath.

Wolfgang ran from the open front door, barking a shrill welcome, and Priscilla came dancing out, Bo'sun George following her.

"Mama, oh Mama! You've comed back!" Unable to wait for her mother to dismount, the child hugged Susan's riding boot and cried ecstatically, "Thank you so much for my paint! It's eggs-whizzit! Oh, but my doll house will be the bestest in the whole county. And England! Slap up to the knocker!"

"Priscilla," said Susan, trying to be stern, "you know Uncle Andrew doesn't like you to use such terms."

"No, but that one must be all right, Mama, 'cause he said it his own self. I heard him!" She drew back to beam up at her mother, then went skipping back inside again, Wolfgang howling after her.

Dodman lifted Susan down and took the reins.

"So the boy came already," she said. "I didn't expect he'd be so prompt. Has my brother seen the paint, Bo'sun?"

"Yes, ma'am." The green eyes twinkled. "He was a bit surprised by the colour."

Susan's smile was rather grim. "He'll be more taken aback when I tell him of the matter. Where is he?"

"Down to the boat, Mrs. Sue. A gentleman's come." He glanced to the house and leaned closer. "Business, I think. They—"

136

"Here you are at last!" Mrs. Starr came onto the steps and hurried to take Susan's parcels. "Oh do come quickly, my dear. You'll never believe what our clever Bo'sun has done!" She beamed approval at Dodman, who promptly became very red in the face and so flustered that he led Pewter around to the wrong side of the house.

Intrigued, Susan followed the little woman indoors. "Whatever has transpired, to win poor George such lavish praise?"

Mrs. Starr turned along the hall towards the withdrawing room. "I vow you'll not credit it. This has been quite a day for paint and paintings. Speaking of which, we were fairly astonished when the boy brought that great tub of paint, Mrs. Sue, after your lectures about economies! Here we are." She turned, her eyes bright with excitement. "Close your eyes now. I want this to be a real surprise. Take my hand. Slowly, dear ma'am . . ."

Groping her way, Susan proceeded obediently, halting when told.

"Now—only *look!*" cried Mrs. Starr, all but squeaking with excitement.

Susan looked, and her eyes opened very wide indeed.

The painting now adorning the wall above the mantelpiece was a far cry from the one Dodman had worked on this morning. The dirty old frame had been polished and was transformed into a richly carven thing of beauty. The raw potato had banished the brown swirls of encrusted grime to reveal a riverbank scene at sunset, the turquoise skies, streaked with crimson, reflecting on the smooth water. A little grove of trees provided a rich background for some carefree picnickers—young men clad in tunics and hose, girls wearing flowing gowns of silk and brocade, their long tresses contained by jewelled nets; while amid the branches and from behind trees, wistful-eyed nude nymphs and dryads peeped at the merrymakers.

"Oh!" said Susan admiringly. "What a good thing you asked the Bo'sun to clean it, Starry. It's very pretty, don't you think?"

"Indeed I do," agreed Mrs. Starr triumphantly. "I suppose it cannot be of any value, else his lordship would not have left it in an unoccupied house. But it does seem a shame it was allowed to come to such a pass."

"And quite typical of that revolting creature," said Susan grimly. "Has Andrew seen it yet?"

"No, but he cannot but be pleased." The little lady sighed wistfully. "What a pity. I suppose we shall have to give it back to Lord Montclair."

"Why? He doesn't deserve it. And at all events, he's abroad, so I understand."

Mrs. Starr stared at her. "Abroad? But—how can that be when you hit him with the brush only yester—"

"It appears that was his brother," said Susan, rather hastily. "Oh, I have so much to tell you, Starry, but I am fairly perishing for my luncheon and a cup of tea."

"Of course you are, my love. I'll put the kettle on at once. Little Priscilla is so excited with her paint, but why ever did you buy so much?"

"Well, actually," began Susan as they started down the hall to the kitchen, "it was quite a bargain, although—" She checked, turning to the gentlemen who came in at the rear door and walked towards them.

"Oh, you're back, Sue," said Lyddford with breezy redundancy.

A little chill crept between Susan's shoulder blades. Their visitor was the foreign gentleman who had been with Sir Selby Trent during her unhappy interview at Longhills Manor.

"I hope you have not mislaid me in your memory already," said Imre Monteil, smiling at her. "Me, I am most delighted by this opportunity to meet you again, Mrs. Henley."

She murmured a polite response, and glancing to her brother, was the recipient of an urgent jerk of the head. Reluctantly, she extended her hand.

It was taken in a clammy white clasp. Monteil bowed to kiss her fingers. Her sense of revulsion was as intense as it seemed unkind and unwarranted, and she had to force an answering smile. "I had not realized you were acquainted with my brother, monsieur."

"We wasn't," said Lyddford. "But"—he gave her a mischievous wink—"we are now."

"How—nice," murmured Susan, freeing her hand from the clasp the Swiss was obviously unwilling to relinquish.

"One hopes ours will be a long and mutually—ah, beneficial association," purred Monteil, his eyes not wavering from Susan.

'Heaven forfend,' she thought, and introduced him to Mrs. Starr.

The little lady dropped a slight curtsy. The Swiss however, bowed low, advanced upon her, and kissed her hand also. *"Enchanté, madame,"* he said with patent admiration.

Blushing furiously, Mrs. Starr excused herself and hurried off to the kitchen area. Susan yearned to depart also, but manners must be observed, and if Monsieur Monteil really was able to throw some commissions their way, it would not do to offend.

"Come and have a glass of Madeira," offered Lyddford, leading their guest to the withdrawing room. "I'm glad you finished your shopping in time, Sue. You were gone such an unconscionable time I began to think you'd popped over to Baghdad or some such place. And that awful paint you bought would bear me out! What on earth possessed—"

They had walked into the long sunny room by this

139

time, and Lyddford paused, glancing at the Swiss, who had uttered an odd hissing sound. Monteil came to an abrupt halt, and stood with shoulders slightly hunched, staring fixedly at the mantelpiece.

"Oh, it's our confounded cat," said Lyddford apologetically, removing Welcome from the mantel.

"I think Monsieur Monteil admires our painting," said Susan. "And I agree with him. Do you like it now that the Bo'sun has cleaned it, Andy?"

Lyddford shrugged. "Oh, I suppose it's all right. I rather liked it the other way. Bit of a challenge to guess what it was."

"Never heed my brother, sir," said Susan with a rueful laugh. "He is hopeless with either art or music; indeed, I think he scarce knows one from t'other!"

"Well, I do," declared Lyddford with a grin. "One's noisy."

Monteil wandered closer to the hearth. "It is most interesting. Did it hang here when you—ah, moved in?"

"No, it didn't," said Lyddford emphatically. "There was another picture here. And why anyone would want to paint a dead partridge slung on a table with its head upside down is more than I can comprehend! Most awful thing! Be dashed if I want to sit in the withdrawing room with a dead partridge! I mean, enough is enough, what? So I dug this one out."

"What do you mean, you 'dug it out'?" asked Susan. "Where was it?"

"In the cellar. All kinds of old rubbish down there."

Monteil said in his soft voice, "If this is the sort of 'old rubbish' in your cellar, Mr. Lyddford, I should very much like to look at it."

Susan eyed him curiously. "Oh dear. That sounds as if you think the picture might be valuable. Is it?"

He spread those long white hands and shrugged. "I think it is a fair copy, madame. For just an instant

140

when first I entered I thought it might be an original, but I see now that the style is not quite as fine as it appeared, and the paint is scarcely aged."

Susan said thoughtfully, "I wonder if Montclair painted it himself . . ."

"Does the fella paint, then?" asked Lyddford, much shocked.

"I have not the remotest notion, save that he was buying some gold-leaf paint whilst I was in the ironmonger's shop."

"Ah, but I believe that would be for his harpsichord, madame," interjected Monteil. "Valentine is a musician *par excellence,* and the harpsichord is a truly magnificent old instrument."

"Be dashed if that surprises me." Lyddford shook his head disapprovingly. "He's just the sort of slippery customer would maudle his brain with music instead of doing a man's work!"

Monteil regarded him with amusement. "You are a gentleman of firm opinions, monsieur. You will forgive if I point out that Frederick the Great of Prussia, and your own King Henry the Eighth were both fine composers, and—"

"There you are then," interposed Lyddford, triumphant. "I don't have nothing against Fred. Never heard much about him, to tell you the truth. But everyone knows Bluff King Hal was a dirty dish."

"Andy," protested Susan, with an eye on the visitor's faint smile, "you must stop and think that Monsieur Monteil is well acquainted at Longhills. Your pardon, sir, if we offend."

"Stuff," said Lyddford. "Monteil likely agrees. But— let's speak of pleasant things for a change. Sue, we've been put in the way of some very nice commissions thanks to this gentleman. A toast is in order." He crossed to the sideboard and poured two glasses of

141

Madeira and one of cider, and distributing these said gaily, "Here's to a long and profitable partnership!"

Honouring the toast, Susan thought, dismayed, 'Partnership?'

After only a very brief conversation, mostly having to do with his admiration of Highperch Cottage, the Swiss took his leave, saying that he was sailing for the Continent early in the morning and must be aboard his yacht before dark.

They walked out onto the front terrace, all three. Lyddford had rung for Deemer, but no one appeared to answer the bell, and muttering anathemas on servants, he went to call up Monteil's curricle.

The Swiss turned to Susan and extended his hand. She shrank from taking it again, but had no recourse. The cold, clammy fingers closed about her own. He stepped very close to her, looking down at the hand he held, and stroking it gently. "Will you believe me, dear lady, if I tell you I have met countless beautiful women and have found them unfailingly vapid, dull—in short, a very great bore. Until . . ." his dark eyes lifted to her face, ". . . now."

Susan fought the urge to tear free and run. "You are too kind, sir," she said, and made an effort to pull away.

His grip tightened. He stepped even closer, lifted her hand to his lips, and watched her as he pressed a kiss upon her fingers.

'If he does that for one more second,' she thought, 'I shall simply have to hit him!'

"Dear lady," he breathed, "you are the loveliest—"

"Good afternoon, Mrs. Henley."

Never would Susan have dreamed she would find that sardonic drawl welcome, but, provided with an excuse now, she pulled her hand away, turned, and uttered a cry of dismay.

Mr. Montclair, mounted on his ugly stallion, was keeping the drooping and bloodstained figure of Señor Angelo from toppling from his bay.

142

"Andy! Bo'sun!" Susan called. "Come quickly!" And running to the Spaniard's side, exclaimed in horror, "Oh! You have shot him!"

Montclair said dryly, "I wonder why I had anticipated just such a considered reaction from you, madam."

Lyddford ran up. "Damn you, what have you done to him?"

Surrendering the mare's reins to him, Montclair's glance turned from Susan's angry eyes to Monteil's enigmatic smile. With a curl of the lip, he rode away.

There was much excitement at Highperch Cottage that afternoon. After Monsieur Monteil departed and Señor Angelo had been tended and ordered to remain in his bed, Susan, her brother, and Mrs. Starr repaired to the withdrawing room for a council of war. Andrew Lyddford's amusement over what he termed "the one-man duel of that blockheaded Spaniard" gave way to fiery wrath when Susan began to tell them of her encounter with Montclair. "Turn him up sweet?" he snarled. "By God, but I won't! Stretch him out stiff is more like it!"

Susan admitted with a guilty little laugh, "I'm afraid I did just that, dearest."

"Good gracious!" exclaimed Mrs. Starr, shocked.

"What?" demanded Lyddford, brightening. "Hauled off and cracked him over the nob with your riding crop, did you? Jolly good, by Jove!"

"Well, not that exactly." Knowing she was blushing, she said hastily, "I'll explain later, but something else happened on the way home that is rather worrisome. She told them of the men who had been loitering about in the woods. "I thought at first they were poachers, but when they spoke, their accents were cultured. I was so frightened when they said they were to watch somebody. Andy—do you think they meant us?"

143

Lyddford scowled and nodded. "'Fraid so. Likely Montclair's having us watched. I wonder what does he expect to discover."

"He must have a very nasty suspicious mind," said Mrs. Starr. "Of course, I could not but notice that you did bruise him rather badly, dear Master Andy."

"And came nigh to adding some more today," he growled. "Did you mark the way the fellow looked at my sister and Imre Monteil? Confounded insolence!"

Susan was tempted to tell him of Monteil's attitude towards her and how repellent she found the man. With true heroism she did not utter any of it, but instead handed her brother the letter she had received from the Longhills solicitors. "More unpleasant news I'm afraid, love."

It was the last straw. Lyddford sprang up, waving the letter about and raging of the villainy of their dastardly neighbour.

When he ran out of breath, Mrs. Starr murmured, "I suppose we must give the devil his due. Mr. Montclair did help poor Señor Angelo, at least, in spite of the fact that he and Mrs. Sue did not part in charity with each other."

"Charity!" cried Susan hotly. "I could not feel charity for that horrid man was he thrown to the lions! He is the most sneering, overbearing, toplofty, sarcastic individual it has ever been my misfortune to meet!"

Although fate had not treated her kindly, she was by nature a kind young woman, not one to hold a grudge, and she seldom took anyone in deep aversion. This fierce outburst caused her companions to eye her in surprise, and Lyddford said shrewdly, "There's more here than meets the eye, don't you agree, Starry? Come along now, Mrs. H. Exactly what transpired that you left Montclair flat on his back? If the crudity dared insult you—"

The grimness in his eyes frightened her, so she smiled and told them the full story of her parting with Mr. Val-

144

entine Montclair, not sparing herself, and joining in the laughter which followed.

Andrew was still wiping his eyes when Priscilla came in search of them. She was dirty, tired, but overjoyed with the results of her painting efforts, and pleaded that they all "simply *must* please come and see. Now!"

"Very well, but stop babbling," said Lyddford, resting a fond hand on his niece's tumbled curls. "You're amazing free from paint, sprat. How so?"

"Starry wrapped me all up in a sheet. We had to put Wolfgang out 'cause he got a little bit painty, but I din't. Oh, *do* hurry! It looks just splendrous!"

Dutifully they followed her to the small room once occupied by the bootblack.

On the threshold Susan checked and stared, wide-eyed. "Oh! The *wretched* man," she gasped.

Valentine Montclair had evidently not left Amberly Down before she did. He must have still been in the ironmonger's shop when she'd sent the paint back with the request for it to be delivered, and he'd seized the opportunity to very effectively spike her guns. Had she really intended to redecorate with the bright red paint, it would doubtless have been judged bold and in questionable taste. But not by any stretch of the imagination would anyone dare to paint the trim on Highperch Cottage the lurid purple that now adorned Priscilla's doll house.

8

"But of course, I instructed Ferry to communicate with the woman at once." Sir Selby Trent's eyes were wide and injured as he closed the door of his display case. "I had thought my promptness might have pleased you, dear boy."

"Pleased me!" Montclair's hands gripped tightly on his riding crop. "I told you I preferred to handle the matter myself, sir. The Henley woman and her nasty little band have stolen a march on us by taking possession of the cottage. It well may be that there is no reasoning with her, but had you not interfered I might have at least—"

"Hoity-toity! Only listen to the lord of the manor!" Arms folded across his powerful chest, Junius leaned against his father's desk watching Montclair contemptuously, and managing to look overdressed in a pair of extremely tight cream pantaloons, a blue coat with big silver buttons, and a neckcloth which had taken his man an hour to perfect. "You don't rule here yet, my poor clod," he sneered.

Montclair stepped closer to him, chin outthrust. "And *you* are here *only* because your father came in an advisory capacity to my brother—a state of affairs which should by rights have ended almost four years ago. *You* have absolutely *no* right whatsoever to interfere in the running of this estate. You had no business to call on Mrs. Henley in Geoff's name, much less to insult and maul her, and break Lyddford's head. Whatever the provocation, neither my father nor Geoffrey would countenance such crude behaviour. I'll thank you in future to keep your meddling out of any matter concerning Longhills."

Junius, whose face had become alarmingly red during this declaration, snarled, "You puny would-be music master! What if I tell you to go to hell?" Standing straight so that he towered over the slighter man, he added, "Or what if I were to very gently break you in half and—"

"Keep in mind that you are at a disadvantage," said Montclair, throwing down his riding crop. "The only time you've ever bested me is when you attacked from behind like the sneaking coward you are!"

Junius swore and whipped back his clenched fist, and Montclair crouched, poised and ready.

Sir Selby sprang between them. "Is this truth, Junius? Did you maul that trollop? I knew you'd struck her brother, but I never dreamed— *Did* you, sir?"

His voice was a hiss of menace, and the glare in the pale eyes sent an uneasy shiver down Montclair's spine.

Junius drew back, and licked his lips nervously. "I— er, merely stole a kiss, sir. She's a buxom wench and—"

"And when her brother sought to defend the chit, you and Pollinger beat him, eh? Do you know how that will sound should this come to a court of law? You damned young fool! *Must* you lust to bed every woman you meet?" As if goaded beyond endurance, Trent's arm flew

147

up and he back-handed his son hard across the face. Junius staggered, then stood with head bowed, one hand clutching his cheek. "I vow to God," panted Sir Selby, "I'd be justified in taking you to a surgeon and having you—" His eyes slid to Valentine's shocked expression. He drew out a handkerchief and mopped his brow. "Get out—you imbecilic animal," he muttered. "And I'd best never again see you dare to attack your cousin in his father's house! Out!"

Another moment Junius stood there. Then, his taut form relaxed and a sly smile dawned. "My apologies, sir," he muttered, and with a short bow went out and closed the door quietly behind him.

Trent shook his head, and walked around his desk. "Alas," he sighed, sinking into the chair and reverting to his usual bland manner, "one has such hopes for one's children, and then—"

"Uncle," Montclair intervened curtly. "Spare me the performance, I beg you."

Sir Selby blinked at him. "Performance. . . ?"

Montclair nodded. "You have outdone yourself; don't spoil it. I have one question for you, however. How close is the friendship between your good friend Monteil and Mrs. Henley?"

"There is none!" Trent seemed to resent the implication. "They are scarcely acquainted. I think he met her here for the first time on Tuesday."

"Do you?" Montclair crossed to the door. "Then I think *you* are the one is mistaken, sir." He went out.

There was no sign of Junius and the long hall stretched out in serene silence. It was all so peaceful and gentle. It didn't seem possible that just a few moments ago, unbridled savagery had reared its ugly head in the elegant study. He could well imagine how shamed and infuriated Junius must feel to have been so brutally chastised in front of the man he hated. As for his father—the veneer of civilization was thin indeed.

148

He muttered, "Phew!" and walked slowly to the stairs, thinking with nostalgic longing of the years before his parents had died. How happy they'd been then. Now Longhills had become a battleground, and he was so confoundedly tired of it all. But there was no use wishing he could escape. There was no escape; not if he was to protect the estate for Geoff.

His troubled look deepened to a frown. The state of the mails was deplorable, but surely Geoff must have received at least one of his letters? It was possible, of course, that he was moving about too rapidly for correspondence to reach him; possible even that he was already en route home. Still, another letter had this morning been despatched to the errant lord of the manor, and if *that* missive didn't bring Geoff back, then there would be real cause for alarm. Actually, the footman had gone off with three letters. The one to Geoffrey, plus notes to Jocelyn Vaughan and Alain Devenish, asking if they would consent to act as seconds in the forthcoming duel with Lyddford. Montclair could picture their reactions. It would take a day or two for the request to reach Joss in Sussex, but Dev's estate was sufficiently nearby that he would likely receive his letter tomorrow. He might very well ride to Longhills at once. Heaven knows how many times the volatile Devenish had been out, but it would be just like him to deliver a stern homily on the evils of duelling before agreeing to act for his friend.

Montclair's faint grin faded as his thoughts turned to the brazen widow and Imre Monteil. Early yesterday morning, the Swiss had said he was leaving for Brussels. Yet this afternoon he'd been at Highperch Cottage, and to judge by the way he'd been slobbering over the Henley woman's hand, one might suppose them to be lovers. His lip curled. The jade had a quality that drew men, that was abundantly evident. First Junius, and now Monteil. A pretty pair of admirers for a lady!

He thought irritably, 'And no concern of mine!' On the other hand, it *might* concern him. Monteil very obviously coveted Highperch. And he was the kind of man who took what he wanted, one way or another. It was possible that he had made the widow an offer for Highperch on the off chance that she might win her ridiculous lawsuit. Imre Monteil would catch cold at that! Mrs. Henley had not the remotest chance of getting her greedy hands on the dear old cottage!

He ran lightly down the remaining stairs and, proceeding to the main block, went to his bedchamber to wash and change clothes. Gould had a note for him. There was no seal, and the direction was a simple V.A.M. The message was brief, the handwriting so blotched and quavery that it was difficult to read, but he deciphered a plea that he meet Barbara in the summer house. She had crossed out the first time she'd indicated, and replaced it with "six o'clock." Under her signature, the round innocent hand had added pitifully, "Please— *please,* Val. We *must* talk about this before tomorrow! Do not fail me—I beg you."

He had no intention of failing her, and folding the paper he frowned down at it. The poor chit had been weeping when she wrote this. Such a timid little soul . . . It was remarkable, really, that she'd found the courage to help him with that demented Spaniard this morning.

He ate luncheon alone in his study, watching the storm that had blown up, but with his thoughts on little Barbara until he turned to his music and all else was forgotten. At half-past four he had an appointment with a tenant farmer. The sturdy man was protesting the fact that his previous complaints had been ignored and debris from the flood still blocked the stream. "It overflows into my barns and the henhouse, Mr. Valentine. Keep it out, I can't. And clear your stream, Mr. Yates won't!" It took some time to calm the indignant yeoman, and it was five o'clock before

150

a vexed Montclair left his study. He had instructed Yates to have the stream cleared weeks ago. Clearly, his order had been countermanded. So another battle loomed. He thought, 'Damn!' but went in search of his uncle.

There was no sign of Trent in conservatory, gallery, or great hall, but when he went to the south wing and approached the Venetian withdrawing room, he heard his aunt's shrill voice, followed by Junius's laugh. Sir Selby was with them, and Montclair's cool request for a private word with his uncle did not please my lady.

"I see no reason for us to be disturbed," she said haughtily.

"None, my love," agreed her spouse. "Come in, Valentine. We may talk in front of our own, I hope."

"We were discussing the wedding," said Junius with a sly grin. "I expect you're fairly panting to hear the details, eh?"

"Not known for your quick wit, are you, coz?" drawled Valentine.

Junius flushed angrily, and Lady Trent snapped, "There is no call for rudeness."

"Nor for Babs to be rushed into something she does not wish," Montclair countered.

"My daughter will do as she is told," put in Sir Selby. "She is obedient to her parents' wishes, as becomes a properly bred-up girl. Come now, Valentine. You know very well all our plans are made. Cannot be making changes now, dear lad."

"Much too late," agreed Junius. "It would be very bad *ton.*"

"*That,* at least, you are well qualified to judge," drawled Montclair. To his dismay the room wavered before his eyes as he spoke. He thought, 'Oh Lord! Not another attack?' and said quickly, "I came to talk to you about Ladies Valley Farm, sir. Hatchett was just here. The property is still being flooded. I told Yates to clear the stream some

151

time ago. And I particularly want the cellar of the old Folly boarded up. It appears nothing has been done in either case. Perhaps you'll be so good as to tell me why?"

"Valentine, Valentine," sighed the baronet. "You never will understand that these things take time. And there is the expense to be considered."

"Expense be hanged! It's a downright disgrace that we—"

"How *dare* you, sir?" shouted Lady Trent, jumping up in one of her swift rages. "And *who* are you, I might add? A snip of a lad who has not yet seen thirty summers! A younger son with *no* authority, who has travelled little about the world and has accomplished nothing save for a babble of useless music! I am aware you and your brother both were indulged as children and allowed to sauce your parents! Certainly your lack of proper unbringing has never been more apparent than when your spleen is turned on your poor uncle who strives with patience and loyalty to safeguard Geoffrey's estates from his brother's hare-brained irresponsible schemes. Apologize at once!"

White with wrath, Montclair attempted a response, but his dizziness had increased to the point that he was instead obliged to clutch at a chair.

"Bravo, Mama," laughed Junius, applauding. "Only look, you've frightened the gudgeon so that he is weak in the knees!"

"You know—damned well—" gasped Montclair furiously.

Quick to seize his advantage, Junius pretended outrage. "Do not swear in front of my mama, you clod," he cried, leaping at his cousin and giving him a shove that sent the weakened man reeling against a table.

Montclair could see two Junius Trents. He knew he was being baited because Junius fancied him too dizzied to give a good account of himself, but he managed to push himself away from the table and clench his fists. Before he could raise them, Junius struck hard.

152

Sir Selby leapt to steady Montclair as he staggered back. "Have you forgot what I told you, Junius?" he demanded, barely hiding a grin.

"I was but defending my mama 'gainst his naughty language, sir," said Junius primly. "You cannot blame me for that, surely?"

Montclair's head was clearing a little. He took out his handkerchief to wipe his bloodied mouth and said in a steadier voice, "You are a brave man, cousin."

"Now only look—you have cut him." Sir Selby clicked his tongue reprovingly. "Could you not see that he was suffering one of his attacks?"

My lady tittered. "Poor Montclair. I vow I must give you a pity party."

Junius howled with laughter.

Montclair's breath hissed through his teeth, and the look in his narrowed eyes caused his aunt to draw back in sudden alarm.

"Now, now—do not lose your temper, dear boy. They were just funning," said Sir Selby.

"We have come to a sorry pass," said Montclair harshly, "if that is—" But he broke off. He was too angry, and a gentleman did not frighten a lady. Even a Lady Marcia Trent. He turned and stalked out of the room, his cousin's mocking laughter following him.

Lord, but she was a merciless harridan! And he was a fool for having allowed the pair of them to make him so angry, for certainly he knew what they were. Striding rapidly across the park towards the summer house, Montclair thought of a hundred ways he might better have handled the matter, a hundred things he might better have said. Still, it was as well he'd left when he had, or he might have said something awful that one does not say to one's own flesh and blood.

153

'I vow I must give you a pity party . . .'

Her harsh voice echoed in his ears. He scowled and dug his hands deeper into his pockets. If only Geoff would come home. Gad, but he missed the old cawker! They could get rid of the Trents then, and life would be bearable again.

When he entered the little copse of beeches at the top of the rise, the sun was going down, sending an occasional beam through the lowering clouds. Homeward-bound birds swooped and chattered, settling noisily into their own particular trees. The air was beginning to be chill, the eastern horizon already darkening to dusk, and a clammy mist was beginning to writhe up from the wet grass. He thought absently, 'It will be foggy tomorrow . . .' and hurried his stride in case Babs in her distraught state had neglected to bring a shawl.

Lost in troubled thought, he roused to the awareness of a faint rustling behind him, and jerked his head up. A lone ray of sunlight followed him and painted his shadow on the grassy ride, but it painted another shadow: a grotesque figure towering high above him, one mighty arm raising a great cudgel high.

Montclair spun around, throwing up his left arm to protect his head. He was too late. Before he had a chance to see who—or what—menaced him, the shadows, the fading light, the woods, were riven into countless whirling fragments. There was pain, brief and terrible. Then, nothing at all.

"Angelo Francisco Luis Lagunes de Ferdinand," repeated Señor Angelo, and started to rap himself on the chest but thought better of it. "Mices elves."

The footman deigned to lower his eyes to a point just above the top of the Spaniard's dark head. 'No card;

talks very odd; no hat; untidy hair; cravat horrid.' Concluding this regrettable silent inventory he restored his gaze to the cloudy skies once more, and intoned sonorously, "Was Mr. Montclair expecting you this morning . . . sir?"

The footman tended to run his words together. Señor Angelo, who should not really have ventured forth on this chill foggy day, found the singsong utterance incomprehensible. He also began to feel rather wobbly on his feet. The stableboy was experiencing some difficulty in controlling the visitor's spirited horse and, amused, the footman turned to watch the contest. Señor Angelo seized his opportunity, ducked past the footman, and occupied the marble bench just inside the front doors. He was a small man and nimble even in adversity, and the footman, tall and secure in his dignified might, did not see the swift manoeuvre and continued to ignore the visitor while enjoying the stableboy's efforts.

Señor Angelo decided that while he waited for Mr. Montclair, he would inspect the premises. With this in mind, he rose, wandered across the great crescent of the entrance hall, and went up a pair of stairs to the landing, from which point the stairs divided into two flights.

The footman, restoring his view to ground level and finding the caller had vanished, wandered out onto the steps and peered about.

"The señor was also peering about. "Charmed theses," he beamed, and chose the left flight.

Thus it was that, humming a little despite his smarting side, he wandered along the east corridor and passed the main staircase just as a lady descended from the upper regions. He halted, glancing up smilingly into the saddest little face he had ever seen. His smile died. He abandoned the bow he had been prepared to make even if it caused his side to split like a sausage, and stepped forward with hand outstretched.

155

"Señorita Trent! Bad somethings was? Tears Angelo de Ferdinand have not can! Must chew splain!"

Despite the garbled English, his eyes held a kindly anxiety that warmed Barbara's heart. She rested her cold fingers in his hand and blinked mistily. "Oh, Señor," she gulped, "I don't want to m-marry him, but— I have no choice! I wish I were dead!"

"Whose marries? What peoples says chew marriage?" Swelling with indignation, he demanded, "Not loving chew theses mens?"

"No, no!" She gripped his hand frantically. "But you see he is very rich, and—" Overcome, she pressed a handkerchief to her lips. "And my cousin—"

"Montclair?" he snarled, bristling. "Chew wanting marriage him, not?"

"No. Val knows how I feel, but he says—"

"*Barbara Trent*! What on *earth* are you doing?"

Barbara gave a whimper of terror and whirled around.

Lady Trent, all chin and frown, was coming rapidly along the hall. "Have you quite taken leave of your senses, Miss Care-for-Nobody? We have been waiting this age!"

Angelo inserted, "Madam—mices elves—"

My lady drew herself up and regarded him with disgust. "What in heaven's name. . . ? Albertson—who *is* this?"

The footman, breathless and irritated, hastened to them. "Slipped past me at the door, m'lady. I been searching all over! Said he wanted to see Mr. Montclair!"

"Nonsense! Mr. Montclair has no wish to see anyone who cannot speak English! Show the person out."

"Madam!" said Angelo, indignant. "Angelo Francisco Luis—"

"This way—sir," growled the footman, taking his arm.

"Hand-un mices elves, oncely at!" cried Angelo, striving rather feebly to escape. "Lagunes de Ferdinand," he shouted after the ladies, completing his introduction. "Meeces wishing—"

Having reached the door, the footman ejected Señor de Ferdinand. Head first.

His ship had gone down in a great storm and he was at the bottom of the sea. Far above him, moonlight shone through the green waters, and the seaweed rippled and swung to the pull of the tide, but down here it was dark. The urge to swim up to the surface grew upon Montclair. He tried to move but pain sank its teeth into him so sharply that he lay still again. He couldn't think very well. Something bad had happened at home . . . And then for some reason he'd been in the woods . . . But where he was now, or why, eluded him. He had awoken several times before this, but the pain had been so excruciating he'd felt sick and had drifted into the shadows again. He sighed wearily. If only he had some water . . .

When he opened his eyes again it was light. A pale murky light. He could smell fog. The birds were singing busily. There must be hundreds of birds. All twittering at once. Such a lot of noise for such tiny creatures . . . And oh Lord, but his head was hell, and he was so damnably thirsty! His left hand was cold. He moved the fingers. They seemed to touch stone. A stone slab . . .

He knew then, and he gave a gasp and his eyes opened very wide.

He was in the Folly! With the shock of it came complete recollection. He'd quarreled with the Trents, and then gone to meet Barbara. But he'd been struck down in the woods by a monstrous creature who had evidently thrown him into the Folly and left him to die. And he *would* die, for no one would think to look for him here. He wondered vaguely who had tried to kill him, but it seemed unimportant. The important thing was that he must get out, or even if his head wasn't crushed, he'd die of thirst and starvation. He tried to sit up, but there was something horribly wrong with his left leg, and his desperate efforts carried so terrible a price that he was very glad to let himself sink into oblivion.

After a long time he awoke again. He was still in the Folly, and he was much weaker. Unless he was willing to just lie here and politely die he must try once more to get up. He lay still, gathering his strength.

Somewhere, very far away, a dog was barking shrilly . . .

Priscilla tiptoed into the clearing. Her fine new friend Mr. Val'tine had told her she must never come here. He'd said it was a bad place and that the lady Fury would boil Wolfgang and eat him all up. She had told Wolfgang about this, but he was in one of his adventuring moods and it was just like him, bold and terrible as he was, to never mind about the Fury. She scanned the drifting mist nervously. If Mama or Uncle Andy caught her she'd really get spanked. Only you didn't leave your friends just 'cause they was naughty. If she ran off and let Wolfgang get eaten up by that horrid Fury, she'd never forgive herself.

She saw him then and gave a gasp of fright. He was right at the edge, his tail waving furiously, barking down into the pit.

Priscilla gripped her small hands before her mouth and whispered, "Oh dear, oh *dearie* me! Wolfgang! Come here at once!"

But her whisper went unheard, and the dog barked louder than ever.

She must be brave. Mr. Val'tine wouldn't leave *his* dog for a Fury to eat up, she was very sure of that! Trembling, she crept forward, calling to the dog, but ready to run for her life if the Fury's terrible face should drift out of the pit. And at last, when she was much too close and her knees were shaking so that she didn't think she could take another step, Wolfgang heard her and ran to prance about her in great excitement, then dart back again.

"No!" she quavered. "Bad dog! Come away from—"

"Priscilla. . . ? Is that . . . Priscilla?"

Half fainting with terror, Priscilla screamed shrilly and ran as fast as her little legs would carry her. The Fury had heard her! And Mr. Val'tine had been wrong. It was a gentleman Fury, not a lady! And he'd known her name and prob'ly had a cooking pot ready, and a list like Mama and Papa had brought home once from a great dinner they'd gone to, with lots and lots of fancy things to eat writ out on it, all in French. Only the Fury's list would say Boiled P'scilla and Wolfgang pudding! Wolfgang was coming now. Howling. She gave a sob of gratitude, but daren't look back lest the gentleman Fury be close behind her with his long terrible teeth and great claws reaching out to take her and pop her into his cooking pot.

She ran almost all the way home.

"He most certainly is *not* here!" Standing on the front steps with Deemer on one side of her, and Mrs. Starr on the other, Susan frowned into Junius Trent's bold grin, and demanded, "Why on earth should you fancy Mr. Montclair would visit us? One might suppose he'd have sufficient sense to know he'd be unwelcome."

Trent leaned forward in the saddle, taking in the widow from the hem of her pale yellow muslin gown to the shine on her proud dark head. "You're fair and far out there," he said. "My cousin ain't one for sense. Nonsense—yes. Sense—very little, alas."

Sir Dennis Pollinger uttered a bray of laughter at this witticism, startling the fine grey horse he bestrode so that he was hard put to it to keep his seat. "Gone and got himself lost, silly cawker," he imparted when he had quieted his mount. "So we're all out looking for him, d'ye see?"

Mrs. Starr tightened her grip on the rolling pin in her hand. "If a grown man cannot find his way about his own estate, he is either ripe for Bedlam or a slave to Demon Rum," she observed tartly.

Junius, not one to waste his time with menials, gave her a bored glance. "Your cook has a point," he said to Susan. "You may take your pick, ma'am."

"I prefer to take my leave of you, sir," she said frigidly. "No such individuals have passed this way this afternoon, I promise you. Good day."

"If you should see him—" began Junius.

Susan curtsied and with one finger under her chin, promised, "I shall spank the wayward boy, and send him home."

They could still hear Pollinger's braying laugh after the door had closed.

Deemer said, "What do you suppose it's all about, Mrs. Sue? Two grooms came looking for Mr. Montclair this morning, whilst you was saying goodbye to Mr. Andrew."

Mrs. Starr's eyes widened. "You never think—there's been murder done?"

"I do not," said Susan. "The man was probably in his cups and is snoring in a ditch somewhere. Quite typical of his unpleasant self."

Panting happily, Wolfgang ran in from the back door. Following, also panting, Priscilla saw them, and ran to plead that Mama keep her promise and take her riding this afternoon. "You said we could go 'smorning, but then you talked an' talked with Uncle Andy, and now the day's almost gone!"

"But—darling, it's getting foggy and cold. I think it would be better if we waited 'til tomorrow, and—" The beam vanished from the hopeful eyes and the small face became resigned. Susan relented. "Oh, all right, you rascal. Martha will help you change into your habit. Hurry now."

Very much the little lady as she guided her pony across the meadows, Priscilla said happily, "Only look, Mama. The sun's coming through the clouds. Will we get a rainbow, d'you s'pose? I like rainbows."

"I don't think so, darling." Susan glanced at the trees that loomed ghostlike through the misted air, and wondered if unpleasant Junius Trent had found his cousin.

"Uncle Andy says rainbows are good luck. Why, Mama?"

"I expect because God painted one in the sky after the great Flood we read about at prayers, do you remember? It was His promise to us not to send quite so much rain again." Priscilla looked solemn, and Susan added on a lighter note, "And there is also a legend that tells of a pot of gold at the end of the rainbow."

The big eyes widened. "Ooh! Then Mr. Val'tine's found it. The rainbow yesterday had one foot right on his house! Oh, how monst'ous grand! I'll have a very rich friend!"

"Priscilla," said Susan thoughtfully, "you haven't seen your new friend today, have you?"

The brown curls danced under the neat little blue hat as Priscilla shook her head briskly. "I pro'bly won't never see him again after Uncle Andy was so dreffully

161

savage to him. An' I was hoping very bad to see him, 'cause I must tell him as he's mistakened about the Fury."

"Mistaken, dear." Susan frowned in irritation. "And—there are not such things as Furies."

"But, Mama, you told me if I had my teeth filed to points I would look like a Fury, and—"

"Yes, but Furies are only in fairy stories really, darling. We make up stories about them for fun, but there are none in real life."

"But there *are,* Mama! There's one in the Folly! I heard it! Honest and true, I did, Mama!"

The little face was so earnest. Heaven forfend whatever she'd heard should cause her to have nightmares again. That *wretched* Montclair—to frighten her so! Somehow, thought Susan, she must put a stop to this horrid business. She said, "Well—if you're sure, perhaps you'd best take me to see this Folly."

"Oh, no, Mama! I promised Mr. Val'tine I wouldn't never go there again, and I wouldn't have, only Wolfgang made me!"

"Pris—cil—la. . . !"

"He did! He did, Mama! I *telled* and *telled* him how we wasn't to go there no more, but Wolfgang is so foxed in his ways, you know, and—"

Susan repressed a smile. "You mean—*fixed* in his ways, I think."

"Do I? Uncle Angelo said 'foxed.' Anyway, whatever it is, Wolfgang is it. A very naughty doggie, I told him. Very stern I said it, Mama. Only, I knew Mr. Val'tine wouldn't leave *his* best friend in hidjus peril, and Wolfgang was hanging right over the edge and barking and barking."

"Edge? I thought you said it was a Folly, dear?"

"Yes, Mama. It was. A long long time ago. But it's all falling down now, and there's a hugeous hole in the middle what goes right through to China, I 'spect!"

162

It sounded most unpleasant. "So you had to go and drag that naughty dog away, did you?"

"No. I called him, only he's so brave he wanted to fight that Fury. But the Fury woke up, and that's when I found out Mr. Val'tine had made a mistake, 'cause he said it was a lady Fury, Mama, and it isn't. It's a gentleman Fury."

With a fond smile, Susan asked, "Did he come out and chase you?"

Priscilla shivered and turned pale. "I don't know. When he shouted my name, only soft and creepily you know, I was *so* frighted! I ran and ran all the way home!"

A dreadful suspicion began to raise gooseflesh on Susan's skin. She reined up, and the child halted her pony. "Dearest, when did this happen?"

"This morning, Mama. When you was saying goodbye to Uncle Andy."

"I see." It was silly, of course, but— "Mama wants you to think very carefully now. Did you *really* hear a voice? Or was it just a make-believe voice?"

Again the determined shake of the little head. "No, Mama. I din't make it up. Not this time I din't. But I'll never go near there again, I truly won't."

Susan hesitated. Valentine Montclair was despicable, and from what Angelo had said the wretch was determined to force his unhappy little cousin to the altar. But whatever he was, whatever he had done, he was a human being, and if there was any chance he had fallen into this Folly of his, he must be helped. Thus, she said quietly, "I just want to—to make sure of something. Come along, sweetheart, show me your Folly. The Fury won't come if I'm with you, I promise. This is a—a *real* adventure, and I need your help. Do you understand?"

"Oooh . . ." said Priscilla, ecstatic.

163

Susan took up the train of her habit and trod carefully across the littered clearing. She had left Priscilla and the horses in the trees, just in case there might be something the child should not see. She thought, 'Which is ridiculous, and I'm just being foolish!' But she went on.

As she drew closer it seemed that the normal sounds of the woods faded and an unnatural stillness enfolded this macabre clearing. The weak sun had gone into hiding once more, and the mists were thickening. There was not a breath of wind, the trees were completely motionless, and the Folly hove up lonely and forbidding against the darkening skies.

The place was positively ghoulish! To think of Priscilla coming here all alone! She found herself holding her breath as she picked her way among the great mossy slabs and then went with careful steps inside the broken walls. The pit loomed before her and she gave a gasp. "Dear God! Small wonder he chased her away!"

It would seem the man had done them a great service. And in return . . . Guilt scourged her but she told herself that, basically, he still was at fault. Such a gruesome hole in the ground should never have been left open. If he had one single ounce of concern for others, he'd have had it sealed up long ago! Anyone might fall into the beastly place! She found herself reluctant to go any nearer, and stood staring uneasily at those sad and broken ruins. What nonsense! There was nothing to be afraid of. In a few seconds she would be laughing at herself because that ancient cellar contained only dampness and—rats? She pushed her qualms aside, ventured to the brink, and peered down.

Heavens, what a pit! It was too dark to see anything much. "Hello?" she called, feeling a perfect fool. "Is anybody there?"

Silence.

She gave a sigh of relief, and turned back to where Priscilla waited.

"Hello. . . ?" The cry was faint and croaking, but she halted and stood as if frozen, an icy hand touching between her shoulder blades. "Oh . . . my heavens!" she whispered, and flinging around, was at the brink again in a second.

"Mr. Montclair? Is that you?"

This time the response was almost immediate. "Yes. Please . . . get help."

He *was* down there! And he sounded so weak. She thought, aghast, 'Small wonder! All this time!'

"Are you hurt?" she called.

A pause, then a feeble, "A trifle. Please . . . water . . ."

"I'll fetch some! I must send for help, then I'll come, I promise!"

She ran to where Priscilla waited. The small face was pale, the eyes behind the spectacles enormous with fright.

"Mama! I been so scared! Did it chase you? You shouldn't of—"

"Darling, listen—there is nothing bad to chase me. But your friend, Mr. Valentine, is down there, and he's hurt a little bit, I'm afraid."

It would have been hard to tell whether the mouth or the eyes were the roundest. "Oh, *poor* Mr. Val'tine! We better help him, Mama!"

"Yes. We must. Only, we're not strong enough to get him out by ourselves. I think I should stay with him. Could you ride home and fetch someone? I know the Bo'sun and Uncle Andy are away, but—tell Uncle Angelo or Deemer; they'll know what to do."

The child whimpered. She looked so little and frightened on the back of her pony, and she was only five. She was, she revealed, afraid to leave her only mama where

165

the gentleman Fury might come back at any minute and eat her all up.

It was quite understandable. Poor Burke had been all tenderness with his child, and Priscilla had adored him. She'd been shattered by his sudden death, and it had left her with the obvious fear that she might lose the other people she loved. It took a moment, but when Susan painted a picture of a great heroine riding bravely for help, the child's active imagination was fired. Beaming, she pushed the spectacles higher on her little nose, and took up the reins.

"Dearest," said Susan. "Mr. Valentine has had no food or water for a long time. When you were here before did you see a stream nearby?"

"No, Mama. But—our picnic might still be there. Starry made one for me and Wolfgang to take in the garden on Wednesday only we camed here 'stead, so we put it in our larder, but then we met Mr. Val'tine and I forgot all 'bout it."

Today was Saturday. Still, it might be usable. Susan enquired as to the location of the "larder," and then sent her daughter off, urging her to hurry but ride carefully.

The larder was a narrow space between two of the great stone slabs which had tilted against each other. Gingerly Susan reached inside and pulled out the small covered basket. Ants had found the cake and bread and jam, but the bottle of lemonade was corked just tightly enough to have kept them out. She snatched it up and ran back to the pit.

Her call brought only a feeble croak in response. Poor Mr. Montclair must stand in desperate need of water, but if she threw the bottle down it might break, or he might be too weak to reach it. She was so near—and she might as well have been a mile away. Fretfully, she thought, 'Surely I can do *something*?'

She began to prowl around the edge. If this horrid pit

had really been a cellar, then there *must* have been stairs, but she could discern only the sheer wall, and she couldn't possibly get down that. And then she saw a slight dip in the far edge that looked too even to have formed by chance. She hurried to it, and knelt, narrowing her eyes in an attempt to pierce the gloom and uttering an exclamation of excitement when she discovered the remains of a flight of steps, the first usable one being about four feet from the top. It looked horribly narrow and crumbly. She bit her lip but there came again a faint pleading cry. "Water . . . please . . . water . . ." All thought of his infamy was gone now, and her kind heart was wrung.

She called, "I'm going to bring it down to you."

"No! Too . . . dangerous. Just . . . lower it and . . ." The weak voice trailed into silence.

Trembling, Susan sent a swift prayer heavenwards. Then she tucked the precious bottle into the pocket of her skirt, turned onto her tummy, and groped downward with her feet. If Mr. Montclair was conscious, she thought grimly, he would have a most excellent view of her pink pantalettes. Her right boot touched the step, and she could feel pieces of debris. The thought of rats recurred. She reached out and was able to grasp a long fallen branch, then she let herself down, resting more and more of her weight on the step until she was reasonably sure it would not crumble under her. She lowered herself gradually, holding her breath, her heart thundering, trying not to think of the black void below. The step was wider and deeper than she'd at first supposed, and she was able to turn sideways. She made her left hand let go, and gripping her branch, lowered that arm slowly, still clinging with her right hand to the top of the pit. She pressed desperately against the wall, grateful that she'd often climbed trees with Andy in her tomboyish younger days, and had a good head for heights.

Using the stick as a probe she found the next step cluttered with leaves and pieces of rock, and she poked the debris away, hoping it was not falling on Montclair, but knowing that if she turned her ankle it must be disastrous. On she went, from step to step, until she had descended to the point where she must make a great decision. If she was to lower herself any farther, she would no longer be able to hold the top of the pit. And suppose there were no more steps? 'Well,' she thought doggedly, 'then I shall have to sit here like a bird on a twig and at least let him know someone is near. No one should have to die all alone in such a place. Even if it is his own silly fault.' She took the next step, pressing against the wall for support, still not daring to look down.

Her eyes were becoming accustomed to the gloom. The rough rock stairs were built against one wall. She could see the bottom now, littered with branches and leaves and chunks of rock, and among them, Montclair, lying sprawled on his back. If he had landed on one of those chunks of the Folly, he must be gravely injured. Praying he was not dead, she started to edge down to the next step.

Threads tickled her face. She thought in horror, 'A web!' Something with many legs scuttled across her cheek. A spider! She let out a shriek, missed her footing, and was falling.

9

ontclair awoke to find that he was still lying in
the Folly; still alone. He had dreamed that
someone came, and that whoever it was had
promised to return with water. And then he'd
sunk back into the dark again. He felt crushed by disappointment, but made no further attempt to try to get up.
He was too weak now, and that last horrible effort had
convinced him that both his leg and his right hand were
broken. He was quite incapable of climbing out, even if
he could stand. He wondered dully if he ever would be
found and given a Christian burial.

His eyes were dim, but something seemed to be moving against the wall. He blinked, peering, and was able
to discern a pale female form floating down through the
darkness. A gasp of shock escaped him. An angel! So his
life really *was* done. It was a sad realization, but at least
it would mean the end of this awful pain and thirst. He
watched the angel, wondering even in his anguish what
he should say when she reached him. She seemed to be
rather new at the business, for she kept dislodging rocks
and stones that came clattering down, several actually

striking him. Now she had stopped. Perhaps she couldn't see where he was.

He tried to call to her, but suddenly a shriek rang out and she was hurtling down.

Angels didn't shriek. In which case she must be human. And there was only one lady who would risk her neck to try and help him. Horror-stricken, he clawed at the slab with his left hand, dragging his battered body up with a strength born of frenzy.

"Babs! Babs! Oh . . . hell! Are you—"

Bruised and battered, Susan said breathlessly, "I am not . . . Miss Trent, sir." She struggled to her knees and made her weaving and uncertain way towards him.

"You!" gasped Montclair. "Good God!" He sagged onto his side and lay crumpled across the slab, panting.

Susan knelt beside him. His beard-stubbled face was liberally streaked with blood. She peered at his head, and recoiled in horror.

He croaked faintly, "Is . . . my skull crushed . . . can you tell?"

"Not crushed, I think, but it's a nasty wound." She did not dare touch that great gash. "I would bathe it for you, but I could only bring lemonade."

"Lemonade . . ." he echoed, stupidly. "Are you . . . really Mrs. Henley?"

"Yes." Shaken, but trying not to reveal that, she said briskly, "I don't wonder you are surprised. Alas, I am not a very efficient rescuer. Neither rope, nor water!" Summoning a smile, she went on. "Now I think we must declare a truce. If I help to prop you up, can you drink a little?"

Her arm was around his shoulders. With all his strength, he tried, but was unable to hold back a groan of agony as his leg twisted . . .

He roused after a while to the scent of violets. His smashed head was resting against a soft and kinder pillow. A bottle was being held to his lips. He managed to

170

drink the stale brackish liquid, sighed in ecstasy, and croaked out the "thank you" that was so hopelessly inadequate. "You fell, I think? Are you all . . . right?"

A pause. He peered upward, trying to see her. Her face was blurred, but he could see the long grey eyes, full of pity; the vivid mouth drooping with sympathy. The dark curtain of her hair was brushing his cheek very softly. And it was so astounding—so past belief that this of all women had come to help him.

"Yes," Susan answered rather huskily. "A bruise or two, perhaps. But you do not seem to have got off so lightly, sir. Are you hurt anywhere else than your head?"

"Leg broken . . . I think. And—right hand . . . bit of a—nuisance."

Her eyes had adjusted to the gloom and she could see that he looked very bad. She had no knowledge of how to set a broken bone and judged it best not to try. Angelo or Deemer would probably send word to Longhills, and they would summon Dr. Sheswell so that the injured man could have expert treatment as soon as he was carried home. However, just in case he was dying she should try to find out what had happened. She said gently, "Help is coming. They should be here very soon. Sir—did you fall?"

"No." He sighed. "Attacked . . . Been here . . . long, long time. Very good . . . of you . . ." The words faded away.

Appalled, Susan bent nearer. "Mr. Montclair—did you see who did this?"

She had to repeat the question before he answered in a whisper. "Giant—giant shadow . . ." And after a pause, "Would you mind . . ."

"What?" she asked anxiously.

"Could you . . . hold my hand—just for a minute. . . ?"

But even as she moved quickly to gratify that request, his blood-spattered head sagged back loosely, and he was very limp and heavy in her arms. She thought, 'He has died, then.' He was too young to die. And especially at the bottom of this horrid Folly. It was his own Folly, in more ways than one, but a lump came into her throat and tears stung her eyes.

"Well, well," drawled a mocking voice. "Beauty and the—er, music master."

Junius Trent's handsome face looked down at her, with Pollinger looming behind him, and Angelo was calling, "Missue! Missue! Findings we having!"

"Thank heaven!" cried Susan fervently.

Trent swung his legs over the side, then checked, his eyes narrowed. "Jove—these steps look crumbly. Doubt they'd support our combined weight was I to haul him out. Can he walk up, ma'am?"

"No, he cannot walk up," she retorted indignantly. "He is unconscious at the moment. The steps supported me, Mr. Trent, and I am no light weight."

"Just the right weight." He laughed, and glancing behind him said, "D'you hear that, Poll? I made a rhyme! Mrs. Henley says—"

Susan could have struck him. "Mr. Trent—your cousin may be dying! Do you fancy you could hurry?"

"Your wish, m'dear, is my command!" Even so, he trod very warily, both hands clinging to the top of the wall until he was obliged to let go. "Egad, what a bloody mess," he said, reaching the foot of the steps and coming over to peer down at Montclair. "Can it be that my beloved coz has expired? Dear me. Well, we cannot live forever, and—"

"He has *not* expired, and I trust will not do so unless he dies of old age before you carry him out of this horrid place!"

Trent chuckled, and bent to stroke her hair. "Much you would care, sweet shrew. So I'm to carry the dolt, am I? As you wish." He bent and gripped Montclair's arm, swinging him upward.

172

Susan uttered a shriek. "Have a care! His arm may be broken, and his leg most certainly is!"

He clicked his tongue. "What a mournful inventory." He dropped to one knee. "Never say I failed in my duty." He pulled his cousin up and then swung him over his shoulder, cutting off Susan's protests by saying, "Now do not rail at me, fairest. I cannot carry him in my arms and negotiate that narrow stair. Do you go first." Susan declining the honour, he said with a grin that if she chose to follow she would be crushed was he to drop Montclair.

"I cannot believe," she said, "that a big strong man like you, Mr. Trent, would be unable to manage such a burden."

This seemed to strike the right chord. Trent climbed up the steps quite well, lowered Montclair to the ground where Deemer and Señor Angelo waited, and turned back to assist Susan to clamber over the edge.

Watching anxiously, Deemer said, "We brought the phaeton, ma'am. And Mrs. Starr sent medical supplies." He opened a valise full of linen strips, flannel, salve, basilicum powder, a pair of scissors, and an earthenware bottle of hot water.

"Thank heaven," said Susan. She knelt beside the victim, and began to bathe the blood from his face.

Trent, who had been quiet and thoughtful, now mounted up. "Well, we'll be off. I expect you can—"

"Be—what?" She jerked around, looking at him in alarm. "Surely you should wait and escort your cousin home?"

"You never mean—all the way back to Longhills? In *his* condition? My dear ma'am, he'd be much better off was you to take him to Highperch."

Aghast, she cried, "That is not possible! I am not able to care for an invalid! Besides, I refuse to take the responsibility! He must be cared for by his doctor, and—"

"But I understood you'd a doctor on your staff," he countered with a sly grin.

"Bo'sun Dodman is away with my brother. And Montclair needs competent medical help at once! No, sir. You must take him to Longhills!"

Montclair moaned faintly.

Sir Dennis said in a shocked tone, "You surprise me, Mrs. Henley, begad but y'do. Poor fella lying here in misery, and you refuse him house room. Cruel."

"Cannot blame the lady," said Trent. "Montclair has treated her badly, and she takes her revenge."

"What a horrid thing to say," Susan flared, wrapping her bandage tightly around Montclair's heavy head. "Hold him up a little please, Deemer. What do you think, señor?"

Angelo trod closer and looked down at Montclair with lips pursed. "Very not goodly," he declared. "Mostly dyings is. Angelo say—"

"Be bled white by the time we get him to Longhills," put in Sir Dennis gloomily.

"I am afraid that the long journey," said Deemer, "and—" He checked, glancing at Trent. "I fear it might indeed be the end of him, Mrs. Sue."

Susan bit her lip. "You could use our phaeton, Mr. Trent," she offered hopefully.

"If you insist, ma'am." He shrugged. "But it had as lief be a hearse."

'Oh, Lord!' thought Susan. 'What*ever* am I to do?'

Dr. Sheswell was a big untidy man somewhere between forty-five and fifty, with puffy blue eyes and a squat nose that seemed too small for his face. His brown receding hair was brushed forward but had fallen into clumps which revealed his bald head. He came stamping into the withdrawing room of Highperch Cottage on this foggy evening, put down his bag, and scanned the larcenous widow. She wore a rose muslin gown that became her willowy figure. A dainty lace cap was set on the thick black hair that fell straight and shining behind her shoulders. He thought it as alluring as it was unconventional. She had risen when he entered the room and stood watching him, tiredness in her face, a scrape on her chin, but her eyes cool and unwavering before his bold stare. He thought, 'No simpering miss, this one. Old Selby's got a fight on his hands!'

Susan wished Andy was at home, and wondered why she so disliked this man. "May I offer you a cup of tea, doctor?" she asked courteously.

"You may, ma'am," he answered in his loud voice. "But I'd as lief have something stronger."

She looked at him sharply, then moved to the credenza, poured sherry into one of the glasses on the tray, and carried it to him. The doctor sat on the old brown sofa and raised his glass. "Here's to a speedy resolution of young Montclair's problems."

"You think he will recover, then?" she asked, returning to her chair.

"Not a doubt, m'dear ma'am," he said with a firm nod. "Terrible thing, I grant you. Terrible. Young fella struck down. Nigh murdered on his own brother's lands! Devil take me if ever I heard of such a thing! But—he's young. Resilient. Strong-willed chap, y'know. Type who heals fast. Up and about in no time, I'd not be surprised!"

Susan stared at him. When she'd left her bedchamber so that Sir Selby and his wife could be private with their nephew and the physician, it had seemed to her that Montclair was very ill indeed. The shock of the blow to the head was of itself enough, she'd thought, to have put a period to the poor man, and when one added the frac-

175

ture of his left leg just above the ankle, and the despair he obviously felt due to his broken hand, she would have been less than surprised had the doctor warned her to prepare for the worst.

"But—I had understood—" she began in a rather confused way.

"Must confess I admire you, ma'am," he boomed. "Yes, by Jove! Admire's the only word." He sampled his wine again. His brows rose and he held the glass up and looked at it with lips pursed. "Damme if I don't admire this sherry as well!" He slanted a narrowed glance at her. "D'ye chance to know where y'brother buys it?"

At such a time the question seemed so trite and irrelevant. Impatient, Susan replied, "I could not say. And why you should admire us for taking in a badly hurt gentleman when our home was nearest to—"

"Come, come, pretty lady," he intervened with a jocose grin. "Everybody knows .there's a—ah, dispute 'twixt y'brother and the Montclairs. To climb down into that hell-hole as you did was passing brave! And then to bring the unfortunate fella here was a splendid thing to do, so it was." He gave her a knowing wink. "I'm very sure Sir Selby and his lady are damned near overcome with gratitude."

She stiffened, resenting the implication. Besides, they had not seemed at all grateful. In fact, when they'd swept in at the door an hour ago, Lady Trent had looked through her as though she'd not even been alive, and they'd both followed Deemer upstairs without so much as one word of thanks. "We did as best we could, but—"

"Did damned well," he interposed, not bothering to curb his language before this scheming adventuress. "Montclair would have died before the night was out had you not found him. And you did right not to try and set his leg."

"Well, so I thought, but Sir Selby and his wife did not seem—"

176

"Ah, you must not mind their manners." He leaned to pat the hand on her knee and said confidingly, "Just their way. Worried, you know. Fairly dote on the boy."

Of course they would have worried. And she had not been very polite to Lady Trent when they'd met on the stairs at Longhills; she could hardly expect the woman to fall on her neck now, especially if they really judged her claim to Highperch to be fraudulent.

She drew her hand away. "I quite understand," she said, wondering if they meant to move Montclair tonight. "It must have been a great shock. And to see him in such pain—but I expect you will have given him laudanum."

"Don't hold with it," he said sternly. "Saw too many young fellas fall under its spell during the war. Drugs. Bad business."

Taken aback, she said, "But—surely it must have been very trying when you set his broken limbs. Anything that would give him some relief—"

"Tush, ma'am. D'ye take the boy for a weakling? Do assure you he ain't. Now don't you worry your pretty head. You ain't responsible."

His cunning little eyes reminded her of a bird of prey. Her bruised knees ached; indeed, she seemed to ache all over, and she was very weary. She thought, 'You're overtired and being silly. Dr. Sheswell takes care of most of the best families hereabouts and is a skilled physician who knows what is appropriate for his patient.' Even so, she said, troubled, "I found him, sir. I *feel* responsible."

"Very commendable of you, Mrs. Henley!" Sir Selby was coming down the stairs, one arm about his wife who looked distraught and held a handkerchief to her eyes.

Susan and the doctor stood and Lady Trent left her husband and flew to throw her arms about Susan and embrace her amidst a torrent of tears and thanks. Mrs. Henley was the bravest creature in the world! She had, single-handedly, saved their beloved nephew! She had

177

risen above petty disputes and arguments, and gone like a Good Samaritan to the aid of the afflicted.

Embarrassed, Susan drew back, only to have her hand taken, bowed over, and kissed by a much moved Sir Selby. "My very dear lady," he said, his voice hoarse with emotion. "There are no words! But we will find some—ah, tangible reward for your courage and generosity, I do assure you!" He turned away, and blew his nose.

"Whatever we did," said Susan, irritated, "was not done with an eye to reward, sir."

"Spoken as a true Christian," trilled my lady, clasping her hands and regarding Susan with a misty smile. "And to have put poor dear Valentine into your very own bedchamber! Compassion! Self-sacrifice! Oh, you are too good—too forgiving, my dear!"

"Yes, indeed," affirmed her spouse, mopping at his brimming eyes. "I hope you will not hesitate to call on us, dear ma'am, should you find yourself short of beds or bedding. Meanwhile, we will make every effort to see that the least possible burden falls on your shoulders. The good doctor will arrange for nurses around the clock, and—"

"But—but," gasped Susan, appalled, "you will want to take Montclair home, sir."

"Take him—*home?*" Lady Trent regarded Susan as though she'd said something sacrilegious. "You cannot *mean* it!"

"No, no. Not to be thought of," interjected the doctor, his face suddenly very grave. "He is in no condition to bear the move. Not for a day or two, at least."

"But—you just said he would be up and about in no time."

"And so he will, I've no doubt. But just at the moment 'twould be best not to move him. It has been a shock. No denying that. You surely can understand, ma'am?"

"Yes, well—I do, of course. But—we are not properly

settled yet, and—and are simply not equipped to care for an invalid. Besides, if you feel his injuries are of a more serious nature, I don't—"

"Pooh! No such thing," declared Sheswell. "Ah, I know what it is. You've heard he's been ailing this past month or two. Set your mind at ease, dear ma'am. It's not—ah, contagious. Rather baffling, medically, but likely only some minor disorder, causing dizziness and weak spells. Comes on poor Montclair without warning. A nuisance more than anything else, but—combined with this unhappy business . . . Better he should be peaceful here, than to haul him all over the countryside."

Mrs. Starr put in gently, "I will be able to help, Mrs. Henley. And we have Bo'sun Dodman, don't forget."

Shocked by such treachery, Susan turned to her friend and met a pleading smile that horrified her.

"Bo'sun—er, Dodman?" echoed Sir Selby, curious.

"The Bo'sun served on Captain Ephraim Tate's man o'war in the Navy, sir," explained Mrs. Starr, apparently unconscious of Susan's dismay. "The Captain was Mrs. Henley's grandpapa, as you may know. Such a splendid gentleman. When he left the Navy, the Bo'sun followed and was Sails Officer on his East Indiaman until the Captain retired. Bo'sun Dodman is in Mrs. Henley's service nowadays. He has a great knowledge of medicine and would easily qualify to become a full-fledged apothecary."

"Excellent!" exclaimed the doctor. "The very man to take charge of the case! I vow, it could scarce be better, do you not agree, ma'am?"

"I do indeed," said Lady Trent. "As if it were planned!"

"B-but . . ." stammered Susan.

"And I do promise, my very gallant lady, that you will be not one penny out of pocket," said Trent.

"Ugh," muttered his wife, staring at the hearth.

Welcome tucked in his chin, stretched, and emerged from the coal scuttle to investigate the visitors.

"The *dear* kitty," gushed my lady, bending to the little tabby.

Welcome crouched, stared fixedly at her, backed away, then fled.

'Oh dear,' thought Susan. "I have no intent to sound unkind," she began, "but—"

"Unkind! Why, I believe there is not an unkind bone in your body, dear ma'am," said the doctor heartily. "And anyone must have a heart hard as stone to insist upon us carrying that poor young man across country at this hour."

"Ye-es. But—"

"Give us a day or two," Sheswell went on, leading her towards the hall. "He's a high-couraged lad, and will give you no trouble, I'll vouch for that."

And somehow it was all settled. Dr. Sheswell promised to send nurses to Highperch at the very earliest possible moment, and left several bottles of medicine with Mrs. Starr, together with firm instructions as to dosages. Sir Selby bowed low over Susan's hand and told her emotionally that he would "never forget" her heroism. Lady Trent embraced her and said that Mrs. Henley was "a good Christian woman—whatever anyone might say!" And they were gone with a clatter of hooves and rumble of wheels and a handkerchief fluttering from the window of the great carriage.

Susan walked back into the house, closed the door, and turned on her devoted retainer. "Starry! Did you not see I wanted none of this? Whatever is my brother going to say? A fine pickle you have got me into!"

Mrs. Starr blinked her pretty eyes and wailed, "Oh, dear Mrs. Sue, I have angered you! I am such a ninny! I could only think of that poor young man, in such pain and not a sound out of him while the doctor tugged him

180

about—so carelessly, I thought. Indeed, I cannot like the man, and it seemed to me—" She broke off, tilting her head. "He is calling, poor soul! I must go!" With a flutter of draperies she ran.

"Traitor!" cried Susan, who had heard no call. Mrs. Starr moaned, and ran faster.

Sighing wearily, Susan began to climb the stairs at a slower pace, her thoughts chaotic. 'Whatever am I to say to Andrew?' She put a hand to her aching head. Perhaps he would be delayed and Montclair would be safely removed to his own bed by the time *The Dainty Dancer* returned. Or she might be able to convince Andy she'd allowed Montclair to remain here hoping to win him to a kindlier attitude. Perhaps he'd even be pleased . . .

"Pleased!" Andrew Lyddford threw up one arm in a wild gesture of frustration and paced to the withdrawing room windows again, while Susan watched him unhappily. "I think you've run mad, is what it is," he raged. "Why in the name of all that's holy did you allow the fellow in the house?"

It was dusk and the room was beginning to grow dark; Deemer came in and began to move quietly about, lighting candles.

"He is very ill, love," said Susan desperately. "It will be many weeks before—"

"Many weeks?" he roared. "I understood you to have been told three days ago it was just for a day or two! And why are you looking so hagged, I'd like to know? Where are the nurses Trent was to send?"

"Dr. Sheswell cannot get the ones he wants. It seems they're working on urgent cases elsewhere and he has had a horrid time trying to find suitable women. Now he is indisposed himself, and there is an outbreak of

181

mumps among the servants at Longhills, so that the Trents are fearful of sending any of their people, and—"

"Good God, what stuff! Is the village depopulated? Are there no willing nurses at—at Tewkesbury, or Gloucester? Indisposed, indeed! Only look at you—worn to a shade! By Jehoshaphat, Sue, you've let yourself be properly hornswoggled! Selby Trent is known for a clutchfist. He likely had no intent of sending anyone and—"

"But he has been most generous, Andy," she interposed hurriedly. "He has sent us a carte blanche for all the village shops. Starry and Martha have driven in twice, and we have plenty of supplies, and—"

"To Jericho with his supplies! Get this pest out of our house is what we must do! And speedily! Aye, I know you think me a regular Captain Stoneheart, but tell me this, Madam Gullible—if his doctor was so sure he would be up and about in no time, why does he still lie up there looking like a death's head?"

"It is a good question, dear Master Andrew," said Mrs. Starr, hurrying into the withdrawing room holding a tray on which was a plate piled high with fragrant biscuits and muffins. "But do pray keep your voice down. The poor young man is in such misery."

Instinctively reaching for one of Mrs. Starr's excellent shortbread biscuits, Lyddford's hand paused and he looked up sharply. "Is the fellow conscious?"

"Sometimes, but not for very long, praise be. These past two days he's been out of his head off and on."

"Good Lord!" he exclaimed, staring at her in horror.

Susan put in hurriedly, "But Dr. Sheswell said he will soon be well and there is absolutely no fear of real danger."

"Aye, ma'am," said Bo'sun Dodman, coming to join them. "Well, I'd be easier could Mr. Montclair get some proper rest, is all. Martha says he has little sleep. He's

182

weak as a cat, his spirits are at low ebb, and he's worn to the bone with pain."

"That don't surprise me," said Lyddford glumly. "His head's broke, his hand's broke, his leg's broke. He ain't likely to be feeling top o' the morning, is he? What baffles me is why my sister allowed him to be foisted off on us."

"Simple kind-hearted compassion, sir," sighed Mrs. Starr, giving Susan a wan and sympathetic smile.

"Simple's the word," grumbled Lyddford. "Trent has access to unlimited funds. Certainly he can provide for his kinsman better and easier than can we. Dammitall, he had no— Oh, your pardon, ladies, but d'ye realize I've work to be done, and the house swarming with invalids and visitors?"

Susan did not at once reply. In her ears was a faint voice pleading, 'Could you . . . hold my hand . . . just for a minute?' He'd only asked it of her because he dreaded to be left alone in that awful pit . . . Or perhaps from the instinctive need of a person close to death to reach out to another human presence. Despite the fact that they despised each other she had tried to help him. And yet . . . She sighed.

Watching her tired face Mrs. Starr gave Lyddford a rare frown and said defensively, "In point of fact the Trents have not come once since they left Montclair here, Master Andy." She started out of the room, pausing to add over her shoulder, "And his affianced bride has never so much as set foot across our threshold, which is pretty behaviour if you was to ask me!"

"Even so, you are perfectly right, Andy," said Susan. "The responsibility was mine, and I suppose I have been very silly. It's none of our bread and butter, after all."

"You've a kind heart, Mrs. Sue," declared Dodman with a fond smile. "And Mr. Montclair's young and seems to have kept himself trim enough. It's not as if he

183

was smashed up inside, or his back broke. Likely he'll
do very well, just as his doctor says. Then the Trents
will be grateful, and maybe—"

Deemer came into the room. Lyddford glanced at him
enquiringly.

"A Mrs. Bentley is here, sir. Says she was sent by Dr.
Sheswell."

"Oh, thank heaven," murmured Susan.

"It's past time," grunted Lyddford. "Come on, Bo'sun
George. We'll get as much work done as we can this evening. I've another cargo to ship day after tomorrow."

Mrs. Bentley, a short rather square woman, waited in
the servants' hall. Susan's first impression of her was of
greyness. Her hair was grey, her eyes were pale and wa-
tery, the shawl pinned over the dun-coloured coat was
grey, and there was a musty air about her. But she
bobbed a curtsy and said respectfully that Dr. Sheswell
sent his apologies for the long delay and that she would
do her best to help the "poor gent."

There was an air of tragedy to the last two words.
Susan eyed her uneasily and asked for her experience. It
was broad and her references were excellent. It was silly
to be prejudiced against the woman only because she
seemed of a rather mournful disposition. Sheswell obviously thought highly of her, and besides, it would be a
relief to be able to get a good night's sleep for a change.
She summoned Martha to conduct Mrs. Bentley to the
small room they'd readied for her arrival, and went up
to look in on Montclair.

He lay as she'd left him, thin and bearded, bearing
little resemblance to the man she'd struck with the
dustpan brush. His right hand and left leg were
splinted, his head heavily bandaged. Somewhere be-

tween sleep and waking, his eyes were closed, but his left hand plucked restlessly at the coverlet and he muttered unintelligibly, his head moving in a feeble but endless tossing.

Mrs. Starr, seated beside the bed, took a cloth from the bowl of lavender water and bathed his face.

Susan whispered, "Does he seem any better to you, Starry?"

The little woman hesitated. "If you was to ask me, Mrs. Sue, he was doing better last Sunday."

"So I thought, though I dared not tell my brother that. Well, at least a nurse has come, so the responsibility is off our hands, thank goodness."

The thought of an uninterrupted night's sleep was luxury, and after saying her prayers, Susan snuggled down gratefully. The fog had come up again, and a profound silence enveloped the old house, blotting out even the slap of the water against the dock. The hush invited slumber, and she was so tired that she fell asleep immediately after blowing out her candle.

She could not tell what woke her, but she was suddenly, heart-stoppingly, wide awake, and listening. The quiet was so intense it was almost a sound in itself. She sat up, holding the bedclothes around her, her eyes trying to pierce the dark. Had Montclair cried out, perhaps? But, of course, if he should, Mrs. Bentley was here now. Martha slept next to the nursery, and would go to Priscilla at once if the child suffered one of her nightmares. Perhaps, she thought, it had just been a bad dream . . . Another moment, and she would lie down again and—

A horse neighed loudly.

Susan's heart leapt into her throat. Pennywise and

Pound Foolish were elderly and seldom woke at night. Priscilla's pony, Deemer's old cob, and the Bo'sun's chestnut gelding were in the paddock on the other side of the house. Andy's big grey, Ghost, was in the stables, as was her own little mare, Pewter. And the neigh had sounded as if the horse stood on the front lawn. Who could possibly be calling at this hour of the night?

She slipped from bed and ran to peep through the window curtains. The three-quarter moon shone through a veil of mist, but there was sufficient light for her to see if anyone was outside. There was no horse on the drive. Nor had she heard the hoofbeats of a departing rider. But there was no doubting she'd heard that neigh.

The minutes crept past. Her feet were very cold and she began to shiver and wish she'd put on her dressing gown, but she would not leave the window to get it. Perhaps it *had* been one of the horses in the paddock. All this worrying must have made her nerves—

The mists on the drive swirled. She gave a gasp as a dark shape rose, seemingly from the ground. Only a glimpse she had—then he was gone, but she was sure it was a man, and equally sure that he'd been watching the house. She flew to the bed, snatched up her dressing gown, and was in the corridor in an instant. A dark figure loomed before her, and she came near to fainting from fright.

Fully dressed, Lyddford said cheerily, "What's to do?"

"Oh, how you . . . frightened me!" she gasped.

"Who did you think I was?" he said, grinning. "Attila the—"

"I saw someone," she panted. "On the drive. A man. He—he was watching the house, Andy!"

"Damn," he grunted and ran to the stairs, Susan following.

Flinging open the front door, Lyddford sprang down the steps, pistol in hand. He ran a short way, stopped in

186

a listening attitude, then came back. "Nobody," he muttered. "You're sure?"

"Quite sure."

He restored the pistol to his coat pocket. "Didn't recognize him, I suppose?"

"No. But he was tall. Oh, Andy, you don't think whoever tried to kill Montclair—"

He put an arm about her. "Don't be a peagoose, Mrs. H. There are a dozen possibilities. Have you forgot those varmints you saw in the woods? Old Selby Trent might have set 'em to see if we're murdering his precious nephew. Or some thief might be after our boat; a gypsy might be after the horses; some bird-witted traveller might have become lost and mistaken the cottage for a tavern . . . Back to bed for you, my girl!"

But Susan noticed that for all his bantering tone, he shot the bolts on the front door for the first time since they'd moved here, and as she walked up the stairs, she heard him repeat the process with the back door.

10

Mrs. Starr removed Welcome from her shopping basket and adjusted her left mitten. "I shall try if I can borrow Mrs. Edgeworth's new book so that you can read it to us tonight, Mrs. Sue. I'll be back as quickly as I can," she added worriedly. "I don't like leaving you alone, with poor Mr. Montclair doing so poorly. And—That Woman. . . !" Her lips tightening, she threw a grim look at the stairs.

There was no love lost between her and their new nurse. It had taken Mrs. Starr less than a day to pronounce that Mrs. Bentley was lazy. The next morning she had complained that not once had she seen the nurse do any more for her patient than to give him the medicine Dr. Sheswell had sent along with her. "There he was at nine o'clock last evening, poor gentleman, tossing and turning and so hot and uncomfortable," she'd told Susan indignantly. "And her, snoring in the chair! A fine nurse *she* is! I declare Señor Angelo could do better!"

Harbouring her own doubts, Susan had spoken to Mrs. Bentley, who had at once dissolved into tears. "The poor gent keeps me awake all night, marm," she

whined. "I got to get *some* sleep *some* time. I mean, I can't go on working me fingers to the bone four and twenty hours out of the twenty-four, now *can* I, marm? Only huming I is. Only huming!"

A trundle bed had been set up in Montclair's room, and Martha and Mrs. Starr took shifts during the day so that the nurse could rest. Martha was up there now, in fact, sitting beside the sick man.

Susan promised to keep an eye on matters while Mrs. Starr was gone, and watched Pennywise and Pound Foolish trot away down the drivepath. The afternoon was overcast and blustery. She glanced up at the building clouds and wondered how Andy was faring at sea with *The Dainty Dancer*. She was not worried, however; her brother had been taught seamanship by Grandpapa, and knew his business.

In the kitchen, Priscilla very proudly presented the composition on which she had been working so hard all morning. It was a pleasant little tale about a lonely rabbit who finds a friend in a kindly but rather domineering hen. Susan marvelled at the warmth of the story, but was touched by the rabbit's loneliness. She praised the work, and Priscilla went off happily with the faithful Wolfgang prancing at her heels. 'Bless her heart,' thought Susan fondly. 'She has a truly remarkable gift with words, but how nice it would be if only she had some little friends to play with.'

A sniff interrupted her fond musing, and Martha wandered disconsolately into the kitchen, carrying a tray of dirty dishes.

"Martha?"

The girl lifted her plain, pale face. There were tears in the brown eyes and her lips trembled.

"My goodness," exclaimed Susan, alarmed. "Whatever is it?"

"Nothing, Mrs. Sue," said Martha in a sort of gulp.

189

"Just me. I'm silly about . . . things." Her attempt at a smile a disaster, she started past.

Susan put a hand on her arm and stopped her. "You are not silly. You may not be clever with arithmetic or writing, but lots of people aren't. You are very good with sick people; you're a hard and steady worker, and you have taught Miss Priscilla how to knit beautifully. Now tell me what has happened."

It was very easy to crush Martha and her bowed head did not lift despite the kindly words. She said with dreary resignation, "She—she says I'm slow and stupid. And I am, I know. But . . . I was—just trying for to help the poor gentleman. He was so thirsty and he tried to reach the water glass and hurt hisself. I ran to get it for him, but—I didn't mean to interfere, honest, Mrs. Sue! She—she was so cross . . . I do everything wrong. Everything. I d-don't know why you put up with me."

Susan was enraged, but rage terrified Martha, so she controlled it and gave the drooping girl a little shake. "What fustian you do talk, indeed. You're one of us and as for putting up with you—goodness! I don't know how we could go along without you! Now you just—" She checked, frowning at the piled plates and glasses. "Are all these from my—I mean, Mr. Montclair's room?"

"Yes, Mrs. Sue. Mrs. Bentley was trying to feed the gentleman, I 'spect."

Susan nodded, and went upstairs, her eyes sparking. Montclair had taken practically no solid food this past week, little more than the brandy and water Dr. Sheswell prescribed. From the look of the dishes on Martha's tray, the nurse had not been stinting herself.

She went into the bedchamber without knocking, and halted.

Mrs. Bentley stood by the bed, measuring medicine into a glass. She was humming some unidentifiable air that made up in volume for what it lacked in melody. Smiling

190

at the spoon, she set it aside, and bent over the bed. "Here we goes, poor fella," she crooned and slid her left hand under Montclair's shoulders, jerking his head up.

Susan heard his choked gasp, and exclaimed indignantly, "Oh, do be more careful!"

The nurse uttered a small cry and straightened, allowing the sick man's bandaged head to drop back onto the crumpled pillows. Susan saw Montclair's mouth twist with pain and the thin left hand clutch convulsively at the coverlet. A soaring wrath possessed her.

"Oh! *'Ow* you did s'prise me, M's Henley," wailed the nurse, one hand flying to her throat and the other slopping the medicine over Montclair. "Bl-blest if ever'n'm'borndays I was more *s'prised*! M'poor heart's beatin' like—like a *kettledrum,* M's Henley, I'm that s'prised."

"Stand aside," demanded Susan, and not waiting to be obeyed, pushed the woman from her path and bent over Montclair. The bedclothes were untidy, the pillowslip creased and damp with perspiration, and he looked desperately ill. She felt his forehead and turned, saying angrily, "He is very hot and uncomfortable. Have you bathed him yet?"

Mrs. Bentley drew herself up. "Doct' Sheswell don't hold wi' bathing when there's fever presh—"

Montclair whispered pleadingly, "If I . . . might have—water . . ."

"Of course."

"That's f'me t'do, ma'am." Mrs. Bentley made a belated snatch for the glass Susan had already taken up. "Now y'mustn't int'fere w'me patient," she added, attempting to force her way between Susan and the bed.

"Nonsense." Susan circumvented this manoeuvre with a jab of one elbow. With great care she raised the dark head very slightly and held the glass to Montclair's cracked dry lips. He took a sip, choked, groaned, and his left hand lifted in a weak gesture of repugnance.

191

"I'll take—" began Mrs. Bentley with another abortive grab at the glass.

"I think not!" Susan lifted the glass to her nose and sniffed. Her eyes flashing, she stepped closer to Mrs. Bentley's aggressive but slightly swaying figure. "Be so good as to explain why there is gin in this glass, ma'am."

"Med'cine," declared the nurse fiercely, but losing her balance for a second. "Y'got no b'sness, M's—"

Raging but keeping her voice low, Susan declared, "You—are—*intoxicated*!"

"Ooooh! Wotta *awfu'* thing t'say!" The nurse darted for the glass.

Susan fended her off, marched to the window, and emptied the contents onto the lawn below. She was greatly relieved to see masts bobbing beside their dock, and the Bo'sun carrying a crate up the back steps.

"M'*med'cine*!" wailed Mrs. Bentley, peering tragically after it. She turned on Susan in a flame. "Oh, you're a wicked woman, you are! Jesslike they said! I was warned, I was, and—"

"Out!" commanded Susan, flinging one arm majestically in the direction of the door.

Mrs. Bentley stared at her, and began to look frightened. "You can't do that," she blustered. "Doc't Sh-Sheshwell says—"

Susan tugged on the bellpull. "You may inform Dr. Sheswell that you were discharged for laziness, drunkenness, ineptitude—"

"*Oooh!* Now she's a'swearin' 't me! A good woman *I* is, not like th'likes of *her* an' she swears—"

"And—" Susan finished, wrinkling her nose in distaste, "dirtiness!"

"Well, I *never!*"

"Your hands are filthy, and your garments little better! As a nurse, madam, you would make a good dustman!"

"If *ever* I—!" Defiantly at bay the nurse threatened,

192

"I'll have th'law onya, see if I don't, fer inf'mation o'character, an'—"

"Ah—Bo'sun," interrupted Susan loftily. "Mrs. Bentley is leaving us. Be so good as to drive her to Dr. Sheswell's house in Bredon, and inform him we were obliged to dismiss her."

Mrs. Bentley folded her arms across her chest, and with narrowed hate-filled eyes and flushed cheeks declared, "Well, I won' go an' y'can't—"

"I can require the Bo'sun to forcibly eject you," said Susan, paying no heed to Dodman's horror-stricken and paling countenance. "But I warn you that unless you leave quietly and at once, Mrs. Bentley, I mean to instruct the constable to bring charges against you for impersonating a qualified nurse! I fancy your credentials would bear some investigation!"

For a moment longer Mrs. Bentley glared at the haughty young face and elevated chin of the notorious Widow Henley. Then she suddenly took refuge in noisy weeping, and with a relieved grin Dodman conducted her from the room.

Susan flew to the water pitcher, took up another glass and filled it, then bent again over Montclair. His eyes were full of pain, but there was a gleam of amusement also.

"She is gone," said Susan, contriving gently to lift his head a little. "From now on, *my* people will tend to your needs, Mr. Montclair. I am only sorry that you were subjected to such a disgraceful scene."

He drank gratefully, then whispered, "Wouldn't . . . have missed it!"

Montclair drifted now in a strange trancelike world, sometimes fathoms deep in a blank emptiness, sometimes dreaming distressing and involved dreams that troubled him greatly. After a very long while, one of his

193

dreams was of a forest wherein he sat watching a forester saw down a tree. But although the forester worked hour after hour, he seemed to make no impression on the tree, which stood there as proud and unshaken as ever. Montclair grew tired of waiting to see it fall and he walked away, but the noise of the saw followed.

He could still hear it when he opened his eyes and discovered an indistinct little scene that blurred into a haze around the edges. A blue canopy billowed over him, edged by dainty lace-trimmed ruffles. He frowned at the matching silken bed-curtains. His bed had a plain red velvet tester with a battlement trim, and red-and-gold bed-curtains. No ruffles. No lace. If Uncle Selby had been meddling again. . . ! Irked, he shifted his gaze in search of the noise. It seemed to be coming from his bed. He tried to raise his head, which was a horrible mistake. After a while, the wavering images settled again, and he peered downward and discovered a small, curled-up shape. Wolfgang snored, evidently . . .

He lay there, staring at the dog, wondering how it came to be at Longhills, and what they'd done to his bed. It was all very perplexing, and the pain in his head prevented him from remembering properly. He'd better get Gould in here. He tried to reach for the bellpull, instinctively using his right hand . . .

After an unpleasant interval, an authoritative voice came through the mists. "Here. Drink this, my poor fellow."

He sipped obediently.

Alain Devenish's face materialized, hovering over him. The usually carefree blue eyes held a rather worried look.

With an amazing effort he was able to say, "Hello—Dev," and heard a faint croak. Good God! Had that been his own voice? "What've they done . . . to my bed?"

"Ain't your bed." Devenish spoke very gently. "Mrs.

Henley's. You're at Highperch, my tulip. Go back to sleep now."

He had a very vague and indistinct recollection of the widow helping him—somehow, somewhere. And he seemed to remember her bending over him, and speaking to someone in an imperious way that had made him want to laugh. But why he thought, confused, should Mrs. Henley have helped him? And what was he doing at Highperch? He whispered, "How . . . long have—"

"About ten days, give or take a day."

"Ten days!" He started up in dismay.

His head seemed to explode. The room swung and dipped sickeningly. From a great distance, he thought he could hear Dev calling someone . . .

A slender white hand was pressing a wonderfully cold cloth to his brow; the mellow voice that held such incredible kindliness was with him again, repeating over and over again that it was all right; that he was quite safe now. The shadow was gone. If he would just lie still and stop tossing about, he would be easier . . . He tried to concentrate on the voice, and gradually he was able to breathe without panting . . .

His eyelids were very heavy, but he managed to open them. It was night. He knew he'd been dreaming, but he did not want to remember the dream and thrust it away with determined desperation. A candle was flickering somewhere nearby. Closer at hand, two searching grey eyes in a tired but lovely face scanned him with concern.

"Are you feeling a little better now?" Susan asked.

He smiled at her, and wondered if she always smelled of violets. "Yes, thank you—but . . . I don't—understand."

"You had—an accident, and were brought here. You suffered a slight relapse, but you are doing much better now. Is that what you mean?"

195

"No. I don't know why—you are so . . . kind to me . . ." But he fell asleep before she could answer.

It seemed a very long time before he heard her voice again, and it was difficult to hear because she was speaking very softly, almost in a whisper. Gradually, he realized that she was talking with Mrs. Starr who sounded very agitated and kept moaning that they "should never have done it! Never!" He wondered idly what "it" was, and tried to open his eyes but was too drowsy to accomplish this.

"You know perfectly well why we did it," said Mrs. Henley with a trace of exasperation.

"Yes. But—but the awful *risk,* dear Mrs. Sue! If you should be found out! Oh dear, oh dear!"

"What could they prove?"

"You know what they would *say!* And the Runners can be clever. If they should even *suspect*— Suppose his family should put two and two together? It is such a dreadful thing to do! I never dreamed you capable of such *ruthless—*"

Decidedly irked, Mrs. Henley interrupted, "For goodness' sake, stop being so melodramatic, Starry! And keep your voice down, do. He might hear us!"

The discussion continued, but the voices were now so low that Montclair could no longer discern the words. Vaguely troubled, he sank back to sleep once more.

The next time he awoke something was nagging at the edges of his mind; something he had dreamed perhaps, and that was quite important, but he couldn't remember what it might be. It was still dark, but he thought it not the same night. For one thing, he felt less discomfort; the aching in his leg and hand was unremitting, but not quite as brutal, and although his head throbbed, it was so bearable by comparison with his earlier awakenings that he could actually think. He lay there quietly, the flickering candlelight and the faint

196

fragrance of violets telling him that he was still in Mrs. Henley's bed. Questions began to form. So many—so unanswerable. And chief among them the dread puzzle of who wanted him dead. Whom had he so antagonized that they were willing to put their own life at risk so as to end his? Had Junius decided to strike again? No, that terrible shadow in the woods had not been Junius. It had been too enormous . . . The very thought of it made Montclair break out in a sweat of horror, and he decided that the solving of the puzzle would have to wait until he regained more of his strength. Meanwhile, he had a great deal for which to be thankful. He was warm and safe. He was also very hungry, which likely meant he was starting to mend, and—

Something was moving in the room. Something or— someone. He tensed and lay completely motionless, straining his eyes through the dimness to that vague, oncoming shape. A man. Creeping towards the bed. He watched the crouching figure draw ever nearer, dark and unidentifiable against the candlelight, but ineffably menacing. The lack of sound was remarkable—not so much as one squeak of a floorboard. He was very close now, and Montclair's heart gave a lurch as the candlelight awoke a glitter on the dagger in the man's right hand. So the would-be murderer had come right inside Highperch and meant to finish what he'd started! Anger scorched through him. He was weak as a cat, but—dammit, he'd not lie here and be butchered without a fight!

With all his strength, he managed to get an elbow under him and heave himself upward a little. At the top of his lungs, he shouted, "No! Get away, you skulking coward!"

His voice was weak, but the intruder uttered a shrill yelp and jumped into the air. The knife clattered to the floor.

"Hell and damnation!" gasped Andrew Lyddford,

197

straightening and tottering to steady himself against the bedpost. "Don't—don't *ever* do such a frightful thing!"

"I—apologize . . ." faltered Montclair, sinking back, exhausted by his great effort.

Lyddford mopped a handkerchief at his face. "I should rather think you might," he said severely. "I wonder I didn't fall over in a fit!"

"I really am sorry. Only . . . well, I saw the knife, you see, and—"

"That's because I was polishing it, but you were so still I got the idea you'd cocked up your toes, so I came creeping to see if you had, and what must you do but let out a yowl like a bloody damned banshee! Jove, if it ain't enough to put the fear of—" His tone changed abruptly. "What the deuce d'you mean—you 'saw the knife'? If you've the confounded gall to suppose I come slithering over to cut your throat, sir, by George but you'll answer to me for it!"

"I am already engaged to meet you, Mr. Lyddford. And you were against the light. I could only make out a silhouette, and the knife."

"Oh." Some of the resentment went out of the proud young face. Lyddford stooped, retrieved the knife, and went over to lay it on the table. "Yes. I suppose it could have looked like that. Sorry if I gave you a nasty turn, but I'd say we're even on that score, at all events." With a grin he came back to bend over Montclair and peer at him critically. "You look somewhat alive. Be damned if I don't think Susan's right and you're going to pull through after all!"

"Your sister has been more than kind, and I'm very sure I've been a great deal of trouble. I believe you've been burdened with me for ten days already, and—"

"Three weeks."

Montclair stared at him. "But—Devenish just said—"

198

Lyddford settled himself on the end of the bed and interrupted, "That was a week and a half ago. And—before you ask me again—no, they didn't have to amputate your hand."

Montclair wasn't quite ready for shocks like that, and he closed his eyes briefly.

"Oh Gad," groaned Lyddford, jumping up and causing the bed to lurch. "I'm as much a disaster as Devenish! I'll go!"

"No. Please." Montclair managed a smile. "I'd be most grateful if you could rather . . . tell me what's been happening."

Lyddford eyed him doubtfully, but the smile was encouraging. He had noted the effect of his earlier sudden movement, and so sat down with care. "You'd not believe the bobbery! When my sister found you, and your cousin hauled you out of there—"

"My—*cousin*. . . ? Trent?"

"Yes. Don't wonder you're surprised. Nasty slug, but strong as an ox." Lyddford grinned boyishly. "Mixing my metaphors a bit, ain't I? At all events, there's been betting in all the inns and alehouses on when you'd snuff it. I wanted to ship you back to Longhills, but you took such a downturn we did not dare move you. You were out of your head for days on end. Raving about music, and birds in harpsichords, and shadows and giants and— Devil take me, I've done it again! Are you all right?"

Weakness was causing Montclair to tremble. He fought it, and said rather inaccurately, "I'm quite all right, thank you. Please go on."

"Well, it's just that from what you were gabbling at, it—er, seemed you hadn't fallen into your silly Folly. Not of your own volition, at least." The long grey eyes (so much like hers) were scanning him curiously. "D'you remember now? What happened, I mean."

"Not much. Just—that I was . . . struck down from behind." His mind was trying to see the shadow. He shut it out. "They believed me, did they?"

"At first they thought you were delirious, and you were, of course. But then you kept on about the East Woods. So a couple of the Runners—"

"Runners?"

Lyddford nodded. A frown darkened his brow and he said rather grimly, "You're an important man, you know. Heir to a title and a great estate. Jehoshaphat— if you'd seen all the comings and goings! Writers from the newspapers; Bow Street; even a couple of high-ranking officers from the Horse Guards."

"Good . . . God!"

"Quite. The upshot was that two of the Runners went to the East Woods and it seems—er, well, they found the place where you'd been hit. Not—much doubt, I gather."

Montclair's brows knit. "But—if I was attacked in the East Woods, why go to all the trouble—"

"To haul you to the Folly? Hmmn. That's what we wondered. I suppose they thought you were finished— Lord knows, you looked it! Horrid sight!—and wanted to tuck you safely away."

It was a puzzle, but he was too tired to worry at it. He asked wearily, "Does my family know?"

"Yes. Your aunt and uncle came when my sister found you. It was at their wish in fact that you stayed here. I do not scruple to tell you I was against it."

"Yes, of course." Montclair said humbly, "I am very grateful to you."

"Mutual, old boy." With breezy tactlessness Lyddford added, "Jolly good of you not to have cocked up your toes. We'd have been in a proper treacle pot! Though to say truth it was our own fault for letting you stay. Bad enough we had to put up with you, Montclair, but I'll not mince words in telling you that you've a weasel's wart for a doctor."

Amused, Montclair said, "Sheswell's been the family physician for years. But—wasn't there another doctor? A red-headed fellow?"

"Right. Our Bo'sun is an apothecary of sorts. He's worked wonders with you."

"I must thank him. I'm afraid I have caused Mrs. Henley a great deal of trouble." His dreams had become so entangled with reality that it was hard to separate them. He half-recalled an odd conversation between Susan Henley and Mrs. Starr, but the memory was so hazy it was likely just another dream. He said haltingly, "I seem to recollect that she was with me often when I woke up. You must all be wishing me . . . at Jericho."

"Oh, my sister's the salt of the earth and not one to hold a grudge under these circumstances. Besides"—Lyddford's voice lost its kindliness—"so long as you're recuperating here, you cannot very well have us kicked out, can you?"

The smile faded from Montclair's eyes, and the faintest flush lit his pale face, but he met Lyddford's suddenly hard stare levelly. "No," he said. "I certainly cannot."

The door opened softly. Montclair couldn't see who entered, but he heard the rustle of silks and then smelled violets.

Lyddford said, "He's awake again, and seems much better this time."

Susan Henley came to rest a cool and investigative hand on the patient's wan cheek. "You've tired him," she scolded.

"I knew I'd be in the suds! That's what comes of trying to help a bit!" With an unrepentant grin, Lyddford said, "I'm off!" and departed.

The widow bathed Montclair's face, held the glass while he drank some deliciously cool barley water, then instructed him to go back to sleep.

Drowsily, he watched her cross to the little table, pull the branch of candles closer, and sit down with her workbox. She began to darn a sock. She had a very pretty way of

201

turning her wrist. He glanced up and found her eyes on him. They really were most remarkable eyes, so clear and— The low-arching brows were lifting slightly. He was very tired now, but murmured, "Why did—"

She shook her head and put one slim finger over her lips. "Hush."

"No. Please—I must—"

"Not more thanks? Heavens, sir, I have been thanked each time you wake up! Have done with your gratitude I beg, and do as your head nurse tells you."

Despite the stern words, her mouth curved to a smile, and he persisted doggedly. "You risked your life to come down those steps. I can't understand why."

Her eyes sharpened and her cheeks seemed a little flushed. She stared hard at her sock, and murmured, "Do you say you—watched me coming down to you?"

"It was the bravest thing I ever saw." He sighed. "I thought—you were an angel."

Her lashes lifted and she looked at him, startled, then said with a smile, "How can you ever have supposed such a thing? I wasn't wearing white."

"No," he said drowsily, "pink."

Susan dropped the sock and when she had retrieved it, her cheeks were very pink indeed. "My habit is pale green, Mr. Montclair."

"Oh. I—thought I saw pink." He sighed again. "Must have dreamed it."

"Indeed you must," she confirmed rather austerely. "Now, go back to sleep."

With each day that followed, Montclair grew stronger. The petite Mrs. Starr and her faithful helper Martha did most of the nursing; they both were kind and gentle, but although grateful for their efficient care, he missed a pair of serene grey eyes and the smell of violets. He slept many hours away, but Bo'sun Dodman came in to check on him several times each day. From him Montclair learned that Mrs. Henley and her brother had gone into Town. Apparently, Lyddford was striving to obtain a position either on the staff of a Foreign Minister, or at the Navy Board, and hoped to enlist the aid of his uncle, Sir John Lyddford, in these endeavours. In view of the unsavoury reputation of the late Lieutenant Burke Henley, Montclair judged the chances for success to be slight, but he said nothing. His chats with the Bo'sun also provided him with a better understanding of the widow's struggle to keep the family together after the death of her grandfather. That it had been a desperate struggle became very apparent, but his attempts to discover the extent of their remaining fortune were deftly turned aside, and since good manners forbade that he question the Bo'sun outright, he was thwarted.

Despite his physical improvement, his spirits were low, a state he fought to conceal. Several bones had been broken in his hand, and the injury caused him constant anxiety. His attempts to move the fingers failed dismally. He knew he should be grateful that it had not been necessary to amputate as he'd at first feared, but he was haunted by the dread that he would no longer be able to play competently. Barbara was another source of worry; and despite their differences, the continued absence of his family troubled him. It was absurd that he should want them to come, but if they had no sufficient interest to do so, they could at least, he thought fretfully, have permitted Babs to pay him a visit.

Alain Devenish, who had been a frequent visitor at first, had not appeared for several days, and Montclair missed his cheerful presence even while he recognized that his friend had a young ward and great estates of his own to be cared for.

Priscilla's short afternoon visits were bright oases through these long days. He looked forward to her coming, and was more and more drawn to the child and charmed by her quaint mixture of solemnity and gaiety. She had a remarkable gift of imagination, and they spent a good deal of their time together in constructing a progressive fairy-tale poem. This fabrication grew more and more complicated, and was a source of much amusement to them both. The child's words were occasionally somewhat unorthodox, but she had a quick ear for rhythm, and Montclair found his work cut out to keep abreast of her in their poetical ventures.

He was anticipating the child's presence on a rainy afternoon a week after Mrs. Henley's departure, when he heard footsteps on the stairs. His heart gave a leap, but then sank again when Sheswell's voice boomed out. The physician had not called for eight days. He was less gentle in his movements than was Dodman, and Montclair nerved himself for an unpleasant few minutes.

The Bo'sun was proud of his patient's rapid progress, and as the door swung open he was saying eagerly, ". . . may not be quite as you'd expected, doctor."

The floor shook to Sheswell's heavy tread. "I can but hope you're wrong, Dod—" The great voice stilled.

Montclair smiled as the doctor stood perfectly still, staring at him. "Good afternoon, Sheswell." His voice was firmer today, and he was able to raise his left hand steadily. It fell back, however, as the doctor did not move but continued to stand as if frozen, his eyes fairly goggling.

"Thought you'd be surprised, sir," chuckled the Bo'sun.

Sheswell gave a start. "Amazed is more like," he exclaimed, coming to take up Montclair's hand vigorously. "By all the gods, I cannot believe it!" He peered into the sick man's eyes, felt the pale forehead, and exclaimed, "You've done exceeding well, Dodman. Jove, but you

204

have! Fever down, some colour in the cheeks, eyes clear! How does the head feel, Mr. Montclair? Still have some beastly headaches, I'll warrant. Have to expect those for a long time to come, and you'll likely find your reasoning confused. Natural. Quite natural."

He proceeded to examine the almost-healed head injury, and the splints on the broken hand and the leg were checked. "Well, well," the doctor said jovially, "you'll be up and trotting about in a day or two, eh, sir?"

"That would be splendid," said Montclair, rather short of breath. "I've been sitting up every afternoon, and I stood yesterday, with the Bo'sun's help."

"I think the doctor's teasing, sir," Dodman put in smilingly.

Sheswell laughed. "Not a bit of it, m'dear fellow. Do him the world of good. I'll have some crutches sent over this afternoon."

"Crutches!" gasped Dodman, startled. "But, sir—how can he manage crutches with only one hand?"

"Perhaps I can get about with just one," put in Montclair eagerly. "Eh, Sheswell?"

"Perhaps, Mr. Montclair. But I think we can contrive to strap the right crutch to your elbow, so you'll have some control over it. Awkward, but it might serve. Meanwhile, we can shorten the leg splints so you can get about easier. Let's have these off now . . ."

The next half-hour was unpleasant, and by the time the doctor left, Montclair felt worn, and fell asleep before he could see Priscilla.

In the downstairs hall, Dodman said hesitantly, "A little rough for him, wasn't it, sir?"

The physician shook his head. "Don't do to coddle 'em, m'dear chap. Sooner they're up and about, the better. Especially in a case like this. You'll be needing some more medicine, I fancy. Wonderful what it can do, ain't it? Not that Montclair was all that badly off, as I said.

205

Still, I'll have some sent over with the crutches. Might be an idea to increase the dosage. Just as a precaution, y'know. You've been managing to get some food into the poor chap by the look of things, eh? Excellent. You're a dashed good man, Dodman. Don't be surprised do I refer some of my less serious cases to you. You ought to get yourself a licence, damme if you oughtn't!"

Dodman flushed with pleasure. Almost, he confessed how he and Mrs. Sue had supplemented Dr. Sheswell's orders, but the physician was so delighted it seemed expedient to leave well enough alone.

That night a keen wind came in from the east, and by morning one might have thought it October rather than early July. The gusts shook the old house and whined in the chimneys, while leaden clouds brought a steady cold rain. The inclement weather did not keep people indoors, apparently. Soon after breakfast Montclair prevailed upon the Bo'sun to shave him, and he was staring somewhat aghast at the reflection of his drawn white face and sunken eyes when he heard a familiar and piercing voice.

Dodman took the mirror and the shaving impedimenta and all but ran from the room. A twittering Martha Reedham bustled about tidying the bed, plumping Montclair's pillows, and smoothing the counterpane. In another minute Mrs. Starr, her lips tightly pursed with disapproval, ushered in Sir Selby and Lady Trent.

Montclair had wanted them to come, but perversely, the recollection of their parting now came so clearly into his mind that he was speechless.

Lady Trent suffered no such inhibitions. She rushed to the bed, bent over her nephew, and kissed his cheek, marvelling that he yet lived, and mourning that they had been unable to see him before this. "If you knew how frightful it has been! The newspapers, and the Runners, and to add to the rest, we have been plagued by an endless stream of pushing people calling themselves your friends, some you've not seen for years, I am very sure! The horrid busybodies! I wonder I have survived it!"

"Truly frightful," agreed Sir Selby, clinging to Montclair's wasted left hand and patting it repeatedly. "You may be assured the criminals will be tracked down and brought to justice! But you look much improved from the last time we saw you. You won't remember that visit of course, poor fellow." His pale eyes scanned Montclair's face narrowly. "Jove, but youth is astonishing! I must admit we were loath to abandon you in this house, dear lad, but you were in no condition to be moved."

Lady Trent's thin lips quivered, and she gave it as her opinion it was a marvel that he still lived. "Heaven knows what these dreadful people might have done," she observed. "Three times we have come and been turned away on the grounds you was too ill to be disturbed, though I doubt you was even told of it, unhappy boy. When first I heard you had been struck down so savagely, I fainted dead away. Did I not, Trent?" Not waiting for a confirmation, she shrilled on. "The strain was . . . dreadful! Almost beyond my powers to support." She vanished into her handkerchief. "We all were worried to death! I vow, I wonder my poor heart did not break!"

Montclair wondered where her heart had been when she'd offered to give him a "pity party," but, helpless in the face of feminine tears, he assured her that he was feeling very much better and was much obliged to Lyddford and Mrs. Henley for their excellent care of him.

"Obliged, is it?" flared my lady, forgetting her grief abruptly. "If my suspicions are correct, Montclair, Dr. Sheswell's instructions have been poorly kept. Why, he thought you would be better in no time, whereas you almost . . . And to see you—like this . . . poor shattered invalid! We ought never to have left you in their hands. But we did what we thought right at the time. Always your best interests have weighed with me. Heaven knows I have *tried* to make a good home for you, little as you've appreciated my poor efforts."

Unable to restrain himself, he said coolly, "To the contrary, I am quite aware of your efforts at Longhills, ma'am. Speaking of which—how is my cousin Barbara?"

Lady Trent's lips settled into a thin line. "She is happily planning her wedding."

"And has been exceeding anxious to see you," murmured Sir Selby.

"Did you bring her with you, then?" asked Montclair eagerly.

"To *this* house?" shrilled his aunt. "I *hope* I am a better parent than to allow my daughter to set foot under this roof while That Woman resides here!"

Trent said, "Babs awaits you at home."

"How relieved you will be to be in your own bed at last," Lady Trent purred. "We have brought your man to help carry you to the carriage. Trent, do you ring the bell and tell them to send Gould up."

Her husband moved to the bellpull.

"I am not ready to come home yet," said Montclair.

"Of course you are ready," his aunt's voice rose. "Why would you wish to stay in this dreadful place when Longhills awaits you?"

"The boy is still weak," soothed Trent. "We must make allowances. But we will keep a very easy pace, dear lad, and you will be carried, so there's no cause for alarm." The all too familiar set of his nephew's pale lips inspired him to add hurriedly, "You really must leave these premises, Valentine. We are far past the date specified for the eviction of the Henley woman and her tribe, and so long as you remain here, we cannot enforce it."

"Good God, sir," exclaimed Montclair, irked. "Do you

208

fancy I shall proceed with an eviction against the lady who saved my life?"

"Saved your life—my hatpin," snorted my lady. "She was extreme reluctant to offer you shelter, which anyone with the least compassion would gladly have done! In point of fact, she only agreed to do so after we paid her a pretty penny! Saved your life, indeed! Pish!"

"Mrs. Henley took some most desperate chances in climbing down into that loathsome pit to help me, ma'am. And—"

"And was it not remarkable," she said with her thin smile, "that a newcomer to the district found you in a place none of the rest of us had even considered? Faith, but one marvels at her perspicacity—or . . . whatever it was . . ."

Montclair's head was aching again, but he met her eyes levelly. "Perhaps you should say straight out what you mean, ma'am."

"My dear wife and I have merely wondered," murmured Sir Selby, "if Mrs. Henley's so magnificent 'rescue' might have been prompted by—er, foreknowledge of the unfortunate event."

"You mean that she and her brother had me attacked and thrown into the Folly."

"She had motive enough, Lord knows," said my lady with a shrug. "Had you died, the ownership of this place would have been bound up in legal nonsense for a great while. Meantime, she has possession. She could have lived here rent-free, indefinitely."

Montclair's hand clenched on the coverlet. "Then how very foolish in her to come to my rescue," he said dryly.

Trent smiled a patient smile. "Perhaps that was made necessary. "One gathers that her little girl had formed the habit of playing near the Folly—"

"A clear case of criminal neglect by her misguided parent," inserted my lady with a smug nod of her head.

"Had the child heard you in the Folly," Trent went on, "and confided in some of the local children, or—"

"Or perchance they had thought you slain," his wife again interrupted. "But when the child discovered you still lived, that sly widow saw her chance for an even better ploy. She would come gallantly to your rescue, bring you here, nurse you back to health, and so win your gratitude that you would give her the house! A pretty scheme upon my word!"

"And an exceeding unlikely one, ma'am," said Montclair frowningly. But Lyddford's acid words came to plague him . . . 'So long as you are recuperating here, you cannot very well have us kicked out, can you?'

Her ladyship tittered. "Never say you have fallen into the hussy's toils? No, I'll not believe you could be so gullible, Montclair!"

He began to feel tired and dispirited, but persisted, "Say rather, I do not believe her guilty of such a scheme."

"Of course you do not," said Trent. "Who could expect your poor brain to function properly after suffering such a wound?"

"You shall have to let us do your reasoning for you, dear nephew," purred my lady. "And I tell you, Montclair, that gratitude is well and good, but one must face reality. Why would a scheming and mercenary adventuress go to so much trouble for a man she thoroughly dislikes?"

"Unless she hoped to profit by it," said Sir Selby.

"Which she has done," declared my lady. "Handsomely!"

Montclair wished they would go away.

11

ntering the house by the rear door, soaked, and aching with tiredness, Susan was rushed at and embraced by an elated Edwina Starr. "Oh, my love, you are safe home! At last!"

"Yes, thank goodness!" Susan allowed the little lady to appropriate the worn valise she carried, and began to unbutton her heavy greatcoat.

Mrs. Starr scolded fondly, "You should have let Deemer bring this heavy bag up for you."

"Andy appropriated the poor man the instant he showed his face at the dock. Is all well? Where is Priscilla? How is Montclair?"

"All is well. Or very nearly," said Mrs. Starr in a low urgent voice as they walked along the passage together. "Priscilla is outside, and—" They had reached the long windows looking out onto the garden court behind the house, and the light of this dull morning fell fully upon Susan's face. Shocked, Mrs. Starr exclaimed, "How sunburned you are! My poor child—we must cover your face with cucumber tonight! Oh, you should never have gone! It has been too much for you!"

"You know it really takes three to manage the barge, Starry, and with Montclair so ill I felt the Bo'sun must stay here."

"Well, he is much better, heaven be praised. No—trouble. . . ?"

"None. Save that we were delayed by a gale and had to ride at anchor off Clovelly for two miserable days." Starting up the stairs, Susan pulled back her shoulders and said brightly, "But thanks to Monsieur Monteil we've a full cargo. The men will be busy."

"And what of the monsieur? Did he come smoothing around you, dear ma'am? Oh, how I mistrust that man!"

"No, but we must be grateful to the gentleman, for he has been more than good." There came the recollection of Monsieur Monteil's ardent glances, the touch of that soft white hand on hers as they had stood on the windy Devonshire beach, and Susan struggled to restrain a shiver. "I'll own he is not exceeding attractive, but—"

"Attractive! 'Tis not his looks, but his *looks* I dislike!"

Susan chuckled. "Oh, Starry, you wretch, you *must* not speak of him so. Andy thinks the world of him, and likely I have misjudged the gentleman. He was the very soul of courtesy—so kind and all consideration towards me. Besides, only think how these consignments help us. Andy says if it keeps up—"

A sudden shrill outburst sent both women's glances to the head of the stairs. Susan gave a gasp of fright. "The Trents? Heavens! Do they visit him often? Have they brought his affianced?"

"This is the first time they've showed their noses since they browbeat you into letting Montclair stay here!"

"Good gracious!"

"Just so! And as for Miss Trent," the little woman sniffed disparagingly, "her ladyship likely judges this an unfit atmosphere for her pure daughter. But *I* judge it most odd. One would suppose a newly engaged girl should brave any atmosphere to be at the side of her betrothed when he is in such straits."

"I think all at Longhills 'most odd,'" said Susan with a sigh. "Only listen to her. You'd best find the Bo'sun. He must get that horrid woman away before she sends Montclair into a relapse again! I'll—" A heavy step behind her brought her spinning around with a guilty yelp.

At the foot of the stairs stood the Bo'sun, wearing a greatcoat and carrying a pair of crutches and a large medicine bottle.

"Welcome home, ma'am," he said breathlessly. "All shipshape?"

"Yes. But it was chancy putting in to our dock, George. It's not an easy river."

"True. But ye'd best stir your stumps, Mrs. Sue. We've company."

Susan nodded to the upper floor and pulled a wry face. "So I hear."

"And more arriving," he said, running an eye down her. "Let me get your boots, ma'am. You'll want to change out of those breeches before you see the nobs, I expect."

Mrs. Starr hurried off, calling for Martha to help Mrs. Sue.

Unceremoniously, Susan sat on the stair. The Bo'sun put down his burdens and pulled off her boots, then took up the valise and followed as she scurried up the stairs.

Two minutes later Martha brought hot water, and with lightning speed Susan washed, Martha brushed out her long hair, a pale lavender gown trimmed with ivory French braid replaced shirt and breeches, and ivory sandals were slipped onto her feet.

"My cap!" she gasped, sliding a carved Indian ivory bangle onto her wrist.

"Oh! Your poor nails, missus," moaned Martha.

Susan glanced regretfully at her ragged fingernails. "I know, I know. I was hoping to get the tar off, but—yes, that one will do, Martha. Quickly!"

She all but ran along the hall, hearing London voices downstairs that were drowned, as she went into her bedchamber, by Lady Trent's shrill voice.

Sir Selby and his wife sat beside the bed. Susan welcomed them politely, but aside from a vague impression that his coat was grey and that my lady wore an elaborate puce gown that made her look sallow, she scarcely noticed them. Her attention flew to Montclair, and her pulses gave the little leap that was so stupid and that had spurred her decision to accompany her brother on the voyage to Devonshire.

He was clean-shaven again, and she was shocked to note how the lack of the beard emphasized the gaunt hollows in his cheeks. A sudden eager flush stained those cheeks; the dark eyes lit up, the amber flecks glowing. He said in a firm voice that surprised her, "Here is my intrepid rescuer come back, and—"

"And Mrs. Henley will be wanting her bedchamber restored to her," interposed my lady, smiling the smile that seemed as if taken from a box and glued over her sneer.

Susan's heart was pounding. They wanted him to go home. Did he want to go? She searched his face and found only that warm smile.

"I fancy you think it past time we should relieve you of your burden," said Sir Selby. "I hope you have not been plagued to death, ma'am. We have brought our coach and shall carry my nephew off, so—"

"Your pardon," interposed Montclair, watching Susan. "But unless my presence here is a great inconvenience, I would prefer to delay leaving until I feel stronger."

"Now, now, dear lad," purred Trent. "We must consider others. And I think we have imposed upon Mrs. Henley sufficiently."

214

Susan shook her head. "It has been no imposition, sir. And I would be sorry to see Mr. Montclair leave us before he is well enough to stand the journey."

"I am very sure you would," smirked my lady, unable to restrain her waspish tongue.

Sir Selby frowned, but his attempt to speak was halted as Montclair lifted a thin hand. "Mrs. Henley is not one to hide her teeth," he drawled. "Did she wish to be rid of me, she would say so."

"I am not sure whether that is a compliment or an insult," said Susan, smiling at him.

"And it is all of a piece," snapped my lady. "My poor nephew is in no condition to know what is best for him, and—"

A loud male voice cut through her words. "Your pardon, ma'am."

My lady did not care to be interrupted at the best of times. This was not the best of times. She sprang to her feet and whirled on the intruder in a passion. "How *dare* you burst into a sickroom and—"

Her husband's quick eyes had noted the small staff one of the two newcomers carried. "Are you gentlemen from Bow Street?" he asked, silencing Lady Trent with a gesture.

A short, sturdy, moon-faced individual with a pugnacious stare and cold dark eyes grunted, "Yussir. Orficers o' the law. I'm 'Obkins, hand this"—he jerked a thumb at his meek associate—"is Limmer. Both desirious o' a word or three with Mr. Montclair, we his. Hif you don't hobject, that his."

"But my dear man, of *course* we do not object," said my lady, all gracious condescension. "As you may well imagine, our most fervent prayer is that the vicious would-be murderer of our beloved nephew should be seized and hung with the greatest dispatch."

The smaller Runner coughed and pointed out with a timid bow that they were unable to guarantee this

215

happy result. "The murderee not having become one, good and proper like, and the law getting so gentle and kindly with evildoers, that the villin might get off with transportation. But apprehend of him we will, m'lady."

"To which hend we got some pertinent questions for to hask," growled his partner.

"Well, we shall not delay you," said Trent. "We were in fact just taking our leave."

"Uncle," said Montclair. "I should very much like to see Barbara."

"But of course, Valentine," said my lady soothingly. "Tomorrow, poor dear boy. Tomorrow morning."

"Come, my love," urged her spouse. "We must not impede the progress of justice. Good day to you, nephew. Mrs. Henley." And with a firm grip on his wife's elbow and a rather sad smile, he moved smoothly from the room and closed the door.

Mr. Hobkins stared pointedly at Susan.

"Mr. Montclair is a long way from being recovered," she said. "Please do not tire him."

This evidently ruffled the Runner's sensibilities, and he observed that he was very sure that Mr. Montclair was "more hanxious than hanyone to see 'is wicked attacker brought to justice. Heven," he added with a grim nod, "hif there's them has *haint* hanxious! Not by so much has a whisker!"

Susan was still mulling over those ominous remarks after she had received an ecstatic greeting from her small daughter and Priscilla had gone off with Martha to change her wet shoes and be de-muddied.

Andrew hurried down the back stairs, looking, Susan thought, endearingly handsome in a brown velvet coat and cream pantaloons, and presenting a very different appearance from the unkempt sailor who'd slunk into the house after the Trents departed.

"I think they suspect us," she told him.

"The devil!" he gasped, paling. "Of not having gone to Town?"

"Of having a hand in the attack on Montclair," she went on, accompanying him into the withdrawing room.

"What fustian," he said scornfully. "As if they'd entertain such a cork-brained notion after you risked your neck to climb down to the poor fellow. Besides, they questioned us all when first Montclair was brought here. By Jove, but they did, and a sillier set of gudgeons I never hope to see!"

She crossed to the sideboard to pour him a glass of wine, and was attacked by a ferocious Welcome who had managed to get the lower cupboard door open and evidently regarded the shelf as his lair. The little cat sprang out, waving his arms to terrify her, then tore off, whiskers bristling and tail held sideways, in high triumph. Laughing, Susan rustled her skirts at him. "Yes, Andy," she said. "And between your threatening to throw them in the river if they didn't stop pestering us, and Angelo confusing them with his incomprehensible answers, I wonder we weren't clapped up then and there."

Lyddford tossed himself into his favourite chair and chuckled unrepentantly. "Don't do to bow down to a trap, love."

Susan carried over his wine. "Well, these aren't the same men. Quite a different proposition to the pair who came at first."

"All tarred with the same brush, pox on 'em." Lyddford raised his glass. "Here's to my excellent first mate *pro tem*! Truly, I don't know how we'd have managed without you, Mrs. H."

Blushing with pleasure, she asked, "Was I really a help? You surely would have contrived better had the Bo'sun been aboard."

"Oh, surely," he agreed with a grin. "But only think

217

how disappointed Imre Monteil would have been! Be dashed if ever I saw a man's face glow as his did when we came ashore at Clovelly! He has a *tendre* for you, my girl! And he's a rare catch, do you fancy him. Rich as Croesus, I hear. Faith, but who could doubt it? That yacht of his must be worth more than everything we own, even if you was to include Highperch."

"But I do not fancy him," she said quickly. "Though I cannot but be grateful for the work he has sent our way. Even," she added with a thoughtful pucker of her brows, "if I don't quite understand his need for us."

"Perfectly obvious. He cannot bring his dashed great yacht upriver. *The Dainty Dancer* is flat-bottomed and far more manoeuvrable."

"Well, I know that, silly. But why must he come upriver? There are many other places where he *could* moor his yacht safely and store his cargo."

Lyddford shrugged. "He wants to store it here. He likes Highperch. Means to buy it, y'know. Made me a most generous offer. Don't look so worried, you foolish chit. This ain't my house."

"No, and it may not be mine, either. But—if it was— Andy—you wouldn't wish me to sell to him?"

"Why not? The sum he offered would buy us a jolly nice home in Town. And certainly, this place needs a great deal of work."

Susan stared at him in dismay. He met her regard gravely, but his eyes danced, and she threw a cushion. "Oh, you horrid creature! You are teasing! A house in Town wouldn't provide us a dock for *The Dainty Dancer*—at least, not a dock we could use!"

He fielded the cushion laughingly, lifted a cautioning hand, and glanced to the open door. "You must not murder me, Mrs. H. We've Runners in the house, don't forget."

She stood. "Yes. And Montclair was sufficiently exhausted after his loving relations left. I must find the Bo'sun and send them packing!"

"Cluck, cluck, cluck," jeered her brother, raising no objection when Welcome raced back in and took possession of his lap.

Susan smiled, and hurried out, taking care to keep her face turned from him, and irked by the awareness that she was blushing.

The men from Bow Street were firing interminable questions at Montclair, and Dodman, representing himself as the sick man's medical advisor, promptly called a halt to the interview. Mr. Hobkins was affronted, and relieved his feelings by accusing Montclair of knowing very well who had tried to put a period to him, and of "deliberately pertecting 'im hor them what done the foul deed." The vexed Bo'sun relieved his own feelings by offering the Runner an extremely uncomplimentary assessment of the silly gumps now posing as representatives of law and order, whereupon the irate Runner took himself off, his meek associate slanting an amused wink at Dodman as he was escorted from the room.

Susan wandered closer to the bed. Montclair was watching her with an oddly speculative expression. Flustered, she glanced at the crutches propped against the chest of drawers. "You are looking very much better, sir," she said. "But not ready for those, I think."

"I've been here for over a month, Mrs. Henley. It is time I was up and about."

She moved a little nearer and smoothed the pillow. "You have had a very bad accident. One does not recover quickly from shock and loss of blood, sir. Nor do broken bones heal in a month."

"Still, my uncle was right. I have imposed on you long

219

enough. Besides, there are things at Longhills requiring my attention."

She sat down on the bedside chair and pointed out demurely, "But you—er, do not feel strong enough to travel."

He chuckled. "Strong enough to travel as far as the windowseat, ma'am. Indeed I look forward to it more than you can imagine. And speaking of travelling, I understand you were in Town. Did you go on your boat? You look the picture of robust health."

"Indeed?" she said, her head tilting upward.

His mouth quivered. "I perceive I have said something dreadful."

"Not at all. There is nothing dreadful about being—big and healthy!"

"Then why do you gnash your teeth when you say it?"

She glared at him, saw the lurking smile, and relented. "Oh, very well. I suppose every woman prefers to be thought of as small and dainty—even when she is—"

"Tall and graceful, and serenely beautiful as any goddess of ancient Greece?"

Astounded, she felt her cheeks grow hot, and stammered in confusion, "The goddess of fishwives, perhaps?"

"Touché!" But the reminder caused him to marvel that he had not seen her beauty in the first moment they met. Or that even in that dirty old mob-cap and apron he'd not realized at once that she was a lady of quality. She was watching him curiously, and he shrugged and admitted wryly, "I was wishing I hadn't said that."

"I wonder if you wish it as deeply as I wish I had not—attacked you."

He froze, and became perfectly white.

Susan had lowered her eyes, and not seeing his reaction, went on. "Though you never did return my poor mob-cap."

220

With comprehension came a deep sense of guilt. Montclair leaned back and stifling a sigh of relief, lied, "I cannot think what became of it."

She smiled to herself. "I noticed how thoughtful you looked when the Runners left. Was that what you were worrying about, Mr. Montclair?"

"No. Actually, I was thinking that it would be nice if you would call me by my name. After all, we are old friends now. Aren't we?"

Her heart gave a little leap. The gentleman was indeed much better! She said pensively, "Are we? Or is this just a temporary truce?"

"It will be far from temporary if I have my way."

Their eyes met and held. It was all Susan could do to remind herself that he was betrothed to Miss Trent and had no business talking to her like this. Even more flustered, she said, "I have been meaning to ask you . . . I wondered if you have thought— I mean, despite what you told the Runners, do you know who—who tried to—"

"To murder me?"

She gasped. "How *awful* that sounds!"

"Doesn't it," he agreed, his mouth grim again. "No, ma'am. I know I am not universally loved, but . . . I'd not realized I was hated."

"It may not be a matter of hatred, Mr.—" His eyes shot to her. She finished with a dimple, "Mr. Valentine. I read a tale once about just such an attack, and the hero asked the victim's wife who would most benefit by the murder."

Montclair said wryly, "Very few people would benefit in my case, ma'am. I have some fine horses, a few prized belongings, an inheritance that could be described as comfortable. And—" He paused.

And what? This *house*? She felt wretched, and rushed

on. "But—but you are your brother's heir—no? If something should befall you . . ."

"The gentlemen from Bow Street had the same notion, Mrs. Henley. But my brother is hale and hearty, and so much the Corinthian with his racing and fisticuffs and all manner of sporting endeavours that he will likely outlive me by ten years at least. Further, he's an exceeding well-favoured man and will likely marry and set up his nursery very soon—if he's not already done so. None of which in the least offends me, for I've not the smallest desire to inherit either the title or estates." He smiled faintly. "Too many responsibilities, and I've other—interests. The next in line after me is my father's younger brother, Hampton. My aunt calls him 'Poor Hampton' because he was so unfortunate as to be severely injured in a riding accident when only eighteen, and although he is the best of good fellows, has never since enjoyed the full possession of his wits."

"How very sad. But after your Uncle Hampton—then. . . ?"

"Then Junius, as my aunt's only son. But—that seems too long a wait, no? And waiting is such a horrid pastime. For instance—I thought you would never come back, Mrs. Sue."

He had lowered his voice when he spoke her name and said it in such a way that it again became necessary for her to duck her head to hide her blushes. And what utter silliness! The wicked man was flirting with her even as he awaited the visit of his betrothed! A fine respect he held for the Widow Henley! She recovered her aplomb and said coolly, "It is nice to be missed. I fancy you must be anxious to see Miss Trent."

He did not look in the least set down, as she had intended, but said with a slight frown, "Yes. Starry told me that Barbara had not called."

"Starry?" Amused, she said, "Now what is this im-

222

propriety, sir? If you've formed a *tendre* for my dear companion, I must warn you that the Bo'sun also has eyes in that direction."

Montclair grinned broadly. "No, has he? What a nice couple they would make. She is a little darling of a lady. And with hands nigh as gentle as . . ."—he gazed up at her—"as your own . . ."

Heavens, but it was a persistent flirt! Susan had to cling hard to common sense. "Perhaps, since Dr. Sheswell says you may be up a little, we can have you in the chair when Miss Trent comes. You will like that."

"I will like to see her, certainly. I am greatly worried about her, you see. She is so terribly alone."

Susan rose, picked up the almost empty water pitcher, and trying not to so dislike Miss Trent, murmured, "What—in the bosom of her family? And now safely betrothed? I would have thought—"

He gave a gasp, and his emaciated hand clamped onto her wrist. He said sharply, "What do you mean? Betrothed? They've never *announced* it?"

How aghast he looked. Had he hoped to keep the betrothal a secret? She removed his clasp, then wandered over to look down at the river again, and *The Dainty Dancer* low in the water, with Andy, Señor Angelo, and the Bo'sun busily unloading Monsieur Monteil's goods, despite the drizzling rain. "Señor Angelo went over to Longhills to see you," she explained. "But you were— well, it was the morning after you were attacked. He had a—a little chat with Miss Trent."

"And she told him she was betrothed? My God!"

One must not be harsh with an invalid, but it was all Susan could do to keep the contempt out of her voice. "You do not seem overjoyed by the announcement, sir."

"Gad, but I'm not," he groaned. "I told her to say no! I might have known she'd not have the courage! Poor little goose."

Susan blinked and wandered back to his side. There could be little doubt but that he was deeply fond of Miss Trent. He desired her, but not as his wife, perhaps. Disgraceful. Yet—the lady did not seem to yearn for wedded bliss either. What a lumpy gravy it was, to be sure! Could it be that Mr. Montclair had been *forced* to make an offer? Curious, she said, "Surely, if you objected to the match, it was *your* responsibility to speak to her parents to that effect?"

"I did speak to them. Much good it did. I offered to run away with her, and had I been there I might have persuaded her . . ."

"Run—*away* with her. . . ?" gasped Susan. "But—but where could you have taken her?"

"To the home of a friend in London."

Fascinated by the outrageous schemes of this gentlemanly-seeming young rake, she asked, "And—would your friend have let you stay?"

Montclair's eyelids were getting heavy. "Oh, yes," he murmured. "She is very understanding."

Her own eyes very round, Susan whispered, "Indeed she must be!"

Montclair had drifted into slumber. She stared at the quiet face for a moment, then went over to close the window curtains before she tiptoed out.

At the foot of the stairs, she encountered Deemer who welcomed her warmly. "Such a sad disappointment for the young gentleman, that his lady did not come," he murmured. "How is he taking it, ma'am?"

"Most—remarkably," said Susan dryly.

After Montclair had breakfasted and been shaved next morning, he sat on the edge of the bed for a few minutes, as had become the daily ritual. Then the great experiment with the crutches began. Dodman watched while the invalid struggled manfully, but it was clear the crutches were not as easily used as one would have thought. When Montclair wavered and almost fell, the Bo'sun ran to steady him and lower him onto the chaise longue by the window. "You did very well, sir," he said with his bright grin. "I reckon it'll take a little time to get the mastery of 'em."

Panting but impatient, Montclair said, "Then let's try again."

"This afternoon perhaps, Mr. Valentine. But for now, you'd better rest for a little while."

Montclair's fuming protests were ignored. The Bo'sun covered his legs with a blanket, laughed at his indignation, and left him.

Scowling across the gardens towards Longhills Manor, Montclair wondered when Babs would come. He brightened when he saw Mrs. Henley walk in the direction of the stables, an umbrella over her head, and her cream gown rippling in the wind. How gracefully she moved, and the silk of her hair blew so softly and seemed the very essence of femininity. That he could ever have thought it anything less than exquisite was— He frowned and sat up straighter. Two men had come to meet the lady and now stood talking with her. Two of the most down-at-heel, disreputable-looking individuals he ever had laid eyes on. Their hats sagged over bearded faces, they both stood in dire need of a barber, and their garments—if they could be called such—were dirty and tattered. Mrs. Sue could have nothing to say to such vagrants and would send them packing quickly. But minutes passed and they did not seem to be leaving.

Barking shrilly, Wolfgang ran up, then began to prance around the strangers. One of them reached down to stroke him. Currying favour, thought Montclair angrily. A fine brother Lyddford was! Why the deuce did the clod not protect his sister from such unwholesome intruders?

The Trents had promised that their daughter would visit Montclair this morning, but when by one o'clock she had not appeared, Susan climbed the stairs to the bedchamber. With one hand on the door, she paused. Why she should care whether the wretched girl came, escaped her. They were the strangest pair of lovers she ever had seen, preferring to run away in disgrace than to wed, and yet apparently devoted! One could only think they deserved each other. Unconvinced and decidedly downcast, she opened the door softly, uttered a faint shocked cry, and ran inside.

Montclair, struggling frantically with the crutches, all but fell into her arms, and she fought to keep her balance as she guided him back to the windowseat.

"Of all the . . . idiotish. . . !" she panted, as he hopped, clinging to her. "Will you be so good as to sit down?"

"I was going to try and come to you." He laughed breathlessly. "But only think how . . . clever I am . . . Have I not managed to—lure you into my arms. . . ?"

She was indeed in his arms. His thin pale face was smiling down at her; he was holding her very close. Gazing up at him, she saw the smile fade from the dark eyes. An intent look succeeded it. The amber flecks were suddenly and devastatingly ablaze. His left hand might be thin but it was like a vise on her arm.

'La, but I am a prize fool!' she thought, and terrified, wrenched away so determinedly that he staggered, half collapsed onto the windowseat, and uttered a small gasp.

"Well, I am very sorry if you have hurt yourself," she said tremblingly. "But the fact that we allow you to stay here, sir, does not—does not give you the right to—to maul me!"

Maul her! Was that how she thought of him? "Thank you," he said, his voice glacial. "One supposes Imre Monteil does not rate such a set-down!"

Susan caught her breath and stood very straight. "I think that is not your concern, sir," she said, and walked quickly to the door.

"Think again, Susan!"

She halted and glanced over her shoulder.

Grim-faced, he was struggling with the crutches. Hesitating, she said, "You have done enough today, surely."

In a swift change of mood, his wry half-smile flickered. "Yes, but if I fall, there is always the chance you may rescue me again."

"Surely, the reward would scarce justify the cost, sir."

"Most assuredly—it *would,* ma'am."

She regarded him steadily, wondering why she was so weak-kneed that she could not resist that tentative smile.

His good hand was stretched out imploringly. "Forgive. Please. I had no right to say that about Monteil."

In some magical fashion she floated back to sit beside him. "He has been very kind in finding work for my brother," she explained. "The income means a great deal to us. Now why do you scowl so?"

"I was thinking that I am an additional charge on you. I hope that my uncle has—"

"He has, so do not fret on that account."

His hand found hers. He asked softly, "About what *may* I fret, ma'am?"

Staring down at their clasped hands, she felt dreamily content, and answering a foolish question as foolishly, murmured, "I don't really know. But—you said you were coming to seek me."

"So I was! And it is a decidedly fretful matter! Whatever is Lyddford about, to allow you to be accosted by every passing ruffian?"

227

She knew she should free her hand. While thinking about it, she blinked at him and said, "Whatever do you mean?"

"I saw you talking to two gooseberry bushes on the drivepath. It made me positively uneasy to see you bothered by such unsavoury creatures."

Laughing, she recovered her wits, drew away, and said, "Oh, you must mean my two new workmen."

"Good God! You were never bamboozled into hiring those two rogues?"

"Those two *rogues,* sir, are veterans wounded on the Peninsula while fighting for their country."

It was a sore point with Montclair that he had been unable to join up. He said irritably, "And I suppose they gulled you into believing they are starving and unable to find work."

"I am not easily gulled," she said, a frown coming into her eyes. "And if you doubt there are such men, sir, you should have a closer look at those who tramp the roads these days."

He well knew the bitter fate of many soldiers and sailors who had fought gallantly for England and returned to face rejection and starvation, but he argued contrarily, "Even so, there have been many kind souls robbed and murdered by ex-servicemen. If Lyddford needs more men, he should have the sense to appoint Deemer to handle the matter, not expect a woman to know how to deal with such fellows."

Bristling, she retorted, "I have been obliged to deal with the world for some years, Mr. Montclair, and am quite a good judge of character, I promise you!"

"You certainly summed me up fast enough," he countered with a grin.

She chuckled, and somehow he was holding her hand again. He said softly, "Perhaps it *is* a good idea to have some more men about, so long as they're reliable. I cannot like you being left so short-staffed here when Lydd-ford is away on his boat. If any unsavoury varmints should come prowling—" A troubled look came into her eyes. His own narrowed. He demanded, "What is it? Have there been such occurrences?"

She hesitated, then told him of the man who'd been watching the house in the middle of the night. "I'll own," she admitted, "I was quite frightened. You may be sure we lock the doors now."

"Good God," he muttered. "I'd best leave here as soon as maybe."

"Why? You cannot know that he was here because of you."

"I'll warrant you did not have such spies hanging about before I came."

"Did you have them at Longhills?"

"We've a small army of servants there to make short work of any intruders." He brightened. "There's the an-swer, by Jove! I'll send for some of my people. You need inside help as well, with all the extra work I bring you. Only look at these poor fingernails."

Susan snatched her hand away, and well aware of what Andy would have to say to all this, said, "I enjoy working in—in the garden. And we will require no more help, thank you just the—"

"Fustian! Do you say you would prefer to have those two grimy vagrants loitering about the place rather than allow me to bring my well-trained servants here? Now that is plainly ridiculous!"

She stiffened. "I must ask that you abide by my deci-sion, Mr. Montclair."

"It is a foolish decision, and I most certainly will not be bound by it! You shall have extra help, madam, so pray put your pride in your pocket."

Unaccustomed to such high-handed intervention, and knowing she must put a stop to this at once, her chin tossed upward. "You do not rule here, sir! And since you find me ridiculous, foolish, and prideful—"

"Er, well—I didn't mean that exactly, but—"

"—you will doubtless prefer to make arrangements to be taken from such an unpleasant atmosphere, as—soon as may be." And with her head high, her hair swinging behind her, and her heart heavy, she left him.

"Women!" snorted Montclair.

Susan gazed blankly at the book, not seeing the little house and the elves climbing cheerfully in and out of the many windows. Outwardly, she was calm. Inwardly, she trembled still. Never with Burke had she felt that wild surge of excited anticipation. Never had Burke's touch made her skin shiver; never had that glow come into his eyes that made her heart feel scorched so that she longed to be hugged closer . . . to be kissed and caressed.

A tremor raced through her. She could deny it and hide it from others, but she could no longer deny it to herself. She was falling in love with a man who could only bring her heartache. Of all the men she'd known she had been so foolish as to single out Mr. Valentine Amberly Montclair, who was hopelessly far above her socially, and far too proud to marry beneath his own rank. A man who had at first been overwhelmed by gratitude, but who was fast recovering his quick-tempered arrogance as well as his health, and had now very obviously decided to amuse himself by flirting carelessly with the notorious widow while awaiting the arrival of his highly born love. If she did not overcome this weakness it would surely destroy her every happiness. Montclair *must* leave! One word breathed to Andy, and he would be gone, and she would be safe. Yes, that was her only hope. She would speak to her dear brother. Soon. But—not today.

She thought wistfully of how gallantly Valentine had borne his suffering. How seldom he had complained, or asked the smallest consideration. How inexpressibly dear had been the light in his dark eyes just now, the tenderness in the deep voice . . . Tenderness from a man who had wanted to run away with poor deceived Miss Trent.

Priscilla said plaintively, "Hasn't you done lookin' at them yet, Mama? You been lookin' an' lookin' and you get drearier an' drearier, an'—"

"Oh!" gasped Susan, returning to the warm and fragrant kitchen, and her patient little daughter sitting beside her at the immaculately scrubbed table. "I am so sorry, darling. Mama was sleepy, I expect."

"You din't look sleepy, Mama. You looked drearier an'—"

"Yes." Avoiding Mrs. Starr's sharp eyes, Susan said hurriedly, "Er, well. Where was I? Oh—this is the tale of five small elves . . ."

12

With typical inconsistency the weather reversed itself. Sunday morning dawned fair and bright, the sun beaming down upon the drenched meadows, flooding Highperch Cottage with radiance, and turning the river into a diamond highway.

Montclair awoke refreshed from a good night's sleep, cheered by the feeling of reviving strength, but in a black humour. Deemer came to tend to his needs and shave him. The mild little man was agreeable but, as usual, uncommunicative. Montclair thanked him profusely for his kindness, and Deemer left, murmuring shyly that he was only too glad to help anyone in trouble. "Always provided," he added with a sudden sharp look, "that they don't bring trouble down upon those I care about."

Montclair smiled, and said nothing, but he was irked. He'd gone out of his way to express his gratitude, and the fellow had turned on him. If these people didn't have enough gall for an army! Here they were living in his house illegally, and they had the confounded brass to set him down when he'd done nothing. Only look at the widow, sulkily avoiding him yesterday and again today, having chosen to behave as if he'd attempted to rape her, rather than simply just holding her for a minute . . . Her hair *had* felt like cool silk, now that he came to think of it . . . And her skin was so clear and fair . . . And very likely she was Imre Monteil's fancy piece. He scowled. The sooner he was back at Longhills, the better. At least, he knew where he stood there.

He reached for the crutches. It was difficult to fasten the strap about his right arm, but he struggled stubbornly, and at last was hobbling about. Twice he almost fell, and after half an hour he was not only worn out, but both his head and his leg were aching fiercely. Still, he lowered himself awkwardly onto the chaise longue before the windows with an exclamation of triumph. He had managed alone. He had got himself across the room and back, having had to bother no one!

Exultant, he leaned back, catching his breath. The breeze blew the curtains inwards, and brought with it the fragrance of blossoms. A swift flashed across the open windows and a blackbird was singing a glorious Sunday hymn. Montclair's ears perked up to those liquid notes. He wondered who played the organ in church on Sundays these days. For the past ten years, since he'd turned seventeen, it had been his pleasure to perform that small duty whenever he was in Gloucestershire. He looked down at the splinted and bandaged right hand, wondering if he would ever again be able to play competently. Once more he tried to move the fingers, but they were stiff and useless. Surely, after all these weeks—

"It's not p'lite to pay no 'tention to a lady when she comes calling," announced a prim little voice.

Priscilla stood at the foot of the chaise longue. She had come straight from church and wore her Sunday best. Her dress, of mid-calf length, was a primrose

233

yellow muslin with a yellow satin sash and three frills at the hem, and under it she wore ankle-length cambric pantalettes trimmed with lace. Her poke bonnet was tied under her chin with a broad yellow ribbon, and on her hands were dainty white mittens. At least they had once been white, but were now rather soiled, probably because of the very large bouquet of spring flowers she carried.

"Especially, such a very pretty lady," said Montclair with a smile.

She looked at him doubtfully. "Am I pretty? Even with my specs?"

"You are indeed pretty. And your dress, Lady Priscilla, is charming."

"Thank you, Mr. Val'tine. Would you like to know 'bout my dress? Mama made it. An' she sewed my bonnet, too." She edged closer and stuck out one leg. "These," she whispered confidingly, "are called pan'lets!"

"They're very dainty," he whispered in turn. "Did you pick the flowers?"

"Yes." She thrust them at him, then dumped them in his lap. "For you. Mama says you want cheering up 'cause your lady din't come." She sat on the edge of the chaise longue, and Montclair thanked her for the flowers and moved aside to allow more room.

"Why din't she come?" asked Priscilla, watching him gravely. "Doesn't she love you?"

"Certainly she loves me," he answered. "All the ladies love me. I am so very dashing you know. Especially just at the moment."

Priscilla stared at the white, haggard face, then burst into laughter. "You look awful, sir," she told him, with the unaffected candour of childhood. "But when you're well, you're nice to look at. Are you going to pick Miss Trent for your wife?"

He chuckled. "She will be a lovely wife for some lucky gentleman. But I think she doesn't want me for a husband."

"Good. Then I'd like to know, please, what your lady likes are."

"Do you mean," he asked experimentally, "which ladies I particularly like?"

She pursed her lips. "That might do, but if I don't know them it won't help much. I mean—d'you like fair ladies or dark ladies? An' must they be fat or thin? And are you in a great big hurry to get yourself marriaged, or d'you think you could wait a bit? Like ten years, or 'bout. And—'sides all that," she added with sudden anxiety, "if it would fill you up with 'gust to marriage a lady with specs."

Touched, Montclair took up her hand and kissed the grubby mitten gently. "Do you say you want to marry me, Lady Priscilla?"

She sighed and burst his bubble. "Not really. To marriage is silly and only for old people. But I'll sac'fice myself for Mama, if it will help her to stop crying in the night." She added kindly, "But I *do* like you, Mr. Val'tine, and I speshly like your eyes, and the way your mouth sort of nearly but not quite smiles sometimes."

"Why don't you just call me Mr. Val," he suggested. "And perhaps, if I knew why your Mama was crying, I might be able to help without your having to—er, sacrifice yourself. Is it, do you suppose, something to do with your Uncle Andrew?"

Priscilla shook her head, setting her bonnet sliding. "It's the same old thing," she said lugubriously. "Money. You *have* got lots of money, haven't you, Mr. Val?"

"I'm afraid not."

She looked aghast. "But—you live in that great big house! And Uncle Andy says your coat's from a wizard, and it must cost lots 'n lots to buy a wizard's coats!"

"Well, you see the house belongs to my brother," he explained apologetically. "I just live there. Er, how much money do you need?"

"Oh, tubs an' tubs! A hundred guineas, at least, I 'spect. So Mama can pay the bills and paint the house and have the roof mended. It leaks in Uncle Andy's bedchamber you know, and makes him shout bad words in the middle of the night." She added in a reproachful voice, "I never would've thought you'd be a big dis'pointment, Mr. Val, but you are. A hugeous one."

"I'm very sorry, my dear. But—perhaps by the time you're old enough to get married I might be able to find a hundred guineas. Would that serve?"

The small shoulders shrugged. "No, I'm 'fraid. I need it now. People make promises 'bout marriaging sometimes, years 'fore they really do, and I was hoping you and me could make that kind of thing, and then I could have the money. But—I s'pose I'll have to find somebody else."

He gave one glossy curl a gentle tug. "I wish you wouldn't, Lady Priscilla. Can't you possibly wait for me?"

She looked glum. "I'll try, Mr. Val. But Mama said only yestiday that things was getting des'prit, and if it keeps on like that, I'll just *have* to sac'fice to somebody else!"

It was with decidedly mixed feelings that Susan shook hands with Miss Barbara Trent at eleven o'clock the next morning, and ushered her into the sunlit withdrawing room. With uncharacteristic malice she had been prepared to dislike the affianced bride and find in her not one single redeeming feature. Confronted by a pale, troubled little creature with a soft, shy voice, and the expression of a frightened doe, Susan experienced a contrary and irritating urge to hug her.

"I know how anxious you must be," she said kindly. "But pray do not be in a pucker. Mr. Montclair is much better. I wish you could go up at once, but Dr. Sheswell is with him at the moment, so instead I shall offer you a cup of tea." She glanced in sudden apprehension to the door. "Is your mama come with you, ma'am?"

Lady Trent having announced resoundingly that she would sooner be seen dead in a ditch than to again be under the same roof with "that shameless hussy," Barbara had escaped that fate. "Mama was unable to come. I brought my personal footman, of course, and your—er, I think it was your housekeeper—took him to the kitchen."

Susan stifled a sigh of relief. "May I tempt you to a cup of tea, Miss Trent? I realize it must be distasteful to you to be here, but—"

Barbara blinked at her. "Because your husband shot himself?"

Susan's jaw dropped a little.

"I can see that must have been very sad for you," said Barbara. "But I do not perceive why you should be held in contempt because of it. Unless you drove him to it. And you do not at all look like a harpy, or—" She stopped, one hand pressed to her mouth, and said in horror, "Oh! I *do* beg your pardon!

Susan laughed helplessly.

Barbara stared at her and thought she had never seen a lady who was more fascinatingly beautiful. And that silvery trill of laughter . . . How long had it been since she laughed. . . ? "It is—is just," she stammered, "that I have been so very—distraught of late. And—and so worried about Valentine. I fear my poor mind . . ." She lifted a hand to her brow in distracted fashion.

"No, please," said Susan. "Such candour is refreshing.

237

I assure you I did not drive my poor husband to his death. At least, I hope I did not." She busied herself with the teapot and handed her guest a full cup complete with sugar and milk as requested. "And of course you have been distracted. I wonder you did not fall into a decline. So newly betrothed and to have Mr. Montclair almost killed on the selfsame day!"

"Yes," said Barbara, beginning to forget her nervousness under the spell of such warm kindliness. "It was frightful. Papa and Mama have told me he is past the crisis now, of course, but one cannot help but worry, and—they would not let me come."

'Because of the notorious widow and this house of infamy,' thought Susan, irritated. "Well, I'm glad you have come now."

"Thank you. My abigail told me Valentine almost died, and—and that you saved his life. How brave you must be."

"No, no. I was merely the one who chanced to find him."

Barbara said quaveringly, "I believe his head was broken. Is—is his mind. . . ?"

"Good gracious—no! He suffered a bad concussion, and when he was thrown into the Folly his leg and some bones in his right hand were broken."

"Oh! Poor Val! He must be frantic! He is a musician, you know."

She looked as if she was about to cry, and Susan pointed out hurriedly that it could have been much worse. "Fortunately he did not suffer any major injuries or compound fractures. The breaks are clean and our Bo'sun says will heal nicely. The gentleman has had a very bad few weeks, I own, and it will likely be a little while yet before he is well again. But his mind is not affected, I promise you!" She was astounded that the poor little creature had known none of this, and im-

238

pulsively patting her hand, said, "Oh, my dear, how dreadful that you have worried so!"

Sympathy, so generously offered, was a rare commodity in Barbara's life, and in her present frame of mind, was devastating. The tears overflowed. Susan spread her arms, and with a choking sob Barbara collapsed into them. She wept unrestrainedly; great racking sobs accompanied such floods of tears that Susan's shoulder was soon drenched. Scarcely the reaction of a girl Angelo had thought would be a reluctant bride. Which was not too surprising—Angelo so often got everything wrong. She held the girl close and spoke softly, and felt wretched, until at last the storm eased.

Barbara reached shamefacedly for her reticule and was surprised to find Welcome in it. That made her smile, and finding a tiny handkerchief she dabbed at her red and swollen eyes while expressing her shaky apologies for such deplorable conduct.

"Never mind about that," said Susan in her serenely matter-of-fact way. "I will not offer my friendship, for I know that I am not quite respectable, whereas you are very respectable indeed, but—"

"Oh," gasped Barbara, clinging to her hand and looking up into her face in a pathetic pleading. "How *very* much I would like to have you for a friend . . . I have none, you see. I hoped to make some when it was decided I should be sent to a young ladies' seminary. But Mama investigated, and found that the teachers were of questionable morals and if The Twig is Bent by Faulted Hands, One Grows a Faulted Tree."

"But—surely you must have *some* friends. Have you no sisters?"

"No. Only Junius. And he—" She closed her lips and gazed miserably at her sodden handkerchief. "I did have a friend once. Our neighbours in Surrey have three daughters; two are married and much older than me, but the youngest is crippled and the dearest thing, with the sunniest disposition, despite her affliction. We used to meet secretly in the spinney that divides our estates, but Mama's dresser (a most disagreeable woman!) caught us, and told Mama, and I was not allowed to meet Hannah again. Papa said that if the Lord had seen fit to visit an infirmity upon her there must be evil in the family, and that I was not to associate with such people."

"Good . . . heavens . . ." breathed Susan. "I fancy Sir Selby would judge that my daughter's poor eyesight is a Divine punishment because of my own sins!"

"Yes, and because of the bad blood she inherited from her father."

"What?"

Barbara jumped at that ringing exclamation, and quavered a terrified apology.

Susan took a breath. "It is I who should apologize," she said, her blazing eyes making that statement of questionable veracity. "I found it difficult to believe that anyone could say such things of a sweet innocent. But— I should not speak so of your parents."

"No. You shouldn't. Nor should I. But then—I'm doomed to hellfire at all events." The sensitive lips quivered and another wayward tear crept down the pale cheek.

"Oh my! What horrid sins have you committed?"

Barbara's eyelashes lowered. She said painfully, "I am f-fat. And—and ugly."

Stunned, Susan gazed at her. Small wonder she was so crushed and colourless. Indignation deepened the flush in her cheeks. Before she could stop herself, she said tartly, "Dear me. And even if that were true, which I assure you it is not, from whom do you suppose your evil tendencies were inherited?"

Barbara peeped up at her. Slowly, a gleam brightened

the reddened eyes. "Ooooh!" she whispered. "I never thought of that!" She giggled, and then they laughed merrily together.

"You will think me evil indeed," sighed Barbara.

"I think we are both being rather naughty. But it was worth it to see you smile. You seemed so very unhappy at a time in your life when most girls are full of joyous plans."

All the animation that had so brightened Barbara's face faded away. "How can I be joyful when I am forced into a marriage I do not want?"

Bewildered, Susan said, "But—I thought you were fond of your betrothed. And he is"—she forced herself to be objective—"wealthy, and—and a fine-looking young man."

Barbara stared at her curiously. "Do you find him so? Mrs. Henley—could *you* be joyful were you to marry such a man?"

It was a home question. Susan's cheeks blazed. "W-well, I— That is—"

"Of course you could not," said Barbara bitterly. "Not if you know of his reputation! But it is too late now. I am betrothed! And only because I am so weak. Such a spineless creature! But what hope have I? My first and only Season was a disaster. Mama says I am most fortunate that such an eligible young man should offer for me."

Searching for something diplomatic to say, Susan pointed out, "Your betrothed evidently does not find you plain and fat."

"Truly, I cannot understand why he wants to marry me." Barbara heaved a deep sigh. "But Val says he supposes that I will be a conformable wife and not interfere with—with his . . . little—*affaires*."

'The villain!' thought Susan, outraged.

Dr. Sheswell came booming along the hall then, and

241

Susan excused herself and went to meet him. He was hugely jovial, and told her that Montclair was making great strides. "A *leetle* concerned by the colour, y'know. And the pulse. But the silly fellow has likely been over-tiring himself with the crutches, and fretting to know who wants to provide him a sod blanket." He fixed her with a suddenly hard stare. "Sufficient to give any man pause, ma'am, ain't it?"

Susan managed to hide her vexation. If this pompous bore fancied there was a conspiracy afoot at Highperch Cottage to rid the world of Valentine Montclair, he was welcome to indulge such nonsense. One might have thought the invalid's improved state of health would have told him otherwise, but Sheswell impressed her as a singularly foolish man who saw no farther than the end of his nose. "Well, Mr. Montclair can rid his mind of such depressing worries for the moment," she said with a forced smile. "As you see, Miss Trent has arrived. He has been extreme anxious to see her."

A grunt was his only reaction to that, and he expressed a wish to consult with Mr. Dodman. The Bo'sun was in the stables with Lyddford, and Susan was far from willing to allow the physician to wander unescorted about the grounds. She considered ringing for Deemer or Martha Reedham, but their sometime butler was busied in the cellar, and Mrs. Starr and Martha were hard at work on the week's washing. She hesitated only momentarily before begging Miss Trent to excuse her for a moment while she showed the doctor the way. The dispassionate lovers had waited this long, another minute or two wouldn't be disastrous surely.

Left alone in the withdrawing room, Barbara glanced around curiously. Val had only brought her here once, but she remembered how shocked she had been by the dreariness of the old house, and horrified to think he would wish to live in such a dowdy place. Hers was not an imaginative mind, and she had been quite unable to picture Highperch thoroughly cleaned, curtains washed, windows sparkling, the furniture taken out of holland covers and polished until the fine old woods gleamed.

Her attention fixed on the painting that hung above the mantel. Lacking so many of the accomplishments her mama had hoped she would acquire, Barbara had a genuine flair for art. She was very shy about her gift, and kept her sketches hidden, dreading lest they be mocked, but she knew enough of the subject to recognize excellence, and was so impelled by interest as to leave the sofa and wander over to the fireplace.

Gazing up at the painting, she murmured admiringly, "Oh, my goodness."

"Theses truth mostly," came a sighful voice behind her. "Goodness. Chess!"

She spun around, and a becoming blush brightened her sad face. "Señor de Ferdinand! How do you do?"

Rushing to take her outstretched hand and hold it with the greatest reverence, he said fiercely, "Miceselves whats you wishes will do. Mostly beautiful lady saying herses-elves 'mire theses. Angelo, he give. Here's and now!" He reached up and began to struggle to remove the picture from the wall.

"No, no!" cried Barbara. "Oh, pray do not! Truly, you are very good, but it belongs to Mrs. Henley, and—"

"Chew like. Chew *havings!*" he declared, by now having succeeded in tipping the picture so that it hung sideways.

"No—really! Oh dear, let me help . . ."

She hurried to stand beside him, but being not even as tall as he, could reach no higher, and the painting, large, heavy, and now considerably out of balance, defied their efforts. The ormolu clock, jolted by de Ferdinand's elbow, fell with a crash into the hearth.

With a dismayed cry Barbara stepped back. "Oh, no!" she wailed. "Whatever will they think of me?"

"Of *chew*?" cried the Spaniard, his dark eyes flashing. "Of chew thinkings they theses lady was beautiful mostly of anys other! Not moment one chew must griefed being! Angelo—mices-elves—he picture buyings!"

That Barbara understood this mangled speech was evident. Her lashes fell, her bosom began to rise and fall in agitation, but the shy smile that curved her mouth so wrought upon the Spaniard that he was emboldened to again seize her hand and press it to his lips.

"Oh, you m-must not," she said, trying without much force to free herself.

"Chew sayings chew not marryings wish," persisted de Ferdinand. "Chaw minds changes its elves?"

"No." She raised suddenly tragic eyes to his ardent ones. "But—it is done now. I am betrothed, do you see?"

He stepped closer. "Lovely lady chew Angelo listen chaw nice ears with! Chew no wish marryings with theses mens, then Angelo—mices-elves—he marryings stopping!"

Awed, she whispered, "You will stop the marriage? Oh, if only you could! But—alas, it is too late."

Even as he began an impassioned denial, she heard quick light footsteps approaching. At once she ran back to the sofa. De Ferdinand sprinted after her. Barbara halted abruptly as a thought occurred. Swinging around she was startled to find the Spaniard coming at her with all speed. They collided violently and fell onto the sofa. Not normally quick-witted, but inspired by desperation, Barbara hissed into his nose, "Tonight at ten, by the summer house!"

Hurrying into the withdrawing room, the apology on Susan's lips died. She received the incredible impression that the man her brother sometimes fondly referred to

244

as "the little Spanish gamecock" had attacked Miss Trent, and that the girl she'd thought to be shy had just bitten him on the nostril. Feeling decidedly out of her depth, she blinked from Miss Trent's pink countenance to de Ferdinand's now upright and rigidly defiant stance.

"I w-was . . . faint," said Barbara. "And—and Señor Angelo, er—helped me."

"Oh." Vastly titillated, Susan added an equally non-sensical "I *am* glad." Her gaze encompassing the painting, which now appeared to stand on one corner, and the shattered clock on the hearth, she asked an astonished "Whatever happened?"

"Mices-elves wishing to theses buyings for mostly beauti—" began Angelo.

"I-I was admiring the painting," interjected Barbara desperately. "I fear I must have disturbed the wire. We—er, tried to straighten it again, and the clock fell. Truly, I am very sorry."

"It was an ugly old clock," Susan declared with commendable grace. "The painting is rather pretty, isn't it? Would you wish to come upstairs now, Miss Trent?"

She led Barbara up the stairs, mulling over how becomingly the girl's cheeks had glowed, and how bright had been the formerly lacklustre blue eyes. And Angelo Francisco Luis Lagunes de Ferdinand had brought it all about. 'Well now, Mr. Rake Montclair,' she thought, 'you had best look to your laurels, or your betrothed may run away with the 'little Spanish gamecock'!

The afternoon breeze was freshening, setting the leaves of the old oak tree to flutter whisperingly, and ruffling Montclair's dark hair. He moved slightly on the chaise longue they had carried into the back garden,

245

and Susan looked up quickly from her mending to see if he was uncomfortable. Dispensing with protocol in these trying circumstances, he wore only a shirt and pantaloons, the left leg slit to the knee to accommodate the splints. He was still too thin, but the slight pucker between his dark brows that always betrayed one of the violent headaches he still occasionally suffered, was not apparent today. In fact, aside from the arm that was carried in a sling and the splinted leg, he looked almost well again.

A week had passed since Miss Trent's visit. It had been a productive week. *The Dainty Dancer*'s cargo was all safely stowed in the cellar, and for two days Andy and the Bo'sun had been busily mending sails. This morning Andy and Señor Angelo had taken the barge to the boatyard near Avonmouth for some much needed work on the tiller.

By mutual if unspoken consent, neither Susan nor Montclair had referred again to the possibility of his returning home. Nor had Dr. Sheswell or the Trents put in another appearance, and although Susan was well aware that this could only be a respite, she was grateful for the present peace.

She became aware that a pair of dark eyes watched her, and averted her own hurriedly.

"Must you always work?" drawled Montclair lazily. "I think I never see you but you are busied at some task. Yet you fly up into the boughs do I dare offer to bring only two of my servants here to help you."

"I like to be busy, sir," she argued. "And besides, I expect your maids have too many tasks already."

He smiled. "More probably it would be the first time they really earned their pay. We have dozens of 'em loitering about Longhills, doing very little."

"A typical male observation," she said in amused chiding. "With a house as gigantic as yours, the poor

246

girls likely slave from dawn to dusk, polishing and dust-
ing and mopping and scrubbing, and—"

"And the butler standing over 'em with a heavy whip,
no doubt! Is that how you envision a maid's life at Longhills, ma'am?"

She laughed. "Not quite that grim, but I fancy your
aunt knows how to keep your servants well occupied."

"Well, that's truth, at all events." In spite of his light
tone the laughter had left his eyes as it always did when
his family was mentioned, and there was a hardening to
the pleasant line of his mouth. Susan folded the tablecloth she had repaired, lifted a yawning Welcome from
her sewing basket, and put the tablecloth in. During
these weeks of his illness she had come to know every
nuance of Montclair's voice, every expression of the very
expressive countenance, and through these last few
summer days they had chatted in an ever deepening
rapport and said much more than mere words. She had
struggled to convince herself that whatever his peculiar
relationship with Miss Trent, it was none of her affair.
She enjoyed him for his whimsical sense of humour and
his easy way of conversing with her. He never ignored
her remarks; he solicited and listened to her opinions—
and if he frequently argued with them he did so as one
would argue with an equal, not with the amused toler-
ance toward an inferior intellect that was so often
shown females by gentlemen. Indeed, in some ways she
felt as comfortable with him as though she'd known him
all her life. And in others— She snipped that thread of
thought and said quietly, "Mr. Valentine, you do not—
that is to say, there does not appear to be a great depth
of affection between you and the Trents."

"Your first impulse was correct, Mrs. Sue. I have no
love for them—save for Barbara, of course."

"Of course." A spark of resentment lit her eyes, but
she went on. "Was your mama excessive fond of them?"

"She scarce knew them. Lady Marcia was sister to my father. He could not abide the lady, and being a very forthright gentleman, told her so to her face during one of their less civilized quarrels. For years afterwards the two families were estranged."

"How dreadful. Were all communications at an end, then?"

"Yes." He said dryly, "It was an exceeding peaceful time." He saw her brows arch, and added, "You are wondering, I think, why my mother appointed Sir Selby as Geoff's Administrator? Her own brothers both had died young, and my papa's surviving younger brother suffered a bad accident many years ago, as I told you. Mama was ill, and she knew that Geoff—" He checked, frowning, then said with his half smile, "Well, he's one of those charming men who always manage to, er— He's a bit of a scamp, and, er—"

'A family trait,' she thought, but inserted shrewdly, "And expert at resting all his responsibilities on the shoulders of others."

Montclair said in a troubled way, "No, really he is the best of men, but—he simply cannot tolerate my uncle. Now that he is of an age to end the Trust and take control, I am sure he will return very soon."

"But meanwhile," she pursued, "your uncle, having been made Administrator, is able to follow his own course while your brother keeps out of the country?"

"Not where I can help it," he said with a sudden fierce scowl. "The deuce of it is, legally he does not really have to heed me. I think the only reason he bothers with me at all is for fear I might appeal to my great-uncle Chauncey. He was my mama's favourite uncle, and is a grand old fellow. He wields no real authority in this instance, sad to say, and lives mostly retired in Wales now, but he is still a power to be reckoned with, and my uncle Selby treads very softly around him." He smiled nostalgically. "You may know of him since your family was Navy also. Admiral Lord Sutton-Newark."

"Yes indeed. I have heard my grandfather mention that name, and with great respect. *Did* you ever appeal to him?"

"Lord, no," he answered indignantly. "A fine booberkin he would have thought me! Unable to deal with such a one as Selby Trent!"

"That is nonsensical! Your brother is older than you, and he could not deal with the man! And Sir Selby has all his retainers, his wife, and his son marshalled against you, and opposes your every wish. I should think—"

Curious, he interrupted. "How did you know all that?"

She hesitated, then said rather airily, "Oh, Señor Angelo is acquaint with Miss Trent, you know, and she—"

"Has babbled all my secrets, has she? Wretched chit!" He checked, then added with a sober look, "No, I must not say that. She is a darling, and heaven knows has much to distress her. I only pray we may deal well—"

"Mr. Val! Mr. Val!" Priscilla ran from the house, her skirts flying, her little face alight and well sprinkled with flour.

Montclair grinned, and shifted on the chaise, sitting up and reaching his good arm to her. "What makes those lovely eyes sparkle so, Lady Priscilla?"

She giggled ecstatically, and ran to be hugged. "I'm going to Tewkesb'y with Starry an' the Bo'sun to get my new specs, and Bo'sun George says he might buy me a ice. An' you know I is not a *real* lady."

"Bless my soul!" he said, smiling into the bright little face. "How you have deceived me! Now tell me what you've been up to with Starry that smells so delectable."

"Oh, we've been cooking. We din't have much time, 'cause Bo'sun George is waiting to drive us, so I must go and put on my bonnet and mittens quick. But I cooked

249

you a special biscuit for your dinner, Mr. Val. Wait till you see it! It's 'normous, and I poked hund'eds an' thousands of currants into it, 'cause I know you like currants."

"Indeed I do. I can scarce wait 'til dinner time. Faith, but I'm glad to know you're such a good cook. If you do decide to wait for me, and accept of my offer, I'll eat well!"

She squealed with delight, jumped up and down twice, bade them both a hurried farewell, then went racing back inside to get ready for the long-awaited journey to Tewkesbury.

Montclair leaned back, watching the flying little figure. "What a sweet child she is," he murmured, fondly.

"Yes," agreed Susan, watching him. "And what is all this about offers, sir?"

He chuckled, and turned his head lazily against the chaise to look at her. "Not quite what you might think, ma'am. I am honoured to inform you that your daughter is prepared to sacrifice herself on the altar of matrimony, and has selected me as a possible mate."

"Good—heavens!"

He sighed and said in tragic accents, "You do not approve! Alas. However, there is a stipulation, so do not worry yourself unduly. Mistress Priscilla considers marriage very silly, and only for old people."

Susan laughed a little uncertainly. "That is not exactly a stipulation, is it?"

"No, but her reluctance to enter such a state is balanced against her need for a rich gentleman, and I had to tell her I have neither title nor a great fortune." Susan tensed at this, a frown coming into her eyes, but far from being an expert in the ways of women, he did not see this danger signal, and blundered on. "She is very sensible, and says that she cannot marry anyone who has less than a hundred guineas."

"Oh." In a clipped voice Susan remarked, "Well, I fancy you told her you are betrothed, which put an end to that nonsense."

"Certainly not! Why should I? Now tell me, ma'am, seriously. You have instilled the proper values into her, I'll not deny. But what do you mean to do with her? She is exceptionally bright and should be educated, for—"

"For what?" she snapped, annoyed with him on more than one count. "The Marriage Mart? Hah! With our reputation to aid her, she'd not get one toe across the threshold!"

His smile faded. "I had not meant to imply that."

"Then what had you meant to imply? You must know that is all women are considered good for in these days. A girl must be educated, certainly. Up to a point. She should speak French and some Latin. She must know her Bible and be able to read the globes. She should sketch nicely, paint, and play the pianoforte tolerably well, and a good singing voice is an asset. And above all, she must be well bred up to know her place in the world, which, as you yourself remarked, is to be a conformable wife and turn a blind eye to her husband's little *affaires de coeur*!"

"The deuce!" growled Montclair angrily. "When did I ever make such a gauche remark?"

Barbara had said that of him, and her confidence must, of course, be respected. Susan evaded hurriedly. "I suppose you will deny that what I have said is truth. But the fact remains that Priscilla will have a vastly better chance of making a good match is she kind and stupid, for a clever woman is considered a threat and unfeminine!"

"Indeed?" he drawled with a curl of the lip. "So your plan for her future goes no further than finding her a wealthy husband! There *are* more important things than money, you know."

251

Stung by his scorn, and driven by hurt and the need to strike out at him, she snapped, "Easy said when you have plenty, but odd as it may seem, I've no ambition to see her marry into poverty and live in a garret."

She had stood as she spoke, and taken up her basket.

Struggling to rise also, Montclair reached for his crutch and responded irritably, "Not that, certainly. But this preoccupation with a good marriage—or in other words, a wealthy one—is—"

"Gauche, I suppose," she interrupted, glaring at him. "Then pray tell sir, what other course suggests itself to you?"

"Lord save us all, ma'am, the child has an excellent mind. Unlike most predatory females she might be content with an average man—even a man with no title and an honest occupation!"

Predatory females! "Oooh!" gasped Susan, infuriated. "Shall I tell you what *this* predatory female prays for, Mr. Montclair? Shall I?"

He bowed precariously, and said at his most cynical, "I am all ears, ma'am."

"Which are precious small of comprehension," she riposted. "I pray, sir, that the day may dawn when the height of a female's ambition is not merely to find a suitable mate!"

Quite as angry as she, he jeered, "Then what shall be the height of this legendary creature's ambition, Mrs. Henley? To enter a nunnery perhaps?"

"To have," she said through her teeth, "some interests of her own! To perhaps be permitted to voice an opinion and not hear it tolerantly sneered at! To be permitted to *hold* an opinion without being thus judged a bluestocking!"

He said hotly, "If ever I heard such stuff! I'll have you know, ma'am, that my mama was exceeding well read! Why, she probably read two or three books a—a day!

252

And discussed 'em with my father! And as to females holding opinions—good God! Have you never listened to my aunt? The woman holds sufficient opinions for a regular army of—"

"Mrs. Sue!" called Martha Reedham from the back step. "Company!"

"How very well timed," said Susan with quelling dignity. "Your pardon, sir."

"Oh—hell!" Valentine gave her his tentative grin. "Sue—please don't rush away angry with me. What the deuce are we quarrelling about? You know I want only the best for Priscilla. I'm just clumsy about the way I say it, I collect."

Her antagonism vanished as swiftly as his mood had changed. She said with a flash of dimples, "Very clumsy. So I *shall* rush away, and leave you to ponder your misdeeds, Mr.—" She started off, glancing at him over her shoulder.

"Mr.—what?" he demanded.

"Valentine . . ." she said provocatively, and hurried to the house guiltily aware that she was as naughty a flirt as he; and that he was smiling after her.

13

It was several seconds before Martha's anxious muttering penetrated Susan's preoccupation. She halted then. "What did you say?"

Martha wrung her apron. "I says as it's them nasty genelmen again, Mrs. Sue. Mr. Junius Trent, and his friend what puts me in mind of a fat snake."

"A poisonous one," muttered Susan. Once again, Trent had timed his visit well. Andy and Angelo were gone, and the Bo'sun had just left for Tewkesbury with Starry and Priscilla.

She told Martha to fetch the two new men who were repairing the stable roof. Glancing to Montclair who was coming awkwardly towards them, she rejected the half-formed thought that he should come with her.

"I'd best help Mr. Montclair up the steps first," said Martha, turning back.

"No! Just hurry and do as I told you."

The kind-hearted girl looked shocked. "But—Mrs. Sue, he won't be able to get up by himself. Not on them crutches."

"I hope not," said Susan in a low grim voice.

254

Martha gave a squeak of fright. "Oh, ma'am! They wouldn't never!" But seeing the cynicism in Susan's face, she panicked and seized her by the arm. "Then you mustn't go in there, neither! Oh, please! Let 'em wait till I find—"

"Hush! Just do as I say. Quickly!"

Martha threw a scared glance at Montclair and flew.

"Mrs. Sue!" called Montclair urgently. "What is it? Who has come?"

She bit her lip, then replied in a pert fashion, "One of my own wealthy admirers. So do not feel obliged to hasten, sir."

She had the dubious satisfaction of seeing him check and stand frowning at her, then she hurried up the steps, praying that this not be too unpleasant.

When she walked into the library, however, both Trent and Sir Dennis Pollinger rose and made their bows with punctilious propriety. Affecting not to notice Trent's outstretched hand, she said coolly, "Have you a message for me, sir?"

His blue eyes, deepened by the blue of the long-tailed coat he wore, sparkled mischief. "Only the sort to be spoken privately," he answered, then laughed. "No, never look so icy, lovely lady. Came to see my lamentable cousin is all. Ain't that right, Poll?"

Susan turned her cool gaze on the large and unlovely baronet. His face seemed even redder than the last time she'd seen it, and his brown eyes slid away furtively the instant they met hers. "Right-oh," he said in his harsh voice.

Susan stepped back as the odour of strong spirits wafted to her. "I can appreciate your anxieties concerning Montclair's recovery, Mr. Trent, but—"

Pollinger gave a neighing laugh and dug his elbow into Trent's ribs. "Anxious are you, Junius?"

"Quiet, you clod," said Trent, grinning broadly. "Allow the sweet widow to think the best of me." He took a pace closer to Susan. "Egad, but you're a picture this afternoon, m'dear. And—"

"And you know all about art, don't you, cousin?"

Susan bit her lip as the icy voice sounded from the hall. She heard Trent's whispered oath. She'd not dreamed Montclair would be able to negotiate the back steps unassisted, but she turned to see him swing himself into the room. He was slightly out of breath, and the dark eyes fixed on his cousin contained a cold contempt.

For an instant the room was hushed, the very air seeming to vibrate with tension.

"As usual, you are in error, dear Valentine," drawled Trent. "I've no more interest in art than in music. Both are fit only for women and old men. I fancy, though, that you're anxious to get back to work on your cacophonous concerto. To which end," a sly smile curved his mouth, "I do trust your hand is better."

Montclair set his jaw and ignored the taunt. "What do you want here, Junius? Say it and your farewells. I prefer to breathe untainted air."

A flush darkened Trent's face, but Pollinger laughed raucously. "He don't love you, Junius. 'Tainted air,' he says. Ha!"

"If you did but know it," snapped Trent, "you fairly reek of whisky, Pollinger! Have your say, for God's sake, and I will entertain the luscious lady."

"The luscious lady has more diverting entertainments," said Montclair, hobbling closer to Susan.

"Such as watching you totter about?" grinned Trent.

"Oh, no. But there are two slugs on the back step who offer her more of interest than do you."

The glitter in Trent's eyes brought Susan quickly between them. "You said you wished to speak with Mr. Montclair, Sir Dennis. Pray do so. He has already been up for too long, and I am sure that his uncle would not wish his progress impeded."

256

The baronet cleared his throat. "Warned you before, Montclair," he brayed. "More'n once, in fact. Getting leg-shackled very soon. Don't like other f-fellas inter-ferin' with my lady. Leave her be or—or I'll be 'bliged to take action."

"Shall you?" said Montclair, interested. "Well, I sup-pose there's a first time for everything."

Junius sniggered. Pollinger, slow-witted and fuzzy with drink, frowned, not quite comprehending the re-mark. "Toldya," he said, nodding ponderously. "Getting leg-shackled, and—"

"Nonsense," said Montclair. "She wants no part of you, Pollinger. Faith, but what lady would?"

Susan stared at him in mute astonishment. The man was a regular Don Juan! Betrothed to Barbara, not above flirting with herself, and apparently also pursu-ing this horrid man's lady!

Pollinger's face darkened. "See here! When I warn a fella—"

"Have a care, Poll," jeered Trent. "If he wants her for himself, he'll likely give you a run for your money."

"Well, he ain't running very fast right at the moment, is he?" Goaded, Pollinger gave an unexpectedly swift shove. Montclair staggered. Trent sprang to support him and said a derisive, "Egad, but you're a crude fellow, Poll. Don't you see this?" He giggled, and kicked the left crutch away.

Inevitably, Montclair fell, but managed to land in the chair behind him.

"Oh! For shame!" cried Susan, and started for him, but grinning triumphantly, Pollinger was also advanc-ing on the helpless man. Montclair swung the crutch strapped to his right arm, and it whacked into Pol-linger's bulging waistcoat.

Pollinger said "Ooosh!" and sat on the floor, clutching his middle and gulping.

257

Junius intercepted Susan, and said seductively, "Well, well, look what I found."

"Let her—go, damn you," panted Montclair, trying to haul himself from the chair.

Junius chuckled and held the struggling girl tighter. "Oh, but I think not."

"That," murmured another voice, "is all too apparent."

Trent jerked as though he had been struck. His eyes shot to the open door, and all the colour drained from his face.

Susan tore free and turned to the newcomer.

Tall, elegant, yet subtly menacing, Imre Monteil stood in the doorway, with Martha hovering anxiously behind him. The Swiss bowed. "I trust I am not *de trop,* dear lady?"

"Not in the least *de trop,* monsieur," she said with a grateful smile.

Monteil waved a dismissing hand, and Martha looked relieved and went away.

"What d'you want here, Monteil?" demanded Junius with a guarded air of resentment.

"I might ask the same of you, my dear. Were you to tell me you came to see your cousin, I could only point out that poor Valentine does not appear to be rendered ecstatic by your visit. And as for Mrs. Henley . . ." He tapped the jewelled handle of his Malacca cane against his lips, his unblinking gaze not for an instant leaving Trent. "I really must urge that you do not again bother her." His voice was very gentle, but something about his smile quite frightened Susan.

Junius muttered sullenly, "Pollinger came to warn my cousin off, is all. From the start he has interfered with the betrothal. Makes my papa deuced angry, I don't mind telling you. And my mama."

"Ah, I comprehend," purred Monteil. "So you are here

258

to defend your sister's prospective marriage, are you, dear Junius? Commendable, but . . ."

Susan did not hear the rest of his sentence. Whatever did the man mean? Barbara was Trent's sister, and she was betrothed to Montclair. Was there another sister, then. . . ? Vaguely she was aware that Junius was assisting Pollinger to his feet and that the Swiss gentleman was escorting the two vanquished warriors from the room. Recovering her wits, she saw Montclair trying to reach his crutch. "Oh, Valentine, you were superb," she said, retrieving the other crutch and handing it to him.

He felt that her praise was ill warranted, for he was sure he'd made a poor showing in front of her, besides which he didn't like the way Monteil was always hanging about Highperch. "Is that why you look so flabbergasted?" he asked irritably, dragging himself upward.

"I was a trifle surprised," Susan admitted. "I'd not realized the Trents had two daughters."

"They don't."

She stared at him. "But—but Barbara is betrothed to—to—"

"To Pollinger," he frowned. "And cannot abide the creature. Small wonder. I'd thought you knew that, Mrs. Sue. Why d'you suppose I kept urging Babs to run away with—" He paused, her stunned expression bringing a belated comprehension. "By Jupiter! You thought Barbara—and *I*. . . ?" He threw back his head and laughed uproariously. "Oho, what a rogue you must have judged me!"

"How pleasant it is to find you so merry, dear Valentine," smiled Imre Monteil, strolling back into the room.

Susan's emotions were rioting, and dreading lest she should betray her joy, she said warmly, "I am most grateful for your help, monsieur. You could scarce have

259

arrived at a more opportune moment. Mr. Trent was behaving disgracefully."

The Swiss was as delighted by her gratitude as Montclair was revolted by it. "I am overjoyed to have been of service," he said, patting her outstretched hand gently, "But I think your patient is wearied and should retire for the nap—no?"

"Yes," snarled Montclair.

"Well, you cannot," said Susan, her heart as light as thistledown. "You shall have to wait until the Bo'sun comes back and can help you upstairs."

"Deemer will help me," he grunted, and added sourly, "Doubtless, you two have much to—talk over."

"*Mais non,*" said Monteil. "I shall myself carry you, dear Valentine. Ah, but what a resentful glare! Is it that you are afraid of being made to look helpless in front of the lady? I assure you, *mon ami—*"

"Go—to the devil," flared Montclair, flushed and furious. And wielding the crutches unusually well, he dragged himself from the room.

The Swiss spread his hands and shrugged ruefully. "Alas—it is that I am clumsy, yes?"

"A little, perhaps." Susan looked after Montclair, her eyes sparkling. "But he has a surfeit of pride, and you meant well, monsieur." She saw Valentine pause in the corridor and start to turn to them. "Indeed," she went on, smiling at the Swiss, "you came very deedily to the rescue, sir."

Monteil's eyes took on the brilliant gleam that was alarming, and even as she knew that she dared not flirt with this man (for whatever reason), he stepped very close, seized her hand, and pressed it to his lips. "To have been of some small service to the lovely widow is its own reward," he murmured.

With a snort of disgust Montclair wrenched around and proceeded towards the stairs, his crutches slamming

260

so hard at the floorboards that it was a wonder they did
not go right through.

Susan's guilty hope that her Swiss admirer would
soon depart proved a vain one. The fact that she was not
an unmarried damsel but a widow with a child made it
quite *convenable* for her to entertain a gentleman in her
home, and Monteil was aware of it. He was not a difficult guest, for he was sophisticated, erudite, a world
traveller, and his conversation was fascinating. She suspected he was going out of his way to entertain her, and
after her earlier encouragement, could scarcely blame
the gentleman. As the afternoon slipped away he still
showed no inclination to leave, and with the dinner
hour not so far distant, she felt obliged to invite him to
stay. He accepted as though she'd offered him a priceless
gift, and Deemer showed him to a hastily prepared bedchamber where he might rest and refresh himself.

Not ten minutes later, Valentine rang his bell, and
Martha brought Susan a message that if it was convenient, this evening he would like to take dinner downstairs. 'He probably thinks it improper that I should
entertain the gentleman alone,' thought Susan, amused.
But she was relieved also, and retiring to the chamber
she occupied until her patient left, she dressed herself
with great care.

She selected a gown of dark pink satin that she'd not
worn since Burke had taken her to a dinner party in
honour of the betrothal of Camille Damon and the Lady
Sophia Drayton. That had been two years ago, just before poor Burke's disgrace had burst upon them so devastatingly. Waistlines had dropped since then, and the
pink satin still had the high-waisted look. She knew it
became her, none the less, and with her hair swept up

261

into gleaming coils on her head, and little curling tendrils beside her ears, she hoped their guests might not notice the somewhat outdated style of the gown. She added an enamelled clasp to her coiffure, and fastening the dainty garnet necklace that was a legacy from her mother, felt as excited as if this was a very special party. She discovered that she was singing softly, and she knew very well why.

He was not betrothed to poor little Barbara Trent! Far from bullying and abusing the girl into an unwanted marriage, he had fought her parents in an effort to spare her. He loved Barbara, but as one loves a dear cousin—not as a sweetheart.

Humming, Susan went down to the kitchen. Starry had left strict instructions with Martha and Deemer before she left, and the tantalizing aromas testified that dinner was well under way. Grateful that she had been spared most of the work, Susan thanked the busy cooks and went off to prepare the dining table. By the time she was finished it looked charming, with fresh flowers brightening the big table and crystal and silverware sparkling. Pleased, she went into the withdrawing room to await her guests, hoping that Starry would get back soon.

It had been a long day, and she fought a tendency to become dreamy. Montclair dominated her thoughts. She reminded herself sternly of his many faults. He personified the artistic temperament with his fiery angers and lightning changes of mood. He was argumentative and cynical and far too full of pride. But—she had also seen a tenderness in his eyes that awoke a frightening emotion in her own heart; he was all gentleness with little Priscilla, who fairly adored him, and he was brave also. When his loathsome cousin had sent him tumbling into that chair, she'd been sure he would be rendered quite helpless, and the memory of how efficiently he had

262

wielded his crutch, and with what a thud Sir Dennis had met the floorboards, made her chuckle.

Valentine was fond of her, she knew that. Fond—or grateful for what she had done; and he was angry because he probably thought Monteil had offered her a *carte blanche*. She sighed faintly. Even if he didn't believe the worst of her, should anything happen to his brother before Lord Geoffrey set up his nursery, Valentine would become Baron Montclair, and a fine uproar it would cause if his lordship stooped to wed the notorious Widow Henley. She was shocked then to realize how far her dreams had carried her, and her heart sank.

Wolfgang, who had been snoozing with his head on her slipper, leapt up and darted from the room, yipping frantically, and a few seconds later she heard the Bo'sun's voice in the front hall, and Priscilla came dancing in, the dog leaping beside her.

Susan stood and the little girl flung herself into her arms, squealing, "Mama, Mama! I getted my new specs and I c'n see better than anybody. Do you like them? Look, Mama!" She tilted her small head upwards, posing, her eyes huge with excitement, and her cheeks bright as two roses.

Putting off the crumpled bonnet, Susan admired the new spectacles, and the child gabbled on. "We had the loveliest time, Mama. Bo'sun George buyed me a ice, and I only dripped a teensy bit on Starry's dress, an' there were so many people, an' we seed the Abbey, which is big, an' the Bo'sun said we went past Bloody Meadows, but I din't see no blood, and Starry was cross with him for using bad words, which he said he wasn't, but she wouldn't talk to him no more, I mean any more, an' he got sad, so I had to ask her to please make him not sad, 'cause I like him better when he's not sad, don't you, Mama? And—oooh! You look *beautiful!*"

Priscilla's admiration was echoed by Mrs. Starr, who

hurried into the room apologizing profusely for their late return.

"We have an unexpected guest," said Susan.

The little lady threw a darkling glance toward the ceiling. "So I heard, Mrs. Sue."

"Did you also hear that the gentleman rendered us a great service?"

Mrs. Starr sighed. "Aye. So we must be properly grateful, I collect. Well, dinner will be ready on time, I promise you."

"It smells magnif'cent," said Priscilla. "An' I'm hungrier than a hogsbody!"

"Priscilla! A well-bred young lady does not use such ugly expressions!"

The child laughed merrily. "The Bo'sun's not a young lady, Mama!"

"Just as I thought," exclaimed Mrs. Starr, scandalized. "That man wants for manners, Mrs. Sue!"

"No, he doesn't," said Priscilla. "He wants you, Starry. I heard him tell you that by the sausages today, an' you said—"

"My gracious, what will the child say next?" gasped Mrs. Starr, and fled, very pink in the face.

Susan struggled to suppress a smile, and watching her anxiously, Priscilla said, "Mama, Bo'sun George really did say that, an' I don't—" Glancing to the side, she interrupted herself. "Mr. Val! Did you see . . . my. . . ?" her words faded into awed silence.

Propped by his crutches, Montclair stood in the doorway. For the first time since his arrival he was formally dressed in a brown tailcoat, cream waistcoat, and fawn pantaloons, and contrived to look elegant, despite the splints, and the fact that he was obliged to wear a slipper on one foot.

He gave a rather embarrassed grin and said, "Deemer valeted me. Ma'am, may I say you look—"

264

His words were drowned by Priscilla's squeaks. "Oh," she cried hilariously, "you look so *funny* in your evening dress, Mr. Val, with your pan'loons all torn, an'—"

"That will do!" said Susan, in a tone she seldom employed to the child. "Apologize to Mr. Montclair at once, and then you may go to your room!"

Shocked and frightened, Priscilla's lower lip trembled as she offered her apologies, then ran from the room with a muffled sob.

Montclair frowned. "I fancy she did but speak truth, ma'am. I must indeed look funny, and she is only a child, after all."

Wishing she had not spoken quite so harshly, and all too aware of the reason, Susan said, "She must learn it is not proper for a child to speak so, but I wish I had not—" She smiled wryly. "But it does not do to turn about, you know, when the damage is done."

"Or the good," he said with an immediate answering smile. "I am very sure she will exercise more caution the next time, and—who knows?—she might feel obliged to tell my uncle his—er, nether garments looked 'funny,' and then the fat *would* be in the fire!"

Grateful for his whimsical lightness, Susan chuckled.

Montclair made his clumsy way closer to her and said in a caressing tone, "Do you know how lovely you are when you laugh, Mrs. Sue?"

He looked really earnest, and her silly pulses were riotous because he stood so close and the amber flecks in his eyes were so bright. Faith, but it was enough to make one doubt one's mental processes! "Thank you," she said. And returning to the sofa, fighting to be sensible, added prosaically, "Deemer was a valet at one time. The poor fellow is a sort of underpaid major domo now, as you've seen, but he valets Andy, and very well, I think."

Montclair had hoped to sit beside her, but the splints

265

restricted him, and the sofa was too difficult to escape from. With a slight frown he lowered himself onto a straight-backed chair. "Yes, Deemer is a very good man. I feel downright guilty that I've taken so much of his time. I cannot think why Gould has not come to me. You'd not object to his presence here, surely?"

For an instant Susan froze. She said, "I must have forgot to tell you, Mr. Valentine. Lady Trent sent word that your man could not come because there is a regular outbreak of mumps at Longhills, and she fears lest you might catch it in your weakened condition."

He muttered, puzzled, "Yet they were eager for me to go home. At all events, I had mumps as a child, so that is no threat, is it?"

"Er—no. But—Priscilla has not had it, you see."

He looked at her steadily. "And if it had not been Priscilla, it would have been Starry, or Martha, or perhaps your brother who has not been exposed to the ailment. Any excuse, eh, Mrs. Sue."

Her heart hammering, she said, "Whatever do you mean?"

"You know perfectly well. Come now, own up. It is very clear that your people are so overworked you have to perform many menial tasks yourself. I am greatly in your debt and most eager to help. I offer you the services of my excellently trained maids, which logically you should accept. Yet you very stubbornly refuse them. Why?"

"Well—that is exactly it, you see," she stammered. "I quite believe that your maids are excellently trained and—and likely most superior, and accustomed to working in a great house, and—"

"Good heavens," he exclaimed. "Do you fancy my employees to consider themselves above working at Highperch?"

"Well—no, of course not. But—well, we go along very simply, and—"

"Which will likely be a welcome change of pace for them." Triumphant, he said, "I shall write a note requiring Gould to bring two girls he knows to be industrious and good workers, which is all we need be concerned with, no?"

"Most certainly not! Sir, there is a great deal more to being a good servant than simply to work hard. I had rather have a somewhat inept girl who is kind and can be pleasant with her fellow workers than—"

He laughed. "Ah—so that's it! You women with your so easily ruffled feathers! Good heavens, ma'am, all they've to do is what they're told."

"And how if they quarrel and scratch at each other all day? I suppose you *men* would not give a button for that!"

"No, of course not. I never saw a group of females yet but what they scratched at each other, however sweetly."

"Oh! Infamous!" she exclaimed, but was unable to repress a smile.

"Then it is settled," he went on firmly. "Gould will bring two maids and instruct them that they are coming here to please *you* and do their work properly. If they don't, only tell 'em you will report their behaviour to me and they'll be turned off."

"As if I would do such a thing to someone else's servants!"

"Lord above! What a storm in a teapot! Then *I'll* tell 'em! But I mean to send for them, I promise you."

She rose, her eyes flashing. "And I promise *you* that I'll have no mumpy servants here! And it is *not* a storm in a teapot!"

"Dear me," murmured Imre Monteil, coming gracefully into the room. "Have you put our lovely hostess out of patience with you already, Valentine?" Smiling admiringly at the flushed Susan, he advanced to bow over her hand. "*Vraiment,* but I cannot wonder at it. Any

267

man who would babble of teapots to a goddess deserves her contempt."

His eyes smiled up at her above the red lips that were touching her fingers again, and she could have wept because by his very intervention and his unfortunate choice of words, this foolish discussion suddenly took on the aspects of a major quarrel. Before she could speak, however, Montclair had taken up the gauntlet.

"Then I must pay heed to your babblings, monsieur," he said stiffly. "I had not thought to have earned Mrs. Henley's contempt, but no doubt the lady finds your wit more endearing than my poor efforts."

"I did not say I held you in contempt, Mr. Montclair," began Susan.

"But of course, for you are too gently kind to make such a remark, even if you felt it," inserted the Swiss, bowing her to a chair and drawing another as close to it as was possible. "For myself I count it an honour and a privilege to find a topic that will please so enchanting a lady."

"Such as buying my house?" drawled Valentine, his eyes glinting unpleasantly. "Is that why you're always hanging about Highperch?"

Susan said hurriedly, "I told you, sir, that Monsieur Monteil has been so kind as to put some business in my brother's way."

Deemer came in with a laden tray. Accepting a glass of Madeira, Valentine waited until the butler had gone out again, then said, "I gather this—er, 'business' has to do with Lyddford's boat?"

"But how astute." Monteil beamed at him. "And I did warn you I meant to offer again for Highperch, you know. Although . . ." he tugged at his lip, his dark eyes flickering from one to the other, "I am unsure at this point as to which of you so charming people I must approach in the matter."

Susan held her breath. Montclair said with a curl of the lip, "There is, I believe, an old adage which says, 'When in doubt—do not.'"

"Is there?" The Swiss looked impressed. "This, I have not heard. *Merci, mon cher.* Always I am grateful to learn more of your language."

Montclair inclined his head in the slightest bow. "And I, in turn, would be interested to learn what your business with Lyddford has to do with Highperch, monsieur."

Susan put in uneasily, "My brother moves cargo for Monsieur Monteil."

Valentine's eyes held steady on Monteil. "Cargo. . . ?"

The Swiss laughed. "Ah, dear my friend, you must not take this simple thing and weave it into the so fascinating Gothic romance. I am closing my London house, and this cargo consists of some of my personal effects, merely. Nothing more sinister than that, I promise it." He waved one of his long hands in a deprecating gesture. "But if your perfervid imagination conjures up images of my involving Lyddford and my dear Mrs. Henley"—his fingers rested lightly over Susan's hand on the arm of her chair—"in gun-running, or the slave traffic, or something equally wicked, you shall come with me into the cellar and inspect my crates."

Susan moved her hand almost at once, but the possessive way in which the Swiss had patted it, the proprietary implications contained in both words and gesture, plus Monteil's continuing air of amused condescension, had fanned the flame of Valentine's hot temper. He said tersely, "I feel sure that I must have mistaken you, monsieur. Certainly no one calling himself a gentleman would store his effects in the home of another, without so much as a by-your-leave."

Susan had long judged Imre Monteil a dangerous man. Now she read a deadly menace in his very immobility as he sat there, leaning forward slightly, his unblinking gaze fixed upon the younger man. There could be no doubt but that he rated his pride high. Montclair as obviously sought a quarrel: there was an icy hauteur in the tilt of the dark head, the disdainful droop of the eyelids, the scornful twist to the mouth. Experiencing the sensation that she sat between two smouldering volcanoes, she tried to think of something to say to ease the tension.

And then, incredibly, a look of dismay banished the glare in the jet eyes of the Swiss. "Do I offend?" he asked anxiously. "I assure you, Valentine, that Lyddford gave his permission."

"And it is purely a temporary arrangement," gulped Susan, as relieved as she was astonished.

"Prior to your taking possession of Highperch Cottage, Monteil?" sneered Valentine.

'Oh, you *idiot!*' thought Susan. '*Why* must you antagonize him?'

"No, no!" The Swiss looked crestfallen, and said sadly, "Ah—but I have been the great fool to have supposed that as my friend you would not object. I quite comprehend the imposition. My crates shall be moved at once. Madame Henley, is it within the realm of possibility that your new men could tomorrow begin to carry my belongings down to the dock to await your brother's return? I am devastated to so inconvenience you, but not for an instant longer must I impose on poor Valentine's good nature!"

Wishing with all her heart that "poor Valentine" was confined to his bed (preferably under strong restraint), or that Monsieur Monteil had gone upon his way, Susan was irked to have been put in so uncomfortable a position. "There is not the need, monsieur," she said. "Since the courts have yet to rule on the matter and *we* live here now, my brother's word is all that is required. Besides, my new men are—"

"Resting, no doubt," interrupted Valentine savagely. "You'll get little work out of them, I'll go bail, for all your much vaunted ability to judge men."

270

"It has not failed me yet, Mr. Montclair," she snapped.

His eyes drifted to the Swiss who watched them smilingly. "Are you perfectly sure, ma'am?"

Susan positively ached for the feel of a solid broom in her hand.

Monteil laughed softly. "Ah, but my Valentine is cross with me," he said with rueful good humour, and shaking one finger at Montclair, added whimsically, "No, no. I refuse to quarrel with you, *mon ami.*"

"Such forbearance can only be admired, monsieur," said Susan, smiling on him with warm approval.

Valentine gave a disgusted snort.

Monteil turned a concerned face to the widow. "My friend is in the right of it, however," he declared. "These new men of yours are the rough-looking fellows at best, and I will own I have worried for your safety, dear Mrs. Henley. With your brother so often away you are quite unprotected here, and there are too many undesirables prowling the countryside."

"I put it to you, Monteil," said Valentine through his teeth, "that I have a fine duelling pistol in my room and am not incapable of firing it in defence of my hostess, should the need arise. Or in any other emergency."

"Good evening, dear Mrs. Sue, and gentlemen," trilled Mrs. Starr, hurrying into the room with a rustle of silks and a whiff of lavender. "I pray you will forgive my tardiness. No, no, you must not get up, Mr. Valentine. I will sit down. There, now you may be at ease. How splendid that you are able to come down and dine with us at last." She shot a knowing glance at Susan. "It would seem you've all enjoyed a lovely chat whilst I kept you waiting, but— Ah, there is the gong."

Rising, Susan could have hugged her. "I expect you gentlemen are famished," she said. "Let us go in." And she thought that it would be remarkable were there no pistols fired across the dinner table.

271

14

The house was very quiet when Montclair struggled down the stairs next morning. His descent was something of an acrobatic feat which involved balancing on his right foot while he swung the crutches one step down, then lowering himself to the same stair. Since his right hand was as useless as his left leg, this was a decidedly hazardous business, with each step presenting a new challenge. When he was three steps from the bottom he lost the knack of it, overbalanced, and descended in a wild hopping rush that left him teetering in the hall, fighting to stay upright, and very much out of breath.

"You are quite mad, sir!"

Pleased with himself despite this harsh verdict, Montclair turned an unrepentant grin on Susan, who was coming in at the front door carrying a basket of freshly cut flowers. The warm breeze billowed her pale green gown of India muslin, and the sun bathed her with brightness, waking a sheen down one delicately contoured cheek and revealing that her grey eyes were wide with fright.

272

Delighting in the knowledge that she had been concerned for his sake, he panted, "And you . . . look the very spirit of summer, ma'am."

"Never mind trying to turn me up sweet, Valentine Montclair!"

"Oho! Cant on the lips of the lady," he laughed, hobbling along with her.

"And never seek to turn the attack to my want of propriety." Frowning at him in a way he thought adorable, she scolded, "Do you *yearn* to be laid down upon your bed for another six weeks?"

"I yearn to be able to get about without being a confounded nuisance to everyone."

"Pride goeth before a fall," she said, turning down the hall towards the kitchen, her long hair tossing in the way it did when she was vexed with him.

"And the Lord helps those who help themselves," he countered.

She shook her head and went into the kitchen, and Montclair chuckled and turned back, determined to investigate the strong smell of paint emanating from the front of the house. He glanced into the withdrawing room as he passed. The sunlight splashed a bright avenue across the floor and his eyes followed it to Mrs. Henley's spinet. Until now he had managed to ignore the instrument, but he eyed it wistfully, then made his way to it. Welcome was reluctant to be evicted, but Montclair banished him from the keyboard, and with his left hand began to play the theme of the first movement of his new concerto. A moment later, the paint forgotten, he had laid the crutches beside him and was sitting rather awkwardly on the wide bench. He dropped the melody into the bass clef and played it through. When he finished, he stared blindly at the keys, lifted his right hand, and tried again to move the fingers. Not by the slightest tremor did they respond. His shoulders slumped. Surely by this time some feeling should have returned? Surely he had not permanently lost the use of his hand. . . ?

A burst of applause brought his head up. Susan, Martha, Mrs. Starr, and Deemer watched him from the doorway. He essayed a slight bow.

"Oh, that was lovely," exclaimed Mrs. Starr.

"Perfectly beautiful," agreed Susan, her eyes alight. "I think I have never heard it before. What is it called?"

"I was going to call it 'Goddess of—the River,'" he said solemnly. "But I may change it to 'Lament for a Dead Painter.'"

Mrs. Starr giggled and shepherded Martha and the butler away.

Susan gasped, "My goodness! Do you say— Did *you* write that lovely piece?"

He flushed with pleasure. "I wish I could play it for you properly."

"It sounded splendid just with the left hand. Will you play it once more?"

"If you will sit beside me."

She came at once to occupy the end of the bench, and Montclair played for her, interspersing his performance with comments. "Here," he said eagerly, "is where the orchestra comes in . . . like so. The solo introduces the second movement . . . and the orchestra enters *pianissimo* in a foreign key—thus . . ."

He glanced up suddenly. "Good God! How I must be boring you! My apologies, ma'am!"

"I resent the implication," she said, indignant. "I find it most fascinating. I wish I could play the right hand for you, but even were you to write out the music for me, I think my talents are too mean to—"

He interrupted, "You play, Mrs. Sue?"

"A little."

"But this is wonderful! If you've music, would you

274

humour me and take the right hand while I play the left. . . ?"

She would, and did, humour him. They played together for more than half an hour, and she was both touched and amazed to see his often grim expression become so open and boyishly eager. This was a Valentine she'd never beheld—so animated, so happily engrossed by their mutual efforts. Often, she stumbled, and they would laugh and try again; several times he suggested different fingering, pausing so that she could follow his advice, as pleased when she argued as when she acquiesced. How he loved his music. Whoever married this man, she thought pensively, would have to accept a competitor for his time and affection; an inanimate competitor, but a merciless one. She stifled a sigh. A competitor she would so willingly tolerate . . .

They finished Mr. Haydn's piece with a rather ragged chord, and laughed together.

Montclair turned a glowing face. "Thank you, Mrs. Sue! You play very well."

"I had thought I was fair—until I heard you, sir." She saw his gaze become sombre as it slanted to his injured right hand, and added kindly, "You will regain the use very soon now; don't worry so."

He looked up at her and said gravely, "I would worry less, dear ma'am, if I dared believe myself forgiven."

"For what? Tormenting my guest last evening?"

"Just so."

"You should ask *his* pardon, sir. Not mine. Although," she added in an afterthought, "you really were very naughty."

He bit back the instinctive reaction, and for a moment they sat in complete silence, gazing at each other. Then he asked softly, "Do you care for Monteil, Susan?"

She had initially thought him a bad man. She realized now that he was also a criminal. It *must* be little short of a crime to lower his voice to that tender note that was almost a caress; to light up the amber flecks in his dusky eyes; and to tilt his dark head toward her so that the finely chiselled cheekbones, the straight nose, the sensitive mouth with its lurking half smile must be forever engraved on her memory. And memory was all she would have. *He* would go back to his great manor house and plunge into his music and forget her. That awareness was so unkind that she was obliged to turn away, her voice failing her.

"You do not reply." He took up the end of her sash, and looked down at it absently. "I wish," he muttered, "that you were not so very beautiful."

Even more flustered, she stammered, "Y-you surprise me . . . Mr. Montclair."

"Do I? Why? Certainly you must know you are beautiful."

"I—I am flattered. But—"

"Nonsense! It would be flattery had you a face like a ferret. But you have not."

"Oh." Afraid that others might hear this conversation, Susan stood and helped him buckle on the right crutch, then handed him the other. "And are you displeased because I—er, do not resemble a ferret?"

He chuckled, and struggled to his feet. "If you did, perhaps Monteil would turn his greasy eyes elsewhere. How long have you known him?"

"About the same length of time as I have known you, sir."

They started towards the front door and he grunted, "Humph. And you store his cargo in my—I mean, in the cellars. Did he tell you why he found such an arrangement desirable?"

"Certainly he makes no secret of his hopes to purchase this house. If he cannot, he says he will buy property somewhere in the neighbourhood."

"One can but hope he will be unsuccessful," he said dryly.

"I cannot echo that hope, Mr. Valentine."

He frowned at the front steps, then said, "It would be much easier for me if I might have your arm, ma'am."

He had not seemed to need a supporting arm when he'd come so precipitately down the stairs, and Susan hesitated.

"You said I was mad when I descended the last time," he reminded her demurely.

"Hmm," said Susan, but she carried one of his crutches and allowed him to put his arm across her shoulders as he hopped awkwardly down the steps. She could feel the warmth of his lean body, and their closeness was, to say the least, unsettling. Then he appeared to lose his balance, so that she threw her arm around his waist, clinging even more tightly.

"That's much better," he said with a grin.

She made no response to this impropriety, but pulled away immediately they reached level ground.

"Alas," he sighed. "So ends the idyll. But I thank you for it. You are ever gracious, ma'am. Even if you have allowed Monteil to pull the wool over your eyes."

"How odd," said Susan, "that I'd the impression another gentleman was doing precisely that. Or trying to."

"Not so," he said, injured. "I merely strive to warn you. Very bad of me, perhaps, but I mistrust the fellow's glib tongue. Lord knows he's rich as Croesus, but—"

"Fair game for a mercenary widow, eh, Mr. Montclair?"

He gave her an irritated look, which changed to a glinting amusement, and reaching up, touched the end of her nose lightly. "This charming article is the barometer of your mood, did you know it? When it is . . ."—he tilted her nose skywards—"elevated, you are very cross with me. When it is—a little uplifted—I have vexed you. When it is . . . down—like that, you are flustered. And when it is neither up nor down—like this—I can breathe easier."

They had stopped walking and stood very close together. His long fingers lingered on her cheek. Susan murmured dreamily, "I must take care never to—to have it cut off, sir. Else—you'd be all at sixes and sevens."

Just as dreamily, he said, "And you'd not be able to breathe."

Still his fingers touched her cheek. So lightly, like the flutter of a butterfly's wings. Yearning to lean into that caress, she laughed instead, and forced herself to move back, saying with some embarrassment, "What rubbish we are talking!"

"Then I shall be very earnest. Susan, if you count Monteil your good friend, may I hope that I can be judged as kindly? I know we did not—ah, see eye to eye at first, but"—he searched her face—"you don't still believe me your enemy, do you?"

She met his anxious regard briefly, then, driven by self-preservation, looked away. "No. Of course not." She thought, 'Only, there is an unbreachable wall between us.'

"In that case, I ask that you allow me the right to help you."

A little pucker disturbed her smooth forehead. "In what way, Mr. Valentine?"

"In whatever way I can. If you are in—I mean, if you need—"

Inwardly cringing, she lifted her eyes to meet his and said candidly, "If I need—money? Is that what you mean?"

It sounded bald, to say the least of it. He was unskilled in what his brother termed frivolity, flattery, and fal-lals. Uncomfortably aware that he was flushing,

278

he balanced himself on his crutch so as to take up her hand. It was very soft and warm, even if the fingernails were discoloured and too short. "What I am trying to say is that—I want to be—more than just a friend to you, dear ma'am." Because he was looking down at her hand he did not see her sudden pallor, or the spasm of pain that flickered across her face, and went on, "I know you are faced with financial troubles and that life is difficult for you, and—er . . ."

'Oh, no!' thought Susan, anguished. 'Do not, Valentine! *Please* do not!' But she said quietly, "And you want to—smooth my path?"

He smiled. "That is one way of wording it, certainly."

It was a way she had heard before. Wounded to the heart, once more she had to turn from him. "You told Priscilla you were not rich."

"One does not discuss such delicate matters with a child. Certainly I can afford to take a—"

'Oh, God!' thought Susan. 'Oh, God!' And desperate to stop him from saying that horrid word, she interpolated, "Do I understand you to say you are . . . are willing to, as Andy would say, tow us out of the River Tick?"

He said heatedly, "You see? You should not even know such a term! Lyddford does not protect you properly, Sue! Dash it all, I—"

"Do wish to . . . protect me?"

"Assuredly! And if Imre Monteil has offered to—"

Very pale, she rounded on him. "Monsieur Monteil has never made me an offer of any kind, sir!"

"Well, he will, let me tell you, which isn't surprising!"

"Indeed?" she said, controlling herself with an effort. "He has been a perfect gentleman, and if—"

"Perfect gentleman, is it? The way the beastly fellow leers at you makes my skin creep! How you can bear to let him slobber over you I don't—"

"*Slobber?*" she echoed, her voice becoming unwont-

279

edly shrill. "Your charm of manner, sir, is exceeded only by your arrogance! Whatever else, *he* does not—that is, I *would* not— And—and besides, when I came to your silly Folly, Mr. Valentine Montclair, it was to help a hurt human being. I did not expect to be insulted in return!"

He stared at her resentfully. "Insulted! However could I have deluded myself into thinking I was being generous?"

"And however can I withstand such noble condescension?" she said, quivering with wrath. "La, but it passes understanding!"

"The devil!" Furious, he swung closer to her.

Susan took a few hurried paces to the rear, but rushed on, "It was not bad enough to insult me, you must say vile things behind his back about a gentleman who has been nothing but kind and—and helpful!"

"Aye, he'll be kind, I'll warrant! And he'll 'help' you straight into the—"

"Yes, malign him—as you mocked my new workmen and called them 'disgusting hedgehogs'! They might not be Corinthian dandies—"

"*Dandies!* Now if that isn't—"

"—but *they,* at the least, have never spoken one improper word to me, and—"

"I should think not, by God!" His eyes glittering, he said, "Only tell me who—"

"—and furthermore, I am perfectly satisfied with their work, so—"

"Work? What work? Be dashed if I've seen them do aught! I vow they're lazier than my lazy gardener, and if what I suspect is—"

Suspect? Now came fear to add to her misery. Facing it bravely, she demanded, "*Now* what do you imply? Of what do you suspect us, sir? Do you think it probable that we have stolen the—the Montclair Mermaid from your fountain, perhaps?"

"Egad, woman, but you're high in the instep! And you speak of *my* pride! All I tried for was—"

"I am all too aware of what you tried for! But do not feel obliged to limit your reviling of us, sir! I heard there was a plot afoot only a year or so ago to kidnap the Prince Regent. Perhaps you think we have *him* tucked away in our cellar!"

She was white with hurt and anger, but Montclair's wrath was cooling, and he said impatiently, "Don't sneer at me, blast it! This is all so ridiculous! I don't—"

"You do not wish to be bored by someone ridiculous," she said with superb hauteur. "But of course. I shall send the Bo'sun to help you. Although perhaps you will not feel perfectly *safe* with him, since you doubtless suspect *him* as well!"

"Oh, I do, for he is always slipping away somewhere. I'd fancied he was—"

"Organizing an uprising of the villagers against you?" she sneered.

"No, you must do better than that, ma'am. Let us have him rather occupying a sinister hut in the woods, where he breeds—ah, man-eating moles, perhaps."

His lips quirked and a dance of laughter came into his eyes. Almost won to an answering smile, Susan remembered his offer, and a fierce pang transfixed her. Suddenly overwhelmed and tearful, she all but ran from him.

Exasperated, Montclair followed her slowly. The ways of women, he thought, were indeed inexplicable. 'And despite all the fustian she spoke, she did not answer my question. She did not say whether she really cares for that wart Monteil . . .'

At the foot of the steps he paused, glancing up. Two ladders, unoccupied at present, were propped against the east front of the house. Jove, if the beautiful but provoking widow hadn't made him forget all about the paint! The trim had been partially restored to a soft

281

cream. He smiled faintly. He'd never really believed she would make good her threat to use that garish red or the purple he had substituted. His inspection was interrupted abruptly, and he cried a startled "Hey!" as he was swept up from either side and carried up the steps.

"Bit too much fer yer, mate?" said a hoarse voice in his right ear.

He had barely time to glimpse a hairy, dirty face under a battered old hat; then he was set down and the even more disreputable individual on his left was shoving the crutch under his arm. 'Mrs. Sue's fine new workmen,' thought Montclair cynically, settling the crutches and scanning a man who might very well be taken for a third-rate pickpocket. He wore a patch over one eye, and the other managed always to avoid a direct glance. His hat was an abomination over an untidy mop of black, greasy hair, and his ragged clothing, several sizes too large, hung loosely from a pair of sagging shoulders. "Worse goin' up than comin' dahn, ain't it, guv," he said in a nasal whine. "We thought as we'd give yer a bit of a hoist, like."

"Good deed fer the day," called the first vagrant, shambling off.

"Yes. Er—well, I'm obliged," said Montclair, eyeing the unlovely pair without delight.

"Cor! Look whatcha bin an' gorn an' done, Seth," called the first man, climbing his ladder.

Montclair glanced down, and swore. There was a generous smear of cream paint on the sleeve of his blue coat.

"Luvva duck," moaned Seth, and taking out a filthy kerchief added what appeared to be coal dust and a scattering of tobacco leaves to the disaster zone.

"Let be," said Montclair indignantly, shoving his hand away.

282

"Clumsy block," leered the first man, dipping his brush in the paint pot.

"Jest tryin' ter be of 'elp, Dicky," whined Seth.

"Your best *help* will be to get back to work," said Montclair, fuming over the ruin of his coat, but unable to scold since the bumbling oafs may have been sincerely trying to help him.

Seth retreated to his ladder, and clambered upward, groaning about his "poor tired bones," and then engaging in a whispered conversation with his cohort.

Montclair frowned from one to the other.

Dicky leered down at him. "Was yer waitin' fer some more 'elp, guv?" he enquired with bland insolence.

'Heaven forbid!' thought Montclair. "I was waiting to see you get back to work," he replied pithily.

"Right y'are, sir!" Seth dipped the brush deeply, and swung it out.

Montclair manoeuvred the crutches desperately, and avoided most of the flying paint. "Take care, damn you!" he cried angrily.

"Sorry, guv," leered Seth.

Dicky pointed out sagely, "Bad luck ter stand under a ladder, mate."

"Worse luck to be impertinent while standing *on* one," snapped Montclair, balancing himself on his right foot and dealing Seth's ladder a whack with his crutch.

Seth screamed loudly and clung to the ladder like a terrified monkey.

Somewhat appeased but with the unhappy conviction that paint was trickling down his forehead, Montclair turned to enter the house. He thought he heard a muffled laugh and jerked about angrily.

The suspects were industriously and soberly at work.

"Confounded hedgehogs," he muttered, and swung himself inside.

For the balance of the day Susan contrived to elude
Montclair. She felt wrapped in a grey despair, and
fought it by immersing herself in the many tasks that
had been postponed owing to the presence of an invalid
in the house. The rugs in the lower hall and the entrance hall were rolled up and carried outside to be thoroughly beaten. She next decided that the furniture
arrangement in the withdrawing room did not please
her, and she required Martha and Deemer to help her
improve it. Meanwhile, the dining room rugs joined
those in the back garden, to be attacked with gusto (and
some whispered imprecations) by the Bo'sun.

At three o'clock, drawn by the uproar, Valentine
peered over the balcony rail into such a maelstrom of
activity that he retreated in horror. He sat at the window of his bedchamber looking out at the golden afternoon and thinking of his brother. Uncle Selby had told
him that when he'd first been attacked, a letter had
been despatched to Geoff's last known address advising
that he was near death. That had been better than five
weeks ago, which meant it was not yet even halfway to
India. By the time Geoff came home he would probably
be completely well again. He was almost well now—except for his hand. He removed the sling he was required
to wear when not using his crutches, and held his arm
out straight. He was almost sure his broken leg had
mended. Surely then, his hand should have healed also,
but his efforts to move the fingers were unavailing.

"Hello, Mr. Val," called Priscilla. "Won't they wriggle
yet?"

He turned eagerly to the child, glad of her company,
and she danced in with Wolfgang beside her, and stared
curiously at the inanimate fingers. "Has you tried bending 'em yourself?"

"No. The doctor said I must not."

"Oh—him," she said, unimpressed.

He chuckled. "You don't care for Dr. Sheswell, Lady Priscilla?"

She shook her head decidedly. "Uncle Angelo calls him a wallet in the wind and says he hides his teeth. Miss Babs laughed and laughed, and Uncle Angelo said his soul she makes sing."

Valentine, also laughing, lifted his brows at this. "Does she, indeed?"

"Well, that's what he said. I wonder if his soul is singing on *The Dainty Dancer*. Do grown-ups always have singing souls when they're in love, Mr. Val?"

He stared at her, then said slowly, "It's a nice thought. Did you make it up yourself?"

"No. Uncle Angelo told Miss Babs 'bout it. I like Miss Babs. She talks so soft, when she's not crying. She does cry a lot." She tilted her head thoughtfully. "Even more than Mama. I 'spect that's why Angelo's always hugging her better."

"Is he, by Jove! Er—do you see her often?"

"He lets me walk over there with him, in the afternoons sometimes. He won't let me ask Mama if I can go after my bedtime."

Incredulous, he asked, "Do you say that Señor Angelo goes to the Manor to take dinner with Sir Selby Trent?"

"No. He jus' meets Miss Babs in that little garden house on the hill."

Montclair thought, 'Why that slippery Spaniard! Junius will break him in half if he catches him!' He frowned thoughtfully. He had promised his cousin he would not allow her to be forced into marriage with Pollinger, but an impoverished Spaniard was scarcely a satisfactory substitute. Unless Babs had given him her heart, of course. And what a bumble broth *that* would be! There was no doubt of Uncle Selby's reaction. As for Aunt Marcia—

285

"'Scuse me, but—do you, Mr. Val?" asked Priscilla, out of patience.

"My apologies, milady. I didn't hear what you said."

"No, 'cause your ears were off somewhere else," she said accusingly. "I asked you where you think Dr. Shes'ell hides his teeth." She leaned closer and whispered with high drama, "I wouldn't be s'prised if it was in the cellar."

Amused, he tugged one of her ringlets. "You scamp. Is this a new story for us to make up?"

"No! I don't want a story about him. Or his friend. I like *him* worse than Dr. Shes'ell."

"Which friend? My uncle?"

"No. The tall man who calls on Mama. He's got dead eyes, and his hands are like lard. Ugh!"

Valentine leaned forward. "What makes you think Monsieur Monteil is a friend of Dr. Sheswell?"

"I seed them together one night. It was all Wolfgang's fault. He'd goed out for a little run, but he din't come back, so I had to find him, only I found them 'stead, over by the bridge, talking whispery. I 'tended they was Roundheads, an' I was a Royalist spy, an' I creeped up on them an' listened to their secret plans."

She crouched, looking very melodramatically furtive, and he smothered a grin and asked, "Were they awfully wicked plans?"

"Well, I couldn't hardly hear them, but I think they must've been, 'cause one of them was cross an' said it should've been done by now."

His amusement faded. Here was more than the child's active imagination. He asked intently, "Do you know what the 'it' was?"

She thought a moment, then said, "I think it was about clothes."

"Clothes? Are you sure, Lady Priscilla?"

"No-o . . . But the other man got cross too, an' said it

wasn't his fault 'cause *they* hadn't gived somebody something. An' he was sorry 'cause it all fitted so goodly an'
would've looked right, an' no one wouldn't have been a
miser."

Montclair frowned. Might they instead have said—no
one would be the *wiser*? Whatever the plot, clothes, he
thought, had little to do with it.

The child went on blithely. "An' then Wolfgang
barked at them and they rid away like cowards, which
is when I saw who they was. An' I wouldn't be s'prised if
Dr. Shes'ell hides his teeth in our cellar, 'cause he
prob'ly keeps 'em in a little jar, like Grandpapa used to,
and doesn't like people to see him take 'em out. 'Sides,
I've heard someone bumping about down there at dead
of night." Her voice lowered again, and she hissed
awfully, "When the goblins an' witches are out! An'
Wolfgang growls, an' he doesn't do that if it's Mama or
some of our people, you know. Can we make our story
now, please? We were up to the part where the princess
finds the unicorn in her coach . . ."

It was taking so blasted long, but if anyone saw him,
thought Montclair, lowering himself carefully onto the
next stair, he would say he'd been very thirsty and
hadn't wanted to disturb anyone at this hour of the
night. He reached back for the crutch and pulled it to
him, but this time he was a shade impatient, and the
armrest clipped the rail with a crack that he was sure
would waken the entire household. Mentally cursing his
clumsiness he bit his lip and sat holding his breath,
waiting. No sound disturbed the silence. Another
breathless moment, then with a sigh of relief, he eased
himself down one more step.

The Dainty Dancer had put neatly into the dock at
four o'clock this afternoon. Lyddford had looked tired,
and the Spaniard not much better, but Lyddford had in-

sisted the cargo must be off-loaded at once. The Bo'sun and Deemer had joined in the effort, and from his window Valentine had seen Seth and Dicky come slouching to assist, looking more ruffianly than ever with paint liberally splattered on their ragged garments.

Valentine smiled rather grimly, recalling Starry's barely concealed look of relief when he'd told her he was not feeling "quite up to the rig" this afternoon and if it would not be too much trouble he'd take dinner in his room. No doubt they were pleased to have him out of the way while the cargo was off-loaded. Martha had carried his tray upstairs and in her gentle warm-hearted way had settled him onto the chaise longue, lit the candles, made sure that books and *The Morning Chronicle* were within easy reach, and spread the napkin across his lap. She'd even given his shoulder a shy little pat. Susan's remarks about servants had come to mind, and he was forced to admit that Martha might be simple-minded, but if she was in his employ he'd take great care not to lose her.

He'd passed the evening reading and listening to the men clumping about downstairs. Several times he'd gone to the big window in the first-floor hall and watched them toiling up from the river with wheelbarrows piled high with boxes and bales that ostensibly contained Imre Monteil's "personal effects." It was past eleven o'clock when the house had quieted. He'd heard the creak of the stairs soon afterwards, then silence had blanketed the old house for another hour. They all had worked so hard; it was to be hoped they'd sleep like logs.

Priscilla's innocent words had decided him upon this course of action. "I've heard someone bumping about down there at dead of night . . . an' Wolfgang growls . . ." He was not quite sure of the significance of Sheswell's nocturnal meeting with Imre Monteil, but he'd long known that the doctor was a tippler. He was beginning to suspect that Monteil was a Free Trader on the side. Possibly, he supplied Sheswell with wines and cognac which had sidestepped the excise tariff. The doctor might have become angered by delays, and Priscilla had chanced upon the two men while Monteil was making his excuses. Who Monteil's customers were did not much concern Valentine, however. The points of concern were firstly, that Susan and her brother might have been gulled into shipping and hiding contraband in the belief that Monteil's cargoes were simple personal belongings; secondly, that the Swiss should have had the unmitigated gall to select Highperch Cottage (admittedly offering the unique advantages of sitting isolated, unoccupied, and on the bank of the river) for a storage and, presumably, distribution point.

When his initial doubts had solidified this afternoon, Valentine had at first thought to seek out Susan and share them with her, but she seemed much taken with Monsieur Monteil. Also, his own offer of financial assistance had sent her straight into the boughs. She was an excessively proud young lady, and resented any criticism of her judgment. Certainly, she'd want to know what he suspected, and if he revealed his belief that she and Lyddford had—however inadvertently—allowed themselves to be dragged into a smuggler's toils, she'd probably be reaching for her broom again and he'd be banished from her presence forever. And despite her apparent preference for gentlemen of the Swiss persuasion, he found that he was reluctant to be banished from the widow's presence.

If that slippery Monteil really had dared to use Highperch for illegal activities, if he had carelessly placed Susan and her brother in danger of being arrested as smugglers, then by George, the man was a scoundrel and must be dealt with! First, however, proof must be found. The ideal time to accomplish this was at night, and now that he had discovered he could manage to get about with only one crutch, he saw no reason to delay.

His undistinguished progress down the stairs having been accomplished, he gripped the end post and dragged himself erect. There was a half moon tonight, and the windows were brightened by a silvery glow, the illumination, faint as it was, making it easier to proceed cautiously down the west hall, past the library and what had once been a study, to the stairs that led to the cellars. It was quite a warm night, but luckily the wind was blustering about, effectively drowning the faint sounds of his crutch and an occasional creaking board under his foot.

He eased the cellar door open, and stood very still, listening. There was no flicker of light; no sound. And then suddenly there came a stir behind him. A rush of air. Something flying at him. His nerves tightened. He braced himself on the crutch, made a grab for the Manton he'd tucked into his sling, and jerked his head around to look behind him. With an amiable trill a small shape tore past and charged full-tilt down the cellar steps. Welcome! Of all the— But the cat was invariably put out before everyone went up to bed. And if Welcome had been put out, who had let him back inside? He thought grimly, 'The Vagrants! I'll warrant the dirty hounds are down there, robbing Lyddford blind!'

He uncocked the pistol, restored it to the sling, and sat down again, using his left hand to settle the splinted leg onto the steps. It was like descending into a black well. The silence pounded at his ears, and he paused frequently so as to listen. He'd have felt so much less vulnerable with the Manton in his hand, even though his left-handed aim would be poor, but he needed his one good hand to guide his leg and pull the crutch. He went on, sitting from step to step in the pitchy gloom, his nerves taut, but not for an instant considering that he had one arm in a sling, and a broken leg, and might at any instant be attacked by a murderous thief. It did occur to him that he must present a properly unheroic picture, and he grinned faintly, imagining Priscilla's mirth if she could see him.

Quite suddenly a faint light appeared some distance ahead. His heart gave a jolt. He whispered a hopeful "Jupiter!" and tried to move more rapidly, his eyes fixed to that hovering glow. He had reached the foot of the cellar steps and was struggling to stand, when the light abruptly vanished. The darkness closed in, seemingly more dense than before. He positioned the crutch under his arm and dragged himself upward, narrowed eyes striving to pierce the blackness, heart pounding with excitement. There came the faintest shuffling sound. And then he knew that someone else was very close to him. He balanced himself and groped for the pistol. His fingers had closed around it when he heard heavy breathing scant inches from his face. He could dimly make out a crouching shape and he shouted harshly, "Stay back! I've a pistol."

The answer was a low, bestial growl. Stunned, he thought, 'By God! It's the bastard who struck me down in the woods!' He jerked the pistol upward. His assailant must have the ability to see in the dark, for before he could fire, the weapon was smashed from his hand. His crutch fell as he staggered. Great arms clamped around him, and again that horrifying growl sounded. His ribs were being crushed; he could scarcely breathe. Struggling frantically to free himself, he was whirled around. He was not huskily built, but his long hours at the harpsichord had given his hands unusual strength, and although his injured right arm was trapped, by the grace of God his left arm was free of that deadly embrace. Sobbing for breath, he swung the heel of his hand at the grotesquely large and dimly seen outline and felt it connect hard with what felt like a man's throat.

A howl of pain and his assailant faltered. With all his

strength he clenched his fist and struck again, this time feeling an eye beneath his knuckles. A choked grunt. The vise that was choking the life from him eased slightly. Fighting to free himself, Montclair was suddenly all too successful. Off balance, he reached out blindly, and the iron stair railing kept him from falling. From the darkness came a snuffling. He sensed rather than saw something flailing at him, flung up his left arm and beat it aside, but his invisible assailant had the advantage of two arms, and Valentine felt the full impact of the second as it caught him across the shoulder, sending him flying. He hurtled across the stairs and crashed against the wall. Half stunned, his head spinning, he was briefly grateful that he had not fallen on his hurt leg again. Heavy footsteps were coming nearer. But the attacker was on a lower level now and Valentine had the advantage of lying half against the wall. Gathering his reeling senses he kicked out blindly, connected hard, and heard an agonized grunt.

Somebody else was coming. If the vagrants were in league with the big man, he was doomed. His bones felt like water, but if he lay here waiting for his strength to come back they'd put a period to him in no time. Dazed and panting, he forced his reluctant body up. A guttural voice full of pain groaned, "Who's . . . it. . . ?" Then the air was split by a shrill unearthly howl, a sound so unexpected and blood-chilling that for an instant Montclair was frozen. He realized then that one of the pair must have trodden on Welcome's tail. A deep cry of terror rang out. He leaned over the rail and sent his left fist in a savage jab towards the sound. He connected in a glancing blow, then his arm was seized and he was jerked over the rail as though he had been a child. Powerless to protect himself, he landed hard and lay sprawled, hearing running footsteps that gradually faded into the distance.

Gradually, his mind cleared, and he lay blinking into

292

the blackness, trying to collect his thoughts. He felt bruised all over, and seemed to be lying on a very hard mattress. There was a sense of urgency. He tried to sit up and a complaining *mew* sounded. Welcome had settled down comfortably on his chest. Memory returned with a rush. The monster had come after him again in an encounter that would surely haunt his dreams for so long as he lived. It was very quiet now. Had both the intruders left? Welcome mewed again, and sniffed with fishy breath at his face. He put the little cat aside, and found the tinderbox in his pocket. Necessity was certainly the mother of invention; he gripped the box between his teeth and was able to scrape the flint with his left hand and awaken a flame.

His eyes sought about desperately. A dark form lay crumpled at the foot of the steps, a candle beside it. Frantic with haste, he dragged himself down to that still figure and lit the candle. The man who lay face-down on the stone floor was slim, certainly not the growling monster who'd tried to kill him. More likely it was one of the vagrants.

Moving as fast as he could, Montclair poured a puddle of melted wax onto the third stair, set the candle in it, then looked about for his crutch. It lay half under the vagrant, for there was no doubt in his mind now about the man's identity. He wondered if he'd killed the rogue. His question was answered by a faint inarticulate sound. The huddled criminal moved, his stocking-capped head lifting slightly. He was probably armed. Valentine crawled with painful haste to the pistol and snatched it up.

"All right . . . you treacherous cur," he panted. "Get up. Slowly. One false move and . . . I shall fire!"

The vagrant struggled to hands and knees and turned a bruised and bewildered face.

Montclair's pistol was aimed squarely between the eyes of Mrs. Susan Henley.

293

15

" **M**rs. Sue?" gasped Montclair, flabbergasted. Susan had suffered through the most miserable day of her life, capped by a hideous encounter with an unseen and nightmarish creature whose great paws had seized her up as though she were a doll. Convinced she was about to be murdered, she'd been too terrified to give vent to the shrieks that had welled in her throat, and then someone else had struck her a cruel blow that had plunged her into unconsciousness. Now, to see Valentine's battered but beloved face quite overpowered her resolution, and she reached out to him, whimpering, "V-Val. . . ? Oh—is it—is it *really* you?"

She looked like a frightened little girl, lying there with her arms outstretched, her dark hair straying in wild strands from beneath that ridiculous stocking cap. Struck to the heart, he threw the pistol aside and clawed his way to her, holding her close as she flung herself into his arms and clung to him, weeping hysterically.

He cradled her clumsily in his right arm and pulled

off the stocking cap, stroking back her hair and murmuring soothingly that it was "all right now," while she sobbed and gulped out tearful little incoherencies.

In a little while her panic eased, and she was quieter. Montclair's befuddled head was beginning to function, and inevitably and inexorably came the questions.

"Val," gulped Susan. "What w-was it? That—that *awful* thing?"

Inestimably relieved that his first question had been answered without the need to have asked it, he managed to give her his handkerchief and she dabbed at her tears. "I think," he said, "it was the same man who threw me into the Folly."

She gave a gasp and pulled back to look up at him. A cut on his cheekbone had sent a crimson trail down to his chin and stained his cravat; his hair was wildly dishevelled, and the shoulder of his coat was ripped.

"Good heavens!" she exclaimed, wiping the blood from his cheek. "Did it—he—come inside the house searching for you, then?"

"I don't know. I thought— Sue—what are you doing down here at this hour, and wearing those—those breeches?"

She realized belatedly how absurd she must look. "I sometimes disguise myself as a man, if I sail with Andy. I can't help with the boat otherwise. And today he needed help with the cargo, so—" She saw shock in his face and changed the subject hurriedly. "Oh, never mind all that. Val, your leg isn't—"

"Broken again? No, I thank God." Remembering how the intruder had hurled him across the steps, he could only marvel that he hadn't broken his neck. "I thought you'd gone up to bed. Have you been down here working all these hours?"

"I stayed to lock up. Andy and the men were absolutely exhausted. And—and I thought I heard Welcome in the lower cellar. I went down there, but couldn't find him, and—and I began to have the most ghastly feeling that there was someone—something else down there . . . in the dark . . . w-with me!" She put her hands over her face, and Valentine pulled her to him again. Shuddering, she gulped, "And then I—I heard someone creeping down the steps, and I was terribly . . . frightened. So I blew out my candle and waited.

"Poor girl. Don't think about it. Come"—he smiled down into her grubby, tearful face—"can you stand?"

Susan peered tremblingly into the shadows. "You— you don't think it—he—is still—"

"No, no. I heard him run off."

She stood, retrieved the crutch, and helped him up. He moved with slow caution, and she said with ready sympathy, "I wonder you were not killed. Valentine! Whatever were *you* doing down here?"

The sudden suspicion in her voice reminded him of just why he had ventured those cellar steps. "I heard someone creeping about," he said in a half truth. "I'd a notion your prized vagrants were down here robbing you blind, so I decided to catch them in the act." He gave a wry smile. "I got rather more than I bargained for."

"Do you say that—with only one usable arm and your leg broken—you came down here all alone—to fight for our sake?"

The look of awed wonderment in her eyes was making him feel about an inch tall. He said gruffly, "Not—entirely. You see . . . I thought . . . Well, I was afraid—" And in a rush he said, "Monteil's a very slippery customer, Susan. I feared he was very likely using you to store cargo that—well, that wasn't what you believed it to be."

Susan's heart sank, but she still thought it the most courageous act she'd ever heard of, and thus her voice was kinder than it might have been when she said, "So

296

you came down in the middle of the night, when you thought we were all asleep, to find out—is that it?"

"Yes. I'm sorry if that sounds deplorable. At all events, I didn't have time to spy. That great brute came roaring and snuffling after me, and I was too dashed busy to—"

Susan closed her eyes, shuddering. "Don't! Don't!"

"You are overwrought—small wonder. And your poor face is so bruised! Gad, what a villain I am! But I'd never have done it had I known it was—"

She jerked her eyes open and stared at him. "*You* struck me?"

"I didn't mean to. It was so dark. And I thought you were some rascally smuggler."

She shrank away from him, her expression one of pure horror.

And suddenly, he knew. He gasped, "My God! You *are* a smuggler!"

How appalled he looked; how stunned. Perversely, she felt as if a weight was gone from her shoulders, and with a small sigh, she said, "Yes. I can imagine how that must appall you. But it is one of the reasons why we wanted Highperch. The proximity to the river, our own private dock, and so far from prying eyes." She smiled tremulously. "Or so we thought."

Valentine's physical distress was as nothing to the searing rage that possessed him. "'So you thought,' is it?" he snarled. "Say rather, 'So you did *not* think'! Good Lord above! Where were Lyddford's wits gone jauntering that he would involve you in such—"

"My brother only went into this for my sake!" she said defensively. "We were left all but destitute after my husband's death. Andy loves Priscilla and me, and—"

"And his love for you sanctions that you should lower yourself to wear breeches? He sees no objection to putting you in danger of being exposed to fire from a Reve-

297

nue cutter? Or have you already had a Navy sloop put a shot across your bows? Dammitall! The man must be mad to—"

"To try to keep us from going hungry? To be without a roof over our heads? Much *you* know of such horrors, Mr. Montclair, coddled and pampered all your days and—"

"Don't attack me, so as to defend *him*! Did neither of you idiots give a thought to Priscilla? What the devil do you think would become of her if you were thrown in Newgate? Did you plan to take her with you into that hellhole?"

The very thought made her feel sick. Tears came into her eyes again, and she began to shake inside. "I— We— She would be—provided for," she gulped.

"Would she now?" he said jeeringly. "By whom? Your devoted admirer, Monteil? Is that the hold he has over you? Is that why you let him paw you and—"

Wrath blazed through her. Before she could stop herself her hand shot out and slapped his face hard.

Taken off balance, Valentine staggered.

With a sob of remorse, Susan flew to put her own dirty hand over his gripping fingers, and look tearfully up into his strained face. "Oh, Val! Why must we always quarrel? I am so sorry!"

Looking down into her woebegone face, his frown faded. "And I'm a proper fool," he groaned. "Of all the times to take you to task when you've had such a dreadful time and are likely feeling poorly."

Her lips trembled. "Only that—my head does ache so," she quavered.

"Of course it does, poor sweet. Gad, what a brute I am!" Bracing himself, he lifted her hand and pressed his lips not onto the fingers but into the warm palm.

A tremor raced through Susan. Her headache was forgotten and her heart began to thunder. What a magic this man wielded over her, even at a moment like this. Mesmerized, she gazed up into his lean bruised face, the dark eyes, now as soft as velvet, the smile of such tenderness that hovered about his lips. He bent to her, and she made no attempt to evade his questing mouth, but raised her face eagerly. Her eyes closed as their lips touched. A flame seemed to enfold her. He pulled her closer. Who would dream the invalid still had such power? Who would dream a kiss could be so sweet, so fiery, so all-consuming? He kissed her again, and again, and joying in his caresses she felt dazed and weak and enraptured, and saw the same emotions in his eyes. But she saw also how pale he was, and when he tried to kiss her again, she pulled back and said breathlessly, "No, sir. You think me—shameless, I do not doubt, but—I'd not have you think me heartless as well. Come. You must get to your bed."

Valentine took a deep, steadying breath. "No. Susan, my lovely Free Trader, so long as we're down here, there's something I must do."

"But you are so very tired."

"And what of you?" He touched her cheek. "How indomitable you are, my dearest. Humour me on this one last point. What do you *really* ship for Imre Monteil?"

At once she stiffened again. "What would you expect?"

"No—pray do not go into the boughs. I don't ask out of jealousy or vindictiveness. I've told you my feelings where he is concerned. I'd trust him as far as I could throw this house. Have you ever *seen* what is inside his bales and boxes?"

Frowning and reluctant, she said a curt "No."

"Where are they stored?"

"Mostly in the lower cellar. But some"—she gestured to the far wall—"over there." She caught Valentine's arm as he started toward the piled boxes. "What do you mean to do?"

299

"Have a look."

"No! You must not! Val—he has been so kind. So helpful. It would be very wrong to interfere with his goods."

"It was very wrong for him to store 'em in my house!"

She argued, but he was adamant, and at length she watched helplessly while he sat on one box and began to struggle with the ropes that contained another. She was sure he wouldn't be able to manage with just one hand, and refused him any aid in what she said was a "dishonourable enterprise." Welcome had no such compunction and came to pounce with great ferocity at the jerking ropes and generally impede Valentine's progress. The strength of his long fingers stood him in good stead, however, and after a tussle he at last pulled the rope away, the cat dangling determinedly from the end.

Despite her aversion to this, Susan's curiosity got the best of her, and she stepped closer. Montclair gave an astounded exclamation when he opened the lid. For a moment Susan thought the dimness deceived her, but then she gave a little cry of astonishment.

"Bricks!" gasped Montclair. "Nothing but—bricks and old sacking! What the deuce. . . ? Sue—let's have a look in another."

This time she did not refuse him, and together they opened two more boxes, one of which was nailed shut so that she had to search around for a suitable tool, finally locating a screwdriver with which to pry the top up. The result was the same.

On her knees, Susan stared in bewilderment into the third box. "Small wonder they were so heavy."

"But why on earth would he hire you to haul such a nonsensical cargo? Unless . . ." He took the screwdriver and chipped off a corner of one of the bricks, then scowled at it.

"No gold?" said Susan with a tired smile. "Does it not strike you that there might be a perfectly simple answer to all this, Valentine?"

300

His scowl deepened. "I am very dense, I fear. What is your simple answer? That the Swiss gentleman is a philanthropist and invents cargoes only to throw some income in Lyddford's way?"

She nodded. "I can think of nothing else. And how very kind that he would—"

"Kind, my Aunt Maria! If Imre Monteil ever did one thing in his life but what there was some ulterior motive, I wish I may learn of it!"

He looked so fierce. She smiled a faint inner smile and, infuriatingly, did not argue.

"No, I do not understand," said Lyddford angrily, turning from the sunny withdrawing room windows to face his sister. "You should have awoken me at once! A fine thing to have murderers popping in and out of the house at all hours of the night! And furthermore, I'd like to know—"

"But I *did* waken Starry. And she and Deemer searched the whole house and secured all the locks. You were so tired, and—"

"And I suppose you were not!" He eyed her pale face and shadowed eyes, inwardly amazed by her courage, but fuming none the less. "A fine night you had, and me snoring like any dullard through the whole! Dammit! If I lay my hands on the man who dared put that bruise on your face, I'll—"

"I reckon as we all feel the same, Mr. Andy," Bo'sun Dodman put in, his ruddy face grim and set. "When we find him there'll be one less murderer roving England's by-ways. The thing is—what was he doing here?"

"Looking for Montclair, I suppose," said Mrs. Starr, seated beside Susan at this morning council of war.

Lyddford ran an impatient hand through his dark locks. "I don't see that. If he meant to put a period to

Montclair, why was he lurking about in the cellar? He certainly didn't expect to find him sleeping down there!"

"I thought the same," said Susan. "Unless perhaps he broke into the house and then decided to steal something from the cargo."

"He'd have had to know we've been off-loading cargo," said the Bo'sun thoughtfully. "Could have, I suppose. But why would anyone want to steal a brick?"

Mrs. Starr observed, "Now *there's* something makes no sense whatsoever."

"Chess," Angelo de Ferdinand agreed from the windowseat. "Monsieur theses bricks he's is wantings, whys it?"

Susan said, "I believe he may have done it out of kindness."

"The devil!" snapped her brother, a flush staining his cheeks. "D'you mean 'charity' by any chance? I comprehend he has a *tendre* for you, but I'll not stand still for that sort of flummery! You may be sure I'll tax him with it!"

"Can't do that, Mr. Andy," the Bo'sun pointed out gravely. "Not unless you're willing to own that we poked our noses in his boxes."

There was a chorus of agreement, and Lyddford muttered that he'd have to think about how to broach the matter. "Meanwhile," he added, "what I'd like to know, Mrs. H., is how you and Valentine Montclair came to be down in the cellar together in the first place."

Susan felt every eye turn to her, and knew her face was scarlet. "We weren't," she said. "Not exactly. I had intended to follow you straight up to bed, Andy, but I sat down to pull my boots off, and fell asleep. When I woke up it was past midnight, and I thought I heard someone in the cellar."

"So you went tripping down there, all alone, and unarmed. Famous behaviour, upon my word! I never fancied you short of a sheet, Susan."

302

"I thought it was Welcome," she said simply.

"Lucky you came out alive," grunted Lyddford. "Both of you. The fact remains that if that murdering hound has taken to coming into Highperch after Montclair, something must be done. And the easiest solution is for our noble guest to go back to his great Manor. No, Sue, don't argue. I'll not have you and Priscilla—or any of us—put at risk here. Montclair can hire an army to defend himself if he chooses. We can't."

Before anyone could respond, Martha came into the room and stood twisting the hem of her apron and looking at Susan in a troubled way.

"Yes, Martha?" said Susan.

"I know as you're all talking, Mrs. Sue," said the girl hesitantly. "But I thought I better come and tell you, just in case."

"Tell us what? Is it about Miss Priscilla?"

"No, ma'am. But she heard it, too. She's outside now, playing with Wolfgang, but—"

"What did she hear?" asked Mrs. Starr patiently.

"Why—the crash. We was in what used to be the study, only it's your sewing room now, you know, Mrs. Sue. And that's right under your bedroom—only it's Mr. Valentine's room now, and—"

Susan tensed. "And you heard a crash, you said?"

"Yes, Mrs. Sue. It sounded like something heavy had been dropped. Or like someone had fallen down, or—"

Lyddford and Susan were already running.

Montclair slept late, awakening to find Deemer opening the window curtains. He felt bruised from head to toe, and by the time, with the butler's help, he was shaved and dressed, he had found ample evidence of the power of the intruder. Martha fetched his breakfast tray, and he ate at the small table before the windows.

It was a beautiful morning, a slight haze draping an ethereal veil over the river and the distant hills, but he scarcely saw the loved prospect. He could see instead the glow in Susan's bruised face as she lifted it to his kiss; feel again the softness and warmth of her lovely body pressed against his. Since leaving Cambridge he'd been too occupied with his music and his endless fight to guard Longhills to have much time for women. When Mrs. Susan Henley had come uninvited into his life she had seemed only a further complication to his already difficult existence. Now, not only was he deeply indebted to her, but if he thought of her as a complication, it was as a most delectable one.

She was very far from being his ideal. That often dreamed-of lady was a soft-voiced, sweetly natured creature with shining golden curls, eyes of cornflower blue, and a rosebud mouth. A delicate and gentle lady who never spoke in anger, or argued with him, but would adoringly agree with any opinion he voiced. Certainly she would not dream of striking him with a dustpan brush! Always, she was impeccably and elegantly gowned. And would faint at the very thought of a lady wearing breeches! She moved with grace and propriety. (And the man who lay in helpless agony at the bottom of a Folly waiting for her to find the gumption to climb down and help him, would die alone!) His ideal was, in short, a lovely dimwit without flesh and blood and human failings, who would bore him to death in a week.

He chuckled, banished his 'ideal lady' forever, and put on her vacant pedestal a tall, willowy young woman with candid grey eyes, a resolute mouth, and long, very straight dark hair that gleamed silkily—when it wasn't tucked under a stocking cap. He smiled again, remembering her face last night, but the smile died abruptly as he recalled the bruise he had put there. It had been unintentional, of course, and she'd understood. Still—it

304

should never have happened. He frowned uneasily. He had criticized Lyddford for exposing his sister to danger, but he himself was no less guilty. If his presence here constituted a menace to Susan and the rest of them, he must leave. The thought of a return to life with the Trents was not enticing, but it was, he knew, past time that he went home. Certainly, little Barbara had stood in need of him, and Lord only knows what Uncle Selby had been about during his absence.

Sighing, he reached for the last crumpet. His outstretched hand checked, and shock was like a physical blow. He had stretched out his *right* hand unthinkingly, and his fingers had *moved* a little! Hope made his pulses race. Perhaps his hand was not permanently damaged after all! Jupiter—he was almost well! He snatched up his crutch, eager to test his leg. He found he was able to lower his left foot to the floor and stand straight without the crutch, and with only a little discomfort. Leaning on the crutch very slightly, he crossed the big room and limped into the dressing room. It was an ungainly hobble, admittedly, but it was a great improvement!

Elated, he swung around, so eager to find Susan and share his triumph with her, that he forgot the need for caution and the crutch pulled the rug into a fold. Thrown off balance, he staggered, and flung his left arm out instinctively. His fingers closed around the handle of a cupboard which was always kept locked. Unhappily, his weight was too much. The handle broke off; he went down, still clutching it, and the warped cupboard door flew off its rusted hinges and crashed down also. He jerked his head away and threw up his arm to protect himself from several cascading bottles.

When the shower ceased, he sat there taking stock of things. Luckily, he appeared to have sustained no hurt, and none of the bottles had smashed. He began to gather them up. There were six, uniformly filled with a

305

dark brown liquid that looked vaguely familiar. Idly, he glanced at the label:

> *"For Valentine Montclair, Esquire.*
> *Give one teaspoonful three times per day.*
> *Dr. K. R. Sheswell."*

A numbness came over him, and he leaned back against the lower cupboard, staring blankly at the bottle in his hand, and trying to fight away the insidious suspicion that was creeping into his mind. He had improved to the point the medicine was no longer needed, that was all. Only—if it was no longer needed, why had old Sheswell kept sending it? For how long had it been withheld? His glance flashed to the cupboard. Suddenly very cold, he could see that there were more bottles still on the shelf. All apparently untouched.

His aunt's voice seemed to scream in his ears: ". . . If my suspicions are correct, Dr. Sheswell's instructions have been poorly kept. Why, he thought you would be better in no time . . ." He had not got better "in no time." He had come very close to turning up his toes, and it had been a long and slow recovery. But—surely the brave and beautiful Susan had not schemed to— He threw his left hand across his eyes, whispering an agonized, "No! Oh, God! Please—no!"

But doubt came to whisper slyly that his uncle had said Susan had profited handsomely. Later, when he'd asked her, she'd admitted that the Trents had made financial provision . . .

His aunt's voice again: ". . . That sly widow saw her chance . . . She would nurse you back to health and so win your affections that you would give her the house . . . Never say you have fallen into the hussy's toils. . . ? I'll not believe you could be so gullible . . ."

He ducked his head and instinctively put both hands

over his ears, fighting to shut out that shrill vindictiveness. "I won't believe it of her! I won't!"

In his misery he hadn't realized he spoke aloud. Nor had he heard the door open, and he was startled when Susan said quietly, "What won't you believe, sir?"

His eyes lifted to hers. She stood very straight, very white, looking down at him with cold hauteur.

It made no sense, he thought in desperation. It *could* not make sense! And then, with perverse and shattering clarity, memory supplied the scene it had denied him until now. The night he'd lain half asleep during the early part of his recovery, and had heard Susan whispering with Mrs. Starr. Starry had said they should never have done something. Susan, obviously irked, had argued that nothing could be proven. And then Starry had moaned, ". . . the Runners can be clever. If they should even *suspect*— Suppose his family should put two and two together? It is such a dreadful thing to do! I never dreamed you capable of such ruthless—" He had dismissed it as a dream, but with a terrible ache of grief he knew now that it hadn't been a dream. He could even hear Susan's final words: "Stop being so melodramatic! And keep your voice down, do. He might hear us!"

It was the withholding of his medicine that had so distressed Starry and made her accuse Susan of ruthlessness. Ruthlessness, indeed! It sounded the death-knell to his hopes, and he was so distraught that for a moment he could neither move nor speak.

Lyddford ran in. "Gad, what a mess! You all right, Montclair?" He stepped over the debris and assisted Montclair to his feet. "Why the deuce have you been flinging all these bottles about?"

"Mr. Montclair found it necessary to break open the cupboard," said Susan, her lip curling contemptuously.

"Break . . . open . . ." gasped Lyddford.

307

"I didn't break it open, Susan," said Montclair. "I was—"

"Dear me," she sneered. "I'd not dreamed there were exploding cupboards in this house. Just what did you expect to find, that you must resort to such methods, sir?"

Sick at heart, he answered, "Not what I did find, certainly. But I'm sure there is a very logical explanation." His eyes pleaded. "Isn't there?"

"Explanation—for what?" said Lyddford, bewildered. "What the deuce is all this stuff?"

"Oh, it is no use your taking that tone, Andy," Susan gave a brittle mirthless little laugh. "Mr. Montclair will never believe you don't know about it."

"By the Lord Harry! Know about—*what?*"

"The medicine," she said, so hurt and angry that she had to fight for self-control. "Mr. Montclair believes we deliberately withheld it so as to delay his recovery."

"*What?*" roared Lyddford, his face reddening.

"I didn't say that," said Montclair. "If you would just—"

"It was exceeding obvious what you *thought*," she flashed.

"Why—why, you *ingrate*," Lyddford howled. "You damned—*dog!* I—"

"Be quiet!" snapped Montclair. "Sue—for the love of God! I fell and the cupboard door broke when I grabbed at it to steady—"

"Like hell!" shouted Lyddford.

Montclair rounded on him furiously. "*Will* you be quiet! Susan—*please*—I know that even now my stupid head is—is confused sometimes. When all the medicine bottles fell out—"

"You put two and two together, and we came up wanting," she said. "La, sir, but your feelings change so rapidly! And how exceeding convenient that you—ah—

308

'fell' against that *particular* cupboard!" Her brows drew down. She said with biting scorn, "For *shame* that you should be so quick to believe the worst!"

She turned to leave, but he caught her wrist. "No! I *don't* believe it! That is—I do, but—but I know you must have had some reason. If you will only *tell* me—"

"Not a word, Sue! Not one blasted word to the carrion!" Lyddford sprang to wrench Montclair's hand away, sending him staggering back to the wall. Through his teeth, he said, "Mrs. H., you will please to leave us. At once! Send Deemer and the Bo'sun up here!"

Susan hesitated, glancing from his livid face to Montclair's haggard one. "Andy—you won't . . ."

"If he was a whole man—by God, I think I'd strangle him with my bare hands! But he'll answer to me, I promise you! Now—*go!*"

She turned and went out.

Montclair watched her in helpless misery. She had offered no excuse. No denial. The cupboard *had* been locked. His medicine *had* been withheld. But he wanted so desperately to disbelieve the evidence of his own eyes. He said, "Lyddford, you must—"

Almost incoherent with rage, Lyddford snarled, "I take leave to tell you that you are a damned *cad* and an ugly-minded— You are no *gentleman!* When I *think*— When I— My challenge to you *stands,* Montclair! As soon as you put off those splints, my seconds will call on you."

Montclair sighed drearily, "I cannot fight you."

"You will, damn you! As soon as you're well, I'll haunt you! I'll shame you until you've no choice! I don't want to see your face until then—or until we meet in court!"

Montclair reached for his crutch. "There will be no need for courts. I told your sister I will not contest your claim to Highperch."

Lyddford sprang forward and seized him by the neck-

309

cloth, thrusting his inflamed countenance forward. "Do not be offering us your damned charity, Mr. High-in-the-Instep aristocrat! If it was only me you insulted, I'd likely simply cut out your liver! But—that you should *dare* to think evil of my sister—! We will defeat you in the courts, sir! Legally! And then— By God, but I can scarce wait to get you before the sights of my pistol!"

Montclair knocked his hand away. "Meanwhile, you might try to keep your so beloved sister from getting herself taken up for a smuggler."

All the colour left Lyddford's face. In a controlled voice far more deadly than his loud fury, he said, "Now—if I thought you meant to betray us like the worthless hound you are—I'd make sure you never reached Longhills alive."

Valentine's mouth hardened. He said bitterly, "I wonder why I should only now recall that you once told me that so long as I was recuperating here, I could not very well have you thrown out."

Lyddford swore ringingly, and his open hand flew at Montclair's face.

It was caught in a grip of steel, the wrist twisted so sharply that he could scarcely keep back a gasp of pain.

His voice cold, Montclair continued. "Which very likely means that I may be the world's most stupid slow-top. But I swear on my honour I shall never betray you—any of you." He flung Lyddford's hand down, took up his crutch, and hobbled into the bedroom.

Holding his wrist in a cherishing clasp, Lyddford stared after him for a moment. Then he kicked the nearest bottle savagely across the floor and stamped, swearing, into the hall.

310

16

All through the week gale-force winds had battered the west country, toppling trees, displacing roofing, restricting the movements of shipping. Today, for the first time the winds had eased, but occasional gusts still bowed the trees and whined around Longhills. Sitting in the windowseat in his bedchamber, Montclair watched the drizzling rain and wondered if Lyddford had been able to take *The Dainty Dancer* out; if Susan had donned her breeches and sailed with him; if little Priscilla was wandering about, missing him, needing him to help finish their long story . . .

His hand tightened on the grubby object he held. Eight days since he had seen the little girl or the wicked widow . . . Eight days. And it seemed more like eight years. He could walk quite comfortably now, so long as he did not walk too far, and his hand was improving rapidly. Sheswell was overjoyed, and declared it was what he had hoped for long since; indeed, he could not comprehend why his medicine, usually so efficacious, had not achieved such results long before this. The thought had caused him to frown and shake his head in mystification. His heart twisting, Valentine had said nothing.

He should be overjoyed also. It was what he had prayed for—that his hand should regain feeling. He'd even been able to play his beloved harpsichord—not well, but a little, and Sheswell assured him it was just the beginning. Just the beginning. Why then must he feel it was the end? Why must joy be a thing forgotten, and grief a constant ache within him?

The question was answered almost before it was asked. Until he found Susan he'd not realized how lonely his life had been. Finding her, he had thought to have found a dauntless lady whose heart was kind, whose nature was generous and loyal, whose bright spirit could always put the sunlight back in his sky. They had bickered sometimes, true, but even the bickering had been comfortable, and how joyous had been the moments when they'd laughed together. Life had begun to look bright again, and full of promise. He had begun to weave dreams of the future . . . glorious dreams. And all the time—

He flung the dirty mob-cap from him and stared unseeingly across the park. Were his suspicions merely another product of the concussion Sheswell said would bother him for months to come? No matter what his aunt and uncle said, nothing would convince him that the lovely Susan and her brother had plotted the initial murderous attack on him. But he could not deny the possibility that Priscilla's discovery of him in the Folly had enabled them to "rescue" him, and then contrive that he would slowly die under their "care." He groaned softly. Could someone so lovely, seemingly so kind and compassionate, be so evil . . . such a clever actress? His heart said no, but the demon called Common Sense whispered that if she was innocent, why had she and

Mrs. Starr held that whispered conversation he'd not been meant to hear? Why had she uttered not one word of explanation? It would have been so simple and he'd been so desperately eager to believe whatever she told him. He'd even pleaded with her. And still she had said nothing.

Tormented by these terrible suspicions, his battle to banish her from his mind was unsuccessful. When he played his music he saw her beside him on the bench of the spinet that beautiful sunny morning, her face aglow as she played the treble and he the bass. The smile in her eyes shone at him from the flickering flames of the candles. Her voice echoed in his ears when he tried to sleep; the tilt of her intrepid chin, the vivid curve of her mouth, the sheen on the thick silken curtain of her hair haunted him day and night. There was no respite, no escape from the yearning for what might have been.

He scowled and his lips tightened. It was no use mooning like this. The idyll—if such it could be called— was done. He had exchanged the cheerful informality of Highperch for the awesome majesty of Longhills. Dammit—what was he thinking? He loved Longhills! He always had. It was his birthplace. Only . . . just now it was also a luxurious loneliness not alleviated by his aunt's barbed remarks, his uncle's smiling insincerity, the sneering hostility of Junius. Only with Barbara could he feel a mutual fondness, and their meetings were few and far between, her parents patently regarding him as a threat, an evil influence on their timid child.

He was to meet with her this afternoon, however. Gould had given him a smuggled note requesting that he await her in the cellar at four o'clock. He could well imagine why. The dreaded marriage must be weighing heavily on the poor girl, in spite of his promise that she would never become Lady Pollinger. Gad, if nothing else

313

offered, he'd marry her himself. He thought wryly that it might offer a solution for both of them.

Despite the rain one of the gardeners was trundling a wheelbarrow across the lawn, leaving a deep rut in the velvet turf. "Stupid clod!" muttered Montclair. At first he thought the offender was the new man, Diccon, but that lazy fellow was not likely to be moving so purposefully, almost as though he was late for something . . . Curious, he crossed to his chest of drawers and sought about until he found the spyglass he had been used to employ when sailing. Returning to the window, he focused it, then swung it ahead of the gardener's fast-moving figure. At first, he could detect only the high shrubs that bordered the cutting gardens. Then the wind whipped the branches apart to reveal a man standing very still among the bushes.

The gardener cast a quick glance behind him, then joined the second man, and the two of them disappeared from view.

Montclair telescoped the glass, his lips tight and angry. The gardener had indeed been Diccon. And the man he'd met so furtively was one of Mrs. Henley's vagrants.

Frowning, he put the glass away. Footsteps sounded in the hall, and his aunt's strident tones shrilled out. The mob-cap was lying on the windowseat in plain sight. Her quick eyes would spot it at once, and a fine time he'd have explaining it away! He leapt to snatch up the betraying cap and thrust it into the drawer of his bedside table, then turned to the opening door. Perhaps he had moved too suddenly and too fast: his aunt's magenta-clad figure rippled before his eyes like silk in a gale. The room dipped and swayed. Uncle Selby's arm was about him. Over the roaring in his ears, he heard the familiar voice, harsh with anger.

"Poor fellow . . . Second attack this week—worse than he was before! God only knows what that unprincipled

314

harpy and her cohorts have done to him . . . Hurry, my love, and send a groom for Sheswell at once . . ."

With a great effort, Montclair fought away the sickening giddiness. "No. Better . . . now. I—don't want . . . Sheswell . . ."

The first cellar was chill and very dark, and stretched off like a vast and deserted warehouse until it was swallowed up by the gloom. Montclair paused to light two candles in a wall sconce. The resultant small circle of brightness pushed back the dark, and neat rows of folding tables that were used for garden parties leapt into view beside him. Most of the articles stored on this level were furnishings and supplies that were periodically put to use. He walked along the clear space between bedsteads, chairs, and chests under holland covers, his mind on the just concluded interview with his aunt and uncle. He had been dismayed by the attack of dizziness, following so soon after the one he'd suffered on Tuesday. For some reason the illness had not struck him since that very bad first week at Highperch, and he'd begun to hope it had run its course. An unwarranted optimism, evidently. However, this particular siege had served a purpose; Sir Selby and Lady Marcia had sought him out so as to discuss the eviction of Mrs. Henley and her family. His flat refusal to instigate such a procedure had infuriated them, but since he was clearly unwell they had been unable to indulge their wrath, and, obviously seething, had left him to Gould's care.

The attack had been sharp, but short, and fortunately he'd recovered in time to meet Babs. Still, he was none too steady on his feet, and trod carefully down the worn stone steps leading to the lower cellar. The darkness was deeper, and mustier, and the silence became absolute. He held his candle higher and called, but there was no sign of Barbara. She must be having difficulty slipping away, poor chit. While waiting for her he amused himself by inspecting the accumulation of unwanted articles that had been relegated to this ignominious retirement. There were quite a number of old paintings, some with quite beautiful frames, all covered with a thick layer of dust. Poking through a pile of crockery and bric-a-brac, he came across a blackened statuette that he found to be a splendid reproduction of the Montclair Mermaid fashioned from what he suspected to be sterling silver. Vaguely irritated that it should have been discarded, he carried the mermaid along with him, and had in short order succumbed happily to the disease that seems to afflict all people who search through attics or cellars crammed with long forgotten, and unexpectedly fascinating articles.

Twenty minutes later he had also rescued a charming inlaid tray, an Etruscan bowl, and a Chinese pottery horse that he thought was very old, possibly of the T'ang Dynasty, in which case it would be quite valuable. Still there was no sign of Barbara, but he was in no hurry, thoroughly enjoying this voyage of exploration.

Quite suddenly, there was a difference in the quality of the air. The rear door must have been opened. Why on earth would Barbara have come down that way when the approach was from the hillside and rather sheer? It dawned on him then that no one but Yates and himself had a key to that door. He swore softly, blew out his candle, and drew the pistol that nowadays he always carried in his pocket. Grim and ready, he waited. There came the scrape of a tinder box, followed by a glow that grew brighter. A tall press blocked his view, but the light was steadier now; the candle must have been put down. A shadow slanted across the room. Montclair caught a glimpse of riding boots and heard the faint jingle of spurs. Not Barbara, that was certain! He strode forward, pistol levelled. "Stand, or I fire!" he commanded ringingly.

The intruder swung around.

"Chew bad being to mices frens," alleged a familiar and somewhat nasal voice. "But chew goodly kinds to mices lady. Mostly Angelo forgiving chews."

Montclair had to fight a ridiculous surge of delight. "What the *devil* are you doing in my cellar?"

"Angelo overlookings theses lamps," said the Spaniard, taking the question literally. "Very old, very finely. Mices elves buyings for loveliest—"

"Good God! What again? Be damned if you ain't a merchant by inclination—always trying to buy something!" Montclair strolled nearer, and glanced at the lamp the señor was holding. Despite the dust it was an interesting piece fashioned of heavy crystal, the shade a series of finely etched panels that were each remarkably beautiful. "Besides, I didn't mean that," he said. "I meant—*why* are you here?" Hope quickened his heartbeat. "Have you brought a—a message for me, perhaps?"

"He is here because I asked him to come, Val." Candlestick in hand, Barbara hurried from the stairs. She gave Montclair a fond smile, but went straight to the Spaniard.

Angelo put down his lamp and bowed to press his lips to her fingers. "Mices loveliest," he murmured with ardour.

"You came," sighed Barbara redundantly.

'Oh, my God,' thought Montclair.

It took a very few minutes to verify his fears. Miss Barbara Trent and Señor Angelo Francisco Luis Lagunes de Ferdinand were deeply in love. The Spaniard followed Barbara's revelation by making an extremely lengthy and incoherent offer for his lady's hand in marriage.

"I'm afraid I didn't quite understand all that, señor," said Montclair as soon as he could break into this dramatic oration. "But I gather you wish to marry my cousin, in which case your application must be made to Sir Selby Trent, not to—"

"No, Val," said Barbara.

It occurred to him belatedly that she had changed from the nervous child he knew. There was a new set to her chin, a brighter light in her eyes, and a becoming colour in her formerly pale cheeks. Being of the personal opinion that de Ferdinand was a little mad, Montclair found it incredible that his cousin could really have given her heart to so volatile an individual. The tender expression she turned upon the Spaniard left little doubt but that she loved him, however, and he in turn regarded her with such slavish adoration that Montclair dreaded what the end might be. "You must realize, Babs," he said gently, "that even if I had a legal right to do so, I could not give you my permission."

"I know exactly what Papa would say," she argued. "And so do you. They all are determined I must marry Sir Dennis Pollinger, and sooner would I be dead."

Señor de Ferdinand uttered a shriek and clapped a hand over her lips. *"Madre de Dios!"* he gasped, forgetting himself in his horror. "Chew deadling be, I yump in rivers! No, no! Angelo firstly deploying theses mens nasty!"

"Destroying, my dearest," corrected Barbara, smiling at him lovingly. She turned to her troubled cousin. "I mean to wed him, Val. Yours is the only consent I care about. I shall elope, if I must."

He frowned. "I know you've been very unhappy, Babs, and I do indeed understand your situation. But I must consider your welfare. We know nothing of Señor de Ferdinand"—he slanted a faint smile at Angelo's anxious and intent face—"save that he's always trying to buy everything in sight."

"For mices loveliest. Chess!"

"I appreciate your motives, certainly. But—señor, this simply will not do. I have no right at all to order Barbara's future, but she is my cousin and her happiness is most important to me. If her heart is set on this, I promise I'll do all in my power to help you, but I'll not see her disgraced by a runaway elopement to Gretna Green."

With several vehement nods the Spaniard drew a folded paper from an inner pocket. "Mices elves buyings theses. Other the days."

Montclair took the paper and scanned it briefly. "Good Lord! A Special Licence?"

"Angelo somethings wanting, Angelo gottings."

Montclair stared at him. "These aren't easy to come by. How the deuce did—" He abandoned that pointless line of enquiry and returned the licence. "Very good. But how am I to know that you don't already have a wife and a well-filled nursery? Or that you—"

The Spaniard gave a snort of wrath, stamped his foot, and drew himself to his full height. "Señora de Ferdinand they's not! Nurseries they's not! Angelo de Ferdinand, mices elves, honour the bull yentleman!"

"I will accept your word that you are an honourable man," said Montclair, contriving to maintain an air of gravity. "But I know nothing of your background, save that you appear to make your home with Mr. Lyddford and Mrs. Henley. Which is certainly not an indication that you are able to support my cousin in comfort."

"Mices loveliest wishings palace, she havings! Herses elves wanting castles or Prinny's vermilion at theses Brightons, she havings! Angelo Francisco—"

"Miss Barbara. . . ?" Winnie's plump and scared countenance peered at them from the steps. "They're looking everywhere for you, Miss," she quavered. "Oh, do come quick! *Ever* so quick, Miss!"

"Chess!" said Angelo, seizing his love's hand. "Comings ourses elves, mices Barbara. Nowly!"

"No!" said Montclair. "If they catch one whiff of this, señor, your lovely lady will be whisked away and you likely clapped up before you know where you are. Babs is underage and her parents have full legal control over her. You'd best get back to your friends, before you're caught."

"He's perfectly right," said Barbara, frantic at the thought of danger to her beloved. "Go now. Val will handle everything, don't worry."

"But, Angelo's wishes—"

"Oh, Miss! *Do* come!" begged the abigail tearfully.

Reluctantly, Angelo returned his key to Barbara and took his leave.

Montclair walked across the cellar with his cousin, easing her apprehensions by promising faithfully that was it at all possible, he would see her safely married to her unorthodox suitor.

"One thing, Babs," he said, as they climbed the stairs. "Where did you get my key to the back door?"

"It's not yours, Val. Winnie persuaded my brother's man to let her borrow it." She whispered desperately, "I beg you will not judge Señor Angelo because he—he sometimes brags a little. He is so kind, so gentle with me."

He reassured her as best he could, but when she left him and hurried after her abigail his steps slowed, his thoughts turning to his own problems. He now had two more pieces to add to his puzzle: at least one of the vagrants from Highperch was conspiring with his lazy gardener, for there could be no doubt that their meeting had been a secretive one. Also, there was the business of Junius having a key to the cellar entrance. In the year 1645, a troop of Oliver Cromwell's Roundheads had discovered the rear door, entered the Manor, slaughtered twenty-five of its Royalist defenders, and set fire to the building so that much of the East Wing had to be re-built. Since then, the two keys to that door had been jealously guarded. His own key (Geoff's, actually) was locked in his desk. He'd seen Yates's key this morning when the steward had opened the safe and grumbled good-naturedly that his key ring all but made him lean sideways when he walked. Somehow, Junius must have got his hands on one and had it copied. Perhaps he only wanted it so as to slink into the house after enjoying one of the wild nights his father would frown upon. On the other hand, Junius was very obviously both obedient to and afraid of Monsieur Imre Monteil. And the Swiss gentleman had a very havey-cavey business rela-tionship with Andrew Lyddford.

He intended to tackle Junius about the key, but the Trents had a dinner engagement that evening, and took Junius and Barbara with them, so he dined alone, plagued by an irritating sense that he had seen some-thing in the cellar that was important, something he should have at once recognized to be of special signifi-cance. Whatever it was, it eluded him. He retired to his study, worked hard at his music for several hours, and went up to bed vexed by the knowledge that he had ac-complished very little of any worth. Gould interpreted his gloomy expression correctly, and was so quietly dip-lomatic that at length Montclair's introspection was pierced. "Am I behaving like a bear?" he asked laugh-ingly. "What a trial I am to cause you to creep about as if on sheer glass."

"You are not a trial at all, Mr. Montclair," said the valet politely, then added with daring, "Only—I wish I might think you happy."

His employer's eyes became veiled. "I have much to be thankful for, Gould. I am alive when by rights I should

321

be thoroughly dead. I live in a beautiful house. I am cared for by patient and faithful retainers. A great deal more than many men can claim, eh?"

Yet even as he spoke those hollow and empty words came another nudge at memory. What in the world was his brain trying to tell him?

After Gould left, he lay frowning at the book in his hands. It had been something in the cellar . . . And it was connected to something he'd said to Gould . . . What had he said? He'd spoken of the beauty of Longhills . . . and of his faithful servants . . . not much else. However he racked his brains the puzzle would not be solved, and at length, frustrated, he slammed the book closed and leaned over to blow out his candle. His outstretched hand checked, and he stared at the water pitcher, his own voice echoing in his ears. ". . . to creep about as if on sheer glass . . ." That was it! Glass! Into his mind's eye came Angelo holding up that crystal lamp. For a long moment he remained stiff and silent. Then, "By God. . . !" he whispered, and flinging back the bed-clothes began to get dressed again.

Everyone had gone to bed when he made his way down to the second cellar, and the dark stillness seemed to press in about him. He had carried a branch of candles this time, and lit those in the wall sconces as he went along. His searching gaze found the lamp at last, and he went eagerly to inspect it. The Chinese student he'd admired at school had been most interested in the manufacture of glass, and from Li he had learned something of the procedure. The diamond-point engraving on the panels of the shade was exquisitely done, the clarity and the hatching, which was without exception worked in a single direction, marking it beyond doubt as having been fashioned in the Netherlands, some time in the sixteenth century. It was a rare work of art. Montclair's breath hissed through his teeth and he began to search carefully through the haphazardly piled articles.

322

When he climbed the steps half an hour later, his eyes were narrowed, his lips a tight line. The pieces of the puzzle were falling together in a way that could no longer be ignored, and always the evidence pointed in one direction. The hurt and disillusion that had racked him were intensified, but now to those emotions was added rage, deep and searing.

Charlie Purvis handed Allegro's reins to Montclair and peered up into the stormy face anxiously.

"You sure you won't let me ride with you, sir? He's awful frisky, and you're not—" He broke off, his sleepy eyes widening as Montclair slipped a long-barrelled Boutet pistol into the saddle holster. "Mr. Valentine," he said in a changed voice, "I don't know what you're about, but it's a wild night and I'm going with—"

Montclair said curtly, "You're going back to bed, Charlie. What I'm about is my own affair, and I shall handle it without interference."

The big bay cavorted, impatient to be gone, but Purvis's hand clung to the bridle still. Montclair's expression lightened. He reached down to grip the Welshman's shoulder. "You're a good fellow, and I thank you for your loyalty. Just in case anything should go wrong, I've left a letter for Mr. Devenish telling him what I suspect. It might be as well for you to take it down to Devencourt. At once. Gould will give it to you, but say nothing of it to anyone else, understand?"

"Aye. I'll be mum as chance, sir."

"Good man. Now—stand clear!"

Allegro reared, snorting, and Purvis jumped away. "Sir," he called, "you forgot your hat!"

But Montclair had already been swallowed up by the blustery darkness.

It was utter folly, thought Susan, wandering across the meadow and lifting her face to the night wind, to brood so about the wretched creature. He was unworthy of one second of her consideration. It was all the fault of Fate, really. Fate was such a cruel trickster. She had married Burke Henley willingly, and she'd been fond of him, but she'd never given him her heart. She had saved it—for a man who in return had despised her!

She was faintly surprised to find that her aimless steps had carried her into the fringes of the woods. She'd come a long way, and she should not really be out here alone, but it was hard to sleep of late, and sometimes she felt a desperate need to escape from her family and the cottage where there were so many reminders of—She frowned.

The moonlight came dimly through the trees, and she had no difficulty making her way back along the rough path. Her steps slowed, and she gazed at a swaying fern. How proud he had looked when he left them. How cold and haughty and unforgiving. She'd begun to dream that he loved her, instead of which he'd made it clear that he judged them a pack of scheming murderers. What a hideous moment of awareness that had been, and what a lesson. Never again would she—

She had been vaguely conscious of odd sounds, and now a great rustling and snapping of branches sounded behind her. Frightened, she wondered if it could be Junius Trent's savage dog. She'd heard several accounts of the animal's viciousness, and the thought of facing such a brute in the woods at night made her very sorry she'd not thought of such a possibility before foolishly wandering out alone. She saw a light approaching and thought nonsensically that dogs did not carry lanterns.

Perhaps Trent was taking his hound for a walk. No, that was silly also. The dog had the run of the estate, and anyway, why would Trent take him out at this hour of the night? It must be at least eleven o'clock.

A deep voice with a foreign accent said, "When master say do, we do."

Whatever they were doing for their master was very likely of a shady nature if it must be done under cover of darkness, and they probably would not be pleased to find they'd been seen. Susan shrank behind a tree, but with horrid perversity the light seemed to be coming this way. If they came too close, they would surely see her! Already it was too late to run away. She could see the lantern bobbing up and down, hear the grumbling voices of several men. And they were headed directly for her! There was probably not another soul in the Longhills woods tonight, but they *had* to choose the exact path she had followed! She was wearing her dark green cloak, and she gathered it around her and with a muffled sob knelt down, crouching very low among the roots, and pulling the hood over her face. Seconds later kneeboots were stamping so close that she could have reached out and touched them, and she huddled there, shaking, scarcely daring to breathe. A Scots voice complained that they'd "hae done better tae ha' fetched the wee carrt closer." Another man swore in French and said belligerently, *"C'est une absurdité!* But thees you will tell us 'ow to do it, *hors de doute!"*

An oath greeted this sarcasm. They all sounded breathless, and the man who had first spoken said a pithy "Many box. Jacques work—not talk."

"Hold on a bit," gasped an English voice. "This accursed . . . thing weighs a ton!"

The last pair of boots halted about six inches from Susan's bowed head. If their owner glanced down he must see her! She prayed with silent intensity.

A noisy collision. A burst of profanity made her shrink, and was cut short by a roared "Get on, damn you! Almost made me drop the lot!"

Grumbling, they moved on, their breathless voices gradually fading away.

When Susan was sure there were no more coming, she peeped up. She could see the last man outlined against the dim light from the lantern, a large box balanced on one shoulder. She thought there must have been five in all, and she gazed after them, trembling, scarcely able to believe she had not been discovered.

The first man had said "Many box." And the Scot had mumbled something about a wee cart. Very likely there were more boxes to be unloaded. When they returned, she must be far from this horrid spot! She clambered to her feet, taking care to make as little noise as possible, and started back the way she had come, but curiosity began to niggle at her. Where in the world could they be going? There were no houses for miles. No buildings at all in the woods—save for that hideous Folly. She peered around, but in the dark it was impossible to tell how close she was to the ruins. Was it possible that *was* where they were going? Could there be a hidden room perhaps, where smugglers met? Intrigued, she began to creep after them. The wind was rising; the agitated branches would smother any sound she might make so long as she stayed far enough distant—just close enough to see without being seen . . .

As it turned out, they went only a short way. She was about ten yards behind them, well screened by the undergrowth, when she heard a crash that made her jump almost out of her skin. She shrank against the nearest tree, clinging to it, her heart in her mouth. What on earth. . . ?

She forced her trembling knees to bear her closer and peeped through the branches.

326

Eerily illumined by the moonlight, and with the wind moaning through the branches, the Montclair Folly looked bizarre indeed. The men were gathered at the pit, the lantern throwing their shadows across the small clearing. Even as Susan watched, a sturdy fellow dragged his box to the very edge. "'Ere we goes, you stupid blocks," he wheezed. To her utter astonishment, he uptilted the box over the pit and another crash split the night. The other men followed his example. It might almost have been a ritual, but if it was, it was weird indeed. The man had spoken truly when he told his companions they were "stupid blocks" for— The light dawned then. He hadn't been referring to his cronies at all! "Bricks!" she whispered, her eyes very wide. Then the boxes being emptied into the Folly were the ones from the cellar at Highperch Cottage, and these men had broken in and stolen them! But why would any thief in his right mind steal boxes of bricks, drive them several miles, then toss them into a pit? Unless these were Monteil's employees—in which case the question still applied.

In another minute they were carrying the empty boxes back again. Baffled, Susan crept after them. A large waggon stood at the edge of the meadow, and several horses were tethered nearby. Her heart sank when she saw a sixth man slouching on the driver's seat, smoking a long clay pipe. If he stayed she would have no chance to cross the meadow without being seen. To her relief, the square-set and powerfully built individual who appeared to be the leader grunted that there was no need for a guard, and that this "lazy peasant" could help with the boxes. The "lazy peasant" protested half-heartedly, but the rest of them shouted him down, the Frenchman, Jacques, saying with a flood of gutter language that there were no troops of riding officers in

327

"thees God-forsaken desolation" and that the sooner they got this done, the better.

Susan watched while they heaved and strained and at last went staggering off once more, each man carrying another box. When their quarrelsome voices were out of earshot she crept from the trees. What it was all about she could not imagine, but she didn't like the look of it, and she daren't take the time to walk home. She must get back to the house before them, and make sure that all was well. Her heart was pounding with nervousness as she crept to the tethered horses and appropriated a mild-looking black mare. The men would come back soon, for there were still more boxes to be unloaded, but if they should notice that one of the horses was gone, she hoped they'd assume it had got loose and wandered off.

She used one of the boxes for a mounting block, and rode across the meadow at a trot, then at a canter, then at a gallop, the wind blowing her hair and sending her cloak billowing out behind her. She reached Highperch with no sign of pursuit, and slowed the mare on the drivepath. Lights were burning in the house. When she'd left, only the lamp in the lower hall had been lit.

The front door was flung open, and her heart gave a leap as Andrew came onto the steps in his shirtsleeves.

"Oh, thank heaven!" she exclaimed, sliding from the saddle into his arms.

"I should jolly well think you might," he cried angrily. "Here I come home a day early and go up to have a word with you, and you're jauntering off somewhere, in the middle of the night, Lord knows where!"

"Yes, yes, but come inside quickly, there's no time to—"

"Here," he interrupted, looking narrowly at the mare. "This ain't one of our hacks, is it? Susan, if you've been creeping about after that damnable Montclair—"

She threw the reins over the pommel, slapped the mare on the rump and sent her trotting off, then seized her astonished brother by the hand and tugged it imperatively. "*Will* you come in!"

Montclair let Allegro have his head and the big bay thundered through the darkness undeterred by the blustering wind. All doubts were gone now. Montclair knew exactly what he would find at Highperch. He was astounded, in fact, that he'd not seen what was all about him. Lord, but one might suppose he'd worn blinkers! The big painting in the withdrawing room, for example; he should have realized at once that—

Allegro snorted and broke his stride. A horse was grazing up ahead. A saddled horse, but riderless. Montclair slowed the stallion and looked about searchingly. The turf stretched out quiet and empty. No sign of anyone for as far as he could see. He dismounted. The black mare fretted a little, but he patted her and spoke soothingly, and she stood docilely enough as he gathered up the reins. She wasn't from the Highperch stables, unless she was a recent acquisition. But she must have come from somewhere nearby, and as a general rule saddled horses were not left to wander about with reins trailing. Montclair swung into the saddle, and leading the mare, sent Allegro on at the canter, his eyes alert for a fallen rider.

"I saw the strangest thing, Andy," said Susan, leading him into the bright kitchen.

"That don't surprise me," he said with a short laugh. "Longhills fairly swarms with strange things!"

"Is Monsieur Monteil here?"

"What, at this hour? Of course not. Why should he be?"

She put off her cloak and laid it over a chair. "Well," she began, "I went out for a walk—"

"And rode home on a strange hack? Mrs. H., have you—"

She put her hand over his lips. *"Listen!"* she hissed.

Two minutes later, Andrew frowned at his sister's worried face, and agreed that it sounded a dashed havey-cavey business. "Tell you what, Sue. Go up and wake Angelo. I'll roust out the Bo'sun and those two louts you took on, and—"

"Good evening, my dearest friends."

Susan whirled around with a shocked gasp.

Imre Monteil smiled at them from the doorway. *"Pardonnez-moi,"* he said apologetically. "The front door it was open, and I took the liberty to enter, since I have rather troublesome news, I fear. A Revenue cutter is at this very moment en route here."

Susan turned deathly pale and gave a frightened little cry.

Lyddford put his arm around her and said hoarsely, "Gad! Have they rumbled us, then?"

"Not so much—er, rumbled, as been informed, *mon cher*. I fear you have a powerful and relentless enemy."

"Montclair!" said Lyddford through his teeth. "Why, that worthless—"

"No!" cried Susan. "Whatever else, I cannot believe that of him! He wouldn't—if only for Priscilla's sake!"

The Swiss gave her a tolerant smile.

Lyddford asked, "How much time have we?"

"With luck, enough. I have contrived, you see, to— divert these zealous gentlemen of the law."

"Jolly good," said Lyddford. "Then your men *were* here tonight?"

Monteil blinked at him. "You heard them? I told them they were not to disturb you! There was no answer when we knocked on the door, so— Ah, but we waste time, and time it is of the essence. Come!" He turned away.

Susan caught her brother's hand nervously, and whispered, "Andy—should we not wake the others?"

Monteil heard, and paused. "I would advise against it, madame. The fewer who know of this, the better." A sadness came into his black eyes. "And you entertain doubts, I think. Have I given you cause to mistrust me, lovely lady? It is but natural, I suppose."

Scarlet, she faltered, "No—you have been nothing but good. Only—"

"Only I am not, alas, of a handsome countenance, and probably seem a thorough villain. Here—" He drew a pistol from his pocket and put it into her hand, ignoring her embarrassed protestations. "Just in case," he said with a twinkle. "Only I beg you will be cautious, dear Mrs. Henley. It is loaded."

Lyddford chuckled. Susan felt very foolish, and held the heavy pistol gingerly as they walked quietly along the hall.

Lanterns glowed in the second cellar when Lyddford swung open the door, and two men who had been nailing up a large crate jerked around and stared up at them.

Again, Susan experienced a twinge of unease. They were big, and roughly dressed, and she had the distinct impression that they were prepared for violent action.

"Vous pouvez être tranquille," Monteil told them, closing the door. "These are my good partners." He offered Susan his arm. "I thought it necessary you see, my dear lady, to move some cargo, and I have instructed my men to prepare for shipment anything that might be—ah, shall we say—of an incriminating nature."

Susan allowed him to usher her down the steps. The cellar seemed bigger somehow, and less cluttered.

Lyddford asked curiously, "But why were your men unloading bricks into the Longhills Folly?"

For an instant the Swiss was as one carven from stone. Then he said gently, "Bricks . . . *mon cher?*"

"My sister—" began Lyddford, but broke off as the upper door burst open again.

Valentine Montclair stood at the top of the steps, looking wild and wind-blown, his eyes glittering unpleasantly, and a long-barrelled duelling pistol aimed steadily at Imre Monteil.

"Well, well," he drawled. "A regular thieves' picnic. How lucky that I found you at home."

17

For a moment they all stood like so many statues, no one saying a word. Then Monteil smiled his strange dead smile. "My dear boy, I—"

"Too late for that fustian," interrupted Valentine. "I know what's in those crates."

"And you informed on us, you ungrateful spy," growled Lyddford, starting forward.

It had been borne in upon Valentine that his hot temper had plunged him into a tricky situation once more. He'd been prepared to tackle Lyddford, man to man. He hadn't expected to face not one man, who would play fair, but four, three of whom he suspected would not balk at murder. Ruefully aware that he should have sent for Devenish and Vaughan sooner, he said coolly, "Better call him off, monsieur, since you're the one my pistol is pointing at."

"But my dear," said Monteil blandly, "even assuming you have found us out—whatever do you propose to do about it?"

"I propose to hand you over to the Runners, sir."

One of Monteil's men stood up. "He ain't handing me

over to no traps," he growled. "If we was all to rush him at once . . ."

Valentine smiled and tightened his finger on the trigger. "Your decision, dear Imre."

"No!" Monteil's voice squeaked slightly. "Wait, you imbeciles!"

"He won't shoot," snarled the second man.

"If he does," cried Monteil, "you know what Ti will do to the man who caused it!"

This threat evidently gave them pause, and they stood motionless.

Watching numbly, torn by conflicting emotions, Susan saw a stealthy movement on the landing. Several men were creeping in behind Valentine. The men she'd seen at the Folly. She gave a frantic little sob, her hand flying to her throat.

Valentine saw her reaction and guessed at the cause. "You fellows behind me," he said, "should know this is a hair trigger. The least jog of my arm and it is sure to go off. If you value your master, you'd best throw down your weapons."

The newcomers hesitated, looking at each other.

Valentine took careful aim.

"Do as he says!" shouted Monteil. *Mon Dieu! He will shoot me!*"

Lyddford cried, "Well, he won't shoot me!" and sprang in front of Monteil.

For a split second Valentine hesitated. It was enough. A savage swipe smashed the pistol from his hand. He ducked, and a large fist whizzed over his head, but another, more powerful one rammed into his back and sent him hurtling down the stairs. He landed hard, struck his chin, and saw stars as he sprawled, breathless.

Susan did not seem to move, but found herself kneeling beside Valentine. He blinked up at her, his eyes dazed, and she said angrily, "Was it necessary to push him downstairs? You might have killed him!"

334

The Oriental who had pushed Valentine, and who looked almost as broad as he was tall, grinned at her.

The Scotsman strolled down the stairs and laughed. "Aye. We might at that, lassie!"

She glared at him, then asked, "Are you hurt, Mr. Montclair?"

He managed to get an elbow under him. His vision was blurred, but he gasped out, "No. You shall have to . . . try harder."

A tall dark man bent and seized Valentine by the hair. *"Regarde qui est là, monsieur!"*

Monteil gave a rather shaky laugh. "Bravo, Jacques!"

Susan slapped the Frenchman's wrist hard. "Stop it, you beast!"

"Oh, but madame she frighten me," he mocked, but he stepped back.

"You came very opportunely," said Monteil. "Surely you cannot have finished your task so soon?"

The fair-haired man answered in a cultured voice, "Bolton's mare wandered off—or so we thought. I didn't like the smell of it, so we left Sam with the waggon and the rest of us went looking for her. We saw Montclair leading her, and followed him here."

"It was well done. You all shall be rewarded." The Swiss tapped the handle of his amber cane against his lips. "But this," he frowned at Valentine, "is a nuisance."

"Nuisance!" snorted Lyddford. "It's damned disgusting is what it is!" He put a hand under Susan's elbow and pulled her to her feet. "Had you not come creeping around like a filthy Excise spy, Montclair, you'd merely have been tossed down the front steps instead of—"

Valentine managed to sit up and propped his shoulders against one of the boxes. "You've more than Excisemen after you, Lyddford. I once thought you a fool to endanger your sister with your smuggling. I little dreamed you were no better than a common thief!"

Monteil sighed and seated himself with fastidious care on a large crate.

Lyddford let out a roar of wrath. "Common *thief*? Damn your eyes and limbs, I'm a Free Trader! One of the Gentlemen! If you were able to stand up, I'd knock you down!"

"And if you are so dense as to suppose that these crates now hold smuggled brandy, or bricks, you're either—a fool, or a liar."

Flushing darkly, Lyddford sprang forward and wrenched off the lid of the box Montclair leaned against. "See for yourself," he snarled, taking out an object and pulling off the wrapping. "You can . . . see—" His words died. He stood there unmoving, staring with stunned eyes at the exquisite jewelled chalice he held.

Susan whispered, "Oh . . . God. . . !"

Monteil clapped his hands. "How very entertaining is this little drama. Exercise your so great gift of the guess, *mon cher* Valentine. Without turning your clever head, tell me what he found."

"Part of England's stolen treasures, which you had the confounded gall to store both here, and in our cellars at the Manor." Ignoring Susan's shocked little cry, he went on contemptuously, "And you're the brains behind the Masterpiece Gang, I'll go bail."

Monteil bowed. "Very true. But, alas, I think there can be no—er, bail."

"What in the . . . devil . . . have you got us into?" gasped Lyddford, turning to face the Swiss as one dazed.

Valentine looked at him narrowly. He was very white, his face wearing a drawn look that could not be a pose.

"Why?" whispered Susan, staring at Monteil in stunned horror. "You are a rich man. Why would you do such dreadful things? Several people have been killed in those robberies."

He shrugged his bony shoulders. "They should not

have interfered. You see, dear lady, I am a vindictive man. Two years ago a very fine gentleman and I concocted a little scheme to—ah, relieve England of the encumbrance of her heir apparent and institute a democratic government. But—"

"Claude Sanguinet!" interposed Valentine. "A murdering ruffian without one iota of conscience or decency! Some of my friends took a hand in that game, and rid the world of the crudity you term a 'very fine gentleman'!"

Ti Chiu lumbered forward. "Ti humbly glad to break man with rude mouth, master," he rumbled, his small eyes glitteringly fixed on Valentine.

Susan gave a gasp and shrank against her brother.

Monteil said gently, "He can do it very easily, *mon ami,* as you should be aware."

Valentine struggled to his feet. His head had cleared and although he was aware of some new bruises, he had come off very lightly compared to what might have resulted from such a fall. He regarded Ti Chiu's might steadily. The man was a condensed Colossus, but not eight feet tall as the distortion of the shadow had made him appear. He said, "So you are the brave man who strikes down his victims from behind."

The little eyes seemed to disappear. The Oriental took a step forward, his great hands curving into claws. "You fight Ti Chiu? Face to face?" he offered, grinning.

"Now that *would* be amusing," said Monteil.

At once the groom crouched. Monteil lifted his cane. "But not just yet," he murmured, and with a disappointed grunt Ti Chiu straightened. "The rest of you men, get the work finished," went on Monteil. "We must be away before dawn."

Four of the newcomers went over to join the other two men in carefully packing the collection of dusty art treasures into the boxes and crates. Ti Chiu stayed close to Monteil.

Valentine, who had prepared himself for what he knew must be a losing battle, relaxed, and said steadily, "So having lost the first round you still mean to take over the throne, do you? I think you will catch cold at that, Monteil."

"It is not my intent," said the Swiss. "I mean to make your country pay me back with interest for the money I lost in our venture two years ago. Also, in stealing her art treasures, I wound her pride. It is, *parbleu,* a small revenge. But it is a beginning."

Staring at him, Lyddford asked, "Why the bricks?"

Monteil smiled. "What is your answer to that, my dear Valentine?"

"I think," said Valentine, "that your benefactor had been storing his booty at Highperch for some time, Lyddford. Like you, he found it an ideal location: isolated from prying eyes, yet with a front door to the river. He had fully expected to buy the place. Probably, my uncle told him he could do so. But at that time my uncle was unaware that Highperch belongs to me. When you suddenly moved in, I fancy Monteil was furious. However, he learned you had a boat, and when he also learned you were short of funds, he hired you to bring many heavy boxes here, telling you they contained his personal belongings. He intended to discard the bricks at some convenient time when you were away, and fill the boxes with the art-works he had stored down here. When the time came to ship his stolen property, everyone would think he had simply taken his own things." He paused, frowning. "Something has occurred to make him move earlier than he'd intended. What, I wonder? Is there really a Revenue cutter on the way, Monteil?"

"Merely a ruse, dear boy," said Monteil expansively. "To get the lovely widow and her brother down here without waking the household. One takes as few lives as possible when Bow Street comes sniffing around."

"Good God!" exclaimed Lyddford. "You're a blasted monster!"

A hearty laugh sounded from the steps. The epitome of elegance in a many-caped riding coat, his high-crowned beaver hat tilted at a rakish angle on his handsome head, Junius Trent called, "I'd resent that were I you, Imre."

Monteil shrugged. "Do I not *en effet* attempt to spare lives?"

Trent sauntered down the steps, his eyes fixed on his cousin. "His—for instance?"

Valentine said contemptuously, "It would be nice to say I'm surprised to find you're part of this nasty little business. Unfortunately, I cannot. May I ask if my uncle is aware you sent your killing machine here"—he nodded towards Ti Chiu—"after me?"

Junius glanced at Monteil. "Are we to be frank?" he enquired. "Before the lady?"

He was asking if they were all to be silenced. Susan felt cold, and tried not to show how frightened she was.

"But of course. Madame Henley will not speak, I do promise you. To do so would be to sentence her brother to death." His jet eyes twinkled at her. "Andrew *is* my partner, you know."

Lyddford raged, "Not in this filthy business!"

"Ah, but it would be most difficult to prove that, *mon ami*. And besides, a wife cannot testify against her husband."

Lyddford swore and plunged at him, but Ti Chiu shoved him back.

Trent chuckled. "In that case, dear cousin of mine, I will give you an honest answer. No. My parents did not know that Ti Chiu was to rid us of you. The credit for that bungle belongs to my Swiss friend."

339

Monteil looked at him thoughtfully.

Puzzled, Valentine asked, "Why, Monteil? As a favour to Junius?"

"I never grant favours," said the Swiss. "The fact is that you displease me on several suits, Valentine. You are an annoyance to Selby Trent, whom I find amusing. He is so delightfully without principles, while presenting such a pious picture to the world. Your friends are unpleasant, and one is judged by the company one keeps—no? Again, you are so impertinent as to address me with thinly veiled contempt. Unwise, *mon cher.* Mostly, however, your stubborn refusal to sell this house has inconvenienced me. Ergo, you must be removed."

"You would kill a man—only for such paltry things as that?" gasped Lyddford in astonishment.

"It is more than sufficient," said Monteil coldly. "However, the Trents may have a more compelling reason, I'll admit."

Valentine stared at him.

"But—surely you have guessed?" The Swiss smiled. "You block Junius's path to the title and the fortune."

"Rubbish! My brother is the heir—not me."

Junius gave a snort of laughter. "Your precious brother, my poor clod, was killed by a tiger six months ago. *You* are Baron Montclair of Longhills."

Valentine reeled with shock, and put a steadying hand against the pillar beside him. Paper white, he gasped, "You . . . lie! Damn you! You *lie!* Geoff's not dead! I—I would have heard!"

"My father learned of it in a rather roundabout way. He has been able to suppress the news because against all advice your stupid brother had journeyed miles into the jungle and told no one where he was going."

"Do you see now?" asked Monteil, amused by Valentine's obvious anguish. "Nobody in this country is as yet aware of Geoffrey's demise. Therefore, your own pre-

340

mature death would have caused no suspicion of foul play, for who would have anything to gain by—er, hastening your exit?"

Junius looked annoyed and said irritably, "If you hadn't taken a hand, his exit would have been *fait accompli* by this time."

"A twist of fate, my dear." Monteil sighed. "Who was to guess he had so hard a skull? Or that the child would go to a spot everyone else avoided, and find him before he obligingly died? If he had ever been found, people would only have thought he must have fallen into the Folly by accident."

Still numbed with shock, Valentine mumbled stupidly, "But—but there is Uncle Hammond . . ."

"Your brainless Uncle Hammond will be easily ruled by the Trents. For—a while, at least." Monteil smiled unpleasantly. "Now you really should not look at me with such disgust, dear Valentine. I assure you your cousin's plan for your—extermination was far less humane than mine."

Valentine tensed, his narrowed gaze darting to Trent.

"Justifiably so." Junius nodded. "I've many scores to settle, and it was such fun to watch his condition slowly worsening. A little taste of hell that he richly deserved. I think, towards the end, he really began to think his mind was affected . . . Didn't you, dear cousin of mine?"

Through his teeth Valentine whispered, "You filthy . . . *bastard!*"

Junius chuckled. "Does the light dawn at last? Yes, dear boy. Dr. Sheswell was once—er, indiscreet with a patient, and by a lucky chance I learned of it. He's been in my pocket ever since. With his help I arranged your first—er, 'attack.' And his 'medicine' did the rest."

"Shocking, is it not?" said Monteil. "For the last few months, Baron Montclair, your loving family has been slowly poisoning you. And that was the trouble, do you

341

see. Too slow. And I was in a hurry, so I sent Ti Chiu to—"

With an incoherent cry of rage Valentine sprang at him.

His attack was as swift as it was unexpected. He seemed to blur across the room, and his hands were locked around Monteil's throat before anyone else could move. Monteil let out a squawk and the two men crashed to the floor. Lyddford snatched a great golden bowl from the open crate, and hurled it at Ti Chiu's head. The Chinese staggered. Beating frenziedly and unavailingly at Valentine, Monteil gulped for breath.

Jacques sprang to his employer's aid, but Lyddford hurled himself between them, shouting, "Sue! Get help!"

Susan was already running for the stairs, but Junius was after her. She whipped up the pistol Monteil had given her. Junius halted, eyeing her uneasily. "I'll fire," she warned, the pistol steady in her hand.

The fair man joined the attack on Lyddford, who was sent hurtling back, to collapse behind a box.

Simultaneously, the Scot and the cockney ran to tear Valentine away. Maddened with rage, Valentine jammed his elbow into the ribs of the Scot and brought his right hand whizzing into a chop across the throat that sent the cockney reeling. Then an iron hand grabbed his left wrist and twisted it up behind him with brutal force. A mighty arm clamped across his throat. A deep growl of a voice asked, "Master? Ti break this?"

Helpless, unable to move, fighting to draw breath, Valentine knew what the answer would be.

"No!" screamed Susan. "Unless you want me to shoot your friend!"

Clutching at his throat, his face livid, Monteil pointed to his amber cane and one of his men sprang to snatch it up and offer it. "Shoot then," croaked the Swiss and tottered towards Valentine.

"Hey!" shouted Junius, blenching.

"I will!" Susan screamed.

Ignoring her, Monteil sent the cane whipping across Valentine's face. *"Saleté!"* he hissed.

The blow was sickeningly painful. Valentine's eyes closed and he sagged in Ti Chiu's grip.

With a sob of desperation, Susan swung the pistol at Monteil and pulled the trigger.

There was a metallic click.

Junius tore the weapon from her hands, his own shaking. "You murdering little doxy! It wasn't loaded! No thanks to you, Imre!"

Monteil sent him a narrowed, rageful glance. "I gave it to her, you imbecile." He called silkily, "Valentine. . . ? You are awake?"

Valentine dragged his head up and met that enraged glare. Somehow, he managed a faint grin.

Monteil hissed, *"Oui.* Break him."

With a delighted smile, the huge Chinese clamped both arms about Valentine's ribs. His grip tightened and he began to laugh softly.

Susan saw Montclair's dark head jerk back, his face convulse. She screamed at the top of her lungs.

With all his rapidly fading strength, Montclair rammed his left foot back at Ti Chiu's shin. His spur struck hard. The death grip eased and the Chinese uttered a shocked grunt. Montclair smashed his right foot back. A guttural snarl sounded in his ear, and he was jerked around. The craggy face was a terrifying mask of rage. One great arm flailed upward. Wheezing, Valentine ducked frantically and discovered that for all his might, the big fellow was slow. The blow that would surely have finished him whipped over his head.

"Idiot!" raged Monteil. "Kill the swine!"

Susan was struggling in Trent's hands; Lyddford was downed. Monteil's unlovely crew made themselves comfortable and watched in amusement as Ti Chiu lumbered in again, scowlingly eager for the kill. There was, Valentine knew, no chance. Breathing hard, he crouched, fists clenched, grimly resolved to sell his life dearly.

"Tally ho!" shouted a familiar voice from the stairs.

"A mill!" howled another equally familiar voice with enthusiasm if not accuracy.

Valentine caught a glimpse of the two vagrants sailing into action. The big Scot grabbed Seth's bushy hair and it came away in his hand, revealing flattened fair curls. *"Dev!"* howled Montclair joyously. Dicky, alias Jocelyn Vaughan, took on Trent, shouting a bracing "Jolly good work, Val!"

So his friends had been here, all the time! He thought gratefully 'I might have known!'

Bo'sun Dodman plunged down the stairs, followed by Deemer, in his dressing gown, clutching an enormous and probably inoperable blunderbuss; and Mrs. Starr, clad in an orange satin dressing gown, hair in curling papers, and rolling pin in hand.

Ti Chiu came on single-mindedly. Immeasurably heartened, Valentine braced himself and drove his fist at the rugged jaw. He had as well have struck a wall of granite. The Chinese launched his great paw in a murderous swipe. Valentine ducked and struck again, then was smashed back as by a battering ram. Dimly, he heard a piercing screech, and saw Angelo fly through the air to land on Ti Chiu's back and beat at his head with verve and determination. The big man did not even seem aware he was there, and lumbered forward.

Clambering to his knees, Valentine knew in a detached way that he was in the middle of a raging battle. The Frenchman kicked at him savagely. Valentine seized the flying boot, brought the Frenchman crashing down, sat on him, and silenced his curses with a left jab.

Gasping for breath, he regained his feet in time to see Susan break a priceless vase over the head of a man wearing a red stocking cap. Imre Monteil was nowhere to be seen. Bewilderingly, the lazy gardener, Diccon, was now fighting Junius for possession of a pistol. Ti Chiu, emitting infuriated grunts, flung Señor Angelo off his back, and the Spaniard landed in the open crate and sank from view. Bo'sun Dodman was knocked down by the cockney's pistol butt. With a squeak of fury, Mrs. Starr cast to the winds all her concepts on the use of violence and bounced her rolling pin off the cockney's head. His eyes crossed, and he lost interest in the fight. The Chinese made a grab for Valentine, who dodged aside and rammed his fist into the big man's midsection. Ti Chiu grunted and advanced inexorably. Vaughan and Devenish ran to Valentine's aid. With one mighty flail of his arm, Ti Chiu sent all three flying. Deemer collected a bloody nose and dropped the blunderbuss. It went off with a deafening roar. The fair man, who was kneeling over Devenish with a glittering dagger upraised, howled and flew backwards, knocking over the lamp. The cellar was plunged into darkness. Gradually, the groans, grunts, thuds, and crashes diminished. Someone scraped at a tinder box and the small circle of light expanded as a branch of candles was lit.

The cellar looked like a small battlefield, with damaged fighting men scattered all about the floor in varying degrees of consciousness.

Alain Devenish hauled himself to a sitting position and explored a back tooth cautiously. Jocelyn Vaughan, flat on his back, lifted his head, his nose streaming crimson, and groaned thickly, "Did we—win, old boy?"

"I'm not altogether . . . sure," panted Devenish, handing down his handkerchief. "That Chinese fella outnumbered the lot of us."

345

"What?" said Vaughan, plying the handkerchief. "Has he got away, then?"

"Must have. Don't see him, my tulip. And he . . . ain't an easy one to overlook!"

"*Aye. . . ! Mamacita. . . !*" sighed a feeble voice from within the crate, and Señor Angelo's rumpled head hove into view.

Diccon, his pistol trained on three battered-looking rogues, called in a brisk, business-like voice, "You people all right?"

They were, Vaughan acknowledged breathlessly, all right.

Both eyes almost swollen shut, and with Susan propping him, Lyddford peered from behind a crate and gasped that he was "perfectly fit," then enquired after Monteil.

"He slid away like the slippery article he is," said Diccon grimly. "A couple of my fellows are hot after him and his big destroyer."

Lyddford asked, "Who are you, by the way?"

Diccon vouchsafed a terse "Military Intelligence. I don't see your friend Montclair."

"Mices fren," sighed Angelo, fingering a split lip, "after goings nasty personable foreign yentlemans."

"No," said Susan quietly. "I rather think Valentine has gone after somebody else."

Bent low in the saddle, Valentine did not feel his bruises or the cold driving rain. He had seen Monteil and Ti Chiu go tearing off in a sleek high-perch phaeton, but the Swiss was not his primary target, and he followed his predatory cousin, his rage drowning out all other sensations. Junius had a good head start, and since he had appropriated Allegro, he maintained his

346

lead and was soon out of sight, but Valentine had no doubt of where he was headed.

Lights were still burning in the great house as he galloped the hack straight across Longhills' velvety rear lawns, reined up behind the great hall, and effected a sliding dismount. He took the terrace steps two at a time. The doors were locked. He kicked savagely and they burst open with a shattering of glass.

Sir Selby and his wife had been walking towards the east hall. They stopped, and swung around. Lady Trent gave a small scream as Valentine ran into the room. His bruised face was further marred by a long welt that angled from his right temple to the point of his chin; his hair was wildly dishevelled, and his clothes were rent and dirty.

Glancing about ferociously, he snarled, "Where is he?"

"Good God!" gasped Sir Selby. "What on earth has happened to you, dear boy?"

Valentine halted, staring at him. "You wicked old humbug," he said between his teeth.

Sir Selby was suddenly very still and watchful.

"How *dare* you! You horrid boy!" shrilled Lady Trent, outraged.

Jimson, the third footman, who had hurried up followed by a lackey, checked, and watched hopefully.

"What kind of murderous thing are you," went on Valentine, pacing towards his uncle, his narrowed eyes savage with rage, "that you could call me your *dear boy*— even while you did your level best to poison me?"

Lady Trent turned white and threw both hands to her mouth.

Jimson and the lackey uttered simultaneous gasps and exchanged shocked glances.

"You are *mad*," declared Trent, blenching, and backing away a step.

Junius ran in from the hall, loading a pistol. "Father,"

he panted, "Montclair knows—" He saw his cousin then, and froze.

"By God, but I do!" roared Montclair, leaping at him.

Junius levelled the pistol and fired. At the same instant, Jimson jumped forward and struck the weapon up, and the ball whammed into the ceiling.

Cursing, Junius whipped the footman into the path of the onrushing Montclair, and fled towards the Gallery.

Jimson stumbled and fell. Valentine leapt over him and tore after Junius.

Lady Trent gave a piercing shriek.

"Don't be a fool, boy!" cried Sir Selby. "You men—Mr. Montclair has gone stark raving mad! Stop him!"

Jimson required the lackey to help him up, and they walked sedately after the combatants.

Glancing over his shoulder, Junius saw Montclair gaining on him, snatched up a lamp, and hurled it. Valentine fielded it with an upflung arm, and ran on. Down the steps and across the gallery went Junius, toppling plant stands, strewing small tables and stools in his wake. Valentine was tripped when an aspidistra crashed at his feet, and went down hard, but he rolled and was up again as his cousin leapt down the steps and disappeared along the side hall and into the South Wing.

There were few servants about at this hour, and the corridor past the ballroom was deserted. Valentine started up the main staircase, and narrowly escaped being brained by a flying bust of the Emperor Vespasian. "Stand . . . and fight, you cowardly dog," he gasped out.

He was tiring, but knew suddenly where Junius was going, and made a mighty effort to catch up. He heard glass shatter as he plunged into Selby's study, and ducked frantically as Junius snatched a heavy Sumatran kris from the display case and sent it whizzing at him. The razor-sharp blade sliced across his upper arm and thudded into the wall. Barely conscious of the sharp burn of pain, Valentine flung himself at his cousin. Junius crashed into the cabinet and it toppled, sending weapons flying. Valentine followed up with a hard left to the jaw, and Junius went to his knees and buried his face in his arms, cowering. "Don't . . ." he whimpered. "Please—don't hit me . . . again!" Valentine stood over him, fists clenched. "Get—up, you—slimy murdering coward!" he panted. Junius moaned and began to struggle up, then pounced to grab a heavy teak sword-stand carved in the shape of deer horns. He spun, and slammed it at Valentine's ribs. Valentine doubled up, gasping. Junius laughed gloatingly, and bent to snatch up a double-edged Khanjar knife. Valentine summoned the last dregs of his strength, locked his hands together and swung them up, connecting solidly under his cousin's chin. Junius was straightened out and went over backwards. He gave an odd, strangled squawk, tried convulsively to rise, then slumped down.

Sagging to his knees again, panting, Valentine saw many legs run in, and heard shocked exclamations. For a minute the room was an echoing blur. Devenish's voice came through the mists. "Gad Val, but you're a bloody mess!" Ragged and battered, his friend knelt, supporting him. Valentine said with breathless indignation, "Talk about . . . pot calling kettle . . . black!"

"Oh, what a lovely brawl," said Vaughan, reeling to join them. "Hey! Diccon! We need a doctor here!"

Valentine gasped, "Dev . . . is she—all right?"

"If you mean the Glorious Henley—yes, dear old boy. The lady is quite safe, but—"

"One of you men," said Diccon sharply, "ride for a doctor. Fast."

"I'm—all right," Valentine muttered. "The Bo'sun will—"

"I think we'll need a proper doctor," said the Intelli-

349

gence Officer, holding up the sword-stand. "I'm afraid your cousin landed on this unpleasant article."

Valentine peered at Junius. "Is he . . . dead?"

Working busily over the huddled figure, Diccon said dryly, "Not yet. I think he won't cheat the hangman, my lord."

The title made Valentine wince. "I will press . . . no charges."

"I understand your desire to preserve your family honour," said Diccon, a note of irritation in his voice. "But this is too large a matter for you to suppress. If Trent was deeply involved with the Masterpiece Gang—"

"He wasn't," said Valentine.

"We'll see that, sir," said Diccon.

Four hectic days later, Susan received Lord Montclair in the withdrawing room at Highperch. She was sure she would be able to control herself, but the shock of seeing him wearing blacks, relieved only by the white neckcloth, almost overset her. He looked less battered than the last time she'd seen him, but the welt was still a livid line across his face, and there was a dulled look to the dark eyes that made it difficult for her to meet them. "I had not expected you to call, my lord," she said, sitting on the sofa and waving him to a chair.

"I had to come." He sat down and gazed at her pleadingly. "Sue—I—"

"I must ask that you address me properly, sir."

So she hadn't forgiven him. Who could blame her? "Yes," he said. "Er—Mrs. Henley, I have come to most humbly apologize for—for what I—"

"For believing we plotted to murder you."

"I—suppose I had come to—to expect it," he murmured. "It seems to have become the national pastime."

She looked at him sharply. A wry smile hovered about his lips. She frowned and he said hurriedly, "I'm sorry. I seem to be handling this badly."

"Is there a good way to handle such an accusation?"

He flushed. "Sue—for the love of God—forgive me! I—must have been mad to have suspected such a thing of you. I had once overheard you talking with Starry, and I thought— But I was a fool! You saved my life all over again when you denied me that medicine. I should have known— How did *you* know, by the way?"

"I had not the least idea," she admitted. "I merely thought Sheswell a stupid man, and the Bo'sun didn't admire his instructions or the effect of the medicine, so we abandoned both and followed our own methods."

"How can I ever thank you? Won't you please be charitable, and ascribe my own stupidity to the concussion Ti dealt me?"

"In view of my reputation, my lord—"

"Must you keep throwing that title at me?"

"It is as well, sir, to keep one's place."

He groaned and threw an irked look at the ceiling.

Her hand went out to him, but was quickly withdrawn. She said in a kinder voice, "I was very sorry to hear of your brother's death. I know he meant a great deal to you."

"Yes. He did. Thank you." He still couldn't accept the fact that dear old Geoff was gone, and his voice shook a little. He recovered himself and said quickly, "I want you to know that I am renouncing all claim to this house, and I—"

"We do not want your charity, Montclair," said Andrew, stalking into the room. "Thank you very much."

"It isn't—" began Valentine, standing to face him.

"Oh, yes it is! That Intelligence man, Diccon— By the bye, did you bring him in to spy on us, too?"

"No, I did not! He was after Monteil. Now see here, Lyddford—"

351

Susan interrupted, her voice calm and dispassionate. "We are moving away, my lord."

"Where?" he demanded, paling.

"Never you mind," said Lyddford. "I don't want you following us and making sheep's eyes at my sister."

"Sheep's eyes! Now devil take you, Lydd—"

"I don't know what else you'd call it, Montclair." He added mockingly, but with his fine eyes very intent, "Unless—is it possible you have come to ask my permission to pay your addresses?"

"Andy!" exclaimed Susan, her eyes flashing with anger. "How *could* you embarrass me so? Mr. Montclair—I mean his lordship—made his opinion of us too clear for me to have anything but disgust for such a declaration."

Lyddford said sternly, "I'll hear his answer, if you please, Mrs. H."

Admiral Lord Sutton-Newark had already visited Longhills, and Valentine's discussion with him regarding the lovely widow had brought a sharp and unyielding verdict. "Unequivocally—and finally—*no!*" had said the old gentleman. "You are the head of the family now, Montclair. You have an obligation to your name, and to all who have carried it before you. You must marry well and with honour! There can be no slightest hint of scandal about your lady. Susan Henley? No, by Gad! *Never!*"

Montclair's head bowed. He said quietly, "No. That is not why I came."

Lyddford gave a bark of sardonic laughter. "I believe that, at least!"

"But there is no reason," went on Montclair, "for you to leave here."

Susan rose to her feet. "There is every reason, sir," she said. "As my brother started to tell you, we learned that prior to my marriage Diccon was slightly acquainted with my husband. He was kind enough to make an investigation for us, and found definite proof that—that your mama did indeed refund the purchase price of this house. You were perfectly right, my lord. We have, in fact, trespassed, and owe you rent for the—"

Montclair stepped closer to her and said with a blaze of anger, "Do not *dare* to say such a thing! You saved my life, and in return I am expected to put you out of house and home and charge you *rent*? If that isn't the most preposterous—"

"I put it to you, sir," interrupted Lyddford, "that I don't like your tone; I don't like your manner; and I most decidedly will not accept your charity! Bad enough," he added grudgingly, "that I've to thank you for clearing me with the Excise people."

Ignoring him, Valentine reached out towards Susan imploringly, but she drew back as if his nearness revolted her. He lowered his hand and asked in desperation, "Where will you go? Please—at least tell me that."

Lyddford stalked over to the door and flung it open. "I tell you goodbye, sir. No more. No less."

Valentine bit his lip and said huskily, "Lyddford—I beg you. Give me a moment alone with her. Only a moment."

Andrew Lyddford was a volatile and somewhat selfish young man, but he was far from being insensitive, and this whole unhappy interview was weakening his stern resolution. He hesitated, glancing at his sister.

Susan turned and walked from the room, her dark hair swinging behind her.

For a moment Valentine gazed after her. Then, without a word, he left the house.

18

"But my good blockhead"—Alain Devenish, who had just wandered into the library after enjoying a late breakfast, leaned forward and placed both hands on the map his friend was attempting to read—"it is positively—*heathen*! Leave your confounded swamp for a minute and attend me! No offense, but—the putrid lot tried to put a period to you! Their own flesh and blood! And you allow them to *remain* here, a full week after their dastardly schemes failed? Blest if ever I heard of such a thing!"

Obediently, Montclair looked up from the map of Amberly Down. "You may believe I'll be glad to see the back of 'em—with the exception of Babs, of course. I insist they keep to the South Wing, and not come into this part of the house, but Junius is very ill, Dev. I can hardly force them to move him when even the doctor from Town said it would be a death sentence."

"The dirty bastard wouldn't be in such a fix had he not planned *your* death in a particularly slow and horrible fashion." Vaughan, who was sprawled in a deep chair reading *The Times,* tossed the newspaper aside and added, "If Diccon has his way—"

"Diccon has his hands full trying to trace Imre Monteil. Besides, Junius is a bad man, I'd be the last to dispute that. But if I pressed charges and the lot came out . . ." Montclair shrugged. "It won't do. The Family, you know."

Devenish nodded a gloomy acknowledgement of the sanctity of The Family. "I know. I suppose you're the head now—eh?"

"Unfortunately."

Vaughan said sympathetically, "Bad luck, old lad. Curst lot of bothersome responsibilities. And with the staff you've got here, and your farms and villages . . ." He shuddered.

"You think it's bad now," said Devenish cheerfully. "Only wait 'til you set up your nursery!" And with an oblique glance at Vaughan, "I suppose your nautical great-uncle wants you to get leg-shackled as fast as may be?"

Bending over the map hurriedly, Valentine murmured, "He said something of the sort. I'm in no hurry. I've to see Babs safely wed first."

Through a short silence Devenish frowned at him, then said with a trace of diffidence, "While Joss and I were having a jolly time being vagrants at Highperch—"

"For which I shall never be able to thank you enough," interjected Montclair, smiling gratefully from one to the other. "When I think of how you hovered about trying to protect me—"

"We were truly noble," nodded Devenish complacently.

"And such splendid painters," mused Vaughan.

Montclair laughed. "The most ruffianly pair of hedgehogs I ever saw. But it's amazing I didn't recognize you, if only for the fun and gigs you had at my expense! Small wonder I warned Su— Mrs. Henley against you. Did you know you scared her half to

355

death one night when she caught you watching High-perch?"

Vaughan threw up his hands. *"C'est mal!* That was our Diccon. He took the night shift whilst we got our beauty sleep."

"And as for being scared to death," said Devenish, "the lady came nigh to causing both Joss and me to swoon with fright when she damn near rode us down in the woods that day!"

Montclair's expression sobered. "You refuse to let me properly thank you, but—"

"Oh, do stow it, you block," snorted Vaughan. "Cease interrupting with all this poppycock, when we want to talk sensibly. Now—speaking of weddings—"

Valentine returned his gaze to the map. "We weren't."

"Yes, we were," argued Devenish. "You said you had to get Babs married off. And—er, as to the Glorious Widow—she is . . . ah, glorious. Eh, my tulip?"

"Mmm," said Valentine, his head bowing lower over the map.

Vaughan said, "Dev and I—we rather thought . . . That is— We don't mean to pry, but—"

Montclair straightened and looked at them gravely. "Thank you," he said. "I'm very grateful for that."

"Oh," said Devenish, blinking at him.

"Er—quite," said Vaughan.

A week later Mr. Yates strolled with Alain Devenish through the sunlit water gardens, and pointed out, "Well, he *is* in deep mourning, sir."

"I fully understand that," nodded Devenish. "But—"

"Do you really, Mr. Devenish? No—please don't think I mean to be insolent. I know you was friends with Mr. Valentine at school. But—you didn't see them grow up, sir. I did. Always fighting, they were. Over nothing, most of the time. But they made it up quick as a wink, and underneath they were as close as brothers can be. Master Geoff was the more easy natured of the two; a bit on the lazy side, perhaps, if I may be so bold as to remark it. But such charm that boy had, sir. Wound us all round his little finger, he did. Aside from their squabbles, which is only natural in two healthy young boys, Master Valentine fairly idolized his brother. Master Geoff could do no wrong in his eyes. 'Til he went flaunting off and—" The steward checked himself abruptly. "I think Mr. Val—I mean his lordship—was counting the days 'til his brother come home. Never wanted the title, he didn't. Or the fortune. He's not one for all the antics of Society, like Master Geoff was. All he wanted was his music . . . Now—" He shrugged.

"That's another thing," said Devenish. "I used to find Lord Valentine at his harpsichord every time I came. I don't think I've seen him in that music room once since the fight at Highperch. Nor has Mr. Vaughan."

"He doesn't have time, sir. Since you two gentlemen left, he works all the hours of the day and often far into the night as well."

"Works? At what? Never say he means to add on to this overgrown hut?"

The steward grinned. "Not exactly, sir, though he does intend to rebuild the family Chapel. It's the land, mostly. He wants each of the estate labourers to be given a cottage and a small acreage so as to grow his own crops. He has been going over the parcels and approving sketches for the cottages. And he's consulting with surveyors and engineers to get that swamp drained at Amberly Down. He means to have the stream rerouted so it flows as it did before the flood. Our tenant-farmers have had a lot of trouble with standing water in their fields."

357

"But—surely all that's your job," said Devenish, frowning.

"Right you are, sir." Yates added wryly, "And his lordship consults with me about it. Constant! Fair wears me out, he does! I don't mind hard work, Mr. Devenish. But—he never stops! It's almost as if—he doesn't dare to stop . . ."

"Hmmn," said Alain Devenish.

Sir Selby Trent was thinner and wore a dejected look. The afternoon sun was slanting golden lances across the gleaming floors of the Great Hall, and he glanced around with a faint sigh for vanished dreams. "It is a sad thing," he said reproachfully, "when a gentleman has to petition for a talk with his own kin."

"Isn't it," said Montclair, waving him to a chair, and marvelling that this devious scoundrel wore blacks and had the gall to affect that ill-used air. "I'm glad you came, sir. I have wanted a word with you before you leave."

"We will depart as soon as is humanly—perhaps I should have said *humanely* possible. But for the time being, my—my poor son . . ." Trent pressed a kerchief to his eyes.

"About Barbara," said Valentine firmly.

Sir Selby blew his nose. "My dear wife is fetching her," he sighed.

"As head of the family, I'll not stand by and see her forced into marriage with the likes of Dennis Pollinger, whether—"

"I wonder you can bring yourself to speak to my husband so rudely, when our beloved son lies on his bed and will likely never walk again." Lady Trent's shrill voice was an instant abrasion to Montclair's nerves, and he thought she looked like a bird of prey as she came into the room clad in severe blacks, as was her daughter.

He stood, and said with icy courtesy, "Good day, madam."

Barbara gave him a look of anguish. He smiled at her, and added in a very different tone, "I've missed seeing you, little one."

She gave a helpless gesture. "Val—I'm so sorry—"

"Do not dare to apologize!" cried my lady militantly. "When I think what we have suffered from all the lies and hypocrisy that have been circulated about us, and—"

"Enough!" His temper flaring, Montclair interrupted, "You know perfectly well what I could have done—and for the sake of our family, have not done. I have nothing to say to either of you, except insofar as Barbara is concerned."

"I had hoped you asked to see us out of Christian charity," murmured Sir Selby, blinking his pale eyes.

"You should have known better," snapped his wife. "Well, I at least shall not mince words. Whatever was done, Valentine Montclair, was done in an effort to save the family name. You may well look ashamed," she added, as Montclair's face reflected his astonishment. "You supposed we did not know how you lusted after that trollop at Highperch!" She overrode his infuriated attempt to speak by the simple expedient of raising her voice another decibel or two. "A fine scandal it would have caused had you brought her here as your wife! My dear son was wrong, I'll admit. But if he caused you to feel a—er, a trifle indisposed, it was only—"

"A *trifle indisposed,* madam," thundered Montclair, causing her ladyship's eyes to goggle as she drew back a step. "Do you fancy me to be a total fool? I was being deliberately poisoned before ever Mrs. Henley moved here! You and your son conspired to bully the lady into

359

keeping me at Highperch, and then sent over poisoned medicine. There is no doubt in my mind but that I was meant to expire there so that the widow and her family could be made the scapegoats, thus killing two birds with one stone! That's why you stayed away; why you kept my servants away, not even permitting my man to come to me! You wanted no possible connection made between yourselves—and my death!"

"Alas," moaned Sir Selby, burying his pale face in his kerchief once more. "This is Monteil's doing! He has planted the seeds of distrust in your poor confused head! Oh, that you would take the word of that snake in the grass, over that of your own dear relations!"

"Not all, sir," said Valentine, breathing hard. "Only those now dwelling under my roof!"

Taking a new course, my lady threw a hand to her bosom and swayed alarmingly. "My heart. . . ! I am . . . going to swoon . . ."

"You'd best wait until I pull up a chair, ma'am," said Montclair dryly, "so that you may accomplish it with grace."

Her eyes opened wide, then narrowed. She crouched, glaring at him so balefully that for a moment he thought she meant to claw him. "Always, you hated Junius," she hissed. "Only because he was everything you are not! You have caused him to be crippled, and broken a poor mother's heart! And you may think you've won! But you'll not interfere in my daughter's life and so I tell you! She will wed Pollinger. And if you *dare* attempt to—"

"The Comtesse de Bruinet, m'lud," announced Prospect from the east door.

Lady Trent gave a horrified little scream and her arrogance crumpled. She threw a glance of stark despair at Valentine. "You won't—"

With a flood of rapid-fire French, Madame la Comtesse swept into the room. She had been in Italy, and had but now heard of *très cher* Valentine's tragic loss. She was *accablée de douleur, affligée* to learn that he had been seriously injured, and now was so cruelly bereaved. She threw her arms wide and, flushing but grateful, he bent to her embrace and thanked her for her kindness in having come to console him.

But what else should she do? she demanded. Was he not her very dear young friend? And did one not go to one's friends were they in trouble?

Apparently becoming aware at this point that others were in the room, she permitted the Trents to welcome her, but the warmth faded markedly from her manner, and a bleak look came into her eyes. She advised Barbara that she looked unhappy and—with a stern look at Sir Selby—that young people should never be made unhappy.

"But I assure you, Madame la Comtesse," cooed Lady Trent, "our daughter is very joyful indeed. Or as joyful as one might properly be under our sad circumstances," she amended hurriedly. "After the proper period of mourning for my dearest Geoffrey, she will be married to a splendid gentleman."

"Ah," said the Comtesse shrewdly. "Is that the problem then, *mon petit chou*? Have you not the affection for this allegedly 'splendid' gentleman?"

"W-well, I—" Barbara's shy voice died away, and her eyes dilated as the French doors opened to admit another caller.

"Mices fren!" declared Angelo, beaming at Montclair. He saw his beloved then, and advanced, his eager eyes encompassing only her.

"The deuce!" exclaimed Sir Selby, starting from his chair, outraged.

"How *dare* you come in here?" shrilled my lady,

361

equally outraged. "Trent, have this person put—" She broke off, her jaw dropping.

The mighty Comtesse de Bruinet had started up from her chair when the Spaniard entered. Now she sank into a deep and graceful curtsy before him. "Your Highness," she murmured.

"Your . . . *what.* . . ?" whispered my lady, stunned.

"Good . . . God!" quavered Sir Selby, staring.

"I'll be damned," muttered Valentine, grinning.

With superb grace Angelo raised the Comtesse and kissed her hand. "My charming Danielle," he said in fluent French. "You are a rascal, and have brought my finest adventure to a close. *Vraisemblablement* it is time. You will be so kind, madame, as to present me to these people." And noting her puzzled look, he explained, "They know me, you comprehend, by a different name."

A twinkle came into her eyes. "So you have been up to your tricks again, have you, sir? As you wish. *Mesdames et messieurs,* it is my honour to present you to Angelo Francisco Luis Lagunes de Ferdinand, Duke of Alberini and Passero, and a fugitive from oppression, even as I."

Montclair's brows lifted. The Duke of Alberini and Passero might be a fugitive from oppression, but if report spoke truly, his royal father had fled his Duchy with a vast fortune, and his palaces in Switzerland and Italy were said to be breathtaking.

From the corner of his eye he saw Lady Trent and Barbara sink into low curtsies, while Sir Selby's hair all but swept the floor. Angelo's amused eyes were on him, and Montclair bowed politely.

The Spaniard winked at him, then crossed to stand beside Barbara. She looked up at him, startled, but adoring. He turned to Sir Selby and said, still in French, and with coldly punctilious good manners, "You would do me great honour, sir, if you would grant me the hand of your daughter in marriage."

"Er— I—" gulped Sir Selby.

"Oh, your *Highness!*" squeaked Lady Trent, in a transport of delight. "We are *honoured*. Truly—*honoured!* Trent. . . !"

Valentine murmured irrepressibly, "But—what about the 'splendid' Pollinger?"

Ignoring him completely, Sir Selby Trent took his daughter's hand and bestowed it upon the Duke of Alberini and Passero.

The morning was hot and sultry, and by noon Montclair was glad to retreat into the cool house for luncheon. He ate in the smaller dining room, alone as always, now that Dev and Joss were gone, the vast table stretching off before him, the silence seeming to press in. As soon as the Trents left, he thought, he would get some dogs. He'd have done so when their old collie, Mac-Pherson, died, save that Soldier would make short work of any pup he'd brought here. He smiled cynically as he considered the imminent departure of his family. Lady Trent was all benevolence now that her plain daughter had made so incredibly illustrious a match, and Barbara had been allowed to visit her cousin several times this past week. Montclair looked forward to these occasions, for aside from his delight at having a little company, sometimes Barbara would speak of Highperch, and he snatched at each crumb of news from his cottage. There had not been much more than crumbs, however. Susan and her brother had been in Town, searching for a suitable house. Priscilla, said Barbara, was quiet and subdued. "But she always asks about you, Val. I think she must love you very much."

Montclair sighed, then stood, impatient with himself. He was allowing himself time to think, and that was disastrous. He must get to work again. He strode across the dining room and into the hall, and caught a glimpse of Yates's blue coat disappearing at speed around the corner into the Great Hall. His call was unavailing. Irked, he started after the man. He passed several footmen and lackeys, all of whom sprang to attention at his approach, but there was no further sign of Yates. The steward must have been fairly flying to have navigated the length of the big room so speedily. He was not to be seen in the south hall, nor in the conservatory. Montclair thought he heard hurried footsteps in the Gallery, but with a faint smile he took pity on his steward and turned towards his music room.

Jimson (now promoted to be his lordship's personal footman) appeared from somewhere and swung open the door, and Montclair smiled his thanks and wandered to the harpsichord. He let his fingers drift over the keys. Did they really plan to move back into Town? Perhaps it would be as well. The country probably held unhappy memories for her. She was so lovely she'd soon have a score of admirers clamouring for her hand. It was only right that she should marry again and settle down with some lucky fellow . . . His aimless music ended in a crashing discord, and he hurried outside.

The air was scorching. Deep in thought, he strolled down the terrace steps, hands in his pockets and head down.

"I wish you hadn't of taked so long to come out," said a small wilting voice. "I waited an' waited an' it's so drefful hot, an' I'm thirsty!"

"Priscilla!" he cried, and dropping to one knee held out his arms.

The child ran to hug him, and Wolfgang came panting over to utter a few desultory yelps of greeting.

"Why ever did you not come and knock at the door?" asked Montclair.

Her big eyes slid past him to scan the house with awe.

"It's so grand," she said simply. "We was 'fraid to 'sturb it."

He chuckled, and suggested that they all go inside for a glass of lemonade. This lure was very well received, and a smiling maid conducted the small caller to a room where she might wash her heated face and refresh herself. Jimson was sent hurrying to the kitchen, and when Priscilla returned she was seated at the dining room table where cold lemonade, fresh fruits, dainty finger sandwiches, and a selection of pastries awaited her. A mat was laid down, and much to the amusement of the servants, a bowl of water and a beef bone were offered to Wolfgang.

"Oooh, scrumptious!" exclaimed Priscilla, her eyes lighting up. She wasted no more time on words, but gave her full attention to the meal until she noticed that Mr. Val was watching her instead of eating, whereupon he was pressed to join her. He helped her dispose of the pastries while they chattered merrily.

Jimson went off with a grin and told the chef it was the first time he'd seen the master enjoy a meal since his friends had left.

"What a hugeous big house," said Priscilla, looking about with interest. "Do you wish it was yours, Mr. Val?"

"It is, now. Do you like it?"

"Not if it makes you sad."

He smiled at her. "Why do you say that, Lady Priscilla?"

"'Cause your eyes got painy when I asked if you wanted it. But it's drefful lovely to hear you call me Lady P'scilla 'gain." She tucked a very sticky hand in his, and said intensely, "I've missed and missed you, Mr. Val, an' I told Wolfgang, an' he said"—she lowered her tone to one suitable for the 'Fierce and Invincible Guard

365

Dog'—"'If Mr. Val won't kindly come an' see us, we must go an' see him,' so here we are."

He took up her small hand and kissed it, stickiness and all. "I'm very glad you're here. I've—missed you, too. And . . . everyone. Is your mama well?"

She considered this while attending to a cheese tart. "Sometimes," she said, muffled. "When she comed home with Uncle Andy, I thinked she'd been crying, but she says she's just tired. Are you tired, Mr. Val?"

"Me? No! Never! Why do you ask?"

"All the grown-ups seem to be tired. Mama's tired. An' the Bosun's tired 'cause he's been painting so much. An' Starry said *she* was tired of always giving him the same answer to his question, so he said, 'Then why don't you give me a yes instead?' So she did. An"—her eyes grew very round and she said in a dramatic whisper—"D'you know *what,* Mr. Val? He *kissed* her! Right in the Still Room! I saw him! An' Starry put her arms *all the way* round him! An' he's so *old!* Older than *you!*"

He laughed and ruffled her hair. "Love doesn't stop because we get old, my lady. If you'd care to come and see some more of my house, I'll show you a picture of my grandmama and grandfather who were deeply in love 'til the day they died. Would you like that?"

"Oh, yes please, Mr. Val!" She nodded so vehemently that the cheese tart in her hand shattered, and he helped her remove a piece of pastry from her hair, sending her into whoops of mirth when he said it was the first time he'd ever gone on a pastry hunt. One of the maids took her off for repairs again, and he was standing at the window musing on how much brighter the afternoon seemed because she was here, when she came running eagerly back to him.

He knew that she must have slipped away without permission, and that he should really take her back at once. But he ignored conscience and invited Wolfgang to join them. The little dog wagged his tail but declined the offer, evidently deciding his guard duties could be postponed until he had dealt with the bone.

The Grand Tour encompassed the first floor only, but took some time. The innumerable chambers through which they passed were all approved of, and Priscilla said of Lord and Lady Colwynne Montclair that they looked as if they were happy people and she could believe they'd loved each other very much. She found the "indoor garden" most to her liking. "Though it would be nicer," she said, surveying the conservatory critically, "if you let some birds come in to the trees and bushes. They're too quiet." She lowered her voice to a confiding whisper. "The whole house is quiet. Hasn't you found yourself a wife, Mr. Val?"

He led her to the windowseat in the front bay of the Gallery, and sat beside her. "I've found the lady I'd like to have for a wife, Lady Priscilla. But I don't think she wants me, and at all events, the world won't let me have her."

Still holding his hand, she gazed up at him. "Why?"

He answered slowly, "Oh—because it's a funny old world, my lady, and I must—play by the rules."

She threw both arms around him and gave him a strong hug. "Poor Mr. Val. I heard the Bo'sun say he wouldn't be in your shoes for any 'mount. Though I don't think your shoes would fit him, you know, 'cause the Bo'sun's a dear, but he's got awful big feet. I'll have to tell him it's not your shoes that's giving you pepper." She frowned thoughtfully. "Starry says I'm not to say your name to Mama, so I 'spect Mama won't like it, an' we'll have to keep it *very* secret 'tween us. But I'd best sac'fice for you. Then at least you'd know you had a lady—somewhere. Would that help?"

He said in a rather husky voice, "Yes, my dear. Indeed

367

it would. Is that why you came all this way on such a hot day? To sacrifice for me?"

Her little face clouded. She pushed the spectacles up her nose and looked at him in sudden deep tragedy. "No. I—I comed to say—goodbye."

His heart contracted painfully. "You *are* moving away, then?"

"No. We're moving away *now*! Uncle Andy and Mama finded a house in Town, and—and Mama says I shall like it. But—" Her eyes filled with tears. "Oh, Mr. V-Val—I don't want to like it! I don't *want* to go 'way. I have a simply drefful time f-finding friends. Look how long it took to find *you*! And now . . . I got to *lose* you!"

Overwhelmed, he pulled her close against him and hugged her tight. "I don't want you to go either, sweetheart."

"I lose all my friends," she sobbed. "I think I—won't have any more. Ever! It's too sad when . . . when you have to—go 'way!"

Montclair buried his face against her tumbled curls and for a moment couldn't say anything at all. Then he asked unsteadily, "When—will you leave?"

"Ever so soon. As soon as the Bo'sun buys some more paint. There wasn't enough in my tub."

He stiffened. "But—I thought— Do you say the Bo'sun is finishing the front of Highperch with the paint you used for your doll house?"

"No," she sniffed. "He started it all over 'gain."

She wouldn't! Surely, however she despised him she wouldn't take her revenge by desecrating the dear old place with that hideous purple?

"I don't like it," Priscilla went on sadly, taking the handkerchief he rather absently handed her. "It's not pretty. But Mama says we must leave you something to 'member us by . . . Why is your face so red, Mr.

Val?" And with the bewilderingly sudden recovery that is the way of childhood, she did not wait for him to respond, but said an excited "Only look at all the carriages!"

With an effort Montclair collected himself and turned to the window.

A long cavalcade was winding up the drivepath; an ornate travelling coach in the lead, followed by three luxurious closed chariots, a phaeton, and a curricle, all piled high with luggage. The final vehicle was a huge coach, so topheavy with boxes and bags it was remarkable it had not foundered. The coachmen and footmen wore an elegant but unfamiliar dark blue livery, nor did Valentine recognize any of the eight outriders. 'Who the devil. . . ?' he thought, and wondered uneasily if Great Uncle Chauncey had decided to move in.

Taking Priscilla's hand, he muttered, "We'd best go and see who this is."

They went out onto the front steps. Prospect, flanked by two lackeys, was already waiting, and several stableboys were running along the drivepath.

The leading carriage halted, the high-bred team snorting and cavorting about. The footmen jumped down and one ran to swing open the door and let down the steps, while the other began to unload valises.

"Good God, Prospect," murmured Valentine *sotto voce,* "we're being invaded! Who the deuce is this?"

Prospect's eyes twinkled. He whispered, "I couldn't say, m'lud, but—"

An extremely beautiful young lady who was obviously in a delicate condition was handed down the steps. "Oh!" she exclaimed, gazing rapturously at Montclair. "Is this my brother? He is *so* handsome!"

Valentine's jaw sagged.

Both footmen were now inside the vehicle. A gentleman was being tenderly supported down the steps. He seemed very frail, and his dark head was bowed as he accepted a walking cane and leaned on it heavily. Then he looked up. From shadowed hollows a pair of dark eyes gazed at Valentine. The pale, sunken face twisted with emotion; a thin arm reached out.

With a choked sob, Valentine was sprinting down the steps to hug and weep and be wept over. *"Geoff!"* he gulped. "Oh—my dear God! *Geoff!"*

"Val," gasped Geoffrey, Baron Montclair, tears gleaming on his cheeks. "Good old Val. You . . . thought me dead, I'll wager! And—and here I am . . . like the proverbial bad penny . . . come to wrest the title away from you, poor old lad!"

"Stupid . . . cawker," managed Valentine.

Priscilla had followed him down the steps and now paused uncertainly. She was considerably shocked to see tears on the cheeks of her beloved friend, for an English gentleman did not weep. Her disappointment was forgotten, however, when from the following carriage came two small children. A little girl, and a boy of about seven with fair curls and a pair of bright green eyes which looked her over appraisingly. "Hello. I'm Theodore," he said. "Have you got any brothers?"

Priscilla shook her head. "No. I've got a dog."

His face, which had fallen, brightened again. "Have you truly?"

"An' my uncle's got a boat," said Priscilla.

"Oh, jolly fine!" said Theodore, his eyes shining with admiration. Clearly, Priscilla was acceptable. He cast about for something equally impressive, but at last admitted regretfully, "I've only got a sister. This is her. Alice. She's four."

Alice had fair curls, a shy smile, and a battered doll. She had something of inestimably greater value. She wore big spectacles. Priscilla smiled at her. Alice held out her doll, and Priscilla inspected it.

"Wha' your name?" asked Alice.

Priscilla told her.

"Can we go and see your dog now?" asked Theodore.

"All right, but you'll have to be very quiet 'cause he's hugeous fierce an' drefful, you know. His name's Wolfgang . . ."

19

Riding across the park with Priscilla perched in front of him, Valentine's thoughts were chaotic. Geoff was home! Dear old Geoff was alive and— if not quite well as yet, was expected to make a full recovery. And what a jolly, lively family he'd brought with him. His beautiful wife, Jemima; her fat and good-humoured mother, Mrs. Bancroft; his widowed brother-in-law, Hamish, whose two children had struck up an immediate friendship with Priscilla; and his sister-in-law, Millicent, a sprightly damsel with auburn curls and mischievous green eyes. The late Mr. Bancroft had been attached to the Ambassador's staff in Calcutta until typhoid fever had carried him off. His family had been intending to return to England when Geoffrey had been carried to their home after being mauled by the tiger, and while recovering had wooed and won the elder Miss Bancroft.

Watching his brother anxiously, Geoffrey had suggested that the South Wing might be ideal for the two Bancroft ladies and Hamish Bancroft and his children, while Geoffrey and Jemima could reside with Valentine in the main house. Valentine had happily approved, but had laughed at "his lordship's" diffidence and told him to stop being such a gudgeon.

Geoffrey had heard about the murderous attempt on Valentine's life, and was full of anxious questions. Valentine was as full of questions, and had yearned to spend the rest of the day with this beloved brother, the report of whose death had been such a crushing blow, and who was now so marvellously restored to him. He had seen concern in his new sister-in-law's eyes, however, and had realized that Geoff was very tired. Also, Priscilla must be sent home. He'd intended to have her driven home, but the news of her mama's infamous behaviour had made it imperative that he take the child back to Highperch himself.

He had been so overjoyed by his brother's safe return, his heart so light that at first he could only be thankful and elated. But a shadow had been cast over even that great happiness. Susan Henley, intending to move away—knowing she would probably never see him again—had been so full of resentment against him that she'd defaced the gentle old cottage. The place where he had come to love her so deeply; where, despite the bad times, they'd known such precious moments. How could she have done such a thing?

"Come on, Wolfgang!" called Priscilla, waving the bone enticingly.

The dog had been attempting to haul his prize home, but it was almost as big as he was, and when the struggle had proven to be an unequal one, his owner had undertaken its transportation. Montclair halted Allegro so that the Fierce and Invincible Guard Dog could catch up, and then they all went on again. Priscilla tossed the bone soon after they reached the drivepath, and Wolfgang settled down with it happily.

Highperch Cottage loomed up beyond the trees, and

Montclair's heart began to beat rapidly. Perhaps it wasn't as bad as Priscilla had said. Perhaps the Bo'sun had mixed the paint so that— "Good . . . God!" he gasped.

"Put me down! Oh, do please put me down!" shrilled Priscilla. He let her down numbly, and she went running off to the stables. "Uncle Andy! Uncle Andy! I finded two new friends. . . !"

Valentine sent Allegro on at a walk, his gaze fixed on the house, rage boiling inside him. The glaring purple trim provided an almost sickening clash with the sandstone walls. The mellow old cottage, always so serenely at peace with its surroundings, was now cheapened and vulgar, so hideous that it hurt him to look at it. He had humbled himself to apologize to Susan, and she, cold and unforgiving, had spurned him. Horribly aware of the depth of his offense, he'd accepted his punishment, and left her in peace. He had perjured himself to the authorities so as to protect her brother, and had gone on loving her, breaking his heart for her these past miserable weeks. While she, remorseless in her wounded pride, had planned to go away and leave him this cruel evidence of her scorn. She knew how much he loved the old place. She must really hate him to have done such a thing. "By the Lord Harry," he muttered, "if ever a woman deserved to be pilloried. . . !"

The deserving woman came out onto the steps. She wore a pale lemon gown and a dainty yellow cap with long ribbons that fluttered in the warm breeze. Folding her hands demurely, she stood watching him.

Burning with hurt and wrath, he slid from the saddle and stamped up the steps. "You wretched, wretched jade," he growled. "You did it to spite me, didn't you?"

"Of course," she said, calm but very pale.

"Did you have to vent your hatred on the dear old house?"

"I had no choice, my lord, since you were not here to—er, vent my hatred on."

He seized her by the arms. "I told you how sorry I was. You knew very well how I felt. Was it not enough to placate you?"

"Not—nearly enough. I wanted to see—"

"See what?" he demanded, shaking her a little. "My hurt that you would do so crude a thing before you went flaunting off to Town? Was this to have been your farewell gift? A tenderness to remember you by?"

She was very close to him, and she smelled of violets, and her grey eyes were so wide—so clear . . . And oh, but he was a sorry fool . . .

"You may have—something more, if you wish," she said, a note of strain in her voice now. "I—we lived here without payment of rent for several months. I feel—you are entitled to—to some recompense."

"Do you? Then by all means fetch me your dustpan brush."

His eyes were saying something very different, and Susan swayed to him. "Would that—satisfy you?"

"No, by God!" he growled.

"I thought not . . ." Somehow her hands were on his chest, and her eyes were soft with a tenderness that took his breath. "And also . . ." she murmured, "I tried to be noble, to push you away. Only—I find that—that I cannot seem to smile . . . any more . . . without you are part of my life."

"Susan . . ." he whispered, his arms slipping about her, and his heart pounding like a kettle drum. "Oh—my Susan. What . . . recompense are you offering me?"

"I— Well, you see I know . . . you cannot wed me. So . . . after Andy moves to the house in Town, I thought—"

He scowled darkly. "You thought—*what*? Why, you shameless wanton! You are offering to be my mistress!"

"Ssshh!" She glanced nervously to the house. "I thought you would be pleased."

"Pleased! Dash it all, Susan Henley, I don't want you for my mistress!"

Her eyes fell. "Oh."

He forced her chin up and said with his lurking smile, "My beautiful, gallant, peerless love. I want you for my *wife*! Will you, dearest girl, do me the very great honour of taking me to husband?"

Susan's lower lip fell. She looked up at him, her eyes glazed with shock. "B-But—Val! I cannot be Lady Montclair, you know that! It is against all sense—all logic!"

The amber flecks in his eyes were more brilliant than she had ever seen them; his half smile broadened into a joyous beam. "There is no logic to the heart, my beloved. How could there be if someone as dear and perfect as you could care for me? Besides, God willing, you never shall be Lady Montclair. Oh, Sue—my adored woman, I am free at last! My brother is come home safe, after all! And has brought a bride who is most decidedly—ah, *enceinte,* so I am very likely pushed right out of any chance at the title."

"My dear, my dear! How very glad I am for your sake! I know how deeply you mourned him."

He kissed her hand. "You also know what it means, my darling. I shall be plain Mr. Montclair again. Thank the good Lord! We can live here, and we may not be rich, lovely one, but I promise you'll not starve. I've a nice inheritance, and Geoff means to settle a substantial amount on me."

"I have a little money too, Val. No, dear, I am serious. Diccon came and told me there is a rather enormous reward for the return of the things in my—in our cellar, so you will not be wedding a pauper after all!"

He scanned her face eagerly. "I think I have just been accepted, no?"

376

"I suspect you have, Mr. Valentine Amberly Montclair."

He hugged her close and murmured humbly, "Most worshipped of wicked widows, I shall make you a horrid husband! When I'm deep in my music, I—I simply disappear. And—my temper is not always exactly—er, tranquil. Will you be able to endure me?"

She looked up at him, her eyes full of happy tears, and lifted her face. Valentine kissed her, hard and long, and they forgot all about titles and estates and smugglers and anything at all except that they loved and needed each other, and that happiness had come to them at last.

Priscilla's shrill screaming jerked them apart. Valentine whipped around. The little girl stood a few feet away, but she was crouched, her clenched hands pressed against her mouth.

Following her horrified eyes, Susan gasped, "Oh! My heavens!"

It was too far, Valentine knew, but he started to run.

Wolfgang was grinding blissfully on his bone. Bearing down on him at top speed came a large and terrible threat.

"Soldier!" roared Montclair, racing full tilt. "Go *home!*"

But Soldier was almost upon the delectable bone and its contemptibly puny owner, and paid no heed.

At the last second, the Fierce and Invincible Guard Dog jumped up and turned to face Nemesis, and quail, shivering.

'Oh, Lord!' thought Montclair, 'please don't let the child see this.'

A horrifying growl rumbling deep in his throat, Soldier lunged in for the kill.

All the hair stood up on Wolfgang's small back. He yapped once, and sprang bravely.

Soldier let out a shrill yelp, and jumped back, one paw flailing at his bloody nose.

Staring in disbelief, Valentine halted.

Wolfgang planted both front paws firmly on his property, and barked a shrill diatribe of canine insults.

His tail between his legs, howling, Soldier sped for home.

Montclair threw back his head and shouted with laughter. He heard peals of merriment ring out behind him, and turned, holding out his arms. Susan and Priscilla ran into them. Priscilla hugged his leg hard. Susan kissed his chin, her eyes full of love and laughter.

Andrew strolled down the front steps with Welcome draped over his shoulder. He relinquished the little cat to Priscilla's eager embrace, and said with his ingratiating grin, "I say, Montclair, I saw the most deuced pretty girl driving towards the Manor when I was coming back from Tewkesbury this afternoon. She has auburn hair and the loveliest green eyes. I wondered . . ."

"She is my new sister-in-law," said Montclair. "And I'll thank you to keep your lecherous eyes from the lady. Furthermore, does it escape your notice, Andy, that I have my arm around your sister?"

Lyddford blinked. "Well, I'm not blind. Why d'you suppose we painted the house that disgusting colour? Or brought Priscilla over to Longhills to tell you about it? You were properly ambushed, poor fellow. Now, regarding your sister-in-law—since we're all going to be part of the family . . ."

Laughing, Montclair planted a firm kiss on Susan's brow.

"By Jove, but we are," he said, and with his arm securely around his love, led the way into the dear old house.